The Riddle of S103

D1807925

By

Peter Maguire

Acknowledgements

I would like to thank my writing group, 'Catchword' for all the encouragement they gave me in the writing of my book which might not have evolved without their enthusiasm and guidance.

I would also like to thank my chief editor, Patricia Ainger, for her considerable expertise, hard work and sensitivity in bringing the story to publication.

Lastly my thanks go to Sarah who always believed in my ability to write and who has been a constant support throughout the whole project.

PM

Contents

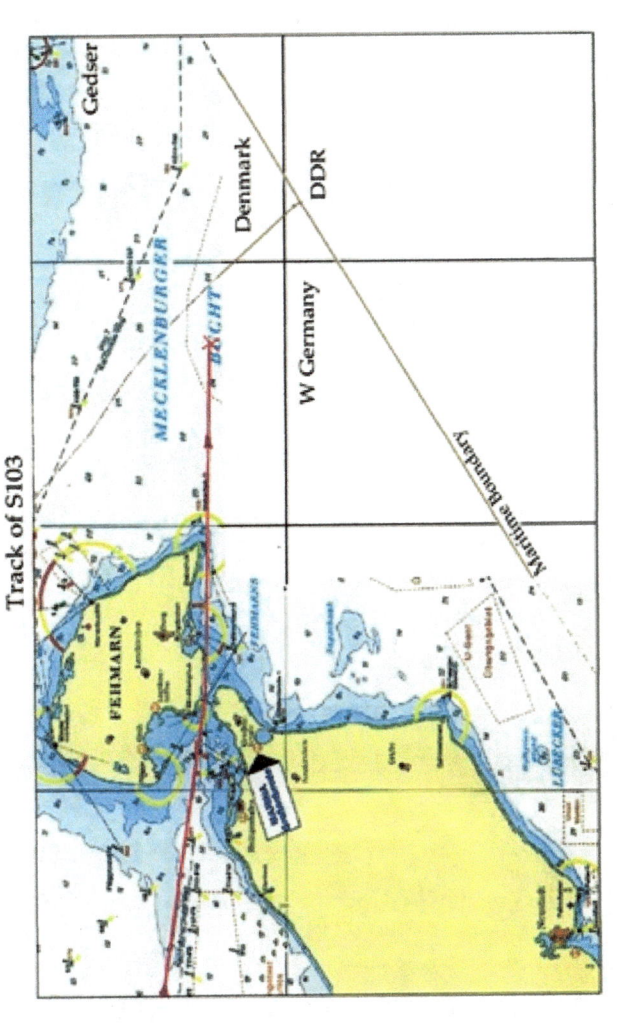

Track of S103

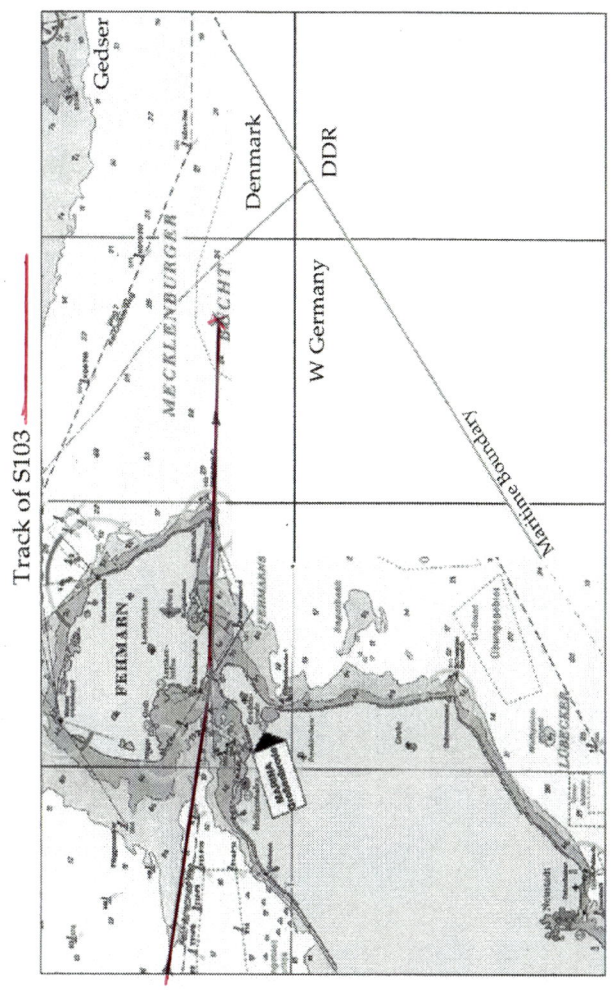

Track of S103

Gedser

Denmark

DDR

MECKLENBURGER BUCHT

W Germany

Maritime Boundary

FEHMARN

FEHMARNS

LÜBECKER

August 1945

The weather in the Ardennes in late January 1945 was cold and miserable. Major Klaus Schmidt of 2nd Panzer division felt tired and battle-weary. Following its transfer from the Eastern Front, he had led his tank battalion throughout the bitter fighting that followed the Allied landings in Normandy then, during the Battle of the Bulge, he and a small number of his tanks had reached the banks of the Meuse, the deepest penetration into Allied-held territory achieved by any German formation. But the Americans had now driven them back almost to the Rhine. His battalion was pulled out for a refit, but the woods into which they had been directed were largely leafless and provided only thin camouflage against the incessant enemy air attacks.

It was still dark when Schmidt awoke, the blankets wrapped around him covered in hoar frost from his breath. He shook them over the end of the truck and jumped out onto the icy ground. This was nearly as bad as Russia. No, in a way it was worse – now there were no replacements for his tanks lost in battle, nor for his men, and they were almost out of fuel. Any minute now the sound of gunfire would start up - the sharp unnerving blast of American artillery shells preceding yet another attack, or the dull thud of his Division's 88 mm anti-tank guns. The inevitability ate into the peaceful silence of the morning. War.

A movement caught his eye and he tensed – the figure of a man appeared out of the gloom, walking purposefully towards him - a Captain. Seeing Schmidt standing by the truck, he stopped and saluted.

'Major Schmidt?'

'It is.'

'The General wishes to see you. Please follow me.'

'What the devil's happening,' Schmidt muttered to himself. Last night's briefing by the Colonel had been precise. General von Lauchert must have pressing reasons for calling another - something must have come up during the night.

Their heavy boots crunched along the rutted, well-used path through the woods as pink clouds in the east heralded the rising of the sun; a solitary blackbird flew out of a nearby tree with a shrill complaining scream. As they approached the four-wheel Command trailer Schmidt noted the presence of a smart Mercedes-Benz 540K cabriolet parked nearby. Black with chromium-plated headlamps, it was the type of car used by party big-wigs. He grimaced. The Captain mounted the steps of the trailer, announced the visitor, and was dismissed.

The General glanced up from the small wooden desk at which he was writing and waved a finger.

'One second, Major.'

For the first time in his career Schmidt found himself alone with von Lauchert. As he waited, his gaze wandered around the inside of the trailer taking in the half-smoked cigarette abandoned in a metal ashtray on the edge of a rack supporting encryption and signals equipment, the maps – their edges tattered from much usage - pinned up on two of the dull brown walls, the whole lit by three well-shielded lamps fixed to the roof which shone an unreal orange light on the workstations. On a hook hung a pair of binoculars, some goggles and a checked woollen scarf. And the General now staring at him ... Von Lauchert's long face, marked with fatigue, had lost none of its look of intense concentration. Schmidt read in his eyes the warning that had he had first registered when the General arrived to take command of the Division: 'If you value your position in 2nd Panzer, don't ever bullshit me'. He waited.

After a long moment, the General spoke.

'Guten Morgen Herr Major, I have a job for you. This is a Movement Order for a special mission that I'm entrusting ... to you.' He indicated the paper in front of him. 'You are to take the civilian car parked outside, and use it to transport a box of secret tank ammunition to Kiel. This box you will first collect from Schloss Bückeberg.'

Schmidt tried to keep his expression blank though his mind was whirring fast.

'You must leave immediately, Major, while we still have an intact bridge over the Rhine. Take extra care to avoid air attack. Don't forget what

9

happened to Marshal Rommel. Even the side-roads are unsafe.'

This said, Von Lauchert finished writing the order, tore it out and handed it to Schmidt.

'Major Kurz will take over temporary command from you. Your driver Beckmeier will be here in five minutes. Talk to nobody about the purpose of your trip. Good luck.'

'Thank you Herr General. I will deliver the box if it is humanly possible.' Schmidt saluted, turned and left the trailer.

He retraced his steps along the footpath in deep thought. Kurz was an untested battalion leader – could he hold them together in what was obviously going to be the last weeks of the war? To put it mildly, Schmidt was unhappy at being separated from his men not to mention that a man of his rank was being treated as a mere delivery boy. And why Kiel? The naval base there could have no interest in tank ammunition. Perhaps it was being shipped to Sweden, they had a vast armament industry.

He frowned as he realised that the most peculiar aspect of the General's order was the provision of a civilian car – why? Though the imposing Mercedes would give him some clout in dealing with any interfering military police he encountered. Suspicion apart, a feeling of relief welled up in him. If nothing else, for a few days he might snatch some decent sleep and get away from the noise of battle and the stench of animal carcases lying unburied in the fields.

Back at his truck he quickly packed some travelling kit and returned to find the driver waiting in the Mercedes.

'You know the roads to Schloss Bückeburg, Driver?'

'Certainly, Herr Major.'

'What gear have you brought?'

'Camouflage netting, food rations, a tent, a stove, beds, and a spade.'

'Good. Then let's be on our way.'

Day was breaking as they left and with it the sound of guns, but the car was already heading east towards the ancient town of Bückeburg.

That Major Klaus Schmidt, Squadron Commander of the 2nd Panzer Division, should be spoken to like that! The words of the man at the Schloss burned in his mind, fuelling his growing annoyance at being reduced to the status of a ... a delivery boy.

He glared at the head of the driver – Beckmeier – nasty reputation from what he'd heard but a good enough soldier. The anger burning slowly inside him, Schmidt turned his attention to the large box occupying the rest of the back seat of the vehicle: it was a standard tank ammunition box, a little battered around the edges and with the usual warnings in black paint. It made no sense.

His eyes narrowed as he recalled the brief meeting he'd had with General von Lauchert a mere twenty-four hours previously. As he went over their brief conversation his resentment was suddenly extinguished by a thought.

The box certainly weighed about the right amount to be what it claimed to be, he'd realised that when he had swung it onto the seat and he'd had enough experience of tank ammo to be able to assess that accurately. But if that is all the box contained then why was it necessary that as high a ranking officer as himself and a ruffian of a driver should be detailed to transport it all the way to Kiel. Surely the next lorry going in that direction would have sufficed. There had to be more to this box than appearances would suggest.

His thoughts playing with this idea, he stared out of the window at the gathering gloom of the late summer evening. The woods bordering the road were still in leaf, casting a false twilight over the roadway. Even as he made up his mind what he was going to do the car slowed.

'What's up?' He asked the driver sharply.

'Need a piss, Herr Major.'

'Okay, pull over then.'

As Beckmeier scurried off to avail himself of the nearest unencumbered tree, Schmidt hurriedly lifted the lid of the box and peered inside. The cartridge cases looked normal enough. He lifted one out. The weight seemed right. He shook it ... no, something was not right. Unscrewing the top, he tilted the tube and a heavy weight loosely wrapped in paper fell into his hand. A touch of a hand and the wrapping unwound.

Schmidt stared impassively at the shiny facets of the jewels revealed ... a stray ray of daylight struck red and blue sparks from the undoubted fortune lying in his hand. He glanced at the papers. They looked like letters, doubtless whoever wrapped the jewels grabbed whatever was at hand. A word caught his eye and he frowned. But before he could read further, a sound outside the car reminded him that he had only moments before the driver would return. An idea blossomed in his mind, he would teach them to treat a man of his rank in such a cavalier fashion. Even as Beckmeier was fastening his trousers, two cartridges found their way into Schmidt's capacious pockets.

An hour later and the car came to a crossroads. Beckmeier stopped the car and reached for the map on the seat beside him. It was nearly full night now. Schmidt leaned over the back of the seats and watched as the man traced the road they had driven by the light of his torch.

'Where are we?' He asked as the driver gave a satisfied grunt, banging his finger on the map.

'Here, Hanover is about two kilometres ... along that road there.' He indicated the road off to their left.

'Can you stop for a moment, please?' Schmidt asked.

'Of course, Herr Major.'

Schmidt climbed out of the car, his legs stiff after the long period driving. He stood and looked around, noting the farm buildings off to the right and set off towards a nearby clump of trees. Once behind a bush, and a quick glance suggested he was out of sight of the car, he hunkered down and stared at the small shadowy hole at the base of a substantial tree. With his penknife he enlarged the hole sufficiently to stuff the two cartridges into it and then covered them with as much soil as he could. He stood and carefully carved a K into the bark of the tree.

Beckmeier was standing by the vehicle smoking a cigarette when he got back. Without a word, Schmidt nodded to him and they resumed their journey.

They reached Kiel just as dawn was breaking.

'You know where to go?' Schmidt asked.

'Yes, Major.'

The address they'd been given was a schloss standing in large grounds owned by Prinz Otto Fürst von Benz. To Schmidt's annoyance, they were kept waiting for two hours while Fürst von Benz ate his breakfast but eventually Schmidt was able to present his credentials. At first the Major was received with calm courtesy but as soon as the Prinz realised that he had a driver with him he became agitated.

'I was assured that only officers of the Wehrmacht would be bringing the box!' he almost shouted. 'Your driver must return to his unit with the car.'

'But I need it to return to my battalion, Sir.'

'Another vehicle will be found for you, Major.'

It seemed that he had naval connections at the highest level so could access a vehicle without any problems. So, the box was unloaded and Beckmeier went off.

'You will stay here tonight, Major.' The Prinz ordered. 'We shall dine together.'

The meal was a nightmare. Whether it was the wine or just the fact of Schmidt's presence, the Prinz seemed to have lost all inhibition and poured out his anger, shame and disgust at what had happened to Germany. As he shovelled food into his mouth, he deplored the criminal behaviour of the Führer, Reichsmarschall Göring, and Reichsführer SS Himmler, speaking in horrifying detail to the appalled Major about the extermination camps in Poland.

Dismissed to his room at the end of the meal, Major Schmidt paced up and down, sickened by what he had learned. Eventually, he forced himself to undress and went to bed though the thoughts roiling in his head drove sleep away. What had he been fighting for? Oh, they'd all heard rumours about the behaviour of the 'Das Reich' Panzer Division in France but they were SS and not an army formation. Now it was clear that evil had penetrated everywhere. If what the Prinz said could be believed, Wehrmacht units in Russia had co-operated with Einsatzgruppen close behind the front and were killing Russian civilians under Hilter's 'Commissar' order. How could such things be? Suddenly he began to be afraid ... what was being done in his name?

A small flame of defiance bloomed in the Major as he marched out to his waiting car the following morning. The horrors of the previous night had transmuted into the realisation that he needed to protect himself. The cartridges of jewels he had buried would be his insurance ... his compensation for being embroiled in such dreadful activities. Any fool could see that the war was going to end soon and with that small fortune he'd be able to set himself up nicely. All he had to do now was retrieve them ...

Autumn 1945

Beckmeier cradled a tin mug in both hands, the warmth it generated meaning more to him than the thin, bitter, pale liquid it contained. He didn't dare think what his wife could have made it from. The wound in his leg throbbed painfully. As he gently moved the leg in an effort to ease the pain, he roundly cursed the RAF plane that had attacked the staff car he had been driving, adding an extra obscenity for the officer who had selected him as driver for the long and dangerous drive across Northern Germany so near to the end of the war.

But at least he was still alive. So many others weren't.

The roar of the brick-crushing machine at the end of the street stopped, filling the air with a silence so profound it almost hurt. He'd managed to find some intact basement rooms and set up home there, but for how long? The machine was slowly but steadily consuming the ruins of the residential district.

As his ears adjusted, he heard the baby making the little snuffling noises that always preceded a burst of screaming.

The wind eddied around the edges of the tarpaulin that was stretched across the door opening making the flames of the tiny coal fire burn briefly brighter; the fire hardly gave out any heat, barely enough to boil a kettle. He stared into the ever-changing red glow and allowed his

17

thoughts to wander back to the many times that he had sat round a roaring blaze in the Russian campaign when his panzer division was resting. Then it had been really cold - bitter, icy winds and snow. He knew all too well that as the Hamburg autumn morphed into winter the cold would become intense and his small stock of coal scavenged from the ruins was running out. He would need to burn some of the many chunks of timber that he had collected, though the woodsmoke might give them away.

He shivered, shuffling the rickety chair he had found in the ruins of an adjacent room nearer to the flames. Perhaps it would serve better as firewood! After all, the seat-back was already half burnt away.

His eyes wandered to the black residue covering everything, walls ceiling, even the floor – the aftermath of the firestorm that had consumed the neighbourhood. Even as the thought flitted through his mind, an acrid smell drifted down into his basement. His nose wrinkled; this place was not fit for pigs to live in!

This was certainly not what he imagined when he walked out of his unit of the Dienstgruppen only a few months ago. He thought longingly of the food, shelter and manual work that made up life there. Again he swore at his bad luck. He'd had to leave, some men in his hut had discovered him stealing and one of them whom he suspected of having been a member of the SS had threatened to beat him up.

So he had deserted and attempted to set up some sort of home with his wife and baby. But none of his bright ideas to support them had worked. He looked at the tired strained face of his young wife, now nursing the baby. Dressed in a drab brown dress under a brown jumper, the jumper stained and darned with thread of the wrong colour, her fair hair matted and hanging down unwashed and unbrushed, she was the epitome of misery. Her eyes caught his but she needed no words, her face said it all.

She was a farmer's daughter used to hard living. Her family home had been nothing more than the top floor of a barn with animals and hens wandering about below, but that was luxury compared with their present situation. How long could she tolerate these conditions? Would she take herself and the baby back to her mother's? Their lack of food, fuel, soap gnawed at him. Once or twice he had managed to steal luggage from the Hauptbahnhof but that frequently produced nothing of value: Reichsmarks from handbags could buy little when the shops were empty.

After liberating some expensive dresses he found in a suitcase, he had persuaded her to get a job in a nightclub in St Pauli. The pay was negligible but she sometimes brought home English cigarettes and sometimes a green bottle of Gordon's Gin that the English soldiers were using as currency but even bartering these was barely enough to obtain the essentials for survival for more than a week.

His frustrated, guilt-ridden desperation turned to anger. To calm himself he picked up a bucket.

'I'll go and get some water, shall I?'

Not waiting for her reply, he brushed aside the tarpaulin and set off to fill it from a tap in the next street. The pain in his leg distracted him, reminding him of the painful exercises that he had been given at the military; the nurses had assured him that exercise was the great healer so perhaps the pain would fade as the muscles became stronger.

His pace slowed as he remembered his time in the hospital ... the first time in his life that he had felt cared for. If only he could do the same for Hilda, make her feel cared for, valued ... but he knew he was failing her. In the army he had only his own survival to think about. Now there were three people and he was in charge. They had to get out.

A large rat ran across the road towards him; it hesitated and ran back. The rat packs were terrifying. Once driving an army car through Hanover he had been attacked by a pack of the aggressive rodents; they had swarmed over the vehicle, tearing off and eating a huge swathe of the canvas fabric that had been pasted to the steel roof. He shuddered at what might befall his child in the cellar. This knowledge driving him, he stumped into the teeth of the bitterly cold wind blowing across the ruin of the street. Night was falling and without street lights he needed to find the tap quickly, dreading the return journey with a full bucket.

Later, watching his wife sleep, he turned over in his mind a plan that had been growing in his mind. Again he saw the flash of jewels in the hand of the Major. He had seen them all right, despite the Major's pathetic attempt at concealing them. To say the least, there was something fishy if not downright illegal about that affair. After all, what was so vital that one of the top tank commanders had been withdrawn from a battle to deliver jewels concealed in such a strange fashion?

Doubtless the owner of the house in Kiel where the Major had delivered the box would be keen to pay for him to keep his mouth shut about it. He smiled at the thought. They may well be still living in the same house. The only problem was how to get to Kiel.

100 km - hitch hiking might be possible. He mulled over in his mind whether to tell his wife. He had to give her some explanation for his absence and the prospect of some relief from their present hardships might help to raise her spirits. He decided to tell her.

1953

'I congratulate you, Herr Schmidt!' von Hessler said, grasping his friend's elbow firmly. 'You have married a beautiful woman.'

Schmidt glanced across the room to where his new English wife was standing chatting to the wife of his company's accountant. She had style, this Englishwoman, and intelligence. Everything that the wife of a successful businessman should be in this post-war period. He smiled and gave his attention to his friend.

'Thank you.' He bowed his head with the grace often associated with large men. 'So what do you think of our new premises?' He waved a hand around the building: the new factory for his growing company Schmidt Elektrodynamik GmbH.

'Very smart.' von Hessler replied.

'Come, let me show you around.'

Chapter 1 Spring 1970

The two men met in the doorway of the restaurant and greeted each other as the long-standing friends they were. They made a strange pair, Elizabeth concluded, watching them despite herself. Klaus, her husband of nearly two decades, the epitome of the successful, self-made businessman – a big man in every meaning of the word, he'd built up a substantial business in electrical equipment. She'd always been drawn to powerful men and Klaus was definitely that. He had money, presence and knew how to apply both to good effect. It had been a sensible decision marrying him. All the same, the man currently speaking to Klaus, Gerhard Frieherr von Hessler, fascinated her – his bearing – his alleged if remote connections to the Hanoverian dynasty that had ruled England lending him a glamour that was only increased by his whispered-about career as an intelligence officer in the Kreigsmarine during the hostilities. As ever, his tall, fair-haired frame was immaculately turned out, looking every inch the aristocrat, even though his family were less affluent than before the war. An anglophile, educated in England, he had perfect English. The subtle lighting in the restaurant highlighted the classical bone structure of his face she decided. As she watched, Klaus turned to point out to Gerhard where she was sitting and, that done, he vanished through the door. She waited, poised and utterly aware of the picture she presented - a calm, graceful lady with an air of authority, dressed in a distinctive green evening gown that perfectly complimented her bright auburn hair. Several of the men in the restaurant had tried to catch her eye in the brief time she had been abandoned.

'Klaus tells me he left something in the cloakroom.' Von Hessler said as he arrived at the table where she was waiting for him.

'Yes, his cigarette case, he won't be a moment.' There was no artificiality about her smile of welcome, it had been several months since they had last met as his business interests had taken him away from Düsseldorf and she was genuinely pleased to see him. 'It is good to see you, Gerhard.'

'You look charming tonight, my dear. But then you always do.' Gerhard said smoothly. He took her hand and, as he bowed over it, their eyes met for a long moment. Not for the first time, Elizabeth found herself wondering what life might have been like if ... but she quickly dismissed that line of conjecture. Klaus was a good husband; they had a good, solid marriage ... at least ... again she rejected the nascent thought.

'Who is this man you want us to meet, Gerhard?' She asked as von Hessler seated himself. 'Shall I like him?'

Von Hessler pretended to consider her question seriously, his eyes twinkling. 'Yes, I think you will. His name is Peter Anson ... well, Lieutenant-Commander Peter Anson RN (Rtd) to be precise.'

'What do you know about him?'

'Quite a bit, actually. He's some years younger than Klaus and I, of course, joined the British Navy just after the end the last war and served for some years in intelligence. Since leaving the Navy, he has acquired a senior marketing role in a multinational company. We met a few years ago when I was working in an advisory capacity in Kiel. Anson was one of the trainees but there had been a cock-up on the accommodation so I offered him a room at my place. It was only for a few days but we discovered we had a fair bit in common apart from naval and intelligence work which had already made a bond between us. We've kept in touch ever since. When I mentioned that I knew Klaus, he immediately asked if I could arrange for a meeting ... it seems he is keen to meet the head of the Schmidt company so here we are.'

His tone was light; but all the same she found herself wondering if there were something behind his words that she was missing. Before she could say more, her husband reappeared and sat down beside her.

'Did you find it, Klaus?' He waved the silver case in answer. 'I'm just asking Gerhard about this man we are meeting tonight.'

'Anson? Gerhard tells me he wants to discuss some business options. But I wanted to have a look at the man first.' Klaus said, glancing at his watch.

'He should be here any moment.' Gerhard said pre-empting the comment he could see forming on the tip of his friend's tongue. 'His plane was late landing.'

'Ah ... we shall forgive him then.' The comment was delivered with a smile. Schmidt was known to be a hard-headed man when it came to business, being late for appointments was not a good career move in his company.

'Is that him?' Elizabeth asked, seeing a strange man appear in the doorway; he was looking around the busy restaurant as if searching for someone.

Gerhard turned. 'Yes, that's him.' He said, standing and raising his hand. He caught the man's attention.

Peter Anson was an attractive man, Elizabeth decided. Typical English type and you could see that he'd been in the Navy from the way he moved! She'd known men like him when she was growing up. Late thirties? Forties perhaps?

'A pleasure to meet you, Frau Schmidt.' Anson said once von Hessler had performed the necessary introductions with the ease and casual formality of the born aristocrat.

'It is always pleasant making the acquaintance of a fellow Englander.' Elizabeth replied. 'What brings you to this part of the world, Mr Anson?'

'Business,' confessed Anson, settling himself at the table. 'Business combined with the pleasure of meeting fellow Englanders like yourself, of course.'

Her eyes sparkled as her husband picked up the conversational ball. 'I hear your flight was delayed, Mr Anson.'

'Please, let's not be formal, call me Peter. Yes, I don't know what the problem was but we sat on the tarmac for over half an hour.'

A waiter appeared wielding menus and the next five minutes was spent in the social dance of selecting dishes and wines.

'I have to say that this is vastly more pleasant than the marketing conference I attended last year in Nürnberg.' Anson said, looking around the room once the waiter had departed, apparently appreciatively.

'Oh, you were there, were you?' Klaus said, his whole attitude somehow sharper, more focussed.

'Yes, you too?'

'Yes, excellent speakers, I thought, but the catering left something to be desired, I thought.'

'Particularly the wine!'

The two men laughed. A bond had been created, Elizabeth realised, exchanging a surreptitious glance with von Hessler.

'How is it you two know each other?' Peter Anson asked with a smile, looking from von Hessler to Schmidt. 'I have to say, I don't associate you with big business, Gerhard.'

'And with good reason! Klaus and I first met at the Kieler Yacht Club in 1960.'

'And he's had me crewing on his boat every year since!' Klaus added. 'But let's not bore Elizabeth and Gerhard with talk of business, Peter, perhaps you would call my office to make an appointment for us to meet ... tomorrow morning if you would?' He said, fixing Anson with his intelligent eyes. Plainly this was more than a casual invitation.

'Of course.'

Their food arrived and the talk became general.

'Peter, Gerhard tells me you have a background in naval intelligence like him.' Elizabeth said at one point. 'How does that help in your work?'

'Well, the business world is not that different from the political one, Elizabeth.' Anson said ruefully. 'Commercial espionage is every bit as devastating to a business and there is a black market in selling new inventions as much as any other commodity. It's a sad reality that nothing is safe these days, especially with technology becoming so advanced.'

'What do you mean?' Elizabeth asked, aware that Klaus had fallen uncharacteristically silent beside her.

'The old days when bugs were large, cumbersome things, easily spotted, are long gone. These days they are tiny ... and highly sensitive.'

She frowned, trying to work out what he meant.

'Let me give you an example.' He said, clearly trying to imagine a scenario for her. 'It's all wireless these days, using miniature tape recorders that can be activated from long distance by a radio signal and made to play back via a radio link.'

'Oh, I see.'

'That means something as innocent as ... as a hardback book, for instance. It could be easily hollowed out and the electronics installed inside. Easily secreted on a bookshelf. You'd never notice it.'

'But how would you find such a thing?' Klaus asked.

'You'd have to be careful not to alert the listeners.' Anson replied, giving his mind to the question. 'As soon as they heard the sound of the search, they'd probably realise ... but if you can overcome that issue ... create a background noise that is realistic – a conversation or perhaps music – something like that. Then you'd just flip open the hardbacks and see what comes up; you could ignore thin paperbacks. I suppose you'd have to work quickly as the bug might be alarmed but once you had neutralised it that should prevent any alarm getting back to the owners.'

'And how would you neutralise such a device?' Von Hessler asked.

'Oh that's easy! Wrap it in aluminium foil. That would effectively isolate it.'

'Is it possible to find out who might have placed such a device?' Schmidt asked.

'If you've got the right equipment, yes. There are people who can do that.' Anson replied.

'It is terrifying the advances being made in technology.' Elizabeth said into the ensuing silence. 'We'll be living on the moon next!'

The conversation turned to a discussion of space exploration.

Dessert.

'Oh, I meant to tell you Klaus, a funny thing happened at the hospital this afternoon.' Elizabeth said, 'I do some voluntary work at the hospital you see, Peter.'

'What was that?' Schmidt asked, reaching for his wine glass.

'D'you remember that woman, wife of your accountant ... she got talking to me at the opening of the factory back in '53 and seemed to think she and I could be bosom friends?'

'Oh yes! I remember, kept ringing you up to meet for lunch. What about her?'

'I saw her ... I don't think she saw me but she was talking to one of the doctors. I caught the odd word. I think her husband may be in hospital.'

'I didn't know he was ill. I'll get my secretary to check. He's a good man. Thanks for the tip.'

'Talking about strange encounters.' von Hessler said, 'I had one earlier today. You'll never guess who telephoned me, Klaus.' He paused dramatically. 'Joachim von Benz!'

'Von Benz? What did he want?' Schmidt asked.

'He wants me to meet up with him though he refused to give me any idea why.' Von Hessler clearly thought the whole thing amusing. 'It is probably a mares' nest; he's not half the man his father was.'

'No, Prinz von Benz was a power to be reckoned with.' Schmidt said absently.

'Anyhow, I have arranged to meet him.' Von Hessler seemed disappointed that his anecdote hadn't conjured a better response from his friend.

'I notice you haven't lost your enthusiasm for English colloquialisms, Gerhard!' Anson put in.

'No indeed! It's one of the more valuable by-products of attending an English public school.'

'I'm not sure that you will see that on a school prospectus!' Elizabeth commented, raising a laugh from the two men.

Beside her, Klaus has fallen silent, blindly fiddling with the last of his strudel with his fork. What is wrong with him? For a frozen moment the thought that there might be another woman paralyzed her. No, it can't be that. She'd know.

Von Hessler looked at his watch. 'This has been a delightful evening.' He said. 'But I shall have to break up the party. Can I offer you a lift to you hotel, Peter?'

'Thank you, that would be most kind.'

Schmidt climbed into the taxi behind his wife and slammed the door. The car moved off.

'That went very well, I thought.' Elizabeth said into the heavy silence.

'What? Oh ... yes. I liked Anson.'

Again Schmidt fell to brooding. Elizabeth felt her impatience growing and the frustration of the last few weeks mounted into a massive tidal wave of questions and doubts that threatened to crash over them both. What was the problem? Was it to do with work or perhaps something she had done? As the car negotiated the streets of the city, the need to say something become overwhelming.

'Klaus, we need to talk.'

He looked at her with that curious half-puzzled half-alarmed expression that so irritated her. The tsunami reared up, the crest threatening.

'I don't think you realise how ... difficult things are becoming between us. Damn it Klaus!' She said, her voice cracking under the strain of what she was saying. 'We simply can't go on like this! I'm your wife for heaven's sake! You've got to tell me what's going on. It's obvious that you have something on your mind ... you're under an increasing amount of pressure and I'm desperately worried about you. Why can't you tell me – surely I'm the one person you can trust?'

He glanced at the driver and turned his gaze on her, annoyed and irritated: a military officer under fire being challenged by a subordinate.

'There's nothing to tell.' He said curtly, nodding his head in the direction of the driver, 'Anyway, what you don't know you can't be made to tell.'

Her eyes widened.

In a low voice she hissed 'Klaus I'm not standing for this. I'm no feeble woman who needs protecting … someone who might let the side down, who's incapable of understanding this "man's game"! We either deal with this together or … or I leave.'

She recoiled at her own words, her stomach churning at the thought … she had never intended to use this, the ultimate weapon but now it was too late. She couldn't call the words back. Her pulse racing, she waited. Someone had to give, and, this time, it was not going to be her.

The painful silence in the car stretched out as the car drove along the empty dark.

Elizabeth knew that she had created an impasse. Yes, he was shocked … angry even … and that had pulled him up short. But what if his pride and temper won? If he called her bluff? What then? Yes, her own frustration, almost despair, had driven her to this impetuous response, but she was not going to back off. She would not be treated like a Personal Assistant who was told only what she needed to know.

The look on Klaus's face pulled at her heartstrings. She saw something of the trapped animal - both abject and dangerous. How to give him a way out?

33

The car pulled up outside their building and in a brittle and almost tangible silence they walked up the stairs to their apartment. As soon as the door had closed behind them, Elizabeth reached out and took hold of his sleeve.

'What is it, Klaus?' She asked softly, her heart in her eyes.

There was a long silence as he looked at her.

'Blackmail,' He said in a low, shamed voice

There was another long silence.

Stunned, she felt no sense of triumph at winning her point. Blackmail? That was the last thing she had expected to hear. He helped her off with her coat.

'Let's have a little drink. I've a brandy I keep for softening up tough customers. I think we both need some.' He said, in a kindly, if brittle fashion. And he ushered her into the living room, disappearing into his study momentarily then re-appearing, executing gyratory turns with a tray loaded with decanter and glasses very much like a high class butler. Involuntarily, she smiled grimly, reminded of how she had been attracted to the play-actor in Klaus when they first met. Now the trait seemed juvenile.

He busied himself pouring the liquid into glasses and handed one to her.

'You are right, we must talk.' He said, seating himself beside her with an air of a man facing the gallows. 'But first, I have to admit that

I've been a very stupid man. I have the best ally in the world and ignore her. Forgive my foolishness, please.' He hesitated, obviously uneasy with the emotional exposure.

'*Prosit*,' said Elizabeth, feeling more than a little mollified, her gesture accepting his apology. 'This is good stuff. Just what I needed.'

She looked at him expectantly.

'It all started towards the end of the war in the last days in April 1945 when I was told to report to headquarters.' He paused, as if reliving the day, then going on to describe the impact the large, open-top Mercedes-Benz with its beautifully maintained shining black paint and chromium plating had had on him, how he had assumed there was a high-up visitor wondering why the hell whoever it was had risked coming so close to the front line.

'Go on.' Elizabeth said, fascinated to hear his story. He rarely talked about his experiences during the war.

'Well, I was shown into General von Lauchert's command truck. To my surprise, he was on his own apart from an aide who was dismissed. This was extraordinary and I realised then that this was not going to be a normal briefing. It puzzled me that there was no sign of the visitor who had arrived in the black car.'

Klaus went on to explain about the box of secret tank ammunition, how he and Beckmeier, his driver, went to Schloss Bückeburg to collect it and of the journey to Kiel.

35

'With hindsight was all very mysterious. The papers authorising the trip included an authority from Kaufmann, the Gauleiter of Hamburg. Even at the time it just didn't make sense.' He shook his head, turning his gaze to his wife's face as he went on. 'It was a hell of a journey though where possible we travelled on minor roads to avoid attacks by RAF 'Typhoons'. He shivered at the memory. 'They would launch rockets at anything moving on the roads. Even when we travelled in convoy protected by anti-aircraft trucks they would fly dead straight into a hail of our fire and hit us with devastating accuracy. It was one of the most unnerving things I ever had to face. There were burnt out and abandoned lorries everywhere. Some had even driven off the road to hide from the Typhoons and had got bogged down. There were holes in the road from high-explosives, dark patches of oil and in places the surface was badly damaged where it had caught fire. Every now and then we met groups of weary troops walking along the edges of the road. None of them were singing marching songs like they used to. It was not a pleasant journey.'

'Go on,' she said.

'I was puzzled by the box; if it was just an ordinary ammo box then why all the mystery? I had to look inside. That's when I realised. The rounds of tank ammunition had unusual features that immediately caught my eye. The joint between the shells and the top of the cartridge cases was covered with a layer of some brown material which I'd never seen before. I noticed that the shells were high-explosive, rather than armour piercing, but they hadn't been filled or fitted with fuses. So I guessed that only the cartridges contained anything special. What also struck me as odd was that the weights were all wrong. By now I was convinced that it was certainly not tank ammunition I was transporting. My guess was right – I prised one open - it contained papers, letters and jewellery. I had no time to read the letters that day, but they were personal, nearly all hand-written, some in English, and all dated before the war. Some had impressive embossed letterheads on expensive paper.' He paused, lowering his eyes.

'What did you do?'

'I … I decided some of the jewels may as well come my way, so buried a couple of cartridges where I could find them again and delivered the rest according to schedule.'

'Oh.'

'I didn't realise the importance of the papers until much, much later. My English was good but the English handwriting was difficult for me to read, though it was obvious that they were from important people, perhaps members of your King's family.'

'What were they about?'

'Things like Anglo-German relations, visits to Berlin; sometimes Hitler was mentioned. They didn't seem terribly important to me. In fact they puzzled me. If the letters compromised the senders, perhaps by their support of the Nazis, then why hadn't the recipients destroyed them? The only purpose in keeping them that I could imagine was that they could be used as bargaining levers to buy protection for aristocratic families when the English or Americans arrived.'

She looked at Klaus in alarm. 'For God's sake, you haven't been blackmailing someone have you? Have you been getting money out of English families?'

Schmidt got up and poured himself another drink. With a gesture he offered one to Elizabeth; she refused with a contemptuous look.

'My God Klaus, What have you done?'

'I'm not the monster that you imagine, Elizabeth. I've been unwise, even a thief, but I'm not a blackmailer.'

There was a simple dignity about Klaus' denial that went a long way to reassuring her. He sat down again.

'There's more to tell. When I worked out the probable motive for getting the letters sent to Sweden via Kiel I became angry. I thought it was just an example of the top people getting away with their crimes while the rest of us are left to rot. So I decided to keep them in case things turned nasty for the Wehrmacht. I even thought I might be able use the letters to show that Hitler had supporters in England in high places.'

There was a silence as she absorbed this statement. As an Englishwoman she was horrified, as his wife she was shocked and fearful.

'But to get back to Kiel, what happened when you delivered the box, did they realise that you had tampered with it?' She asked, battling to control her rising anger at the mess he had got them into.

He shrugged. 'The address we'd been given turned out to be a schloss standing in large grounds ... it was owned by Prinz Otto Fürst von Benz.'

Her eyes widened. Suddenly she realised why von Hessler's revelation over dinner had hit Klaus so hard.

She stared at him, though plainly he had been whisked back through time, reliving the memory.

'He sent Beckmeier away and insisted that I stay the night.' Klaus went on, struggling to find the words to describe what von Benz had revealed to him at that awful, awful dinner.

'I couldn't believe what he was telling me ... how it was all lies about the labour camps, how the Jews were being gassed within hours of arriving, their belongings stolen and their bodies burnt. I began to be afraid for my own skin.'

She looked at him aghast.

'Klaus, you're frightening me. You weren't personally involved in those atrocities were you?'

In a quiet voice with a deep sigh and a slow shake of his head he replied 'No, no I never was.'

There was a long pause as they looked at each other.

'Thank God!' She whispered, her voice quavering.

'Believe me, Elizabeth, I was never a Nazi. Yes, my father insisted that I join the Hitler youth but he said it was essential if I was to be selected for a commission in the Army. Already there were young officers who were strongly Nazi and the movement was growing powerful but my father saw through the lies. I remember he told me that the NSDAP was a political party with a capital P. The N stood for National but, he said, they had no right to represent the Nation. The S for Socialist meant only state control - just like the Bolsheviks. He emphasised that I should believe nothing they told me, but should just pretend.'

'He was a wise man.'

'Yes, but when I realised what was going on I could only think of how my father spent so much effort on pulling strings to get me into the army – and all to what purpose? My career would go the same way as his.'

'What do you mean?'

'He had been a professional soldier but his career ended abruptly in 1918 and he bitterly resented the way the politicians had capitulated at the end of the war. He'd marched home apparently undefeated with the bands playing. And then came the unbelievable humiliation of the Treaty of Versailles, the dismemberment of the army, unemployment, inflation - you know the story. He'd believed in von Hindenburg, that he would lead us – fat chance! The man was no match for Hitler.'

Elizabeth was suddenly aware of the huge intensity of his feelings. In an almost inaudible voice he said: 'Hitler talked of the great Thousand Year Reich but a thousand years is how long it will take the world to forgive what we allowed to be done in our name.'

She sensed the dark force gripping her husband. Words seemed inadequate. Their eyes met, his pleading silently for her understanding.

'It's an extraordinary story, Klaus.' She said in as normal a voice as possible. 'What happened next?'

'I was given a staff car with a navy driver and we set off back though I had great difficulty finding my unit again as the Americans were advancing fast and there was total confusion. My Colonel demanded to know what had been going on. Why had General von Lauchert ordered me to go to Hamburg? I clung frantically to the tale of having to make a special delivery of secret experimental ammunition. I assumed that Beckmeier must have already been grilled by the Colonel but in fact he hadn't returned. It was thought that he had deserted or been killed. We carried on fighting until I was captured.'

'When was that?'

'Only a few days before the surrender. Months later when I was released I made straight for the guest house where we'd stayed on the journey to Kiel. It was very difficult in those days.

I had no car and taxis were difficult. Reichsmarks were useless and I had no coffee or cigarettes and such like as a means of paying. I needed to find those jewels. In the end I borrowed a bicycle I found at the back of the guest house and set off for the woods. I remember it was so peaceful. There was little traffic and I could hear the birds singing. The woods were in full leaf and the bright shades of green set off the silver bark of the birch trees. It took me a couple of hours to find the spot where I had buried the ammunition but I was vastly relieved to find that it was undisturbed. That's when I first seriously read the papers. Deciding it wasn't safe to leave them there, but unwilling to have them in my possession until I was sure that General von Lauchert, the Prinz in Kiel or even the tired old Colonel in Schloss Bückeburg was not going to start asking questions, I buried them again a little way away.'

'Why didn't you hand them over to the police there and then?' interrupted Elizabeth. 'They were not your property.'

'Elizabeth, for God's sake let me finish the story before you start criticising. You wanted me to tell you everything. Now I am, so please let me finish.'

He paused and glared at her. She glared back.

After a painful interval she took a deep breath and said: 'Go on.'

'Well, then I heard that the old Colonel had died. He was presumably one of the few who knew exactly what was in the cartridges and how many there were and I figured that by the time the box reached Sweden, or wherever it was intended for, it would have been difficult to pin down who had interfered with the contents, so I waited another year and then decided to recover the buried cartridges. I extracted the letters but decided not to do anything with the jewellery until I was sure that the Colonel's widow wasn't going to find me. But then she died and no-one came looking for me, at least not until much later.'

He got up, found a packet of cigarettes, pulled out a couple and offered one to Elizabeth.

'I read the letters again. They were indeed compromising, not just for political reasons but also because two of them were love letters. One was from a member of an aristocratic English family who was almost certainly married. It was passionate and addressed to a lady over here. Another was from an Englishman to a young man on an English Navy ship. This also was compromising. There was even a letter from the Gestapo to the father of a friend of mine about the disposal of concentration camp prisoners. Of course there was nothing I could do with them. So I did nothing.'

'You must burn the letters and give back the jewels' said Elizabeth. 'This is all too dreadful. Why did you keep them?'

'Well, for a start, I didn't know who the jewels belonged to. The country was completely devastated and, believe me, you hung on to anything ... anything that you found, no matter what or how. You don't know what it was like ... people were living in bombed out ruins; it was a time of immense, universal suffering, grinding, unrelenting poverty, utter chaos. You never knew what the next day would bring. I kept them without much real thought and as the years went by I tried to forget them.'

He swallowed audibly.

'Then Beckmeier appeared. You remember the man with the limp who came to the door last year? That was him. He'd been wounded on the return journey to my unit and ended up in hospital. Somehow the wretched man had realised there was something hidden in the cartridges and taken a round from the box for himself, hiding it in the car when I wasn't looking. He left this with his sister on his way back before he was attacked, and recovered it a year later. He even went back to the woods to search for the others but of course he couldn't find them. Some years later he sold some of the jewels from his cartridge to a dealer of dubious reputation who identified that they were part of the original crown jewels of the Kings of Wurtemburg and extremely valuable.'

'What!'

'Yes, I know ... because of this they were easily recognisable and consequently impossible to sell. It was then Beckmeier started looking for me. With a common name like Schmidt he found it difficult, especially as I'd lost touch with my old comrades in 2nd Panzer so they were no help to him. Then he saw my name somewhere and discovered this address. He called to see if he recognised me and of course he did. Then the trouble started.'

Elizabeth shook her head in disbelief. 'I don't understand, Klaus, you're a sensible competent businessman yet you have been behaving like a small-time crook.' She looked away and then glanced back at him. 'Oh my God! I hardly feel I know you. I'm sorry, this is all a horrible shock. But, go on Klaus, what happened? What did he say?'

'Beckmeier threatened to go to the police but he had no concrete proof and anyway he was implicated himself so I called his bluff. Then he told me that he'd traced the 35 year-old younger son of Fürst von Benz ... that's Joachim who telephoned Gerhard. It seems he claims he remembers my visit and the delivery of the box in 1945. This was bad news because I'd no idea how much the son knew about the contents and whether he was aware some had gone missing. There was no way of knowing how much information would come out.'

'But apart from Beckmeier, no-one knew you had anything.' Elizabeth said, relief colouring her voice. Then she saw his face. 'Did they?'

'I'd sold a gold locket to a dealer in Hamburg in 1947.' He admitted. 'That could have been easily traced back to me. Beckmeier's aim was to accumulate evidence implicating me and then blackmail me.'

He paused and pulled at his cigarette before continuing.

'That was when I made my biggest mistake. I decided to buy him off with one of the smaller jewels. I thought if I gave him money he could bleed me dry but the jewels would cost me nothing. But of course he came back for more. So I set up a trap for him and he was arrested. The second time I had actually given him some modern pieces that I bought especially for the purpose. When he blustered, claiming that I had stolen them from a 1945 consignment being delivered to Fürst von Benz, the police decided that he was lying and didn't believe any of his story.'

A guilty expression crossed his face.

'It was unfair I admit, but I had to stop the man.'

'Did it?'

'Partly ... I may have temporarily neutralised Beckmeier but he has friends. He'd told them the story and now they're sniffing around. I don't know how much they know.'

He paused and then added 'Well now I've told you everything.'

Elizabeth stared at him. She drew heavily on her cigarette and looking away slowly blowing out a plume of smoke.

'I can hardly believe it. All this time you've kept silent. My God! What have you done? What have you done, Klaus? You've put everything you've built at risk – our marriage, your business ... everything. I never dreamed you

46

could behave like this.' She paused and nothing was said for several seconds.

And then with a sigh she looked straight at him 'Is there a bug in your study?'

'I don't know ... after what Anson was saying tonight, it's possible.'

'Let's go look.'

'What now? It's nearly two in the morning!'

'We'll only lie awake wondering if we don't.'

'Anson did mention that wrapping it in foil would mask it.' Klaus said, appearing to take comfort from the fact. 'Let's do it.'

Stopping only to collect the foil from the kitchen, they soon stood in the doorway to his study. Her finger on her lips she mimed that they had better not make any noise, but then Klaus grinned and gestured towards the record player. As Beethoven's Fifth exploded into the room, they began their search.

It was Elizabeth who found the device, stowed inside what purported to be a Dutch dictionary. They stared at it, feeling both exultant and slightly sick, then quickly wrapped it in foil wrap.

'So I was right ... I am under surveillance.' His voice was curiously resigned.

'What now?' She asked as he stopped the music.

'I suppose I could pass it to Anson ... I'm meeting him tomorrow. Maybe he could find out who ... who planted this.'

They walked slowly back to the lounge carrying the strange, metal-wrapped object.

'Klaus, is this just commercial espionage or is it linked to those jewels or perhaps the papers you found?' She reached for a cigarette and lit it, her hand shaking.

'How the hell do I know? You seem to think that if someone has been bugging the place I must automatically be guilty of something. It's ridiculous!'

'Is it, Klaus? After what you've just told me? You haven't exactly kept within the letter of the law have you?'

'That's got nothing to do with it! It's probably one of my competitors.'

'Come on Klaus, you don't really believe that do you? They'd have bugged your office, yes, I can believe that, but your home?'

He offered no reply; she realised he was backing away from her again. She aggressively stubbed out her cigarette, and stalked up and down the room fighting down the urge to smash something. However, as she thought through what she'd learned, it dawned on her that shady characters like Beckmeier and his friends were extremely unlikely to resort to bugging his study. A mob like that wouldn't have that level of sophistication, surely. So who could it be? It felt sinister – the work of a big organisation. And they would hardly be interested in a few pieces of jewellery, even if they had royal antecedents.

Still Klaus said nothing. Suddenly feeling that the air in the room felt stale, she left. His eyes followed her, something like despair engulfing him.

Chapter 2

Schmidt left for the office as usual, the foil package in his briefcase, leaving Elizabeth pacing the floor desperate to do something but unsure what. An idea struck her. She reached for the telephone.

'Gerhard, are you busy today?'

'Well, I have that idiot von Benz coming this morning but apart from that, no. Why?'

'Could we meet for coffee this afternoon perhaps?'

'Not afternoon tea?' He teased. 'Don't say you have lost the habit, Elizabeth!'

She laughed, if a little perfunctorily.

'No, not at all ... I just thought you might prefer coffee.'

'What time would suit you?' He asked, wondering why she was so lack lustre.

They arranged to meet at 4pm; von Hessler stared at the telephone for several minutes after the call was ended.

'Yes, of course.' Anson strove to keep the surprise out of his voice.

As Schmidt's secretary gave him directions he tried to work out why the promised meeting was being held in a restaurant. He'd heard that

Schmidt was conventional ... it was hardly conventional to hold meetings in restaurants. What is going on?

Curiosity burning inside him, he found his way to the discreet entrance on the river embankment and, after giving Herr Schmidt's name to the smart waiter, he was led into a long airy dining room where the vast array of windows filling one wall permitted an impressive and very attractive view across a sweeping bend in the wide river. A series of square tables covered by pristine white tablecloths was ranged along the windows and the room was filled with the hum of conversation from the obviously well-dressed and equally well-heeled clientele. Schmidt rose to greet him.

'Good morning, Peter. You had no problem finding your way here, I hope?'

'No, none at all, thank you. Your secretary gave very clear instructions.'

'Excellent! First food, I think, and then we can get down to business.'

However, the conversation over hors d'oeuvres centred on the state of the German economy and Anson began to suspect that his host was keeping to generalities for a reason though what precise reason completely baffled him.

The main course arrived.

'Who are you really working for?' Schmidt suddenly asked in an almost menacing fashion.

'The company whose name appears on the card I gave you,' said Anson with mild surprise.

'Lieutenant Commander Anson, shall we dispense with such absurdities? When an ex-member of English Intelligence starts taking an interest in me I want to know why.' He paused, his eyes searching Anson's face. 'You must understand that I know I'm being watched, my movements monitored and my telephone tapped. Why do you think I suggested we meet here?'

Anson looked at Schmidt with considerable astonishment. What the hell's going on? Gerhard never mentioned that Schmidt was under any sort of covert surveillance. He decided to play for time.

'I can only repeat what I've just told you,' said Anson looking straight at Schmidt. 'And I assure you that my position is not influenced by any commercial interests other than those of the company that I now work for. The fact that I was in British Naval Intelligence has no bearing whatever on my wish to meet you. You have to believe me.'

Anson felt under scrutiny as Schmidt digested this. But all the same, he liked Schmidt's style - it was much the same as his own - direct and open.

'Lieutenant Commander, you interest me. I am reliably informed that you undertook some intelligence work in Hamburg a few years back. Yet you claim you are now working for a commercial company ... only a fool or a very honest man would expect me to believe that.'

Anson thought quickly – this sounded like a case of commercial espionage and the man clearly wanted him to look into it. That would be easy enough to uncover. Might be the Stasi over the East German border, though. Either way, it would be an opportunity to get closer to Schmidt.

'You will have to trust me,' responded Anson. 'That's all I can say.'

'Your English code of honour is not what it was, Lieutenant Commander. Do you really expect me to trust you when you admit nothing? If you tell me nothing then I have to assume that you're not my friend.'

'Herr Schmidt, you know as well as I do that the capitalist system works on trust. You do business with men you trust not to cheat you more than a certain percentage. Okay, so criminals operate within the system, but only for so long. They are discovered and the rest of us go on trusting, because if we didn't the system would eventually grind to a halt. It cannot function without reasonable honesty.'

Schmidt stared at him for a long moment then appeared to come to a conclusion. 'Excuse me for a second,' he said. Heaving his bulk out of his seat, he crossed the room, exiting through a door.

Perplexed, his senses on the alert, his thoughts whirring, Anson sipped his wine and gazed out of the windows apparently engrossed in the sight of the endless procession of heavily-laden boats plugging upstream against the fast-flowing muddy brown water on the busy Rhine. Out of the corner of his eye, he saw Schmidt reappear and pausing to speak to two men he obviously knew, make his way back to their table. For all he said about choosing a public place for their meeting because he's fearful of being watched, surely a place where he would not be recognised or observed would have been more sensible. This isn't making any sense.

Schmidt seated himself.

'Anson, you've persuaded me. Now we can talk in private.'

He tapped the top pocket of his suit and Anson caught his meaning. The man had been taking no chances - their conversation had been recorded via radio link to the men on the other table. Bastard! That was unexpected to say the least!

'Following our conversation over dinner last night, my wife and I carried out a little search of my study at home. And we found this.' Schmidt produced the foil-wrapped bundle and, carefully ensuring it stayed contained, passed it across to his astonished guest. 'Can you take it and find out where it came from? I need to know who it is behind my surveillance and before you ask, I cannot trust anyone in the security business here. They have been infiltrated by all sorts of people - criminals, policemen, intelligence men, arms dealers, even the Mafia. They have fast computers that can decrypt coded messages. Nothing is safe. That's why I need somebody completely outside the system, outside West Germany ... and you drop into my lap if you will pardon the expression. With your experience you could be a valuable man for me. I can make it worth your while.'

Anson tried to cover his surprise; this was an opportunity that would not come his way again! He thought fast; of course, there may be unpleasant consequences ... the gambler in him urged him on.

'You make it hard for me to refuse, Herr Schmidt.' He said with a smile. 'I still have friends in intelligence so maybe I can help you. But first I will need to make some phone calls.'

Immediately Anson regretted his impetuosity – something that had got him into trouble in the Navy and one of the reasons he had left. You idiot! You've virtually promised you can call on naval intelligence resources! Who can you possibly expect to help you in the UK? And what do you know the murky sea of commercial espionage? If indeed that was what it was. .

Even more frustratingly, after this surprising turn in the conversation Schmidt made no further mention of his concerns. Despite this, Anson found himself enjoying the rest of the lunch. Schmidt was an accomplished and entertaining raconteur.

Anson drove back across the city somewhat lost in thought. What an extraordinary man

Schmidt was. To sit there quite calmly and admit he was under surveillance by an unknown organisation or power ... and it had to be something big if the type of bug he'd handed over was anything to go by. The Britisher had only glanced briefly at the technology but even he could see that it was not a tin-pot affair.

This whole affair was becoming dangerous. He had better cover his tracks. Annoyed with himself he belatedly realised that his meetings with Schmidt may had been noted ... he may even have been tailed. A change of hotels would be a sensible precaution. Driving up to a large one not far from his own, he swung into the car park and, throwing the car key under the seat, he walked in, registering under his own name, paying for one night in cash. That done, he took the lift up to his room and sat down to think. He waited half an hour before ringing the desk. Had anyone made enquiries about him? No, sir, not for him personally. However, there had been a routine police check.

'What sort of check?' asked Anson. He was assured that it was one of the random checks during which the police noted down names of people with foreign passports.

A chill ran down his spine. Coincidence or not, this was sinister. A random check with anything but random timing. Whether they had been real policemen or not was irrelevant, what was clear was that he was up against a professional organisation who were used to moving fast.

Leaving his key in the door he calmly walked down to the restaurant. The waiters were wearing white shirts and black bow ties. Removing his jacket as the head waiter led him to a table he sat down. Menus were produced and the waiter left him. Quickly grabbing his jacket he got up and whisked through the door into the servery. An open door led to the kitchens and a food preparation room. Beyond that he could see the staff entrance. Taking a DM20 note out his wallet he folded it tightly and walking briskly up to the doorman slipped it to him.

'Don't tell the wife,' he said with a broad wink as he put on his jacket.

Out in the street there was little traffic and he spotted a taxi rank at the junction with a main road. The taxi set him down well past the entrance to his own hotel and he walked round the block as a precaution. Then he went in and sat down in the foyer. No-one appeared to be taking the smallest interest in the people coming and going, and after waiting for several minutes he collected his key and set about the task of finding an expert to look at the bug.

Chapter 3

As von Hessler waited for his visitor to arrive, he reflected over what he knew of Joachim, the son of old Prinz von Benz, a man von Hessler had known for many years. Unlike his late father, Joachim had a stiff manner that went a fair way to explaining why von Hessler disliked him. That, and the fact there was something slightly pathetic in his insistence on formal behaviour and excessive politeness; it was almost as if he was perpetually reminding people of his status. Perhaps due, in part, to the loss of the bulk of the family estates at the end of the First World War when the family had fled East Prussia by sea as the Russians advanced and taken up residence in the property near Kiel, owned by his grandfather.

Joachim had been only a boy at the time and had taken the collapse of his secure, privileged world badly. The family's long-standing tradition of sending the younger boys to Cadet Schools had broken down when such schools were abolished at the end of the Great War, so Joachim had been forced into the Hitler Youth just after the start of the Second World War though he had never fired a shot in anger. Defeat had left him stranded with no loyalties, a vague, aimless pacifism and profound sense of alienation from mainstream German culture. Conrad Adenauer and the men from the Rhineland who were leading Germany were not his sort of people. They lacked the Code of Honour that was part of the consciousness of a

58

special and personal relationship with the old Emperor, and when he died in Holland in 1941 the family had gone into mourning. As he mused over all this he realised that, to say the least, he was not looking forward to their meeting. He sighed deeply. The things that honour and status demanded of one!

Half an hour later, Gerhard, his affable expression firmly in place, watched as the tall and gangly Joachim entered the room. It offended his fastidious side that his visitor was wearing an ill-fitting suit of plain medium grey and sporting a trilby hat out of which sprouted a large blue-green feather, almost as if this execrence was intended to compensate for his otherwise nondescript appearance. Plainly, he was in an agitated state.

'May I offer you a drink?' Von Hessler asked.

'Schnapps ... please.'

While pouring the drink, his host watched under his eyelids as the young man lit a cigarette, his hands shaking. Once he'd got it lit, he sucked on it hungrily then sat down. Almost immediately he got to his feet again and started to pace the room, collecting his glass en route.

'Gerhard, I need your help. A ... a ... I don't know ... a criminal, I suppose you'd call him ... a horrible, coarse man ... he came to see me.' The eyes staring at von Hessler were full of terror. 'Gerhard ... he threatened me ... and my whole family! Normally, of course, my elder brother would deal with this but he's in America. It's an unbelievable story. The man claims that we're hiding valuable jewels that belong to the Bundesrepublic ... he speaks of war crimes and that we're bribing the police for protection, laying false accusations against one of his friends. A whole torrent of accusations! He demanded that we hand over the jewels otherwise ...' Joachim swallowed, obviously recalling the man's words. 'He threatened dreadful things! What the hell am I going to do?'

'Steady on, Joachim, for a start, why don't you sit down? I can't concentrate with you walking up and down like that.'

Joachim collapsed into an armchair and von Hessler continued. 'Now let us break this down. First of all, what are these jewels?'

'This man asserts that they were delivered to my father by an army officer called Schmidt towards the end of the war. He was driven to Kiel by a man who seems to be behind this criminal.'

'Do you know if this is true?' asked von Hessler, his mind working furiously.

Joachim shrugged helplessly. 'My aunt vaguely remembers a car arriving with an officer and driver towards the end of the war, but she saw nothing of any jewels.' He paused. 'In fact I think I remember their visit and the officer staying the night. But I heard nothing of any jewels either. I sort of remember seeing a large steel box with military markings on it, but that's all.'

'What did this officer look like?'

'He was a big man wearing a hat but it was nearly dark so I can't say that I saw much of his face. But I do remember the silver tank insignia he was wearing; he must have been from a Panzer unit.'

'What about the rest of his accusations?'

'Absolute nonsense. I asked the man what evidence he had but he just went on uttering vague threats'.

'So how did you react?'

'I told him that the whole story was complete and utter fiction. That my father was dead and that we had very little money. I impressed on him that it was nothing to do with me and that I intended to call the police, reporting this blackmail attempt. He laughed so I told the gardener to ring the police there and then. This obviously convinced him I meant business; he very quickly drove away. I didn't have the sense to take his registration number so when the police came I could only give them a rough description of the man.'

'What was he like?'

'Nothing special ... a commonplace sort of person, average height and so on. The only distinguishing feature that I could remember was his limp.'

'So why are you concerned about him now?'

'Well, wouldn't you be if you were threatened by a criminal? That story he told about a Panzer officer is actually true. What if the rest of it is too?'

Von Hessler thought for a moment as the younger man downed his drink in one gulp.

'My advice is that you should sit tight and do nothing. You called his bluff ... that may be enough. Let me know if or when something does happen and I'll see what I can do.'

Von Hessler stood up to signal that the interview was over and with that von Benz had no choice but to leave, though he was looking as tense as when he had arrived.

Just after two in the afternoon the telephone rang.

'Ah Peter ... how did your meeting with Klaus go this morning?'

'I need to talk to you Gerhard.'

Von Hessler frowned. 'Then talk.'

'I think it might be ... more friendly if we met up.' Anson replied, choosing his words carefully.

'Let me think, I'm meeting Elizabeth at four ...' Gerhard mused. 'Um ...'

'Really?   May I gate-crash your rendezvous? She's such a charming lady, I'd love to get to know her better.'

Von Hessler, every sense suddenly alert, analysed that statement carefully. 'Of course, my friend, we'd be delighted to see you.' He said, keeping his voice light, he mentioned the name of the cafe. 'See you at four then.'

Elizabeth arrived at the rendezvous before the others and sat smoking nervously trying to make sense of the message von Hessler had left that Anson would be joining them. Whatever could that mean? She was not left in the dark very long. The two men arrived virtually together and, as soon as all three had obtained their coffees, Anson dropped his bombshell.

'That bug you found.' He said, looking Elizabeth straight in the eye. 'I got some experts to look at it. They examined it; they'd never seen one as sophisticated as that. They reckon it could even have been a CIA job, would you believe.'

She gasped going pale.

'What bug?' Von Hessler asked.

'The one Klaus and I found in his study last night.' She said, reaching for her coffee and taking a long draught to steady herself.

'What I want to know is what your husband has been up to that would be of interest to a mob like that.' Anson said.

'I reckon I might have the answer to that.' Von Hessler said, suddenly realising the import of what von Benz had told him earlier. 'I saw von Benz this morning.' A glance at the silent woman sitting near him answered his tacit question. 'I see you know the story, Elizabeth.'

'Klaus told me about it last night.'

Anson looked from one to the other in confusion.

'You tell him, Gerhard.' Elizabeth said, reaching into her bag for a cigarette.

Although von Hessler only related the bare bones of the story, it still took several minutes in the telling.

'That still doesn't explain why a government organisation would be interested.' Anson said, his brow furrowed as he tried to assimilate the meaning of what he had just heard.

'There were not just jewels in the box.' Elizabeth said, going on to explain about the papers.

'Ah ... now that makes more sense.' Anson said with a heavy sigh. 'What a mess!' He went on to explain what had happened at the hotel after his meeting with Schmidt.

'That could be mere coincidence.' Von Hessler pointed out sceptically.

'It could.' Anson agreed, nodding his head slowly. 'But all the same ...'

'Yes, it seems so very unlikely.' Von Hessler sighed. 'That explains your tone on the telephone this morning, I suppose.'

'Gerhard, what are we going to do?' Elizabeth asked.

'Well, first of all, we have to do some serious thinking.'

'Not an easy process with so many imponderables. I suggest you think out the next move.' Anson put in.

'Aha, now we see the English mind at work. Offload the thinking to the continentals while you get on with the action. Ratiocination is hard work Old Boy; sub-contract that bit eh?'

'Gerhard, why do you have to think in caricatures? Any more of your obscure English words and we'll have to communicate in French at least then we'd both be on the same level. But enough of this. What do you think is going on.'

'I shall quote your Winston Churchill - it's a riddle wrapped in a mystery inside an enigma. What we know is that Klaus is up to his neck in something dangerous, Peter. After von Benz left me I did a little digging, forgive me Elizabeth, but I needed to find out if what he had told me about Schmidt had any basis in truth. And what do I find? Schmidt's old army service records have disappeared!'

'That's absurd!' Elizabeth cried, quickly hushing her voice.

'Gerhard, are you telling me that something sinister is going on inside intelligence circles?' Anson asked.

Von Hessler shrugged. 'Something is going on, either on an official level or in the grey area inhabited by such people as Nazi-hunters. That's my alarming conclusion.'

'God! But who could have the power for such a thing?'

'Exactly.' Von Hessler stared at the Englishman. 'But Klaus has asked you to help him, you say?'

'Yes, but I'll have to tread carefully. It could well be that the bug issue is nothing to do with ... with what you just told me. It could be commercial ... some sort of espionage to do with his business.'

'Klaus hasn't been involved in anything like that!' Elizabeth exclaimed.

'With respect, we don't know that, Elizabeth.' Von Hessler countered. 'If it's illegal exports we could easily come up against the CIA which would at least add up with what we currently know ... and God knows who else. We need to discover precisely who it is after him, and, perhaps more importantly, who we can call on for help. The disappearance of his records raises a definite question over my old friends in intelligence. A mole or is it a beetle?'

'Mole,' said Anson 'And my overwhelming problem is that I have a marketing job to hold down with a Director on my back. A man called Hendriks. It's easy for you aristocrats with your connections right through to Buckingham Palace!'

'I am sure Klaus will finance you, Peter.' Elizabeth said firmly. 'And he's sure to put some business your way.'

'If nothing else that should keep your Director happy.'

'Hendriks is no fool, Gerhard. He has a mind like a knife. He'll wants plans, strategy, refined tactics, progress reports, analyses, *und so weiter, und so weiter*. One new contract won't satisfy him. I can hear him say 'One swallow doesn't make a summer.' He's a hard man. I tell you what - you could ring up the palace. The Queen probably owns half the shares. Her people will know exactly who to ring and get him to back off.'

'Very funny! But let's get back to earth, shall we, Peter?'

But their banter quickly way to a more sombre mood as Anson bleakly laid out the case as he saw it.

'We've almost no hard information to work on, Gerhard. I've no idea who is blackmailing Schmidt or why – leaving aside that wartime story and I don't like the sound of the papers you mentioned, Elizabeth - and not a clue about who he has working for or against him. We have no idea who removed his record file and worryingly no idea if that hotel police check at the hotel was coincidence or not. I don't feel we can trust any official agency at this stage.' He shrugged his shoulders. 'There could be moles anywhere. It's not a pretty picture.'

Von Hessler raised his eyebrows and added a wry smile. Anson took a deep breath, trying to get his thoughts in order.

'Why would Klaus's file be missing?' Elizabeth asked, plainly out of her depth.

'That suggests someone wants to cover up his war record.' Anson said, working through the data logically. 'Yet it must have been scrutinised by the Americans before they released him and that means we are not talking about war crimes here.'

'Klaus was never a Nazi.' His wife assured them.

'So it can't be Nazi-hunters after him.' Von Hessler concluded taking a sip of his nearly cold coffee. He waited for Anson to go on.

'There can only be a handful of people who have the authority to access these records, remove them and also cover their tracks.' Anson said slowly, frowning as he tried to get a grip on this fact.

'We might get a lead via the police hotel check.' Von Hessler said. 'I've some friends who can find out if it was just a random check. Of course if it wasn't …' He let the words hang.

'It would have to be another inside job.' Anson finished for him. The two men exchanged a glance.

'But your biggest problem is getting Schmidt to talk. Elizabeth, you got him to tell you about the blackmail … perhaps you can apply a little more pressure and find out if there is anything else that is behind all this.'

'I can try.' She said anxiously.

'I intend to speak to him myself about what von Benz said this morning.' Von Hessler said.

'Talking of that, what do you think von Benz will do next?'

'I don't know ... he's something of a loose cannon. He could do anything.'

Von Hessler discovered the answer to that three days later when von Benz contacted him to arrange another meeting.   By this time, von Hessler had concluded that the whole plot relating to the jewels and the papers might have been connected to an upper class plot of some kind. It was undeniable that Von Benz family had a hand in attempting to get valuable jewels out of the country in 1945.   But did they know who owned the jewels?

What was true was that some members of the upper class, including his own extended family, had behaved very strangely during the final stages of the war, though to be fair, their earlier track record was mixed at best!   Some had remained aloof from the Nazis and Hitler but many had joined the SS after Himmler had offered them honorary membership. Many had been motivated by Hitler's aim to restore German self-esteem and discipline, others had been attracted by the Führer's hatred of Communism and his promises to restore the monarchy. Very few had joined the Resistance and those that had were amateurish in their efforts to say the least.   That bomb plot against Hitler for instance. A complete fiasco! And they had paid dearly for their failure to organize action in Berlin after the explosion. Planning had been half-baked, useless, and hindered by the Oaths of Loyalty army officers had been forced to make to Hitler. It was entirely possible von Benz had fallen in with this or a similar plan.

Von Benz arrived in a calmer state of mind this time.

'I've tracked down Major Schmidt of the Panzers.' He exclaimed with barely suppressed excitement.

'Oh?' von Hessler froze.

'Yes, he lives in Düsseldorf. I went to see him.'

'I see. So tell me what happened.'

'I came straight to the point and told him that I knew he had illegally acquired some jewels and that I was considering going to the police.' Joachim's arrogance was tangible.

'What! What on earth did you think were you doing?' exclaimed von Hessler.

'That's easy to explain. Obviously, he set those criminals on to me so I thought the man needed putting in his place. I told him I had been present when he delivered jewels to my father in 1945 and that as the jewels had failed to reach their intended destination, I concluded that he had stolen them.'

'That was certainly a provocative move.' Gerhard commented dryly. 'How did he react?'

'At first he just stared at me. The silence began to be oppressive and I started wondering if perhaps I had made a mistake.' The reluctant admission swiftly changed into triumph. 'But then he leaned across his desk and asked me in a low voice what I planned to do about it.'

'I'll go to the police, I told him again.' The confidence von Benz shown suddenly faded. He frowned, confused. 'Then he proposed that we went to lunch where we could talk in private. That puzzled me ... I thought perhaps he was intending to bribe me to keep quiet but when we got to the restaurant, which was a very quiet place overlooking the river – rather nice really - he told me that I was getting into deeper waters than I realized and that I should be careful.'

A pair of puzzled, frightened eyes looked at von Hessler. How did your father produce a son like you?

'Schmidt spoke of what he called publicity of an unfavourable kind affecting both my family and other aristocratic families. He even suggested that someone was in a powerful position in England; in fact a family that he advised me not to fall foul of, might be involved. Then he reminded me that we are still in some ways an occupied country.'

'What sort of unfavourable publicity?'

'He mentioned some papers, letters, which might compromise my family both politically and morally. Naturally, I didn't believe him. But then he said he would send me a sample copy which would resolve any doubts I might have.'

'How would you know if it was genuine?'

'That's what I said but he said the originals could be validated by ink and simple and conclusive tests on the paper. There are forensic laboratories that do such work, you know.' He paused and something like chagrin spread across his features. Von Hessler wondered what was coming. 'Gerhard, he looked at me so ... so contemptuously! Me! A von Benz! And he laughed and told me I was out of my depth!'

'Why?'

With a sheepishness that said much about the man's mindset, he went on. 'It seems that both our discussion in the restaurant and the conversation we'd had in his office had been recorded. He told me to go back to Kiel and forget what I'd said as I hadn't a single shred of evidence against him. Then he threatened me, warning me that he had powerful friends.'

'What an extraordinary story. What are you going to do?'

'I've already done it,' admitted Joachim. 'I was so annoyed with his threats that I drove straight down to Bonn and walked into the British Embassy.'

'What!' Von Hessler closed his eyes ... was this man a total imbecile?

But Joachim was not listening. 'It's an awful place. Looks almost like a factory. I knew enough to realise that if a member of the English Royal family was involved in this somehow then would be keen to act. The official on duty started off being politely sceptical but as soon as I mentioned the Royal connection, he sat up and started to take notice. He passed me on to his superior and I related the whole story.'

'My God, Joachim! Was that wise?'

'Schmidt could be dangerous especially as he claims to have protectors, presumably corrupt police or criminals. He's got to be neutralised before he does some serious damage.'

'So you believe his story about the letters?' Von Hessler said, suddenly realising where the bugs could have come from. Not the CIA at all ... but UK intelligence!

'Yes, yes, I do. He was very convincing.'

There was a brief silence.

'So what was the outcome at the embassy?' Von Hessler asked, trying to contain his emotions.

'The official said he would speak to the ambassador and they would probably get in touch with me again.'

'Joachim, I can't say I'm at all happy about all this. I know Schmidt. He had a reputation in the Panzers as a tough character. I suppose that's why he was chosen to get the stuff to Kiel.'

'You know him?' Von Benz looked at him in horror, plainly, he did not know how to take this information.

'Look, why don't you leave this all to me from now on? The matter is acquiring an international dimension. It'll need careful handling.'

'Well, I suppose you're better placed than I am, especially as you know Schmidt. It would be a weight off my mind if I did leave it to you.'

Von Hessler waited while the arrogant, idiot of a young man visibly weighed up the benefits to himself.

'Perhaps it would be sensible to leave it in your hands, von Hessler.'

'Joachim, if I take it on it means no further action whatsoever on your part. Is that clear?'

'Yes, yes, all right. If you insist.'

'And you'll leave everything to me?'

'Yes. Haven't I said so!'

Another silence.

'I will of course keep you informed, particularly if anything comes up that might affect your family.' Von Hessler said slowly. He sighed. 'If and when the British embassy gets back to you, I suggest you tell them that I am looking after your interests and refer them to me.'

After von Benz had departed, von Hessler sat down to ponder the situation. That aristocratic idiot's crazy attempts to get his own back on Klaus had dragged in the British embassy – what action would they take over the letters? Was the English Royal family actually involved? True, they had many historic connections in Germany, not to mention that there had been strongly validated stories concerning a member of the blue-blooded Mitford family and her association with Hitler, so it was a possibility. Most alarmingly, the letters could pose a threat to the honour of the von Hessler family. .

He grimaced as he recalled evening visits at his father's house in Kiel made by his uncle and some senior members of the SS trying to convince his father to put his name behind the Nazi dream. His uncle had been the only von Hessler to back the regime actively; it was a matter of shame that the other family members tried to forget. But what if the papers now come to light had originated with him? His blood ran cold with shame at the thought. He sighed. Now he had an impelling personal reason to act in this matter. The key lay in finding out what had happened to the ammunition box and its contents; it must be found.

He heaved another deep sigh. It was time to see if his friends in German Naval intelligence could help. The fact that von Benz lived near the naval base at Kiel would have facilitated the business of getting jewels out of the country; could the navy have been involved?

A little after six that evening, Anson called. 'I'm heading back to the UK tomorrow, Gerhard. Unavoidable, I'm afraid.' He said. 'Just thought I would call and let you know.'

'Have a good flight. I'll keep you posted on that little project we discussed. It looks like it might keep me busy for a while.'

'Really? Well, don't overdo things. You don't want to damage your health there's some very nasty bugs going around.'

'Oh I reckon I know where they are coming from. I think you may be more at risk than I!'

'I'll be careful to avoid infection then. Please pass my regards to your friends.'

'Will do.'

Chapter 4

The new *Bundesmarine* was a shadow of the wartime *Kriegsmarine* and now largely occupied in little more than minesweeping and patrolling the Baltic. However, a cadre of intelligence staff had been retained and von Hessler had kept in touch with them. Now was the moment to see what they could unearth.

The first move would be to discover if any naval ships or U-boats had sailed over to Sweden just before the end of the war. He reached for the phone.

A few days later a phone call provided the information that there had been almost no serviceable U-boats left in the Baltic at the salient period. During the final Russian advance most had been sent on rescue missions to eastern ports or had been dispatched to Norway.

'However, there were a few S-boats still hanging around in Kiel.' His informant said.

Von Hessler's spirits rose – S-boats were extremely fast and could easily have made it to Sweden during the hours of darkness.

'Yes, records show that one set off for Trelleborg in Sweden on 4 May 1945.' The voice went on. 'But it was sunk by enemy aircraft off

Fehmarn Island. I can't find any evidence that any other S-boat tried to make the crossing.'

'Any survivors?' von Hessler asked.

'Yes, two crewmen survived: the wireless operator Mallmann and engine technician Hennig.'

'Von Hessler scribbled these names down, it was obvious that any cargo on board would now be at the bottom of the sea.

He terminated the call and sat looking at his notes, intrigued. Where was the wreck lying and in what depth of water? He knew some divers working for a ship repairing company in Kiel. That they could be asked to find the sunken S-boat was a tantalising thought.

But first he needed to track down the surviving crew members. Despite his best efforts, he drew a complete blank on Mallman's whereabouts but Hennig's home address in the records was the same as that given in the local phone directory against that name. Von Hessler called the number and smiled when the man who answered the phone confirmed that he had been a crew member of S 103. Quickly concocting a tale regarding research into the history of S-boats, he requested an interview. Hennig agreed to see him.

The next morning, feeling that he was finally getting somewhere, he set off to see the Maschinenstabsgefreiter of S-boat number 103.

There was a definite spring in his step as he set out into the fresh June morning. The stone cottages of the fishing village were bathed in sunlight, the grey of the stonework set off by the brilliant red and yellow of the flowers in the pots and tubs that lined the pavements. Raucous gulls circled overhead, squawking and breaking out into furious squabbles. Von Hessler thought back to his naval days when he had looked out over this same Baltic from his office in Kiel.

He had to go carefully. Hennig was now the only known survivor from the stricken boat and he might clam up if questioned in an insensitive way, and fail to provide the vital clues which would enable the wreck to be located. Von Hessler pulled on the bell of the grey stone cottage. The door was opened promptly by a short well-built man with a neatly trimmed grey beard and an expectant look on his weather-beaten face.

'Come in, Herr von Hessler,' said Hennig warmly and showed him into the snug little sitting room.

'It is kind of you to see me,' said von Hessler. 'I hope this won't bring back too many unhappy memories for you.'

Hennig hesitated; his firm features betrayed a trace of anxiety. 'I've never talked to anyone about the sinking – not even my wife.' For a moment he looked down at the threadbare carpet. Then he straightened up and faced von Hessler.

'That was a bad time but I have happy memories as well. We were a good crew, worked well together, did our job. I can show you a photograph of them, if you like.'

He went to a battered old desk and pulled out an envelope. In it was a dock-side photograph of the crew of S103, the captain, the navigator, the helmsman, gunners and torpedo men, the wireless operator and cook, and Hennig himself, the man in charge of the engines. They looked so young, thought von Hessler. Some were smiling but even so he detected signs of strain in some of the faces. The photo was probably taken towards the end of the war, he decided, by that time a mere handful of the original hundred or so S-boats were still operative.

There was an awkward pause. Von Hessler had planned to start a general conversation about life in the Kriegsmarine but, faced with this photo, he changed tack and asked to hear more about the crew.

'All dead but me and Mallmann the wireless operator. It was almost the end of the war and we'd all come through with no serious injuries. It seems so wrong that they should have died then.' Hennig stopped and looked hard at him. Von Hessler could see that even after 25 years he was still grieving.

But the man was going on. 'A few more days and all of us would have been safe. Every time I put to sea today I ask myself 'Why just me and Mallmann? But Herr von Hessler, you didn't come here to talk about the crew, did you? You want to know about that box we were taking to Sweden. That's what I think. I reckoned there was something funny about it at the time. What was it all about?'

Von Hessler cursed silently. He should have foreseen this. He'd have to tread carefully.

'You're quite right, Herr Hennig, it was an unusual cargo. Firstly because its exact nature was kept secret, and still is a secret for that matter, and secondly because of the strange circumstances surrounding the attempt to get it to Sweden. I ...'

'But why now? Why has it come up after all this time? After twenty-five years?' Interrupted Hennig.

'A good question; I wish I had the answer.' He said in an honest, man-to-man way. 'Questions are being asked by a variety of people – the police, people in Bonn, even foreign governments. That's why I'm here today. Nobody seems to know what was in that box. Was it dangerous? Maybe radioactive? Was it biological? Nobody seems to know. The first thing that we need to find out is what happened to your boat. The naval records tell us almost nothing.'

'Well that's no secret,' said Hennig. 'We were shot up by those RAF bastards. They caught us napping. She sank in less than five minutes. Me and Mallmann got away in one of the life rafts and a fishing boat picked us up early the next morning.'

'How did it all start?' asked von Hessler. 'Why don't you tell me the whole story from the beginning?'

Von Hessler anxiously pondered what was going on in Hennig's mind. His face had the look of a perplexed yet determined man. Was he aware that he was the key to the search? Did he think his information might be saleable, that there might be a reward? He waited impatiently for the outcome of the man's internal struggle.

The uncomfortable silence was broken only by the ticking of the marine chronometer on the wall. The minutes passed, then, apparently coming to a decision, Hennig began speaking.

'Well I'll tell you. It all started when the skipper called us into the office and told us that we was to do a trip to Trelleborg that night. Our navigator was right surprised. Not at all happy. He said there would be no cloud cover and a nearly full moon – it would be suicide. But the skipper said we was to leave at 2300 hours come what may. I was told to make sure we had enough fuel to get us there at high speed. When I asked him how fast, he said I was to reckon on 30 knots. I can tell you, this worried the navigator even more. At that speed our wake would be visible for miles! I threw in my three ha'pence about problems with the cooling water intakes and said that continuous cruising at 30 knots would be seriously pushing it. But the skipper wasn't to be shifted.' He shook his head at the memory. 'But at least the sea was calm and we wouldn't be knocked about too much at that speed. So I supervised fuelling, checked the lubricators on the three stern glands, checked the air pressure for the starters and we waited. About an hour before we was due to leave a big car arrives on the dockside and two men carries a big steel box across to us. They put it in the skipper's cabin which was odd in itself.'

'Why do you say that?' interrupted von Hessler.

'Cargo would normally go in the storage spaces or in the torpedo tubes. Often things like ball bearings were packed in quite small boxes and we could easily find places to stow them. But we never put stuff in the skipper's cabin.' He stopped uncertainly. 'Shall I go on?'

'Of course, please do. You're being most helpful.'

'At exactly 2300 hours we cast off and in no time we were up to speed. I remember the night was warmer than usual with good visibility and the skipper stayed on the bridge. Our navigator was used to doing the trip and he spent very little time looking at the charts and was up with the skipper. I did my engine checks every hour on the hour. The gunners were keeping a sharp lookout or so we thought, you see, we had no radar so we had to rely entirely on them.'

'At 30 knots I imagine there wasn't much room for navigational errors,' said von Hessler. 'I wouldn't like to do the passage inside Fehmarn Island at that speed in the dark.'

Hennig hesitated, did he perhaps realise that he was being coaxed into revealing their route ... whether they had sailed inside or outside the island?

'You're right, but that cursed moonlight was working for us at that point so we could easily pick out the shoreline either side of us.'

A surge of relief tsunamied through von Hessler – now he knew their route and their speed.

All he needed now was precise timing and Hennig was about to oblige. It was all he could do not to grin broadly.

'I'd just started my second engine check when it happened. There was no bloody warning. Nothing. Suddenly shells tore into us from the stern. The lights went out and the engines coughed and died one after the other. The smoke and fumes of the high explosives filled the engine room and made me choke. I got an eyeful of diesel that was spraying out from a ruptured feed pipe. Then the emergency lighting came on and I could just make out Mallmann groping for the handrail on the companionway. Everything had gone silent and for the first time I heard that damned aircraft. It had come up behind us without a shot being fired by our gunners. The deck was a terrible sight. That plane had well and truly strafed us. Some of the men were groaning, I remember one screaming, others just lay unmoving, silent. The skipper and navigator were crumpled on the floor of the bridge.'

Distress was evident on Hennig's face and he made for the door. This was a moment that von Hessler knew all too well. Several times he had had to stop a debriefing to allow a ship's crew to recover. A rush to the lavatory often followed. But he had not expected it this time. It was over a minute later a grim-faced Hennig returned with a bottle of schnapps and filled a pair of stubby glasses. Without a word he poured two generous quantities; they drank them down. The two men looked at each other, unspeaking. Words seemed superfluous. And then Hennig continued.

'Mallmann starts to undo the lashings on the forward life raft. Two men are crawling up to the other life raft and releasing it. But the noise of the aircraft's engine isn't dying away as I hoped and I realise it's turning. The bastards swing right round and come in low on our port side. Mallmann and me heave the life raft clear of its brackets and shove it into the water on the other side. I see the other two men get theirs overboard but that was on the side that was facing the plane. We jumped into our raft and lay down flat on our stomachs waiting for the second attack. There's a burst of cannon fire followed by a deafening explosion. That must have been some of our own ammunition. The boat was on fire. We unshipped the paddles and put as much distance between us and S103 as we could.'

Hennig stopped abruptly, poured out some more schnapps and threw it down his throat.

'It went down quickly. We were too paralysed to do anything for several minutes. Then in the moonlight I picked out the other life raft and we paddled over to it. It was low in the water and both men were gonners. We couldn't do nothing for them.' Hennig stopped again, staring out of the window. The only sound was the squawking of the gulls outside. In a low voice he went on: 'She sank fast. Later we was picked up by a fishing boat.'

He seemed exhausted by this reliving of the traumatic time.

Von Hessler stood up and went over to the window. He looked out over the peaceful Baltic at a fishing boat chugging slowly out of the harbour. He could think of nothing to say. But the business had to be finished. He turned to Hennig with one last question.

'Do you know what course you were steering after you cleared Fehmarn?'

Immediately he knew the question was a mistake. Hennig's face clouded and then darkened.

'Why do you want to know that?'

'I want to get a complete picture of the whole journey. It helps to put all the pieces together.'

'Yes,' Said Hennig, 'and it helps you find the wreck of my boat and that precious cargo that you're after! Well you'll get no more help from me. I've told you too much already. That boat is a war grave and you're not going to touch it. I'll see to that.'

Von Hessler had met angry reactions to his questioning before. Some U-boat commanders had become positively truculent when he had queried their complaints about defective torpedoes. He was used to taking it from a *Kapitänleutnant* but not from a *Maschinenstabsgefreiter*. He looked hard at Hennig and for a moment his mind wandered. The man had stirred up a feeling that he recognised. It was the discomfort of facing someone of greater courage than he suspected lay within himself. He felt reluctant to go on, but the intelligence officer in him reasserted control and he switched back to the multi-level thinking needed to keep ahead in an interrogation. The man might stir up trouble with the *Bundesmarine* and was worth placating.

'Please take my word, Herr Hennig, that we have no intention of disturbing a war grave. In fact we know from the records that all the bodies of the crew were found apart from yourself and Mallmann, so I am glad to assure you that the question of a war grave does not arise. It has been extremely kind of you to answer my questions and I won't bother you any further.'

'And what about that extra man.' said Hennig.

Von Hessler battled to conceal his astonishment and raced through possible responses. This was something that he had not foreseen. Even though he could dismiss a body left in the wreck on the grounds that its existence was not backed by any official record curiosity got the better of him.

'Tell me about him,' he said. 'You must have an idea who he was.'

Hennig's face in turn was giving nothing away.

'Why does it matter to you?'

'Well for a start it might have been Martin Bormann.' Von Hessler suggested slyly.

'Not a chance,' said Hennig. 'He was tall, straight, fair-haired. He'd a posh accent ... haughty but different from a SS man such as Bormann. The captain treated him with respect like he was a senior officer. And he had a briefcase with a gold shield on it ... I remember there was some initials below the shield and the last letter had a little 'v' before it. He must have been a 'von Something'.'

Von Hessler did his best to conceal his astonishment. He needed time to adjust to the extraordinary turn that the investigation had taken. For a second or two he said nothing while Hennig stared at him. But he decided that further questioning would only annoy the man; it was time to leave. Abruptly he got up and offered his hand.

'I really must get back to Kiel,' he handed his card to Hennig. 'Please let me know if you remember anything. Thank you for your time ... you've been most helpful. '

Von Hessler drove back fast and exuberantly to Kiel his mind mulling over the information he had extracted from Hennig. He seemingly had everything needed to establish the position of the wreck. On reaching home, he went straight to his study and pulled out a chart of the Baltic hurriedly plotting the wreck's likely position. His buoyant mood evaporated. The spot he had marked was very close to the maritime boundaries of with both Denmark and East Germany. It was now clear that establishing its exact position was crucial and he had to be doubly sure that he had not missed anything. He decided to ring Anson. He was fresher at the intelligence game and one of the people he could trust.

It took a quarter of an hour to get hold of Anson who, according to his secretary, was just finishing a meeting in his office. He hung on, practising the words he would use.

'Gerhard, how are you?' Peter's voice said eventually.

'Peter, old boy, you are going to need a chart of our Baltic to make any sense of this conversation.'

Von Hessler heard laughter at the end of the line.

'Equipped as I am to deal with most contingencies, my dear Gerhard, I have to confess that I do not have Baltic sea charts in my office. I'm in the business of marketing chemicals not ships! But I do have a large atlas. Will that do?'

'Of course. Open up the page covering Kiel, Fehmarn Island and the tip of Sweden. OK?'

'Hang on ... yes, I've got that.'

'Now I'll tell you what I've learned from Maschinenstabsgefrieter Hennig.'

'Who's he?'

Von Hessler quickly explained. 'I think I can trust him – he seems to be a precise, disciplined character who takes pride in his job. The sinking of S103 is strongly engraved on his memory and I reckon he's an accurate witness. I set out to get precise details of speed, course and

89

distance travelled by his boat and he didn't disappoint me.'

'That's something of a surprise.' responded Anson. 'Surely he was only the engine mechanic; how would he have that sort of knowledge?'

'Well just listen to this. First let us deal with speed. Before they set out, the skipper insisted on cruising at 30 knots despite objections from the navigator, and I suspect Hennig would have set the throttles to achieve very close to that. Then, by one of those chances of fate, the RAF attack took place exactly at the point when he was starting his second round of engine checks which he did at hourly intervals. He told me that he had done these precisely on the hour so we can confidently conclude that the boat had been out for almost exactly two hours, which at 30 knots gives us 60 nautical miles travelled. OK so far?'

'Yes,' said Anson in a guarded voice. 'I'll give you that.'

'Now we come to the course steered. Heading for Trelleborg they had a choice of going inside or outside Fehmarn Island. He said he could see land on both sides of the vessel which means they went inside the island. After that they had to turn north and I couldn't get much more out of him. In fact he clammed up on me. But looking at the chart it now seems obvious to me. They would have had to clear Gedser on the tip of one of the Danish islands so I can make a pretty good guess as to where the navigator would have put the waypoint for the northward turn.'

'Hold on, Gerhard, while I check the map. Yes, I see what you mean. What about currents?'

'Hennig told me at the start that the sea was calm so there can't have been much wind to stir up currents along the Fehmarn channel, and as you are no doubt aware the tides are minimal in the Baltic. It looks like a straightforward plot to me. Agreed?'

'It looks too easy. I smell a rat. You'd be bursting into song by now if there wasn't a catch. What is it?'

'*Mein Gott* Peter, your antennae are working well even down the telephone. No attenuation at all, if that's the right word. I'm impressed. The catch is a big one. My plot shows the wreck uncomfortably close to East German waters.'

'How close?'

'Just a seamile or two.'

'I see. That is a bit of a setback. But I can't see any reason to question the accuracy of your plot. It looks right to me provided you're correct about Hennig. Are you sure about him?'

'Absolutely sure. He is a seadog of the old sort and I would trust him any day.'

'Then we'll have to stick with your findings. There is one thing you haven't told me – what depth of water are we in?'

'Twenty four metres, so at least it's within an aqualung diver's limit. But the second catch is that the East Germans have banned almost all underwater exploration in their part of the Baltic and the Bundesmarine is under orders to avoid boundary incidents. So I'm going to have a much harder time persuading my naval friends to locate the wreck using their sonar gear, let alone getting them to mount a diving expedition.'

'So what do you propose?'

'I think I'll have to go right to the top. As you know I've met Rear Admiral Lange several times at the sailing club; I thought I'd approach him. He was the man with the piercing eyes that I introduced you to last year.'

'Well, good luck to you on that one, Gerhard. He seemed a formidable character to me. Watch your step - and keep me posted. If I didn't have a job to do I'd join you. Anyway, the best of luck.'

Several hours on the phone to his friends resulted in a highly satisfied von Hessler presenting himself at the Admiral's brand new offices three days later. There was little resemblance to the comfortless, wartime bureaux that he remembered. Now there was a thick carpet on the floor where before there had been linoleum. The furnishings were modern, the filing cabinets in the outer office veneered in an expensive-looking wood and the only sounds were the discreet throb of air conditioning and the subdued, distant voices of the staff. Had it not been for the presence on the wall of a large chart of the Baltic, Gerhard would have reckoned he was at the Headquarters of Siemens or Mercedes Benz, the only other evidence of naval occupation the bulky, government-issue fire extinguisher and some racks of electronic gear.

The Admiral was a handsome, well-built man with no trace of grey in his dark hair. His challengingly intelligent eyes focused on von Hessler as the latter expounded the need to discover the contents of the ammunition box.

'Herr von Hessler, before I let you go any further I have a question – who exactly are you working for?'

'For myself, Admiral. My enquiries started when I was asked to help an English friend of mine with something entirely unconnected with the navy. I got drawn in and now it has awoken my professional naval interest, and I can't let it drop.'

'So you have become a sort of naval Sherlock Holmes?' There was a hint of mockery in the Admiral's voice. 'But this is not fiction and we're in the real world. You are asking me to authorise an operation the like of which I am expressly forbidden to undertake. Not only because it is outside my operational limits, but also because it involves an underwater search that will look like espionage to Ulbricht's people. Willi Brandt is a friend of mine and he will not be amused if I upset his opposite number.'

'Would you be prepared to ask him?' said von Hessler grasping at the faint chance that the Admiral might be tempted by a challenge.

The faint smile in the Admiral's eyes clearly revealed his appreciation of von Hessler's tactics.

'You rate this mystery box rather more highly than is warranted by the evidence that you've so far produced. Can it be of such importance that I should raise it with the Chancellor of all people?' Clearly he suspected something.

'Well Sir, I can only repeat that a number of foreign agencies are showing interest in it. Someone somewhere knows more about the contents than we do and I have an uncomfortable feeling that we might be sorry if they get to the wreck first.'

'Who are 'we' in this context?' asked the Admiral.

'Prominent members of our society, royal families, even our own government.' Von Hessler replied, meeting the man's eyes. Choosing his words carefully, he went on. 'The war-crimes people or the press both here and abroad could make trouble. Whatever was in that box in 1945 was sufficiently vital to persuade General von Lauchert and others to ship it out of the country. I need hardly point out that the key player in the planned transport of the box was the Kriegsmarine. Somebody with authority sanctioned both the trip and the presence of that supernumerary crew member, possibly someone with an unsavoury reputation. I suggest that we find his briefcase before someone else does.'

'If he has an unsavoury reputation then he joins the pile of other Nazis on the scrapheap of history. Why should the Navy concern itself with him?'

'Well Sir,' replied von Hessler smoothly, 'he might have been a senior naval officer.'

The Admiral screwed up his eyes while he ran the tip of his forefinger up and down his nose.

'I can see why you were in intelligence, Herr von Hessler.' He paused and looked even harder at his visitor for several seconds before continuing. 'I think you had better give me that piece of paper with the co-ordinates of the wreck.'

The admiral looked at it and put it in his pocket.

'I am not going to make any promises. I cannot take it through official channels. If I do mention this to the Chancellor it will have to be off-the-record. Consequently I must ask you to give me your solemn word that you will not disclose this conversation to anyone, anyone at all. Do I have your solemn word?'

'Admiral, you have my solemn word.'

'One more thing, Herr von Hessler - I don't want you inveigling yourself into my office again. I will get a message to you within the next three weeks, but that will be the end of our discussions. Is that clear?'

'Entirely clear, Admiral.'

Von Hessler made his farewells and left the room, ignoring the curious glances of the secretaries working in the outer office. How many times had they seen men looking a little grim, even shocked as they emerged through that door? The thought amused him.

Two weeks later he discovered that his efforts to involve the navy had been in vain, word reached him that there would be no help forthcoming. It was strongly hinted that the Chancellor's Ostpolitik was sacrosanct and that nothing that could possibly be interpreted as a hostile act by the East Germans would be considered.

Denied naval co-operation, his only viable option was a commercial salvage company. Gerhard started to make enquiries among local firms. However, as soon as he suggested that the wreck lay close to the limits of West German waters he met immediate refusals. One company led by an ex-diver became almost abusive reminding him that the fate of any diver caught in an act that could be deemed espionage was to lose his head.

'You exaggerate!' Von Hessler protested.

Though his mood changed as the man reminded him of the British diver, Commander Crabbe, whose headless body had been found in Portsmouth harbour in 1956 following the visit of the Russian cruiser Ordzhonikidze.

Obviously commercial help was going to be costly and his enthusiasm did not extend to cover the signing of fat cheques. The only possible source of money was Klaus Schmidt. Perhaps it was time to take another plane to Düsseldorf and disclose his plans. It would not take much to persuade Klaus of the dangerous implications for him if others got to the wreck first.

However, before he could make his travel arrangements he received a call from Admiral Lange's office informing him that he would be receiving a visit from one of his staff officers. The following day a Kapitänleutnant Fricke presented himself. Taller than von Hessler, he had piercing eyes that reminded Gerhard of Admiral Lange.

Von Hessler escorted his visitor to the large drawing room with its collection of neo-classical and Biedermeier furniture, most of which showed the ravages of time. On the walls hung some unrestored paintings in gilt Rococo frames, and a faded early Bechstein grand piano on three luxuriously carved legs stood in one corner of the room. There was a hint of furniture polish that suggested the room not been used or ventilated properly. It was as bad as an antique shop!

Adjudging the rather disdainful expression on Fricke's face to be reaction to his surroundings, Von Hessler offered the man a particularly uncomfortable seat. He was unaccustomed to being interviewed by another professional, particularly one who was responsible for Intelligence under Admiral Lange, and the thought disturbed him. Fricke immediately took charge of the conversation.

'Herr von Hessler, three days ago a *Volksmarine* hydrographic survey vessel was seen steaming up and down their side of the Bay of Mecklenburg in roughly the area where you suspect lies the wreck of S103. It appeared again the next day. This is unusual and a departure from their normal procedures.'

He paused with an enquiring look on his face.

'*Scheiss!*'

For once von Hessler was at a loss. Who could possibly have alerted the Volksmarine? There must have been a leak. But where?

'Maybe it's a coincidence,' said von Hessler, attempting to cover his alarm and immediately regretting saying it.

'There are no coincidences in the intelligence business, as I am sure you would agree,' said Fricke dismissively, raising a sceptical eyebrow. 'Exactly how many people possess information relating to S103?'

'As far as I know, only Admiral Lange, Hennig who was the Maschinenstabsgefreiter on S103 and myself. Nobody else. No one else has even the faintest clue as to the location of the wreck.'

'You are quite sure about this?' asked Fricke with an undercurrent of menace.

'Quite sure,' responded von Hessler making little attempt to conceal his irritation.

'Well, at least that narrows the field.' Fricke paused.

Von Hessler realised that his list was far shorter than the man had expected. Ought he to have to included Chancellor Brandt? Or Schmidt? Or Anson?

'How do you rate Hennig? Is he likely to have disclosed anything?' Fricke asked.

'I doubt it. In fact he objected strongly to the idea of disturbing the wreck, describing it as a war grave. He has no idea of the significance of the stuff on board and certainly isn't the type to go shooting his mouth off. He told me he hasn't even talked to his own wife about the sinking.'

Fricke sat silently staring at the painting of a von Hessler ancestor in court uniform on the wall opposite. The thought occurred to von Hessler that the Kapitänleutnant was treading carefully and his spirits rose.

'I imagine that I am not very popular with the Admiral,' said von Hessler in an attempt to draw out him out.

'The Admiral is being tight-lipped but, rest assured, you are not in any sort of trouble, Herr von Hessler. The people who are likely to bear the brunt are in Bonn and very near the centre of government. But this is a 'hot potato' as the English would say and I should not say any more. What I would advise you to do is to stick strictly to your promise to the Admiral and, furthermore, to extend it to include this conversation.' So saying, he rose to take his leave and without a smile shook hands and left.

Von Hessler closed the heavy oak door behind him, turned round and leaning his back against it let out a long sigh of exasperation. He had not liked Fricke. He was offended by the way the man had pointedly copied his own habit of using English colloquialisms with his reference to 'hot potatoes'; information doubtless gleaned from reading his file before the visit. Something about the man reminded him of an SS officer he had come across when on home leave during the war. The man had called to see his father and Gerhard had made such an unpleasant impression that he'd been surprised that his father had anything to do with him.

With an effort he dragged himself from contemplation of this thought and started working on how this latest occurrence would impact on his plans. He would be watched, no doubt about that, and Mecklenburg bay would inevitably be under surveillance by both East and West German navies as well. If one of them locates the wreck and finds its contents, the consequences could be … catastrophic. Thank God he had 'adjusted' the wreck's coordinates before writing them down on the piece of paper that Admiral Lange now had. If this was the information that had reached the Volksmarine then they had been looking in the wrong place. He managed a thin smile.

All the same, he had to work fast.

This is going to be expensive but Schmidt ought to foot the bill after all it's his fault you are involved. Von Hessler poured himself some schnapps and sat down to review the situation. Naval intelligence was certain to interrogate Hennig and they might uncover the true site of the wreck. We can only hope that they annoy Hennig sufficiently to make him clam up. Time was of the essence if he was to exploit his information before the Bundesmarine digested theirs. But if he found the wreck surely Schmidt would be at risk as his theft from the box would inevitably be discovered. Yes, Schmid was bound to be uneasy at the prospect of others getting there first and that should provide good reason for financing its recovery as soon as possible.

If not a salvage company, then who? Perhaps a hydrographic survey organisation would agree to search for the wreck. How much of a risk premium would they demand to cover the hazards of East German interference? And how was he to organise anything without coming up against the formidable Rear Admiral Lange? Not to mention how he would get around the problem of legal ownership of the box and the fact that the wreck was presumably still the property of the Bundesrepublik? It looked as if the recovery operation would have to be clandestine, undertaken at night in small unobtrusive boats to avoid radar detection. It had to be worth a try.

Eventually, Von Hessler located a small survey firm that was willing in principle if unenthusiastic in practice. They had had problems with the Volksmarine before and were reluctant to go nearer than five miles from the boundary. It seemed their radar was not good enough to detect the small rubber dinghies used by the inshore frontier patrols nor did it give sufficient warning if and when trouble was on its way in the shape of bigger vessels.

He needed another brain to bear on the problem. Peter Anson's naval experience was fifteen years fresher than his and he had the advantage of a relatively low profile. Alarmed by the information leakage disclosed by Fricke von Hessler was now reluctant to use the telephone; his only option was to meet Anson in Amsterdam before going on to Düsseldorf. They arranged to meet in the Hilton hotel at Schipol airport.

Naturally, von Hessler's plane was late and at first glance he failed to pick out Anson from among the assembled business men filling the reception area. Then he remembered Anson's habit of hiding behind a newspaper when wanting to avoid chance meetings with acquaintances – he'd probably be in the lounge. Ah! There in a corner of the room pink Financial Times was being held up by someone in a corner seat. Von Hessler smiled.

'Hello Peter old boy, glad to see you again. Taking the stock market's temperature? However I have some even more interesting business for us to discuss.'

'Hello Gerhard, and what might that business be?' Anson replied, folding the paper as von Hessler seated himself.

'It concerns our man Schmidt.'

'You don't say! I was wondering how long it would be before that man appeared on your radar again.'

'My God! You've hit it right on the head there! Radar is precisely the problem.'

'Tell me,' Anson invited.

'A great deal has happened since we spoke on the phone. My attempt to get the navy involved has seriously back-fired. The East Germans have sent out a survey ship.'

'What?'

'There's been a leak somewhere. Fortunately they don't appear to have found anything ... so far. But the result is that I've got to move double fast and find that wreck before they or anyone else does. I've found a survey company who are capable of locating it but the snag is they were warned off by the Volksmarine once before and now don't like going too close to East German waters. When I gave them a rough idea of where to look they cried off. They claim their radar isn't good enough to detect the small boats of the inshore frontier patrols. So they won't take the job on. It's a pretty kettle of fish as you would say.'

'That's not good. Look, I'm no radar expert but you surely could bring in someone who could sort out the problem. Or you could try a different survey company.'

'But that could take three or four weeks; time I haven't got.'

'Why the hurry? Admiral Lange is not going to do anything and you say the Volksmarine don't appear to have found anything.'

'Peter, I need to get moving on this as soon as possible. My knowledge of the wreck's probable location is a wasting asset. Our comrades over the border are hard to read. They might do anything – even carry out a search in our waters if they thought they could get away with it. My plan is to tell Schmidt the whole story and persuade him to pay whatever it takes to get these nervous surveyors into action. After all, it's in his best interests to find the ammo box before anyone else does. If anyone has a list they could discover that some of its contents have gone missing.'

'OK point taken. But it seems to me, that you're over-keen to get results. I'd go cautiously. That man Schmidt could lead you into dangerous territory, Gerhard. But I take your point about moving quickly. How about keeping an eye on the Volksmarine from the air?'

'That's an interesting idea. I'd not thought of that. I wonder if the survey people would accept it,' von Hessler mused, thinking through the idea. 'Klaus Schmidt has his own plane but we know that someone is watching him so that could create difficulties. They'll be keeping an eye on that plane.'

'Well I can fly. If Klaus is willing to foot the bill, I could charter a plane. After all, I doubt I'm going to be noticed, at least by your Admiral and his men.'

'That's an excellent idea, Peter! We're finally making progress. But are you sure you want to get involved?'

'Why not? We've been in some scrapes before and survived. Remember Leipzig? Besides I need to get in some more flying hours now the weather's good.'

Von Hessler lowered his voice. 'Before I go there's another thing I need to mention – the involvement of our friends across the border means that we'll have to invoke tight security procedures from now on. We'll have to restrict information to those who need to know. For instance when I've got accurate coordinates for the wreck I'll keep them to myself.'

Anson looked puzzled. 'So what coordinates did you pass to Admiral Lange?'

'I have to confess that I made some slight adjustments to the figures.' Von Hessler's eyes were dancing with mischief.

'Well I'm damned!' Anson laughed. 'You old devil! Spreading mis-information amongst Admirals, eh? My God, that's something I never aspired to!'

As Von Hessler headed for the air terminal for his onward flight to Düsseldorf a little later he felt buoyant. Not only did the plan contain just the right mixture of excitement and conspiracy to appeal to Schmidt, but it also had a chance of escaping the attentions of both the Bundesmarine and whoever was watching Schmidt himself.

Arriving at Düsseldorf he hired a car from a small firm outside the airport and drove into the town. Leaving the vehicle in the extensive tree-lined car park at Schmidt's corporate headquarters, he entered through the glass and chromium revolving doors. Stainless steel furniture gleamed from across the pale marble floor of the spacious hall. Greeted by the steady gaze of a platinum blonde receptionist (whom he felt might almost have been chosen to fit in with the décor) he gave his name and was informed that Herr Schmidt himself would be coming down shortly. He waited. With the well-rehearsed movements of an actor making a stage entrance, the bulky figure of Klaus Schmidt swept out of the lift, barely slowed down to shake hands, and escorted von Hessler out of the building into a waiting limousine in which they were wafted to a discreetly expensive restaurant.

It was obvious that Schmidt was a valued customer and the two men were shown to their table with that charming mixture of affability and deference which is the mark of the successful head waiter who proceeded with professional dexterity to place large elaborate menus in front of them, while a junior waiter arrived with a bread basket and carafe of water. An equally large wine list was presented to Schmidt who, having confirmed that his guest would start with white wine, ordered a bottle of number 12 without referring to the list. Almost immediately the wine appeared in a large cooler standing on the floor and the brief ceremony of uncorking and tasting was performed. Schmidt took a large gulp of the wine which jarred on von Hessler to whom this was sacrilege, his preference being for the slow savouring of what he recognised was a good wine.

'So what is this astonishing development that you have for me, Gerhard?' asked Schmidt, putting his glass down.

'Klaus, this involves you personally. You can probably guess what I mean if I tell you that that idiot Joachim von Benz has been to see me.'

Schmidt's ebullient manner vanished, his face clouded. He lowered his voice and mouthed some imprecations. Von Hessler decided to press on with the story before Schmidt's temperature rose any further. He had decided to conceal Elizabeth's involvement in the affair but von Benz's activities had rendered that obsolete anyway.

'I'm here today to put a proposition to you, Klaus. Von Benz spilled out the story of the ammo box to his father and your part in it ... and how he came to visit you.'

'Oh.' The two men eyed each other warily.

'Precisely, but leaving the connotations of that aside, the obvious naval involvement intrigued me so I made a few enquiries. The result is that I think I've a good idea where your ammo box ended up. It's at the bottom of the sea a few seamiles from Kiel.'

'Good God! Where is all this leading?'

'Don't look so alarmed Klaus. My proposition's quite harmless. If you are willing to foot the bill, I'll recover the box. I want nothing for myself beyond your agreement that we open it together and anything inside that could damage the reputation of my family or friends is destroyed immediately. Let's face it we both have ... shall we call it 'an investment' in that box; we should help each other.'

Schmidt ceased eating and sat immobile looking at von Hessler, his face reflecting a cascade of emotions. He reached for his glass and swallowed a mouthful of wine. 'I think you had better start again at the beginning, Gerhard. What exactly did von Benz tell you?'

'Well, to start with he described how in 1945, when he was a boy, he saw a Panzer officer arrive at his house in Kiel. Then he detailed how a man visited him earlier this year who he identified as a criminal type, who claimed to know all about the box and its contents and who tried to blackmail him. This man claimed that you were the Panzer officer involved and, according to von Benz, he knew what he was talking about. Then I began to realize that it was probably all true. Isn't it?'

There was a long pause as Schmidt looked out of the restaurant window. Then he turned to von Hessler with a grim smile.

'Of course it's bloody true. I'm not going to be so stupid as to deny it to a man with your brains and your background in intelligence who also happens to be a friend.' He paused for several seconds and then continued. 'I accept your offer and its terms, Gerhard. I don't really have any choice do I? The stuff in those cartridges could do serious damage and I don't just mean chemical explosions. The letters I saw are dynamite.'

'Dynamite for whom? Are you talking about my family?

'God knows! But as you've told me yourself, your family has connections all over the place, so it's not impossible.'

'But you know my family's always been above suspicion. Always.'

'I was only making a general remark' said Schmidt

'OK , let's get down to the details. This has to remain secret, Klaus and we have to keep tabs on who knows what, especially the plans. Information needs to be given out strictly on a need-to-know basis. Is that understood?'

With a wave of his hand Schmidt signalled his assent, after a second added 'Not a word to Elizabeth.'

Ignoring this last, Von Hessler continued, his voice low.

'Already too many people are in the know. Both the Bundesmarine and the Volksmarine are on the alert, British intelligence has got involved and God knows what is going on with our friends on the other side of the Iron Curtain. The problem is that the boat and its cargo are lying on the bottom of the Baltic close to our maritime boundary. If we're going to salvage that box we've got to move fast. And it's going to cost money, big money.'

'How the hell did all these people get involved?' Schmidt asked, his face now registering alarm.

'I'm not sure, though there has been a leak right up at the top in Bonn, which incidentally I find hard to credit although I have it on good authority. It's possible that my research into naval records which led me to discover details of the boat where it was sunk set off an alarm somewhere. Just how much information von Benz's 'criminal' has is unknown. I've already enlisted Peter Anson to help.

'That's good.'

'Yes, he has the great advantage of being an outsider and will probably escape surveillance from any outfit operating here in West Germany. Which brings me back to security – who else knows the history of the box?'

'Elizabeth knows; I've told her the whole story. But I'm sure she'll keep her mouth shut.' He frowned, thinking hard. 'The big unknown is the man who drove me to Kiel with the box. His name is Beckmeier. He's doubtless the one behind all the blackmail attempts. I think he's out of jail now.'

'He's bad news, but I suspect there are bigger people involved than Beckmeier,' said von Hessler. 'And speaking as an ex-intelligence officer this operation is as leaky as a sieve. The whole thing could blow at any moment so it is vital that we find that boat. The first thing to settle is money. As soon as I mentioned that the salvage job was near the maritime boundary I met objections from all the commercial outfit, all of which added up to big money. Persuading anyone to carry out the minimum underwater survey is going to be costly and the salvage job will have to be done by aqualung divers at night and they'll want danger money for that. We are in for tens of thousands of deutschmarks.'

'I'll pay whatever it takes,' said Schmidt decisively. 'If it stops any more blackmailers climbing on my back it'll be worth it. You go ahead.'

'Are you really giving me *carte blanche* to run the whole thing?' Von Hessler stammered, attempted to conceal his astonishment.

'I am,' said Schmidt. Then he added as an afterthought: 'But it's going to be one hell of a gamble. You might not find the box or worse, someone else might find it first.'

He let the sentence hang.

'I'm damned sure it's there and if we move fast enough we'll get it. We can take it back to my place in Kiel, go through it and then decide what to do. If some of the contents compromise my family or friends then they go into the incinerator *tout de suite.* '

'*Naturellement,*' responded Schmidt with a wave of his hand. 'And, who knows, the contents might include some dollars to help me pay for the expedition! Who knows!'

Klaus seemed keen to keep on the periphery of the operation. This surprised von Hessler who had expected him to want to take an active part in the salvage operation. Was he distancing himself in case things went wrong? Despite these misgivings, the meal finished on a lighter note. Schmidt appearing to be in an expansive mood again as they talked in the back of the car on the way tot the airport for von Hessler's return flight.

He flew back to Hamburg in a strange mood. He sensed a darkness in his friend Schmidt that he had not spotted before. Was Schmidt's money clean? Von Hessler felt as though he was being driven irrevocably into a world populated by blackmailers, suspect dealers and covert government agencies. This was not his milieu. He was the latest generation of an old Hanoverian landed family which had a long tradition of diplomatic service to the crown. This had culminated nearly two centuries ago with the award of his inherited title of Freiherr. He shook his head. Times were changing – already he had moved from a combat role in the navy into intelligence work and had acquired a taste for it. But the thought that his own family might involved in this stuck in his throat? For the sake of his name, he must carry on with the search for S103.

With the money issue resolved, things began to fall into place. The survey firm agreed to Anson's scheme for aerial surveillance and he provided them with a transmitter/receiver working on aircraft radio channels so they could talk to each other. He took the skipper aside and promised him an envelope of cash on condition that details of the wreck location were passed only to him, and impressed on the man that the crew should have absolutely no sight of the wreck co-ordinates displayed on the Decca Navigator equipment.

Two nights later, well before dawn, von Hessler drove down to the docks and parked his car at the back of the shed where the survey company had their office. The only sign of activity was a dim light showing in a window and the hum of a diesel engine some distance away. Opening the boot, he hauled out a bag containing his oilskins and walked around to the front of the building. A mercury vapour lamp cast its cold light over the empty dockside. He tried a sliding door, but it refused to budge. In the end he had to hammer on it to gain entry. This did not improve his already jangling nerves. Upstairs he found the skipper poring over charts while engaged in a discussion with the navigator about the search plan. The man looked up.

'Good morning Herr von Hessler. Looks like we're going to be lucky with the weather. Not much low cloud and fairly calm water.'

'Splendid! That's what I wanted to hear. We need good flying weather. Have you got that radio working?'

'No problem at all. We got Kiel air traffic control loud and clear on it yesterday and we heard the Englishman Anson talk to them.' He gestured towards the plan on the table. 'The plan is for us to cover a square four seamiles wide starting west of the maritime boundary and moving east.'

'Sounds like a long trip.' Von Hessler said, glancing at the map, his eyes narrowing as he took in the area suggested.

'It'll take as long as it takes,' said the skipper with a shrug. 'The halfway point would be about two and a half hours if that's any help. Well let's get on board.'

Von Hessler donned his oilskin coat and followed the crew down to the dockside where they all climbed onto the boat. At 4 am they cast off; as anticipated the pre-dawn sky was clear and the sea relatively calm.

'We've established contact with the plane.' The captain said, as they struck out into clear water. 'I've told them we should reach the search zone in about four hours.'

Them? Von Hessler listened hard to the next radio exchange … yes, that sounded like Schmidt's voice in the background. He was obviously up there with Anson.

The aircraft reported an absence of Volksmarine craft so the monotonous search pattern commenced. On the bridge the skipper plotted their position on the chart using the latitude and longitude data from the Decca Navigator displays. At intervals he ordered the helmsman to alter course by ninety degrees and slowly but surely the pattern of the square search was marked on the chart. Periodically he looked over the shoulder of the operator watching the green sonar display. Time slowly dripped by.

Two anxious hours had elapsed when a shout from the operator grabbed everyone's attention. Taking the helm, the skipper reduced speed to a crawl as the operator guided him closer to the source of the sonar echoes. Von Hessler gazed at the display which was showing a wreck whose length roughly matched the 35 metres of an S-boat. It was located five nautical miles from the maritime boundary with East Germany and lying in 24 metres of water. It had to be S103!

A a buoy fitted with a battery-powered light was dropped over the side to mark the wreck and then the skipper passed the Decca Navigator figures to von Hessler. He had what he needed!

His spirits high, he drove immediately to the airfield at Kiel-Holtenau where Anson had landed the Cessna 150 and jubilantly related the news to the two men sitting in the airport restaurant. Schmidt listened intently with a grave face and for a second Von Hessler could clearly see the Panzer Major leaning out of his tank taking in a situation report about a reconnaissance that had been made in the face of a dangerous enemy. It was a weird experience. He looked at Schmidt quizzically, waiting for a comment … approval even.

'A good morning's work, Gerhard,' responded Schmidt, breaking into a broad grin.

Von Hessler nodded his head in recognition of the comment.

'Our problem now is to get the salvage job done before the battery in the marker buoy goes flat. That gives us forty-eight hours – two nights; otherwise we'll have to do it in daylight. I've got divers lined up who are prepared to work at night using a rigid inflatable boat with an outboard motor. The plan is to leave from Grossenbrode towing the inflatable and transfer into it just off the tip of Fehmarn at Staberhuk. It's right under the nose of the radar station but I'm hoping they won't bother with us. From there it should take us no more than an hour to get to the wreck if we make 10 knots.'

'Why does it have to be an inflatable?' Anson asked.

'It has several advantages but the main one is that it has a smaller radar signature. It's very low in the water and the rubber hull tubes make poor radar reflectors. There's also the fact that divers find them easier to climb back into. The sea hasn't had much chance to warm up yet and they are going to get cold down there so it makes things a bit easier for stiff muscles.'

'You say *we* are planning to do all this, Gerhard,' said Schmidt. 'Does this mean that *you* are going out in the boat? '

'That is my intention. I'm going to navigate because I'm the only one who knows exactly where the wreck is, and I'm keeping those coordinates to myself. In any case someone has to be aboard to make decisions.'

'Navigating in a small boat in the dark isn't going to be easy,' said Anson. 'It sounds like a tough proposition to me. I presume you won't have a Decca navigator to help you.'

'No I won't, but there are light towers on Fehmarn, Gedser in Denmark and Bastorf in the DDR. They'll give me a good fix using a hand-bearing compass. I've only got to get us close enough to spot the marker buoy. Navigating in daylight without those lights would be a nightmare spotting the marker buoy will be so much easier at night.'

'What will you do if the Volksmarine put in an appearance?' said Schmidt with a provocative grin. 'How much ransom money are you expecting me to produce?'

Von Hessler snorted with laughter.

'Klaus, I'm sure you can find anything they're likely to demand! Don't worry. We're much more likely to be escorted back here, or even to Denmark. The wreck lies close to the Danish boundary. I'm more worried about the weather. If the sea gets up we'll have to delay with the risk that the battery in the buoy goes flat.'

His amusement vanished, Von Hessler looked straight at Schmidt.

'Klaus, it's on the beach that I'll need your practical assistance. The lead diver refuses to land stuff from the wreck. He intends to drop it off in shallow water, leaving us to take ashore. He's adamant that if anyone is going to get into trouble it won't be him. So can you produce someone who is prepared to get wet?'

'How wet?' enquired Schmidt.

'Very wet. I'll be wearing a thick wetsuit. As you know, the Baltic is damn cold and whoever is coming in with me will need one if he's not going to freeze.'

'Looks like a job for one of my young assistants in the Hamburg office. He goes snorkelling, has all the kit and can swim like a fish. And he'll keep his mouth shut,' added Schmidt with a slight air of menace.

'Right. I'm planning to do the job tomorrow night so you'll need to get him primed. The weather looks good and the team of divers is standing by. Can you get your man up here by say 20 hundred hours?'

'Yes, I think we can arrange that,' said Schmidt after a moment's thought. 'I'll spend the day in the Hamburg office and drive him up myself.'

'We'll rendezvous at Burgstaaken harbour on Fehmarn Island.'

'Okay.'

They bade each other farewell and von Hessler watched as the plane took off heading back towards Hamburg-Fuhlsbüttel airport. As he drove home he felt the familiar surge excitement reminding him of planning operations he'd carried out during the early part of the war. Thank God nobody was going to die in this one!

The next day dawned bright and clear. Von Hessler drove into Kiel threading his way through the docks and met the diving team leader König in the company's office in a shed near the dockside. König was a solidly built man with a trim grey beard and a comforting air of competence and authority. He discussed his plans for bringing up the box and briefcase from the S-boat while he watched his van being loaded with air cylinders and diving gear.

'I've dug out some old S-boat plans and we shouldn't have too much trouble finding the skipper's cabin provided she's not upside down. 24 metres depth is no problem for the divers and water visibility should be okay now that the spring plankton blooms are dying away.'

'Do you think the box will have survived a quarter of a century at the bottom of the sea?' asked von Hessler with a questioning look.

'It's hard to say,' said König pausing for thought. 'If it was made of steel it could be anything from virtually intact to completely rusted away. As for the ammunition itself it depends on what the cartridge cases were made of. If they're brass then they should be okay.'

'What about the leather briefcase?'

'Well surprisingly enough, you may be lucky there. The bottom of the Baltic is nearly dead; there's not much biological activity due to lack of oxygen. As a result there are quite a few ancient wooden ships down there with little or no sign of decay so it's entirely possible your briefcase may well be intact, barring a few worm holes.'

'Let's hope so,' said von Hessler. 'That briefcase is as important as the ammunition.'

'The ammunition goes overboard the minute I detect any customs boats moving in on us – understood? That's a condition we've agreed – yes? What's in that briefcase?'

'Herr König I can assure you that there will be nothing of the slightest interest to customs officials. Only papers and documents. It was the property of a civilian, maybe a senior government official, certainly not a smuggler.'

'Okay, I won't dump the briefcase, but I'll pray that you're right otherwise we'll be in trouble. In fact it might help to put them off the scent if we keep it on board. Incidentally we did a salvage job for some archaeologists last year and they put the paperwork that we brought up straight into a refrigerator to stop mould growth.' He paused, 'On a different tack, are you sure that you're up to handling the navigation? It's not going to be easy in the dark in an inflatable.'

'You're absolutely right, it isn't going to be easy. But at one stage in my naval career I had the job of getting a man ashore from a U-boat in the dark and on that occasion there were no lights at all to take fixes on so I reckon this trip is going to be simple by comparison.' von Hessler assured him, warming to his theme. 'Our first leg takes us up to a waypoint I've put in off Staberhuk where we transfer into the inflatable. The second leg is true east for about ten seamiles. I've already made a note of the bearings on the chart for the lights on Staberhuk, Gedser and Bastorf. Those three will give me a good fix for the position of the marker buoy. The only think I need is an accurate compass,' He finished. 'Have you swung the compass on the inflatable recently?'

'That we have,' said König. 'The outboard motor is the only chunk of iron but it's at the other end of the boat and produces almost no deviation. We can sometimes see effects from the steel air cylinders but we tend to ignore them.'

'But will they affect my hand-bearing compass? I might be sitting close to those cylinders.'

'If you're worried about it, I can swap them for aluminium ones and we'll stash them well forward. That should take care of it.' Then König hesitated, 'You do realize that this is going to be a tough trip? With the greatest respect you are not as young as the rest of us. An hour each way at ten knots in a rubber boat can be punishing. It could be bumpy and it's certainly going to be wet. You're going to need a thick wetsuit at the very least and some good oilskins.'

'Thank you for your concern Herr König, but I must remind you that I am an experienced sailor. I keep my yacht *Jasmine* in Kiel and I've made passages of 15 hours or more in her in tough conditions. Last year I sailed her to Copenhagen along the same stretch of water as we plan to cover tonight … and with a fair bit of wind. So you need have no fear.'

König's concerned face relaxed into a smile. 'Only checking,'

Von Hessler arranged to meet the van in the harbour at Grossenbrode on the mainland where the motor cruiser was berthed, then went home to organise the kit needed for the trip.

His housekeeper had filled a food-box and a flask of coffee though with the familiarity of the long-standing servant, she expressed her alarm at the idea of his venturing out into the open sea in the middle of the night. It was not easy calming her fussing but her obvious concern made him stop and think. Was his irresponsible streak surfacing again? Even his old chum Peter Anson who shared his sense of adventure had been cautious about this expedition. Was he being stupid?

He reassured himself; the weather forecast was good and he'd done everything he to frustrate interference by the local authorities who might challenge his right to salvage material from the wreck. At worst they might lose the ammunition box if it had to be dumped.

Damn it, he thought, I'm going to pull off this job right under the nose of Rear Admiral Lange and the chaps in the radar station at Staberhuk to say nothing of the Volksmarine. He laughed. Oh to hell with the consequences!

In this confident frame of mind, he drove to the little harbour of Grossenbrode on the tip of a tongue of land that stretches out to the Island of

Fehmarn and parked alongside the van that was already being unloaded by König and his divers. Each man carried a kit bag and an air cylinder and moving in single file they carefully picked their way along the quayside avoiding the piles of nets, ropes and the general detritus left by decades of fishing. They passed a row of deserted fishing boats tied up alongside each other for the night. The still air was heavy with the smell of decaying marine life. No-one was about and an evening hush had fallen over the harbour.

Quietly the trailer was unhitched from the van and pushed over the cobbles down the slipway into the murky water. The big inflatable floated off and its painter was attached to the motor cruiser that lay alongside. The divers' gear was loaded into the motor cruiser while the four men got into their black wetsuits and yellow life jackets and climbed on board. Von Hessler was taken back thirty years to the time when he had practised beach landings. There was the same absence of casual conversation; the same quiet air of competent men who knew what they had to do.

The motor cruiser skipper selected switches on the control panel for navigation lights, instruments, radio and pumps, and started the engine. All was ready.

A nod from von Hessler and the order was given to cast off the mooring warps and the vessel started moving slowly across the harbour following the breakwater towards the entrance, steering between the red and green channel marker buoys that were becoming visible in the fading light. As they left the harbour they aimed for the flashing buoy marking the end of the mole and swung round it heading north-east. A moderate sea was running with a warm southerly breeze, and over the land they could see the last pink traces of the sunset. The skipper pushed open the throttle and the boat surged forward. Von Hessler ordered a course of 072 magnetic as they headed out into the Bay of Mecklenburg.

The sea was now an inky blue barely distinguishable from the sky where a few wisps of cloud drifted, occasionally obscuring the half-moon. In the distance, they saw the navigation lights of sea traffic bound for Lübeck and, low down on the horizon, the Staberhuk light on the tip of the island. A ripple of uncertainty ran through the team as they stared into the dark immensity. They cracked a few jokes but conversation quickly petered out. Von Hessler wondered if they had been infected by his anxiety. This was nothing compared with the operations that he had planned and sometimes engaged in during the war, so why was he so anxious? It must be his age. He put the question aside and concentrated on calculating a back-bearing on the lights of the harbour entrance in order to check their progress. The compass read the reciprocal of 072 – good - the helmsman was holding course, there was no drift due to cross currents.

He stared back over the phosphorescent wake of the boat to where the inflatable was riding well, yawing as each wave cruised under it, pitching and rolling with a mesmerising rhythm. Ahead he could see the light on Staberhuk. The first stage of the plan was unfolding; in twenty minutes they would transfer to the inflatable and the real action would begin.

As the light came closer he could pick out a faint white line of surf surging around the boulders that littered the shore.

'Not the place to try beaching a boat, particularly a torpedo boat,' said König. 'This stretch is a menace.'

'Oh? It sounds as if there's a history behind that remark.' responded von Hessler.

'You're right. Herr Navigator. A torpedo boat of the Imperial Navy ran aground here in 1900. It was after that they built Staberhuk Light.'

'Navigators had a hard time in those days,' remarked von Hessler. 'No radar, no Decca, no electronics.' Just like tonight, his inconvenient thoughts added.

The cruiser's skipper eased back the throttle, and watched the red neon on the spinning disc of the echo-sounder as the reading gradually dropped to 5 metres. He cut the throttle and shouted to one of the divers to release the anchor. Painters were unhitched and the inflatable brought alongside. Each man let himself down and sat on the rubber hull tubes. Fuel cans and air cylinders were passed across and then the diving gear, kitbags and lifting bags.

125

At 10pm precisely König pulled the starter rope on the outboard motor; it fired and settled back, burbling reassuringly. Then he turned to von Hessler.

'OK Herr Navigator. Got our position? Are we all set?'

Von Hessler called for a course of 093 magnetic and König opened the throttle; they were underway. The boat accelerated, its bow lifted and started to plane. Behind them the light on Staberhuk receded.

'Attention everyone,' said von Hessler, 'we're going to cross the shipping lanes leading into Lübeck. They can't see us on their radar so keep a sharp lookout. Watch the bearing of any ship closing on us. If it stays constant for more than a couple of minutes we're on a collision course. Give me a shout if you spot trouble and I'll check with my compass.'

Steering the new course of 093 meant the seas were now coming broadside on and the roll of the boat was comfortable with only the occasional dousing of spray. The breeze was southerly for which von Hessler was very grateful, shuddering at the thought of crashing from wave top to wave top which would have been the case had they been driving into an easterly; an hour of that would have been unendurable.

He took a back-bearing on Staberhuk light and was reassured that König was holding a good course. The powerful outboard motor was driving the boat at 10 knots so he was confident that they could steer clear of any merchantmen bearing down on them but once they were stationary over the wreck it would be a different matter. Tied up to the marker buoy they would be unable to manoeuvre and, even if the dive was shorter than the 20 minutes maximum stipulated by König, that was a long time to be at the mercy of the merchant ships. He scanned the horizon at frequent intervals, checking the many lights that he could see, some fixed, others on merchant ships slowly moving and fell into ruminative mood. Was there really a chance that his family might be involved? Was this a good enough reason for sticking his neck out to help Klaus Schmidt in this enterprise? Why was he still taking the sort of risks that had caused his father to say in exasperation: 'Gerhard, I suggest that you grow up!'. Even his housekeeper disapproved of his driving … maybe he should have given up sports cars long ago. In the Kriegsmarine he had been accused by senior officers of ignoring danger. Now he was putting four men at risk. Was that a responsible thing to do?

He became aware that the cold was seeping into his bones, the motion beginning make him queasy, the spray obscuring his goggles. With a jerk he forced himself to concentrate on counting the flash sequences of the lights. Doing this through binoculars sitting in a rolling boat was difficult. Bastorf light was flashing every 9 seconds way off to starboard. Was he going to be able to pick out the light on Gedser on the tip of the Danish island ahead?

The two divers in front of him had fallen silent. He suspected they were not enjoying the ride and had nothing to take their minds off the risks in front of them. It was far too soon but they were already searching the sea ahead for signs of the wreck marker buoy.

Still no sign of the Gedser light.

He asked König to slow right down while he swept the North-eastern horizon, feeling the confidence of the other men ebbing away.

There it is!

A pinpoint of light!

He grabbed his hand bearing compass aiming it into the darkness and waiting for the next group of flashes. The motion of the boat made it difficult both to hold a steady aim and prevent the compass card from swinging but then he saw it again – three white flashes: the sequence of the Gedser light repeated at 20 second intervals! But the card was swinging and he failed to get an accurate reading. With an oath he turned towards Bastorf light to the South. He aimed the compass at the vague colour change marking the horizon, and waited for the flashes. This time the card was barely swinging and the light came up almost dead in line with the compass sight. Thank God! He had an accurate reading.

'We're on track Herr König,' he said in a matter-of-fact tone hoping to mask his relief. 'I'll need another sight in 10 minutes. Then we start looking for the marker.'

'OK Herr Navigator, on we go' said König briskly as he opened the throttle.

At least this activity had driven Von Hessler's queasiness of his mind. But it worried him that the last successful sight had been a more or less fluke. How many sights would he have to take before he was able to establish their final position within visible range of the marker? Holding their course on 093 from Staberhuk would take them straight across the wreck site, but he still needed the cross-bearings to know when to stop.

The journey continued.

Laboriously they went through the process again and again, sometimes he needed three attempts to get an accurate fix, a tedious process that occupied several minutes and provoked frustration among the divers. However, they pushed on steadily east, slowing down at intervals until finally von Hessler called for a complete stop. He took sights on all three lights in turn and then repeated the process a second time.

'This is it,' he said tersely, looking around for the buoy ... it had to be here somewhere.

'What's that?' shouted one of the divers. 'On the port bow. I can see something.'

König steered towards it and soon they picked out the tiny point of light on the yellow buoy.

'Excellent work, Herr Navigator,' said König. 'I wish I knew your secret!'

Von Hessler was beginning to like König.

'There really isn't any secret Herr König,' he responded. 'Perhaps it's something I share with Napoleon's Generals. He insisted that they had to be lucky.'

The boat went slowly ahead as a diver hauled the buoy on board. Torches flashed as König and the two divers buckled on their air cylinders, checked their aqualungs, slipped on their fins and pulled down their masks. The anchor was dropped overboard and the two divers eased themselves into the water. In the darkness von Hessler could just make out the hand signals they were making while König watched them from the boat. And then they disappeared below the surface.

The waiting had begun.

'Those two can manage,' said König as the boat gently rose and fell on the water. 'They both have experience with wrecks and Fritz is a real expert. I'll only go down if they get into trouble.'

'What sort of trouble?' asked von Hessler.

'Disorientation is one danger. Once you're inside a wreck you can lose your bearings, particularly if it's on its side. They have to keep in sight of each other and keep track of the way back out. I don't reckon there's much space inside an S-boat.'

'Talking of confined spaces, have you ever done a U-boat?'

'No, and I never would,' said König. 'For those that did it was a grim business. I can tell you that if there had been any corpses in this one I would've had a job finding divers. Taking the *Deutschland* apart was enough for me. It was one of my first jobs. She was sunk near Lübeck, upside down, but the crew got out.'

'Did you get involved with clearing the liner *Cap Arcona*?' asked von Hessler.

'No thank God! As you probably know, that one was crammed with prisoners from *Konzentrationslagern* such as Neuengamme near Hamburg. The RAF sank it two days before the end of the war; thousands drowned.'

'Yes, I remember getting the news. It made me sick. I knew something was brewing when Gauleiter Kaufmann took the liner out of naval control even though he was acting under orders from Hitler. The war had less than 48 hours to go. I heard they were mostly Jews on board. It's ironic that it was the Kriegsmarine who allowed the Jews to escape across the sea from Denmark in '43 then almost as many were later drowned in the *Cap Arcona.*'

'What exactly happened in Denmark?' asked König .

'As you probably know our Maritime Attaché in Copenhagen warned the Danes at the end of September about Hitler's order to round up the Jews in Denmark. A few days later our Rear Admiral gave a verbal order to patrol boats to sit tight in their bases. I had the job of passing on the order to some of the local commanders. In that way we allowed seven thousand Jews to get away in fishing boats to Sweden.'

'I'm glad I was too young to fight,' said König rubbing his beard.

'There's a lot that I try to forget,' muttered von Hessler, disinclined to continue the conversation. Then an ugly thought entered his head. What if the body of that supernumerary crew member of S103 was still down there. Would they abort the dive? It seemed all too likely. His imagination all too easily pictured a corpse rearing up alongside the boat. To shake off the image he asked König about his other diving experiences.

As they talked the two men automatically scanned the sea around them. So far, the occasional ship had passed some distance away. The wind had dropped to nothing and the only sound above the slosh of the waves was the deep hum of far-off marine engines and once, as an unladen ship passed in the distance, they heard the regular thump of propeller blades breaking the surface of the water. The inflatable rocked gently in the swell and bubbles from the divers' breathing could just be seen caught in the moonlight. An unpleasant odour wafted briefly across the boat, evidence of the algal and plankton blooms that had consumed all the oxygen in the surface waters and were now decaying.

Von Hessler scanned the horizon again. In the distance he thought he detected something. Raising his binoculars he realised he could see red and green navigation lights close together.

'I don't like the look of that,' he said, waving a hand. 'It's coming straight for us.'

'Let me have a look,' said König and took the glasses from von Hessler. For what seemed an age he sat concentrating and immobile. 'I don't like it either. It's a big one. I can see the deck lighting.'

He handed the glasses back and picked up the searchlight. The ship's port and starboard navigation lights were of equal intensity, that meant it was still pointing straight at them. Von Hessler felt his heart rate increasing. König remained silent, swinging the searchlight widely from side to side in the hope that someone on board would see them. By now they could clearly hear the low threatening throb of its engines.

'We'll have to move,' said König, 'Get the marker overboard. I'll do the anchor.'

Von Hessler grabbed the yellow buoy and heaved it over.

'The anchors stuck fast,' shouted König. 'Use my knife. I'll start the motor.'

Von Hessler grabbed the diver's knife and sawed at the rope. Already he could hear the menacing sound of water boiling up around the ship's spherical bow that poked out just above the surface like a giant torpedo. König rammed the motor into forward gear and the rope tightened as the knife cut through the last strands; the inflatable leapt forward. But it was too late.

The big ship's bow wave crashed into them, spinning their small craft round and nearly engulfing them. The motor spluttered and died as the turbulent water flung the boat against the bows spinning it round yet again. The red plates of the hull ripped past them, slicing through the hissing water as razor-sharp barnacles bit into their rubber hull. König quickly seized a paddle and attempted to push the fragile craft off, but it was jerked out of his hands.

Then came a new, terrifying sound - the regular, deadly pounding of propellers. It rose in intensity, filling their heads, deafening as it pulsated through their bodies. Bitter salt water flew in his face - freezing, blinding, smarting on his skin - as an unbidden, terrifying image flashed through von Hessler's mind: huge slicing blades and water staining pink. For a second, he froze and then, above the chaotic, brutal tumult, he heard König shout: 'Watch it! Hold fast! In terror, he fastened his grip on the lifelines as the pounding reached a mind-blowing crescendo and the inflatable reared up in the churning maelstrom, balancing for an eternity on end before collapsing back onto the surface of the sea again, the two men soaked but safe inside it.

The violent movement ceased as quickly as it had begun and the pounding slowly died away. The two men relaxed their grip on the lifelines and paused to regain their breath. The ship steamed on, unconcerned.

'*Bastarden,*' spat out König repeatedly, his eyes following the retreating ship as it slowly dissolved in the darkness. Then he turned towards von Hessler.

In a quieter voice he said, 'Now we have to find that marker buoy. I don't suppose you switched its light back on did you?'

'Not a chance,' replied von Hessler. 'Not a cat in hell's chance.'

'Silly question,' said König 'Never mind, we'll find it. That is if I can start the motor. I'll leave it to drain for a minute.'

They waited, hoping, then with a pull on the starter rope it roared into life. But despite motoring round in circles there was no sign of the yellow buoy.

König gave a low grunt, 'This is beginning to look serious. There's only one way we're going to find that buoy. We'll have to recall the divers. When the divers come up they'll follow the buoy rope so when they flash their torches we should spot them. At least that's the theory.'

He rummaged in his kit bag, produced a waterproof thunderflash, pulled the igniter tab and tossed it into the sea. He held up his hand. After a few seconds they heard a perceptible thud.

'At least they'll know we're still around. They should hear that bang if they're not more than 300 metres from us. If it's more than that we'll have to wait for them to come up and hope that we can see their torches. Or maybe we'll hear them.'

König cut the motor and they listened, peering into the empty darkness. He looked at his watch. 'Eight minutes to go. If they stay down much longer they'll need a decompression stop on the way up.'

Then with a splash a lifting bag surfaced not far from them, the spray of water glinting in the moonlight. That was quickly followed by two blobs that had to be the heads of the two divers. The sound of their voices travelled across the water and König started the motor making towards them. He grabbed the lifting bag and the attached box and tried to haul them into the inflatable but, it was too heavy for him to manage alone. Von Hessler lent over to help and between them they managed to get it aboard. The second diver was holding up a briefcase with both hands.

'Watch out,' He shouted 'It's in a dodgy state. The handle has come off.'

'Pass him that net,' said König. Von Hessler complied and watched anxiously as the diver pushed the briefcase into the net, then pulled a single round of ammunition from the carrying bag that was clipped to his knife belt and pushed it into the net with it. They manoeuvred themselves back on board and started to remove their cylinders.

'Any problems?' König asked him.

'Not really. Getting that ammo box out was a bit tricky. It's damned heavy and for a moment I wondered if the lifting bag would cope. I had to inflate it almost to its maximum.'

'You two did a good job. Well done,' said König.

Von Hessler felt like shaking their hands but restrained himself. This was just another night's work for them, after all. Then he remembered the corpse that might have aborted the dive – he had got away with it again. Perhaps he really was blessed with good luck.

König unbuckled his air cylinder. 'Well, I won't be needing that tonight. Cut the rope on the marker, Fritz, and we'll get under way.' Von Hessler could just see the grin on his face.

'Course, if you please Herr Navigator.'

'Staberhuk,' Shouted von Hessler, pointing, 'as fast as you like.'

König opened the throttle and they headed towards the coast steering on the Staberhuk light.

Von Hessler examined the contents of the net with his torch. The briefcase was coated with a repellent grey slime which precluded further examination for the time being. The big round of ammunition he transferred to his kitbag. They passed Staberhuk and as they moved along the coast König throttled back.

A rendezvous had been arranged with the motor cruiser in the fishing harbour of Burgstaaken on Fehmarn where Schmidt had agreed to pick them up in his car. The land was dark with just one or two pinpoints of light showing from houses along the beach. The people of Fehmarn were sensibly tucked up in their beds. It seemed irrational, impossible even, that it should be so.

König brought the boat closer to the beach then finally stopped, grabbed one of the paddles, thrust it down into the water, and touched bottom. 'OK we've got a metre. Now we have to find the first of the groynes, so keep a sharp lookout.'

'I see it!' shouted one of the divers, waving a hand. 'There, we're almost on it.'

Von Hessler peered into the darkness as the boat inched ahead. He could just pick out the pile of dark grey stones edged with white foam that formed the groyne.

'I can't see any sign of customs' patrols so this is where we do the drop, Herr von Hessler. We're off the village of Meeschendorf and there's a road that you can bring a car down. Going west this is the first groyne you come to, so you should easily be able to locate it from the beach.'

The two divers lifted the box and lowered it slowly into a net held open by König; it gently sank out of sight into the water followed by the net holding the briefcase. Then they headed back into deeper water and set course for Burkstaaken harbour.

Rounding the mole at the entrance to Burgstaaken they motored up to the fishing fleet moored in the little harbour. Against the quay lay the motor cruiser, its skipper reclining in the cockpit comfortably smoking a pipe. Quickly passing up the diving gear, the men scrambled on board. König exchanged a few words with the skipper and turned to von Hessler

'Your friends have just arrived,' he said, pointing to where a black Mercedes had just parked nearby.

'Then I'd better get moving before it gets too light. You've done an excellent job, Herr König. I am much in debt to you and your boys. *Auf Wiedersehen.*'

He handed his borrowed lifejacket back to König and leapt ashore, glad to feel the solid ground under his feet as he walked across to the car; the fleeting spectre of the spinning blade still haunting his memory, he tapped on the window. The door opened and the bulky figure of Klaus Schmidt emerged.

'*Mein Gott,*' said Schmidt, 'you look like a real diver, Gerhard. How did it go?'

'Pretty well, Klaus. Though it was a bit more exciting than I anticipated. We were nearly chopped in half by a merchant ship. Apart from that, everything went like clockwork. The loot is in shallow water off a groyne near Meeschendorf. We can get there by car.'

'OK, in you get. This is Hans Richter, my right-hand man in Hamburg. Have you found it on the map yet, Hans?'

'No problem. The groynes are clearly marked, Herr Schmidt.'

'Very good, off we go. I'll be glad to get out of this place. The smell of rotting fish is making me ill. Tell me about the condition of the box, Gerhard. Is it in one piece?'

'Well I haven't had a chance to examine it properly yet, but it's certainly in one piece. They tell me that there's not enough oxygen down there for much rust to form but everything is covered with slime. The briefcase looks OK. But I'll have to get it into the fridge as soon as possible.'

'The fridge? Why?'

'The reason is quite simple. The paper experts in the University tell me that I must do this to prevent mould growth affecting the documents. I want to be able to read the damn things.'

'You'll be lucky after 25 years in the sea. Sea water does things to paper.'

'We'll see,' said von Hessler, feeling suddenly exhausted.

A few minutes later Hans parked the Mercedes and they walked down to the beach, von Hessler's joints complaining as he forced them into action again. As anticipated, the groyne was just visible against the sea. Hans returned to the car and after a minute reappeared in his wetsuit. Von Hessler led the way into the water alongside the groyne feeling for the nets with his feet.

'I have it!'

He and Hans grasped the net between them and carried their unwieldy, heavy load onto the beach. Schmidt examined it with a torch.

'Damn me!' said Schmidt, 'I never thought I'd see that box again. Spread out that plastic sheet in the boot, will you, Hans, and we'll load it.'

'I'll get the briefcase,' said von Hessler.

The sky was brightening in the East as he walked down the beach again following the line of the groyne. Elated by a sense of achievement that his plans for S103 had succeeded although this gave way to a vague feeling of concern as he re-entered the water. What was in the briefcase? There was something mysterious about the shadowy aristocrat to whom it belonged. Suddenly spooked, he scanned the dim shoreline - still deserted. Their activities had not attracted attention from coastguards or customs. Thank God!

But he needed to hurry, concerned that his black wetsuit would stand out against the pale sand, he waded quickly into the water towards the end of the groyne. There was not enough light to see anything on the seabed and a whisper of doubt crept into his mind. Was he going to find it?

He was already up to his waist, exploring the surface of the sand by swinging his foot around in an arc but he could detect nothing apart from an occasional boulder. Then he struck what felt like a sharp piece of metal with his ankle, the shock nearly overbalanced him. Although the pain was dulled by the coldness of the water ball the same it was intense enough to make him fear that his skin had been pierced. He swapped to the other foot and continued his search.

A pink glow began to suffuse the sky in the east, feeding his fear that he would be seen by early walkers on the beach. He swept his foot around as widely as he could. It slammed into the net, becoming entangled in its mesh. Helplessly, he fell sideways and went under, water flooding into his mouth. He paddled furiously with his arms trying to recover but the foot trapped in the net hampered him. Frantically he kicked out trying to free himself, but only succeeded in getting both feet enmeshed. Now floating in the water, he tried backstrokes, splashing in the water attempting to pull himself clear. But a sudden wave went over his head and he went under for the second time. As the water closed over him, weariness seized him and he lost all sense of orientation. He tried not to breathe the water, but his throat had gone into spasm and panic seized him.

His kicking became weaker and weaker. The fear evaporated, becoming an almost joyful resignation ... the pain in his ankle ceased ... his taut body relaxed ... above him the pink glow of the sky spread out its glory, a visual requiem. So this was death ... a sense of wonderful peace lapped over him like a wave.

He thought of his father. Would he meet him now that he was leaving the world? Carried by a mysterious force, accelerating him smoothly, soundlessly, he floated. The pink glow morphed into yellow, then to purple and then coalesced into mysterious shapes that formed, reformed and pulsated before shrinking away to merge into the darkness. The sensation of movement increased, the bonds of gravity loosening and dropping away.

All sensation was fading; consciousness no more than a string of memories. A white veil flew towards him flanking the blue sphere of an earth that seemed no longer relevant. Then the sphere dissolved into the eternal infinite darkness and everything ceased.

At first the agony seemed to come from outside himself, from a distant part of the universe, formless and utterly remote, but gradually it spiralled inwards, concentrated and moving closer, entering his body and centring in his chest. Sounds began to reach him – strange noises and voices that he could not identify. A pink glow suffused his vision again.

He opened his eyes and saw blurred faces peering at him. A woman wearing a white coat asked him something but he her words made no sense. He tried to speak but the effort was too great. The bright lights hurt his eyes; his whole body ached. Confused and somehow disappointed, he stared at the ceiling above him and gingerly tried to move his fingers. Some instinct made him attempt the same with his legs but the hurt in his chest increased so he abandoned that trying to focus on the woman ... she looked extraordinarily beautiful, he thought ... her lovely eyes staring at him.

'Where am I?'

'You're in hospital,' The vision replied, 'in Burg hospital. You nearly drowned but you're going to be all right. I'll turn down the lights and you can sleep.'

He sank down into the warm comfortable darkness again, secure and safe.

When Von Hessler awoke again, his body aching, it was to the sound of subdued voices. He opened his eyes to see a man in a white coat looking down at him.

'What happened?' He croaked.

'You nearly drowned. Your friends saved you.' The doctor seemed to be speaking slowly and checking that he understood his words. His face expressed a well-practised concern as he continued. 'You had a narrow escape. Your heart nearly stopped. Fortunately the young man that rescued you was trained in the army and gave you cardiopulmonary resuscitation. The X-ray showed that he cracked two of your ribs in the process. But he did well.'

'God in heaven,' said von Hessler softly.

'All your vital signs are good so your stay here will not be an extended one.'

'How long have I been here?'

'Twelve hours. We had to sedate you. How are you feeling now?'

'Tired. What time is it?'

'Two o'clock. Would you like to receive your visitors?'

'Not yet.' He answered automatically, closely followed by the question: 'Who are they?'

'Herr Schmidt and the young man who hauled you out of the water. They're staying in a hotel just around the corner. I suggest that you tell the nurse when you would like to see them. You are going to find those ribs extremely painful for a while so I would suggest you avoid unnecessary movement; even activities like laughing or coughing will hurt, I'm afraid. If you need more painkillers, just ask. I will be back to see you later this evening.'

'Thank you Herr Doktor.'

With a prolonged glance at the chart at the end of the bed, the doctor nodded with satisfaction, turned and left.

Floating on the sea of sedatives, Von Hessler dozed off, dreaming of ships smashing across his body, crushing his chest and awoke abruptly unsure which was dream and which reality.

Slowly he remembered the events of the last 24 hours and a glow of satisfaction warmed him. He had outwitted a whole bunch of officials, customs men, navy patrols, even Admiral Lange. As he contemplated his achievements, he felt his strength returning - he was not going to stay in that hospital an hour more than he had to!

Grabbing the call button, he waited for the nurse to appear and then asked her to contact his visitors. Half an hour later she returned and ushered in Schmidt followed by Hans. This was the first time that he had seen Hans in daylight. He was wearing a smart dark grey suit; a well-built young man, almost a younger version of Schmidt himself. The resemblance was strange.

Schmidt strode up to the bed, 'My dear old friend, you gave us a terrible shock! Thanks be to God. Hans was not far behind you.'

'Yes, I am told it is due to you that I am here now.' Von Hessler said, looking at the young man. 'Thank you.'

Hans flushed and muttered something incomprehensible.

Schmidt looked round the room sniffing the hospital odour of antiseptics and floor polish and obviously finding it wanting. 'The hotel is sending round some flowers to cheer you up, Gerhard. Do they let you drink in here?' Without waiting for a response he grinned like a boy and went on, 'I will slip in a bottle of something to help your recovery. Unfortunately, Hans and I have to leave tonight. Is there anything I do for you before we leave?'

'The briefcase ...' said von Hessler, ignoring Schmidt's question. 'Did you get it?'

'Of course,' said Schmidt. 'Hans persuaded the hotel to stick it in their refrigerator much to the astonishment of the staff. He put it in a transparent plastic bag and labelled it *Property of Schmidt Elektrodynamik GmbH*. Of course they think we are mad.' Then he added with a broad grin, 'my Company's reputation is in ruins! He spread out his hands in one of his expansive gestures. 'But it's a small price I'm more than happy to pay if it helps my old friend.'

'And the box?'

146

'Safe in the car. But now we have seen you, we must go. I must get a plane back tonight. The doctor has forbidden you to drive, so I've arranged for a taxi to take you back to Kiel when you're fit to travel. The Company will of course meet the bills for the taxi and the hospital. I'll telephone you tomorrow. I hope those ribs of yours recover quickly. Hans doesn't know his own strength.'

And with a wave the two men departed.

Von Hessler ruefully contemplated the next few days alone on a remote Baltic Island. He wondered how his friends would have fared if this had happened to them. They would have had wives bringing flowers and stopping for a good long chat. Why had he never married? The carefree bachelor life had long since begun to pall. He was only 50 and from a distinguished family ... and had no children. There must be women around who would fall for an older man. Twenty years ago he had had girls chasing after him but then came the sad affair of the broken engagement. Had it affected his outlook? He wondered if he had been put off by the failure of so many of his friends' marriages, all those bitter divorces, and angry children. What had gone wrong? He was dismayed by the atmosphere of failure that seeped from the fissures in society whose latest eructation was the Baader-Meinhof gang. Unconsciously trying to dismiss these dismal thoughts, he made to turn onto his side but stabbing pains forced him to lie back again.

Perhaps he bore some of the responsibility? His family had been leaders of their culture three hundred years ago when a von Hessler had been a general in the army of the Elector of Hanover. But they had become complacent, mere spectators. They had watched while von Bismarck wove his plots. Then came the Great War, the Weimar Republic and then Hitler, and what had his father done? Wearily he dismissed the thought. There was already enough pain in his body. Schmidt's rapid-fire conversation had exhausted him; he dozed off.

Chapter 5

Klaus Schmidt inserted himself into the passenger seat of the big black Mercedes and sank back with a contented sigh. Hans started the engine and they moved off.

'So now back to Fuhlsbüttel. I'll get the last flight to Düsseldorf. You can take the car home and bring it down to HQ tomorrow, Hans, but put it in your garage and don't let anyone near it, that box in the boot has to be kept away from prying eyes.' He paused and glanced at his assistant, 'That was a good night's work, Hans.'

'It's the first time I've done real heart massage, Herr Schmidt. I was sure he was a goner when I didn't seem to get any water out of his lungs. I thought he can't have drowned and must have had a heart attack due to sudden immersion in cold water.'

'What did the Doctor say?'

'He said it was difficult to detect a pulse in someone suffering from the onset of anoxia and his heart may not actually have stopped.'

'Better safe than sorry, even if it means a few cracked ribs. It was a bit of quick thinking Hans. You did a professional job there.'

'Thank you, Herr Schmidt.'

The flat countryside of Schleswig Holstein, its fields dotted with the familiar sight of black and white cattle rolled past as Hans drove fast along the newly-opened autobahn that bypassed Neumünster. As a young man Schmidt had cycled along the local country lanes visiting his mother's family and the farmhouses, in which most of them had lived, were still there, unscathed by the war.

His professional eye noted that this was good tank country - his Panzers would have had a field day! His mind went back to the war, seeing his gunner destroying American Sherman tanks one after the other in quick succession in Normandy. For a moment he was back in action swinging the periscope to monitor the advance of his squadron, issuing commands over the radio, keeping a watchful eye on the Panzergrenadiers supporting his battalion. The familiar roar of the tank engine loud in his ears, he smelt again the pungent fumes of burnt shell propellant. In those battles his armour had been the best, but slowly their fighting strength had ebbed away as, slowly and steadily, their numbers were depleted; there were no replacements once they had been put out of action rendering that last year of the war a miserable, drawn-out nightmare.

His mind turned to the cartridge cases in the box in the car boot .He wondered what he would find when he opened them up and what problems they would conjure. Beckmeier's threats had taught him something. This time he was going to be extremely careful.

Hans dropped him at Fuhlsbüttel airport and while waiting in the departure lounge he rang Elizabeth and gave her a resumé of the events on

Fehmarn Island. She was horrified by the news of von Hessler but he calmed her, assuring her their friend was on the road to recovery.

This done, he boarded the Lufthansa flight to Düsseldorf and settled himself in one of the ample seats in the first class compartment of the Boeing 727. He rejected the glass of *Sekt* offered by the air hostess, consulted the wine list and ordered a half bottle of *Moët & Chandon* together with a copy of the *Bild-Zeitung*. Elizabeth had banned 'that awful tabloid' at home, whereupon he had protested, not very convincingly nor successfully, that he needed to keep abreast of the rubbish that formed the opinions of his workforce. He extracted a Havana from his cigar case ready for the 'No Smoking' sign to be switched off and studied the shapely model featured on the front page of the newspaper.

It was late when the plane landed at Düsseldorf. He felt relaxed – it had been a successful trip and he had the ammunition box to himself.

Elizabeth greeted Schmidt in her usual restrained fashion.

'Had a good flight, Klaus?' she asked as he pulled off his coat.

'Yes, all went very smoothly.'

'Tell me about it.'

She noticed a moment's irritation on Klaus's face. 'It's a complicated story. My first job was to sort out the marketing people up there who are always too conservative. I don't think they have a real feel for things tucked away up in that corner of the country. Whoever drops in on people in Hamburg? They lack contact. It's not on the way to anywhere.'

'Klaus, that is not what I mean! Now tell me the full story. I rang the hospital after you called and had a brief conversation with Gerhard but he sounded incoherent.'

'I expect that is the painkillers they are pumping into him. Well, as he probably told you, he successfully located the wreck. Despite what he said about it being easier than he expected, it can have been no sinecure! Navigating in the dark with only a hand-bearing compass while sitting in a rubber inflatable sounds like a serious challenge to me.'

'I suspect Gerhard secretly enjoys a challenge.'

'Oh yes. There's more to that man than people realise. My psychologist friend Carl once described him as a *puer aeternus*. A boy who never grows up – you know the sort.'

'A Peter Pan character, you mean?'

'Eh? Oh ... yes, very much so. He's forever attracting the girls with that title of his but all the same, he's no dilettante playboy. There's a tough core inside him - would have made a brilliant Panzer commander, but he chose the Navy.'

'But you like risk-takers like him, Klaus.' She fell silent for a second. 'It's funny how these fast drivers often meet their end doing something prosaic like drowning in a metre of water.'

'You're right. He nearly did this time.'

'He told me on the phone that someone called Hans pulled him out of the water. Who is this Hans?'

'He's my right hand man in the Hamburg office.'

'You've never told me about him,' said Elizabeth with a hint of complaint in her voice. 'What's he like?'

'Oh nothing special. Another of these rising young men that one has to encourage. He's an aqualung diver and I thought he might be useful. I'd no idea he was going to be absolutely vital.'

'So did you bring anything up?'

'Not much. The ammunition box was corroded to hell and much of the contents lost. They brought up the briefcase that Gerhard was keen examine and he's taking that home.'

'What are you going to do with the stuff you did get?'

'We're going to open it up and see what's inside, then decide what to do with it.'

A determined look appeared on her face. 'Which will be to restore it to its rightful owners.'

'I doubt there'll be anything to restore,' said Schmidt briskly. 'In any case it depends who the owners are.' His face coloured, 'One thing is certain - nothing's going to Ulbricht and his comrades in the DDR.'

'I'm not going to be diverted, Klaus. The moral principle is clear. Precisely how you interpret it is not the point.'

'Well my dear, let's see what's in the cartridges before we fall out over them. After 25 years at the bottom of the Baltic anything can have happened. Let's have a drink.'

Klaus poured her a gin and tonic and a beer for himself while Willi prepared a late supper.

'Tell me about Gerhard. How did he seem when you left him.'

'Pretty poorly. His cracked ribs are hurting. When I last saw him, he was doped up with painkillers, couldn't concentrate. The doctor doubts that his heart actually stopped. And he didn't get much water into his lungs.'

'Poor Gerhard, cooped up in a hospital miles from anywhere and no-one to visit him,' she said ruefully. 'I've a good mind to go up and see him. I can stop off in Hamburg and see my old friends from the Consulate.'

Elizabeth noticed the wary look that crossed Klaus's face. What was in his mind? Perhaps he hadn't given her the whole story. Hmmm ... if so, that was another good reason for going up there. Willi announced supper and they moved into the dining room.

'Open a bottle of *Bernkasteler Doctor,* please Willi.'

'Very good sir,' responded Willi with impeccable gravitas, but revealing the tiniest hint of surprise.

Elizabeth noted the wine, usually only reserved for important guests. The fact that Klaus was unusually talkative during the meal only served to increase her unease and she made up her mind to undertake the trip to Fehmarn.

The next morning she rang Burg hospital again. Von Hessler sounded tired but brightened up when she announced her plan to visit him.

'I'll get the train.' She told him. 'There's just the one change at Hamburg.'

As she put the telephone down, she felt a lightening of her spirits.

The following day Klaus gave her a lift to the rail station, carried her bag into the carriage and folded her mohair coat and placed it in the luggage rack. A little puzzled by this uncharacteristic solicitude, Elizabeth settled back in her seat, prepared to enjoy the journey. As the Bundesbahn train left the station (dead on time, of course), she pulled out a new novel from her handbag, the latest Iris Murdoch: *A Fairly Honourable Defeat.* She enjoyed reading English novels finding German authors overly occupied with existential *Angst.* Apart from that, the title resonated - she sensed there was a battle looming with Klaus over the disposal of the ammunition box and its contents. Who was going to be defeated? And would the outcome be honourable?

A short taxi-ride got her to the hospital in Burg and she was shown in to von Hessler's room. He was asleep. Moving quietly so as not to disturb him, she sat down beside the bed and contemplated the face on the pillow. He looked older, somehow more wise. She reassured herself – doubtless the shock and fatigue of his night's work. After all, Gerhard was still a comparatively young man, fifty, only nine years older than herself. A bunch of yellow roses filled a vase on a small chromium plated trolley though there were no letters or Get-Well cards to be seen on the bedside locker. Everything in the white-walled room was clean and clinical, the odour of disinfectant overwhelming.

A nurse bustled in to take his temperature and woke him. Elizabeth watched his face as he blinked, looked around the room and saw her. He broke into a broad smile while the nurse counted his heart rate and measured his blood pressure.

'Very good.' said the nurse patting him on the arm possessively.

'How good of you to come, Elizabeth. Already I'm feeling better. Did you have a good journey?'

'Yes, it was easy and trouble-free. Now tell me all about your escape from death.'

'Do you mean my pathetic attempt at drowning or my being run down by a Russian killer ship?'

Elizabeth chuckled, as he intended. 'Both? It sounds like an episode from an American thriller!'

She listened, enthralled, as Von Hessler related the tale of his trip out into the Baltic night – the navigational problems, his conversations with König, the narrow escape from being run down, the divers bringing up the box and the briefcase. His words conjured the lights in the darkness, and the tiny, vulnerable rubber boat at the mercy of the huge merchantman. Tactfully, she admired the composure of König, the professionalism of the divers and the skill of their navigator. It was all vastly different from Klaus's business conquests. But underneath the magic of the tale was a dark, haunting reality – the very real menace of the sea and the deaths of those who sank into its cold embrace. She shuddered to think that Gerhard might have joined them. For a moment she was silent.

'You are a lucky man. Two scrapes with death in one night. You must be a survivor ... or born to be hanged!'

'Ouch! Don't make me laugh! It hurts!' He moved awkwardly on the bed before going on. 'You know I sometimes wonder about that, Elizabeth. Neither of my parents survived into old age. My mother died when she was 35 and my father at 55.'

'Was that the war?' Elizabeth asked gently.

'Yes, in my father's case. He was presumed killed in the last raid on Kiel on 2nd May

1945 just three days before the cease-fire. My mother died well before the war when I was six. It was actually my sixth birthday. She died of a stroke.'

'God, how awful for you! It must have been a dreadful shock.'

'Yes ...' His eyes stared into the black void of memory for several seconds. 'What made it worse was that my father wasn't home either. He was on his way to Sweden by sea when it happened and it was three days before he could get back home.'

'That must have been terrible!'

He grimaced, dismissing the past with a shrug. 'But talking of boats going to Sweden, I managed to retrieve the briefcase, but I've not yet had a chance to look in it yet. Doubtless, Klaus told you that we brought up the ammunition box. It was mostly intact, I think. Klaus took it.'

'Yes, he says it was in a pretty bad condition and that some of the contents had fallen out. Gerhard, tell me about this chap Hans. Klaus said he's one of his right-hand men in the Hamburg office.'

'So I understand. He's a friendly, big solid sort of man, very confident. Klaus was quite avuncular with him. In fact he even asked his advice on something when we were loading the box into the car and that's not something I've heard him do very often. Why are you interested?'

'It's just that Klaus has never mentioned him before which is odd in itself. Next time I'm in

158

the Hamburg office I shall ask to see him. What's his surname?'

'Richter, I think, or something similar. I've managed to write him a letter. It was a bit of a struggle and I don't have his address but I felt it was the least I could do to thank him for saving my life.'

'If you like, Gerhard, I can drop it into the Hamburg office. It will give me an excuse to discover something about him.'

'Come on. Tell me why you're so interested.'

'Never you mind,' said Elizabeth with a smile.

Her attempts to read Iris Murdoch on the return journey were interrupted by bizarre images of a rubber inflatable at sea on a dark night in which two men were discussing the terrible sinking of the liner *Cap Arcona* that Gerhard had mentioned. As so many have, she puzzled over the connection between the nation that produced Goethe and Beethoven and the men who drove those prisoners onto that death-ship. Why had the RAF attacked it? Hitler was dead, Berlin had fallen, and resistance was in the last stages of collapse. It seemed ... unnecessary.

Her musings were interrupted by the train slowing down as it approached Hamburg Hauptbahnhof. It took her back to the time had arrived at the same station in 1949, fresh from

England, ready to start work in the consulate. She had been horrified as the train rumbled past mile after mile of the filthy, brick-strewn wasteland of the city, its beauty and grace consumed by a fire-storm during the RAF raids in 1943.

She'd booked a room at the Hotel *Vier Jahreszieten* and, as she walked up to the entrance she recalled the consular reception where she had first met Klaus. Once in her room, she picked up the phone and rang an old friend from the consulate days, inviting her and her husband for dinner. She was intending to enjoy her few days of freedom!

The next morning she visited the offices of *Schmidt Elektrodynamik* and asked at reception for Hans Richter, recognising him from von Hessler's description as soon as he appeared. He walked confidently towards her - a young man sure of his position, aware of his ability to command.

She held out her hand 'Herr Richter?'

'Frau Schmidt,' he bowed. 'To what do I owe the pleasure of your visit?'

'I have a letter for you from Herr von Hessler.'

Richter registered some surprise as she extracted it from her crocodile skin handbag.

'But that's not the only reason. I would also like to thank you personally for saving his life.'

'Frau Schmidt you are very kind, but I assure you it was at no risk to myself. It was quite automatic. I just did what I was trained to do.'

'And you did it very well by all accounts. It can't have been easy working in almost complete darkness.'

'I try to do my best,' said Hans deprecatingly. 'Let us not stand here. Can I offer you a cup of coffee?'

'What a good idea, I'd love one.'

Richter led her in the direction of his office and offered her a seat. Elizabeth noted the Swedish furniture and the expensive carpet. He lowered himself into an executive style chair behind a large, virtually empty desk; plainly, he operated a clear desk policy!

'This is very pleasant.' She said, looking around. 'So how long have you worked for my husband's company Herr Richter?'

'Since I left university and finished my military service - about four years. I have been very happy here and enjoy the work.'

Elizabeth was fascinated, this young man had the same assurance, almost panache, as her husband. She noticed a photograph of a young woman on his desk.

She pointed to it – 'Your wife?'

'No, my fiancée. We plan to marry soon. Then I shall leave home; we plan on living outside the city.'

'I suppose that will be a big change for your parents. Do you have brothers or sisters still at home?'

'No, there's just me and my mother. I can't remember my father. He left home when I was very little.'

'She will miss you.'

'I don't think she will really. She has a very active social life and a very good friend.'

A young woman quietly entered the room and served them coffee in a delicately moulded Rosenthal porcelain service. Elizabeth was glad of the diversion to try to straighten out her thoughts Clearly, Hans already filled a senior position which made it all the more incomprehensible that Klaus had never mentioned his existence.

They made small talk while the coffee was consumed and then she made to leave.

'You must tell me when your wedding is fixed and I'll send you a little present.' She said rising.

'That would be most generous of you, Frau Schmidt. I'll write the date on my card and then I'll sort out a car to take you to the station.'

After a brief word on the phone to a driver he escorted her out to a large Mercedes. It took her to the Hotel where she collected her bags, and then to the Hauptbahnhof. Once in the train she examined the card. His home address showed that he lived in an apartment in an expensive Hamburg suburb. She pulled out the copy of *A Fairly Honourable Defeat* from her handbag and tried to immerse herself in it. But the ammo box and its contents kept intruding.

Elizabeth awoke, unrested, disturbed and disorientated after a poor night's sleep. Klaus was worrying her, the uncertain morality of the world of commerce in which he moved seemed to be changing him. He was starting to exhibit some of the less acceptable traits of the businessman, was less concerned with the welfare of people and more with making money ... not to mention that he seemed less interested in her. She sighed. In the past, whenever he came in late he'd never proffer any explanation and this she had accepted. But now he was for ever producing unnecessary explanations. It made her wonder.

Over breakfast she decided to say something. She waited until Willi had brought in the toast and orange marmalade. 'Klaus I'm not happy about this ammunition box. We're not going to have another Beckmeier calling on us, are we?'

'My dear, don't over-dramatise. Of course we won't!' He was annoyed, that was perfectly clear. 'You needn't worry, I've learnt my lesson! In any case there's nothing much left in the cartridges. Twenty-five years in the sea have rotted most of the papers. There are no jewels if that's what you're thinking.'

'Where are you keeping them?'

'They're in the safe at the works. Gerhard warned me that 'God knows who' could be after the stuff – even the Stasi. I'd be an idiot to try and dispose of anything.'

'Well let's hope that we don't attract the Stasi of all people. You will tell me what you find in those cartridges, Klaus? Promise me.'

'Yes, yes, I will. But remember I've only had a chance to open up a few of them so far.'

Elizabeth was not reassured. Schmidt got up from the table, leaving his cup of coffee half finished, he grabbed his coat without putting it on and hurriedly left the apartment. It was her turn to feel affronted. Honestly! That sort of childish behaviour was absurd from a man of his age! She sighed and went to the phone, hoping to catch von Hessler while he was still in the hospital. After a considerable delay she was put through.

'Gerhard, how are you this morning?'

'The ribs are still bad, but the medics have warned me that mending is a long process so I'll be on painkillers for some time. It was so nice seeing you here though, did you get back all right?'

'Yes I did. Oh, I called on Hans Richter and delivered your letter. It quite surprised him; I don't think he was expecting it. He's getting married soon and I've promised to send them a little present. I understand that he's living with his mother at the moment. They're in an expensive apartment so he must be earning a good salary. But that's enough of him, let's talk about you, Gerhard. I'm concerned about your involvement in the disposal of those cartridges. You know what happened last time with that driver Beckmeier and

164

then with von Benz. I don't want any more of that.'

'Well everything depends on what's in them. Until we open them up but as Klaus agreed we'd do them together, it'll have to wait until I can travel.'

'Gerhard, I'm sorry to tell you, he's already opened them. He told me yesterday that all those years in the sea have taken their toll and there was nothing of value.'

She waited several seconds for his reply.

'Elizabeth, I don't like the sound of this. We had an agreement. What's he up to?'

There was another long silence and then she blurted out 'He's straying off the straight and narrow again, to put it bluntly.'

'Elizabeth, I don't want to worry you unncecessarily, but Klaus is not going to get away with this. There is a lot at stake and as soon as I'm up and about, I'm going to take steps to stop him.'

'We both have to try and stop him, Gerhard, but I think it's best if you leave it to me, at least for the time being. I'm intending to talk to him when he gets in tonight. I've got to nip this thing in the bud. But what you need is rest - you sound furious and that won't help your recovery.'

'You're absolutely right. The more I think about it, the more angry I get. My reason for proposing the salvage trip was that I feared the emergence of more compromising letters, and not just those involving my own family. Klaus has already used some to threaten young von Benz. I don't trust him with those letters.'

'Leave him to me, Gerhard. You concentrate on resting and get those ribs mended.'

Elizabeth put down the phone and lit a cigarette. She needed to think. Klaus could manoeuvre adroitly to avoid breaking the civil law but the moral law was another matter. Its rules were precise – 'Thou shalt not steal' – but they were not always easy to apply. She thought about the morality of a starving man who could steal food without invoking legal reprisals aware that since the revolution in France stealing food from a shop was not a criminal offence. All the same, a kleptomaniac woman could be convicted for shoplifting, and yet she could be just as desperate in her own way as the starving man.

Klaus's set of values had always worried her. He believed in *finders keepers*. He would argue that insurance premiums were a way of making money out of other people's fear of loss, so why shouldn't he do the same. If people didn't insure their property they only had themselves to blame.

She knew that with him an appeal to moral law was not always effective and she was tired of him fighting with her over matters of principle even though she suspected that underneath he often really agreed with her. Was her difficulty in understanding him rooted in her failure to appreciate how much winning mattered to him? When he got angry he could be unpredictable and talked of 'collateral damage' – an army term he employed to describe the side-effects of an action on innocent bystanders. The more she thought about it the more tense she became.

By the time she left the hospital to go home after her afternoon's work, she felt fairly confident that she could handle Klaus but a residual doubt lurked. What if he returned in one of his tense, impenetrable moods? She might have to delay things until after dinner. However, when he came in he was exuberant, giving her a hug and immediately started to tell her how he had landed a big electrical contract from the Rheinbahn, the Düsseldorf tram operators, in a fight with Siemens. As her lack of enthusiasm permeated through his excitement, he stalled..

'My dear, you don't seem to be your usual self. Is anything wrong?'

'Well, yes, there is something, Klaus. But let's talk about it after dinner. Go on, tell me about this contract. How big is it?'

'Massive! It'll keep the factory going for four years and the margins are good. The Rheinbahn think they are taking a risk using a smallish supplier, but we're local and that won the day. My friends in the Industrie Klub are going to be impressed.'

They moved into the drawing room and Schmidt asked Willi to open a bottle of wine.

'I'm so glad for you, Klaus. I'm glad for both of us. Will it help your finances?'

'Yes indeed. The banks like deals with public bodies. No chance of the customer going under and pulling down their suppliers so I won't have any trouble raising the working capital which is often the snag with these big contracts.'

While Klaus steadily consumed half the bottle of wine, they chatted until Willi announced dinner. Elizabeth looped her arm through his as they went into the dining room.

'Klaus, my dear, now that your financial problems have been eased, you won't need that stuff from the cartridges, will you? So you just hand it over to the authorities. Or, if you prefer, you can leave it to me to do it.'

Her last remark surprised Elizabeth. It seemed to come from nowhere.

'What did you say?' said Klaus in astonishment.

'I've thought this thing through, Klaus and I've decided you really ought to hand that stuff in. I have to live with myself, and you have to live with yourself.'

'Is that a threat?'

Klaus was defensive; she was going to succeed! Purposefully, she sat down at the table, unfolding her napkin. Then she looked directly at him.

'It depends how you interpret it. Let's call it a domestic deal. You think about it – it's a win-win situation, we both come out of it with something.'

'Good God! .... you really mean you'd report the salvage operation? Don't forget Gerhard is involved.'

'He won't object. He's done nothing illegal - merely acted as navigator. You took the cartridges.'

Schmidt banged his arms on the table. 'Damn me, Elizabeth!   You expect me to hand over the proceeds after financing the whole thing?'

'Klaus, your financing it puts Gerhard in the clear. If there's anything of value in the cartridges, and you say there isn't, then you'll get the standard salvage fee which should cover you. But that is beside the point. I've made up my mind and I'd rather not have a long discussion about it.' She knew she sounded like a Victorian Aunt, and kicked herself.

Schmidt stared at the table for a few seconds. 'So,' he said 'it's take it or leave it?'

'Yes Klaus, I'm afraid it is.'

'You should be on the Supervisory Board of the Company.' He growled, pouring the last of the wine into his glass, picked it up and, stared at it pensively, swirling the contents around. Elizabeth watched as mixed emotions flitted across his face – anger, defiance, even a hint of resignation. T hen he raised his glass.

'Here's to Panzer-General Elizabeth Schmidt, the hero of Fehmarn.'

Elizabeth gave him a wry smile. It had been a narrow victory, barely conceded.

It was two days later, when Willi brought her an SAS airline ticket that he had found on the floor of Klaus's study, that she started to wonder about that victory. Willi had been apologetic, thinking that the ticket might be important.

'No, that's fine. I'll look into it, Willi.' She said, dismissing him.

It proved to be the remains of a recently-used ticket, the bottom carbon copy of which was illegible. Klaus usually flew Lufthansa so where had Klaus been? Sweden was the first country that came to her mind when SAS was mentioned and Sweden was probably the boat's destination. It had to be something to do with the sunken boat.

Chapter 6

The days in hospital passed slowly for von Hessler, his only diversion the telephone calls that came from Schmidt, his housekeeper and from Elizabeth. The latter puzzled him; for some unaccountable reason she spoke in English. Increasingly he felt the need to get back to Kiel.

Despite the pain from the cracked ribs, he decided to make the journey and returned to find his housekeeper Frau Graubal in sceptical mood and not entirely sympathetic. It dawned on him that perhaps the fact that he had returned by train had aroused her suspicions. Did she think that his fast driving had once again caused an accident, and his story of the drowning was a cover-up? Although this amused him, he could hardly blame her – the connection between drowning and cracked ribs was not obvious, but he felt too tired to go into long explanations. When he asked her to store the briefcase in the refrigerator her look changed from scepticism to astonishment. He poured himself a drink, asked her for an omelette, and took his aching body to bed.

Anson rang the next day to say that he was in Hamburg and would call on him the following morning. Von Hessler was glad. He liked Anson – he was one of the few men that he could talk to without shadows from the past looming up. Unlike himself, half his friends had been party members and at the back of their minds lay dark territory that they were unwilling to explore.

Later the diving firm rang to remind him that he had left his kitbag on the motor cruiser and that it was now in their office. Something else he needed to retrieve!

Anson arrived in one of his impeccably tailored charcoal suits, carrying a florid 'Get Well' card.

'What's all this Gerhard? He said, indicating the sling von Hessler was sporting. 'I thought you had chest injuries.'

'I have, I have. It's easier to wear a sling than to try to stop people shaking my hand which hurts me like the devil.'

They moved into the orangery, and settled into a pair of wicker chairs placed between the orange trees planted in wooden tubs at intervals all along the stone floor. The morning sun streaming through the large windows set off the bright orange of the fruit against the dark green of the leaves and released the delicious fragrance produced by the blossom.

Frau Graubal came in to enquire if the guest would like coffee and remonstrated, rather pointedly, with von Hessler about the state of the chairs which she declared were only fit for a bonfire. Anson grinned and watched her ample figure walking back to the kitchen. Von Hessler waited until she was out of earshot.

'Frau Graubal thinks I'm made of money. When I tell her that I can't afford both her and a new set of chairs she waves her arms in the air and goes on about my expensive collection of motor cars.' He grumbled fondly. 'I really ought not to tease her though; she's very kind. You should see the way she dotes on her grandchildren.'

She returned carrying a tray with coffee percolator and cups. With interest, Anson examined the flowers in the pots and troughs distributed around the walls of the orangery.

'What on earth are those?' he said looking closely at a group on particularly tall stems. 'They look like bird's heads. I've never seen anything like them.'

'My dear fellow we've been growing them for centuries, apart from a period when your damn bombers blew in the glass in my greenhouse. There're called 'Bird of Paradise' flowers in English, or in Latin *Strelitzia reginae.* They're named after Charlotte von Mecklenburg-Strelitz, the lady who married your George the Third. Hence the *reginae.* Frau Graubal's husband sees to the grounds here and he's very proud of them. In fact they're something of a family trophy.'

'It's a very unusual trophy! What do you mean?'

'Well, Queen Charlotte's mother was Frederike Prinzessin von Hessen-Darmstadt. She's one of my ancestors, so there you are.'

'Oh! Very good, Gerhard, I'm impressed! But now you must tell me about your adventures. I gather you pulled off your little expedition and I must say I didn't think you would. No trouble with the Volksmarine?'

'No trouble at all. However we did have a serious brush with the Merchant Marine as you may have heard. They tried to sink us ... though doubtless it was not deliberate. Their watch-keeping is abysmal. They deserve to steam straight onto a sharp rock – going fast.'

'Probably a Russian ship,' Ventured Anson. 'They think they own the Baltic. You were bloody lucky!'

'You can say that again! But that wasn't the only near-disaster that night. The chief diver refused to land the stuff we got up from the S-boat, so he dropped it in nets off the end of a groyne near the village of Burgstaaken. I went in to get the briefcase and got my feet tangled up in the net and all but drowned. Klaus's chap, Hans Richter, saved me though he was a bit over-enthusiastic – these big chaps don't know their own strength! – hence the cracked ribs. Anyway I've got the briefcase here but I haven't been able to open it. I'm reluctant to lift anything heavy and the thing's waterlogged. You coming like this is a godsend!'

'You want me to get it?'

'If you wouldn't mind.'

Anson hurried off and returned carrying the briefcase in its plastic bag, at the bottom of which slopped a pool of filthy water. Slime could still be seen clinging to the briefcase.

'I think this needs sponging down. I'd better find a tap. Back in a minute.' Anson said.

Patiently, von Hessler took a sip of coffee and gazed out of the windows at the neat flower beds where red and yellow tulips were just starting to lose their petals. He must remember to congratulate old Graubal on a fine display.

Anson returned carrying the briefcase now cleaned of the slime it had accumulated at the bottom of the sea.

'Gerhard, you need to see these initials.'

He put the briefcase down on the floor and turned it round to face von Hessler. The initials read: *PHUM v H.*

Von Hessler looked from the case to Anson and back to the case unable to speak. He leaned forward and stared at the initials as if hoping to change them. Then he turned to Anson with the same stare. Slowly he put a name to each initial. 'Paul Heribert Ulrich Manfred von Hessler.'

In a choking voice he added: 'My father.'

For a moment the two men were silent.

His face a mask, von Hessler struggled to regained his composure as he struggled to come to terms with this fact.

'You know what this means?'

Anson shook his head. This was all beyond him.

'I was told ... I've always believed my father was killed in that last raid on the docks in Kiel on the 2nd May ...' He frowned. 'But if he was on board the S103 that obviously can't be true!' He struggled to adjust his thoughts to accommodate this information. 'Could he have

175

survived the wreck? No ... Hennig was clear on that, only two of them survived.' A wave of filial grief washed over him as he felt his father's death afresh. Then another bombshell struck his struggling mind. 'What in God's name was he doing on that boat, Peter?'

He slumped back in the chair and seemed unable to continue.

'I need a drink.' He said desperately, turning to Anson.

He couldn't help but notice the surprise on Anson's face as, with energy he hardly knew he had, he hauled himself to his feet and went into the house, returning almost immediately clutching a bottle of whisky and some glasses.

'Here, let me help you with those.' Anson said quickly, removing them from von Hessler's grip. 'You sit down.'

A peaty aroma drifted across the table as he uncapped the bottle.

'The Macallan', that was my father's favourite scotch,' von Hessler muttered, staring at the bottle. 'D'you know the very moment that Hennig told me about the supernumerary crew member I had a strange, eerie feeling.' Suddenly energised he leaned forward. 'What's in that briefcase, Peter? What are we going to find? What was he doing in Sweden? What's in that ammunition box?' Clutching the glass, he slumped back into his chair.

Anson remained silent.

'Do you know Peter, there was always something about my father that puzzled me. I could never put my finger on it... Deep down I couldn't completely trust him... I've never told anyone before.' He took a gulp of the amber liquid. 'D'you know something? I'm scared what I'm going to find in that briefcase. You know I loved that bloody man. Still do.'

'Take it easy, Gerthard! Your father wasn't a war criminal. That's never been suggested ... has it?'

'No. But he was up to something! All those trips to Berlin ... those letters from SS HQ that he didn't want me to see.'

'Aren't you jumping to conclusions? Not every letter from the SS meant another train of *Untermenschen* departing for 'resettlement' in the East. Himmler was planning to take over the Reich, not just run the SS, he must have had. He planned a scheme for a civil administration ... that isn't a war crime.'

'You're talking about Himmler as if he was just a crafty politician, not a mass murderer.'

'No I'm not. I'm trying to point out that you cannot classify every single action of Himmler's as murderous. It's entirely possible that he might have been negotiating with the West behind Hitler's back asnd that is just the sort of thing your father would have been drawn into with his diplomatic skills. How do you know that he wasn't involved in the bomb plot? If they'd succeeded in killing Hitler that would have made your father almost a hero.'

'You're a good fellow, Peter. I wish I could believe you.'

Von Hessler studied the golden liquid in his tumbler, and took a sip. Silence descended again, the only sound the twittering of sparrows in the trees and the far distant sound of a ship's hooter filtering through the open windows.

'You're right of course.' He said with a faint sigh. 'We have to look at the evidence.'

'Can I do anything?' Anson asked.

'Yes, you can open that briefcase for me and we'll see what's in it.'

The metal of locks was bubbled and blotched, corroded by the long immersion. Seeing there was no access that way, Anson cut the straps with a knife and gently prised it. Inside were limp discoloured papers clinging together in two sheaves, one in each compartment. Gingerly, he lifted the first batch out, laying it flat on the table. The top document of the first sheaf was indecipherable, showing only traces of the ink of the original hand-written text.

'These are extremely fragile.' Anson said needlessly as von Hessler touched the side of a page. 'Probably best not to try to attempt to separate them.'

He turned his attention to the second sheaf, laying it on the table beside the other. The top letter was clearly readable, typed on high quality writing paper. Anson read it out -

'It's headed with the address Headquarters of the SS, Prinz-Albrechtstrasse, Berlin, and addressed to The Ambassador, The Embassy of the Deutsches Reich, Stockholm. It's addressed to the ambassador and dated 19 April 1945.'

Von Hessler closed his eyes and leaned back in the chair.

'What does it say?'

'The bearer of this letter, Freiherr von Hessler, is to be given every facility to deposit material in the embassy safe and to make arrangements with reputable Swedish banks to deposit material and documents in their vaults. Heil Hitler! It's signed Heinrich Himmler - Reichsführer SS.'

Von Hessler listened with a frozen, expressionless face.

'Perhaps these are the documents,' he said, pointing to the table. 'We'll have to wait and see. I daren't try separating them. I've already arranged for a curator in the university to deal with any waterlogged papers. He's an expert on archive recovery and he's been working with the Danes on a freeze-drying technique.'

'I should think the material Himmler's referring to is in the ammunition box with some more documents,' said Anson.

'And the box is now in the hands of my friend, Klaus Schmidt. I wonder if he'll be tempted to open it. God, if he gets at it, how much is he going to tell me about its contents?' said von

179

Hessler wearily. Then he remembered the single round of ammunition he'd stowed in his kitbag. The bleak look on his face changed.

'Peter, is there any chance you can get into Kiel and get my kitbag? One round fell out of the box and the diver shoved it in the net that we used to lift the stuff up from the wreck. I found it lying on the bottom of the inflatable and shoved it into my kitbag. It may give us a clue as to what's in the others.'

'Of course I will. Give me the address and I'll get over there straight away.'

As Anson left, von Hessler sat back in his chair and closed his eyes. Scenes from the past drifted across his mind. He heard the sound of his father's voice introducing him as a little boy to Field Marshal von Hindenburg. The Field Marshal was a big man, nearly as tall as his father, but older with white hair.

More memories surfaced.

His father's despair as he read the text of the telegram that President Hindenburg had sent to Hitler in 1934 congratulating him on carrying out the murderous Röhm Putsch! He remembered his father's admiration for Dietrich Bonhöffer after his powerful sermon the Sunday following the Putsch when, unlike other churchmen, he abhorred the murders and called for repentance by the German people. Again, he heard the anger in his father's voice when Hitler took command of the armed forces and compelled them to take a personal oath of allegiance to him. His words 'Gerhard, the army is finished!' came back to him. How could he have been a Nazi?

The painkillers and the warm sun sent him into an uneasy doze from which he woke to find Anson sitting beside him, the black kitbag by his feet.

'You're back with us then, Gerhard?'

'Have I slept long?'

'A couple of hours. Long enough for me to pick up your bag and head back here. Those divers told me they'd had an exciting time on your trip! They seemed rather impressed with you. They thought you came out rather well for an old man of 50.'

'Cheeky young pups!' Said von Hessler, grinning despite himself. 'Did you see König, the chief diver?'

'No. He was off visiting a yacht chandler. One of the divers told me with a big grin that he was buying radar reflectors. He's keen not to be run down again! Hardly surprising from what you tell me.'

Von Hessler turned his attention to the kitbag.

'This is it,' he said as he hauled out a single round of 50mm tank ammunition. The smooth surface of the brass cartridge case had aged to a dark brown with a layer of damp orange rust covering the steel shell. The joint between them was sealed with a finger-width band of brown gutta-percha. 'That's interesting,' he muttered to himself. 'Someone's taken special precautions to

181

stop water ingress. Peter, can you get a wood chisel from the workshop. We need to get this stuff off. Herr Graubal will show you where to go.'

Anson returned with a chisel and pared off the sealant with some difficulty. Then he gently inserted the chisel into the joint and gradually levered out the shell. The inside of the cartridge case was dry and from it he pulled out a roll of documents, flattened them, and handed them to von Hessler. He flipped through them quickly. 'These are in Swedish from three different Stockholm banks all dated 3rd August 1939, one made out in triplicate.' He handed them back to Anson. 'What do you make of them?'

'They look like pre-printed 'Letters of Authorisation' to me. They've got hand-written serial numbers entered in the two boxes in each of the letters. Those signatures at the bottom are over the titles of senior men; this one is a *Direktör*. But I'm afraid I'm not much help when it comes to reading Swedish.'

'Well at least we know why the ammunition was heading for Sweden. I wouldn't mind betting there are more such letters in the other cartridges. No wonder Schmidt agreed to finance the trip. Do you know I've a feeling that he's not going to play fair with me.'

'That wouldn't be a complete surprise, Gerhard! But these letters are not much use without the keys to the safe deposit boxes, I wonder where they are.'

Anson took the cartridge, shook it and out fell a bunch of three keys.

'There you are - now we're getting somewhere. These keys are numbered. If I read them out, you can see if the numbers on the forms correspond.'

Each key number matched a figure on one of the forms.

'Gerhard, you do realise that there is frequently more than one person authorised to access deposit boxes and each will have a key?'

Von Hessler glanced at Anson with a determined look. 'I do. It seems I'm due for a trip to Stockholm.'

Anson stood up and straightened his jacket and glanced at his watch. 'I must get back to base. Don't get up. Let me know if there's anything more I can do. It's just possible I could fit in a trip to Stockholm, but perhaps it's better for you to go as soon as you can face it.'

'Don't worry. I'll fill myself up with painkillers. Keep in touch Peter and thanks for coming.'

Anson departed with a wave of his hand. Von Hessler leaned back in his chair and ran his hands over his face, closed his eyes and tried to relax. He listened to the steady hum of bees working around him. Then he levered himself up, walked slowly across the lawn to the flower beds and stood contemplating the alternating purple and white alyssum that formed the border. He caught a whiff of the scent from the flowers. The bed looked so calm and orderly - old Graubal was a good gardener. For a moment he envied the man his uncomplicated role.

The resonant sound of a high flying aircraft drew his attention and he looked up at the vapour trail forming behind it in the blue sky. It was flying north, probably to Stockholm. Abruptly he turned and retraced his steps. He glanced at the two sheaves of wet letters from the briefcase. The top copy of the first sheaf was drying out in the sun and curling up and with great care he peeled it off. Now he could read the Foreign Ministry heading of the letter below. The Wilhelmstrasse address had been overtyped and substituted by another. His face tensed as he read:-

To the Reichs Ambassador, Stockholm,

19 April 1945

Dear Ambassador,

By order of the Führer arrangements are being made under the direction of Reichsführer SS Heinrich Himmler to remove by sea the inmates of lagers Nauengarme, Fürstengrube and others in Gau Hamburg. Gauleiter Kaufmann has taken control of passenger liners Cap Arcona, Thielbeck and Deutschland to enable this movement. These ships are currently lying off Neustadt.
You are instructed to inform the Swedish government that the safety of these ships is in the

184

hands of the Kriegsmarine and that any distress signals from these ships will be prompted by attempts by prisoners to escape and are to be ignored.
Heil Hitler!

Joachim von Ribbentrop
Aussenminister
This letter will be handed to you in person by Paul Freiherr von Hessler.

Not knowing what to think, von Hessler put down the letter and went into the house. He gasped with pain as he banged his shoulder against the door post as he moved into the study and sat down at his desk. Unable to sit still he got up and lurched towards the barn in which he kept his collection of cars, selected the key for the gleaming new Aston Martin and lowered himself carefully into the driving seat. The dark green car's aroma of paint and leather reminded him of the time as a boy when his father had proudly demonstrated his magnificent new Isotta Fraschini. He turned the starter switch and checked the array of circular dials spread out across the dashboard like the instrument panel of an aircraft. He blipped the throttle and the growl of the big V8 engine reverberated through the barn. The concentration needed to drive the world's fastest production car would distract him ... and he needed distraction. He backed the vehicle into the yard, swung it round into the drive and out through the delicately wrought iron gates. Then he put his foot down and held the pedal to the floor. For a few seconds the exuberant acceleration of the car lifted his mood. In the driving mirror he saw the cloud of black smoke from the spinning tyres. The smell of burning rubber brought a grim smile to his face.

All too late, he spotted a woman on a horse trotting towards him. Frantically, he slammed on the brakes, all four tyres protesting, and came to a halt with only a few metres to spare. The horse's head flew up and it turned away, its legs skittering, hooves clattering on the road as the rider struggled to regain control. He saw the fear in the flaring nostrils and the whites of the animal's eyes. Mortified, he watched as the rider gradually calmed the animal and forced it to turn towards him and continue on its way, snorting and panting, wet with sweat. He shook his head and grimaced in abject apology to the rider. Surprisingly she gave him a forgiving smile and he watched in the driving mirror as the horse and rider trotted off down the road. The irony of the incident hit him – she, the young woman dealing firmly with a crisis, he the older man trying to escape from one and creating another.

The autobahn to Kiel was still under construction – there was no real chance of driving at speed on the local roads. Anyway no matter how fast he went he could never leave the crisis behind. Instead of tearing along roads, he should be looking inside himself.

Turning the car round he drove slowly back into the barn and returned to his study. Pouring a stiff measure of whisky he noticed that his hand was shaking. He picked up the glass and looked curiously at the agitated liquid – he had seen unsteady hands before when debriefing top U-boat commanders – men of the calibre of Günter Prien and Otto Kretschmer. Wearily he sat down again at his desk and stared unfocussed at the row of family photographs placed across the top. He saw his father in Diplomatic Corps uniform, looking squarely at the camera. How had he become involved in the transport of those thousands of camp prisoners? How had this honourable man become a messenger of death? There must be an explanation.

He had obviously left Berlin just before the last escape route was blocked by the Russians. Perhaps he'd had no time to read the letters and documents in the briefcase. Perhaps someone had inserted von Ribbentrop's letter at the last minute unbeknown to him. The place had been swarming with SS since Himmler had established himself in Flensburg to the North. Maybe he used the letter to persuade the SS to allow him to board the S-boat. Perhaps he had he intended to destroy it once he was safely out of their reach.

Von Hessler was seized with a fierce determination to establish the facts and if possible to clear his father's name. Going indoors he sat down in the study and listed what had been unearthed so far. Then he drew out a plan of campaign and it was rapidly apparent which actions were needed.

First he rang the university and arranged to hand over the sodden papers to the Curator of Archives to see if he could dry out and separate them successfully.

The next move would be a trip to Sweden to examine the safe deposit boxes, so he searched out the SAS and Lufthansa timetables for flights to Stockholm.

But the central mystery remained - who had planned the trip to Sweden? His father, perhaps? Or von Benz's father or even the old Colonel at Schloss Bückeburg ... all those men were dead. Only one man remained who might still be alive – Klaus Schmidt's commanding General. He picked up the phone and rang the Curator of Archives again. Would he be able to discover who had commanded the 2nd Panzer Division at the end of the war? The answer came back in a few minutes – the name he wanted was General von Lauchert and, as far as the clerk was concerned, he was alive and well, and living at an address in Bavaria.

Von Hessler seized a sheet of writing paper and quickly penned a letter to the General explaining how the death of his father had come about, and his hope that the General would be able to help him to unravel some of the mystery surrounding it.

Von Hessler booked a starboard window seat in the First Class section of the SAS Caravelle to Stockholm so as to secure a good view of the Bay of Mecklenburg on the flight to Sweden. Shortly after take-off from Hamburg the city of Kiel appeared below and then the island of Fehmarn. He could just make out the dark lines of the groynes on the beach ... the beach where he had very nearly drowned.

Life was strange! Only a few days previously he'd been lying in hospital on that remote island ... never could he have imagined that he would be looking down on it from 25,000 ft. Stifling the chuckle that threatened, he shifted in the seat, trying to ease his cracked ribs.

Despite the pain, his hospital stay had been a pleasant experience – the facilities good and the staff caring and efficient. But, he reluctantly admitted to himself, it's not that, is it? It was the appearance of Elizabeth Schmidt – you hadn't expected that. She's had always kept her distance in the past, but this time she had been *sympathisch*. She was an attractive woman. Why the devil had she fallen for Klaus? Sure, the man was an attractive rogue, and could be good company although not quite the gentleman, his fastidious self added. But Elizabeth ... she was made of finer stuff and she was stronger. Was it just his fancy that the ardour in their marriage was cooling? It was an intriguing thought that led him into some hitherto unexplored areas of thought.

His pleasant musings were interrupted by the 'Fasten Seatbelts' signal and the plane landed at Stockholm-Bromma on time It was a crisp morning, though colder than Hamburg and he was glad to feel some warmth from the sun. A taxi took him to the West German embassy in Skarpögatan. He was disappointed by the uninspiring building – certainly not one that a half-decent architect would have conceived for a site that overlooked the water in a central part of the capital. Nor would the old Kaiser have settled for anything so unpretentious. But the fact had to be faced that the building had been constructed by a divided country emerging chastened from a disastrous war.

Scandinavian style was evident in the ambassador's office - pale colours, functional furniture, Orrefors glass displayed on a glass shelf, the greyness only relieved by a bowl of red carnations placed on a large antique desk of gleaming mahogany. Doubtless, the ambassador's personal attempt to introduce some warmth into his clinical surroundings.   He was an old acquaintance of the family, an elegant and distinguished man with the polished manner of an old-school diplomat who welcomed von Hessler with a firm handshake and an open smile.

After an exchange of family news von Hessler raised the subject of his visit.

'I'm here, Dietrich, on a mission of some delicacy. I've discovered papers of my father's which show that in the last few days of the war he

190

set off for Sweden by sea, heading for Trelleborg. He never arrived.' Von Hessler paused, discomfited.

It was the first time he had related the story and he was unprepared for the emotional impact it made on him. Battling to control himself, he turned to look out of the window. In the middle distance he saw the ancient houses that had been re-erected on the grassland of the Skansen open-air museum. It resembled a model landscape he had made as a boy with his father's help. With patience and understanding, the ambassador waited while his visitor tried to recover his thread.

'It's virtually certain that my father ... that he died during the crossing. He was travelling in an S-boat that was attacked by the RAF. His body was never recovered.'

'I am so sorry, Gerhard. I take it that this is a recent discovery. How long have you known?'

'Only a few days,' said von Hessler. 'He was carrying a briefcase of documents, which I've just recovered. They make remarkable reading,' and again he paused. 'They were written by men like Joachim von Ribbentrop.' He stopped abruptly the name of Heinrich Himmler sticking in his throat. 'I don't understand why he was making the trip and I need to find out more about it – that's why I am here.'

The ambassador looked concerned. 'How can I help you?'

'Well, I was wondering if your archives would show any previous trips he might have made.'

'I'm afraid I'll have to disappoint you there; our archives are in Bonn. I can get access for you, but I warn you that researching them calls for patience, perseverance, time and perhaps most importantly, plenty of luck.' He smiled. 'You have all of those – of course. The first thing you'll need to examine will be the visitors' books. I'll get my people to check if they appear on our archive list.'

'That would be a great help Dietrich. There's also an indication that he was bringing over 'material' for storage in the embassy vaults, although there's no mention of what that consisted of. Would there be anything left here now?'

'Not a chance,' said the ambassador shaking his head. 'Anything in the vaults of the old embassy was long since cleared out and sent back home. And I dare say Allied Military Government or the Control Commission picked over everything.' There was a brief silence as the two men acknowledged what that would mean. 'I'd give up on that one if I were you. Let me check where the visitors' books are.'

The ambassador made a phone call'

'You're in luck, Gerhard. The books for the period 1944 - 1945 are still here. I've asked for them to be brought up.'

'Excellent!' Von Hessler said, his spirits lifting. 'So what's occupying Stockholm's attention these days?'

'Not a great deal. We don't see much of the cold war up here. Everybody's watching how Willi Brandt's Ostpolitik is developing. They think he'll have his Moscow treaty within a few months and end up with a Nobel Peace Prize, so that will keep me busy looking after him for a couple of days.' He chuckled ironically. 'We have occasional problems with Russian submarines but the government makes a fuss and they keep clear for a bit.' With a grimace the ambassador pointed to a row of gold-embossed invitation cards on a side table. 'I'm busy doing the rounds of diplomatic receptions – they're hard work. Constantly meeting the same people dulls the excitement. I'm looking forward to some leave.'

After a discreet knock at the door a secretary entered with the red leather-bound visitors' books embossed with an eagle clutching a golden orb which bore a swastika. The ambassador examined them, page by page and shook his head. 'That takes us up to the end of hostilities. There's no visit from your father recorded here.'

'So that means his fatal trip must have been very special. I was hoping that I could establish a reason for it based on a history of previous trips and their dates. Obviously not. Pity.'

The conversation reverted to family matters and after a few minutes von Hessler bade farewell to the ambassador.

He took a taxi to the Skandinaviska Banken building where he casually informed the lady receptionist that he needed access to some deposit boxes.   The interview room he was taken to was furnished with a table, two chairs and a telephone. It lacked windows or decoration apart from a pair of early photographs hanging on the dull white walls that showing some be-wiskered members of an old banking dynasty.   After a few minutes a young clerk entered and in deferential tones asked for his card and then for his Letters of Authorisation, these he examined briefly and departed. A further wait ensued and von Hessler began to feel irritated. At least the bank could have provided some reading matter even if it was in Swedish.

An older man entered carrying a file, introduced himself as a manager and waved towards the chairs. Unusually for a Swede he claimed to be an indifferent German-speaker and they agreed to communicate in English.

'Herr von Hessler, you will appreciate that we have certain rules with which we must comply and I must therefore ask to see your passport.'

'My passport?' Von Hessler expressed surprise. 'I fail to see what my passport has to do with examining a box for which I have a Letter of Authorisation signed by one of your Directörs?'

'It is to protect your interests and those of the other holders of Letters for that box,' was the curt reply.

Other holders ... the words hung in the air.

Von Hessler controlled his antipathy towards officialdom and with a stony face produced his passport which was examined and returned without comment. Then the Letters and key numbers were laboriously compared with items in the file. Satisfied, the man made some further entries, shut the file, stood up and silently motioned von Hessler to accompany him.

Walking a shade too rapidly the man led the way along a corridor to a lift, and they descended to vault level. With a flourish he produced a bunch of keys and opened a steel gate, waved von Hessler through and locked it again behind them. A further door was unlocked and the two men entered a narrow strong room lined with bronze-coloured deposit boxes; there was a felt-covered table at the far end of the room. The manager ran his eye up and down the tiers of boxes, turned a master key to release a box which he pulled out and laid on the table, before turning to face his visitor.

'You may access the box. I will wait outside the door until you have finished. Then I will replace the box.'

With that he left the room.

Von Hessler inserted his key and raised the lid. It was empty. The trail was cold.

'Damn and blast,' he muttered to himself in English.

Someone had visited the vault ahead of him ... someone provided with the necessary credentials. He walked out to the waiting manager.

'There is nothing in this box. Who else has had access?'

'I cannot say.'

'Why the devil not? You have just asked me for my passport to protect my interests as you so clearly stated. It is in my interest to discover who has emptied that box.' In an icy tone he continued 'Let us now discover whether this 'protection' of which you speak has any teeth or is just a meaningless fiction.'

The manager hesitated. Perhaps he was unsure how well connected von Hessler was after seeing the title 'Freiherr' that appeared on his card. Normally he used it only for booking tables in restaurants and such like, switching to the word 'Baron' in London - it usually secured him a good table at the Savoy or at Boulestin across the Strand. He was on the point of saying that he would be escalating the matter when the man spoke.

'I cannot give you names but I can give you the dates and times.' Sweat beaded the man's forehead.

Von Hessler nodded regally.

'The most recent was three days ago; before that was over 25 years ago on 21st July 1944 and then 1st September 1939. The charges for the box have been paid regularly every five years.'

As von Hessler walked back into the strong room the words 'bloody crook' escaped him. Schmidt had got there before him – there was no other explanation. He closed the lid, withdrew the key and returned to the waiting manager. He frowned.

'Who pays the charge for the box?'

'I have no information as to the payer. Payment is by drafts drawn on Coutts' in London.'

'Then that concludes our business,' said von Hessler with asperity.

He needed time to think. As he strode towards the next bank in Norrmalmstorg he mused over these dates. The first was the day after von Stauffenberg's unsuccessful attempt on Hitler's life on 20th July 1944, and the second coincided with the start of the invasion of Poland. Whoever travelled to Sweden on those dates was obviously well informed and in a position to travel without hindrance. Who was it, and who had issued those drafts on Coutts'? There was plenty to think about.

Norrmalmstorg: the sunlit green of the young leaves on the trees stood out refreshingly against the white and pale grey stone of the buildings around the busy square. He drank in the atmosphere of understated wealth that permeated the place, an expensive part of Stockholm.

At Kreditbanken he was received cordially and introduced to an affable young manager who escorted him to the vaults. The deposit box revealed a folder with a red wax seal which he immediately broke, drawing out a sheaf of documents. Encouraged, for he had half expected to find nothing, and consequently a little excited, he quickly scanned them.

The top one was an opened blue envelope carrying a British stamp containing a private letter in German. Below it were more handwritten letters, again, mainly in German. The remainder consisted of Bearer Bonds issued by American states and corporations. Von Hessler hurriedly stowed the folder in his bag, thanked the manager, and hurried to the third bank where, almost with a sense of relief, he found an empty box, presumably Schmidt again. But it was a relief that he did not have to face reading yet more letters implicating his father with Nazi leaders.

The ache in his chest warned him that the painkillers were wearing off; it was time to take a taxi back to Bromma where he quickly checked in and a few minutes later boarded the aircraft. He strapped himself into his seat, looking forward to a glass of champagne and the attentions of the fair-haired air hostesses.

As the miles sped past, his mind played with the contents of the hand-written letters. What dreadful new light would they shed on his father's affairs?

Where next? Düsseldorf perhaps? To see Elizabeth and confront Klaus, or maybe Bavaria to see General von Lauchert. No, Amsterdam - to talk to Peter Anson. He could give a detached view of the latest developments, valuable because it was from someone outside his immediate circle.

Two days later von Hessler boarded a Boeing 727 for the flight to Amsterdam-Schipol to meet Anson, grateful beyond measure for the fact that there were no hidden agendas with Peter, few subjects to be avoided, no baggage from the past. The past was lying heavily upon him that morning.

The discovery of the letter from von Ribbentrop had brought to the surface an uneasy guilt that he had long buried, now exposed - fresh and raw – it fed the horror first felt at his full and final realisation of the fate of the Jews. Like so many, he had tried to distance himself when ugly rumours first circulated, arguing that his *Kriegsmarine* was fighting a clean war, maintaining their independence until near the end. After all, Admiral Räder's refusal to force his officers into the party was one of the reasons he was replaced by Dönitz. Hitler distrusted the Navy and the feeling was mutual. Like his father he'd had no time for that lower-class rabble-rouser.

But the discovery of his father's dealings with Himmler and von Ribbentrop over the shipping of the Jews in the *Cap Arcona* turned all this on its head. He had to talk to someone, to reveal his sense of contamination to another human soul. He would tell Anson, but fear pulled at him – could he go through with it? Well, he would find out when he sat down face-to-face with the man.

He asked for a newspaper, determinedly immersing himself in the arguments over Willi Brandt's Ostpolitik. However, as the plane landed his dread returned. Anson was, as usual, hiding himself behind a newspaper in one of the brown armchairs in the lounge of the Hilton Hotel.

'Good God!' said Anson, taking one glance at his friend. 'What on earth is the matter?'

Saying nothing, von Hessler led the way to the coffee shop where they found a secluded table and sat down. Leaning forward, he immediately opened the conversation.

'I need to talk to you, Peter. Firstly I need your opinion on the results of my foray into the Stockholm banks. I had three Letters of Authorisation to open the deposit boxes and what did I find? Two of them empty – cleaned out three days before I got there. Three days! It can only have been Klaus.'

'Wow,' exclaimed Anson. 'Does he know that you've got that round of ammo that fell out of the box?'

'I haven't told him, so I don't see that he can know. But before we get onto Klaus, let me tell you what I found in the third box – these letters and American bearer bonds. Look at them!' He handed the letters to Anson. 'The German ones are a riddle. They are nothing but family letters written in a man's hand; I can't for the life of me see why they needed to be got out of the country. They're utterly banal – no meaningful information at all. Just Aunt so-and-so did this last week and Uncle so-and-so did that.'

Anson handed back the letters. 'They could be coded messages. Have you thought of that?'

Von Hessler scanned them again. 'I should have thought of that ... I suppose it's possible. If so then I've got a problem. There's no clue to the sender's name, no surnames and the address is vague and variable. It's going to be a tough one.' His breath whistled out through his teeth as he contemplated the problem. 'Now have a look at this English one. It's pre-war.'

Von Hessler watched his expression change to amusement.

'Oh my God. We're into deep water here. This reads like a love letter and I'm pretty sure I know who wrote it. It's to a young midshipman from an English naval officer who was very well-connected. He was in a top job by the end of the war. He might even be a distant relation of yours.'

'Par for the course, old man. My family has a long history - we tend to take that sort of relationship in our stride. Come to think of it Klaus must have found similar letters in the ammo he purloined at the end of the war and threatened to use against that ass von Benz. And he's much closer to your Royals than I am.'

'What are you going to do with it?'

'Burn the bloody thing. But that won't help if Klaus has similar letters and uses them as bargaining chips. He could sell them to the *Bild-Zeitung*. They'd give them front page treatment, might even displace the naked girls.' He said cynically. 'God forbid what he might do if we push him too hard!'

'Before you set about burning anything, Gerhard, I've got some interesting news. I had a visit a couple of days ago from a chap who's been put on Schmidt's case by our intelligence people.'

'What?'

'Exactly. It was all rather odd. My secretary showed him in; he placed a card on my desk and walked straight out again without saying a word. How about that?'

'What did it say on the card?'

'It carried the name AJP Hutchison of Hermag Security GmbH with a Bonn address. On the back he'd scribbled 'Meet you in the car park in 5 minutes'. So I wait five minutes before going out and Hutchison beckons me over to his car. He apologises for what he calls 'the cloak and dagger stuff', tells me he's 'on Her Majesty's business' and invites me to lunch.'

'What sort of chap is he?'

'Probably a retired army man. Well dressed. Pretty bright. We met in a modest restaurant and I noticed his choice of the cheaper items on the menu. Hermag Security must keep a tight rein on expenses – probably on some Civil Service scale. He told me that our intelligence people, MI6, were anxious to keep an eye on one Klaus Schmidt whom they gathered I knew, and that they would be very much obliged if I would do just that.'

'Astonishing! How did you react?'

'I reacted by saying that I thought my intelligence activities had come to an end when I retired from the navy and he gave a sort of shrug by which I think he meant: 'Don't be so naïve.' So I asked him what the story was and this is what he told me – they're worried about dodgy deals that

Schmidt has done, or is about to do, over some potentially embarrassing correspondence that originated in high places. They don't know anything of the contents but he said our Bonn embassy is expressing a keen interest and Downing Street has passed the word.'

'I'll be damned,' said von Hessler. 'Things are hotting up. I'm not sure I like this. What are you going to do?'

'Well I warned him that Schmidt is the key to significant business for me, and stressed that keeping an eye on him would not be easy – the man is a canny operator and habitually carries a miniature radio transmitter or tape recorder which he uses during negotiations. I also said that he can be unpredictable.'

'But you've agreed to do it?'

'How can I refuse? In any case Schmidt's attempt to flog Royal correspondence to some dealer that MI6 has their eye on is not something I can turn a blind eye to.'

'Are they going to pay you?'

Anson laughed. 'Only expenses. In addition to that, if I land myself hot water they're unlikely to help me out of it.'

'Generous bunch. Do they know about me?'

'Yes, you're on their radar, but Hutchison thought I should keep you in the picture.'

'How much do they know about my part in the salvage operations?'

'I doubt if they know very much. But I got the impression that some rumour is doing the rounds of the intelligence community. He dropped a hint about the Stasi which in turn could involve the KGB and hence automatically the CIA. That East German hydrographic survey boat's appearance can't have been a coincidence.'

Von Hessler waved to a waiter and ordered more coffee.

'It's daft asking you to keep an eye on Klaus now. As your proverb says, the horse has bolted! He'll have sold any bearer bonds he found; that's if they're still valid. Heaven knows what else was in those boxes - gold deposit certificates, dollar accounts, Swiss bank accounts. What do you suggest I should do now?'

'Well, people are still looking for the cash and gold that went AWOL at the end of the war despite the best efforts of the Reichsbank and the American army. If he makes a move to sell, he could land himself in trouble. But that's his problem. I don't know why you're looking so tragic about it Gerhard. Think what this might mean to Elizabeth? And those letters you've got? Not to mention, on a personal note, what about my contract with *Schmidt Elektrodynamik?* He's not signed that yet.'

'I'm a *dummkopf* for getting involved,' said von Hessler shaking his head. 'I'll have to confront him but before that I'll have to tell Elizabeth and that's not going to be easy.'

He stopped awkwardly and pulled out his airline ticket.

'I'll have to watch the time. Excuse me for a minute.'

Levering himself out of his chair he walked out and through the lounge. Around him were men in dark suits holding earnest discussions, at their feet or on the tables, briefcases, some similar to his father's. Across the room he spied a group of four men seated around a table. It seemed to him that three of them had the faces of top Nazi leaders, and the man with his back to him was his father. In shock he nearly collided with a waiter carrying a tray.

He fled along a corridor, down a staircase, hardly seeing where he was going, then found himself in the toilets. The chamber appeared to be empty. Relieved, he leaned on a wall, relaxing his body against it and shutting his eyes. On his forehead he felt the soothing coolness of the tiles - and then the warmth of his father's hand. He heard his father say '*You're going to be alright. It's only a fever*'.

'*Is meneer OK?*' Asked a passing Dutchman in a red tracksuit, jerking von Hessler from his reverie.

'Yes, yes, thank you. Just a headache,'

When he got back to the coffee shop, he sat down and looked straight at Anson.

'I've got more to tell you,' he said in a lowered voice; he took a deep breath. 'After you left me that day, I examined that pile of sodden

205

letters ... I ... I found one from von Ribbentrop. It appears to show that my father was ... helping the Nazis ....actively.'   He swallowed, looking anxiously at Anson.

'Shit!! God! How awful! You must feel pretty shaken.'

'Bloody awful!   I'm going out of my mind, Peter. I feel I'm being encircled by dark and dangerous forces.'

Von Hessler put his elbows on the table, and covered his face with his hands. Memories of the raids on Kiel came back to him, the destruction, the smoke, glowing embers and the acrid, sickening stench. That last raid of the war ... and the report that his father was missing. He dropped his hands and looked into the distance.

Anson quietly responded 'You look as if you're taking the whole weight of Nazi atrocities on your shoulders.'

'You would - if you were in my shoes. You ended the war celebrating. Our people had to creep into the cellars and beg and steal. We had the Nürnberg trials and the Denazification Courts. You came out unblemished.' He saw the puzzled, embarrassed look on Anson's face.

'Steady on old man. What about Dresden? What about sending the Cossacks back to Stalin's Russia and certain death? As for concentration camps, we invented them. We set them up in South Africa and thirty thousand Afrikaner women and children died of disease, not to mention twenty thousand blacks. You should talk to my boss

Hendriks – he's a Dutchman who lived for a time in South Africa and understands Afrikaans.'

'But that wasn't a deliberate, cold-blooded extermination policy,' said von Hessler with the first trace of energy in his voice.

'Perhaps not, but the end result was the same.'

'I must say you don't pull your punches. You don't sound like a typical Englishman.' Von Hessler said, feeling the weight lifting slightly. 'It must be your wife, Elke's, influence.'

'Possibly, but it's more likely from Hendriks. He believes all nations have a dark side - Russians, Japs, British, take your pick. They all ran camps. Look at Russia and the deliberate starvation of the Kulaks. More to the point, he understands the primal forces that drove the Nazis; they're complex ... and they're universal. And that comes from a Dutchman who lived through the destruction of Rotterdam by the Luftwaffe *after* a cease-fire had been negotiated.'

'You're very kind, Peter. Your man Hendriks has a point, but that doesn't make it any easier, particularly when you're the latest nation to join the list of murderers.'

Von Hessler relapsed into silence and watched the other man staring into his coffee cup for what seemed an age.

Then Anson said 'That von Ribbentrop letter - how can I help? Have you checked its authenticity?'

'I got my man in the university to run tests in his lab. The only thing that raised a question in his mind was the reference to my father that was typed in below the signature, he thought it could have been an addition. However it was definitely typed on the same machine. Spectroscopic analysis of the inks match and he even compared the signature with a letter in his archive. It's genuine, all right. There's one relief – that letter was in the briefcase and not in a cartridge, and it was dated as late as 19th April 1945. That means that whatever earlier stuff Klaus has got might predate my father's first involvement with Ribbentrop ... assuming it was his first..'

'If your father is implicated before that it complicates your next move.' said Anson reflectively. 'Schmidt could hold some aces and he'll play them. But he has to be careful, someone's watching him and he knows it. It could be Beckmeier and his crooks, it could be our people, even the Stasi. But you have an ace as well - he doesn't know that you've got that cartridge and that you're on his track. And of course there's Elizabeth and from what little I know of her, I wouldn't mind betting she's on your side.'

Von Hessler pulled out his airline ticket again and checked his departure time once more. He frowned. 'Yes, I wonder how much she knows. I rang her the other day and suggested we met. She used English, presumably in case Willi was listening. In fact, I'm going on from here to rendezvous with her in a Düsseldorf coffee bar.'

'Well I'm damned, Gerhard! Watch out that Klaus hasn't put a detective on your tail! But at least you're not meeting in a hotel. Did you tell her what it was all about?'

'No I didn't. She seemed uptight which put me off a little and then she reacted oddly when I mentioned I'd been to Stockholm. She started to ask me all about it, and then seemed to lose interest.'

'What are you going to tell her?'

'Basically I'll tell her most of what I've discovered. I won't disclose that I've got that cartridge; I'll let her think that the letters came from the briefcase. I'm wondering if she knows that Klaus went to Stockholm, and how she'll react when I tell her about what I discovered.'

'I've got to stop him using those letters, if necessary by threats, even if it upsets her. I'm just not prepared to risk exposure of my family and friends, particularly now my father's involved.' His eyes burned with fervour as he said these words.

'And I guess you're hoping that Elizabeth will keep you briefed on what Klaus is up to. You want to watch you don't get romantically entangled!'

Von Hessler shook his head and grinned. 'You know me Peter – the eligible bachelor who never gets the girl though I have to say I could fall for that one ... given sufficient encouragement.

Anyway, enough of this talk. I've got a plane to catch.'

He shook hands with Anson, picked up his travel bag and set off back to the airport with a springier step.

Chapter 7

Needless to say, Elizabeth arrived early for her morning rendezvous with von Hessler in the coffee bar in Tonhallenstrasse. The disquiet that had been steadily growing in her mind over the past few weeks was not at all dispelled by the anxiety she sensed in his voice when he called to make the appointment. She awaited his arrival nervously.

Over and over again she had berated herself for not dissuading Klaus from taking part in the recovery of the cartridges from the sunken boat. She had relied on it being no more than a wild goose chase, something that Gerhard would never summon sufficient energy to see through. She had been proved wrong on both counts.

Gerhard in particular puzzled her. Chasing all over the place ... with his painful ribs, too! There was more to the man than just a charming aristocrat.

'Am I beginning to admire him?' She asked herself for the millionth time trying to explain away the frisson of excitement she felt at the prospect of seeing him. 'I must watch myself.'

Von Hessler strode in and she immediately found herself comparing his tall figure with the rotundity of her husband. He was wearing a suit of Prince of Wales check with a cut that looked English, probably Savile Row. She greeted him, unaware of how attractive her smile was.

'Dear Gerhard, how are you feeling?'

'I won't be playing tennis for a while yet.' He said with a rueful smile. 'But I'm not too bad. Next time I try drowning I must find a less muscular rescuer!' Filing his ongoing curiosity regarding Hans Richter for the future, he ordered coffees and sat down.

'Elizabeth, I can't tell you how much I appreciated you travelling all the way up to Fehmarn to see me; I feel pretty much that my recovery started the moment you arrived. Looking back it all seems like a dream. I never suspected that Klaus and I were going to be involved in anything quite so dramatic.'

'To be honest neither did I,' said Elizabeth. 'In fact if I'd known where it was going to lead I would have tried to talk both of you out of it. I'm afraid the outcome is not what I was expecting.'

'Why do you say that?' He asked, dreading what she was going to say.

Elizabeth paused. She wondered how he would take her reply.

'I'm not sure that salvaging those cartridges was a good idea. Gerhard, I'm almost certain they were being got out of the country for highly dubious reasons. I know you risked your life twice that evening but I have to say I think it would have been better to leave them where they were.'

There was a slight tightening of his jaw, but apart from that his face gave nothing away. He sighed and stirred his coffee.

212

'I'm inclined to agree with you, Elizabeth. I suspect we've brought up Pandora's box.'

'That bad?'

He took a mouthful of coffee before replying.

'The paperwork mentions arrangements for various items to be deposited in Swedish banks.' He said, keeping the comment as general as possible.

'Did you find out anything in Sweden?'

'What I found in Sweden was ... was evidence that doesn't of itself prove anything.' He paused again. 'But, to be blunt, it does makes me wonder what Klaus is up to.'

'Oh God! I knew it was going to end up like this! Klaus is up to his tricks again.'

She blew out a stream of smoke watching as it dissipated in the draught from the kitchen. Why had she married this man? Why hadn't she waited until she had more understanding of men? And of herself? All those things she had found attractive about Klaus – his boyish exuberance, his foolish play-acting ... they'd been superficial, hiding the reality: the dark masculine side of him at first exciting – like a dominant bull – and just as dangerous.

Aware that von Hessler was watching her intently, she somehow found something reassuring about the way he kept silent. She read the concern in his face.

'There's something of the Mafioso about him, Gerhard, he can be totally unprincipled.' She muttered as she stubbed out her cigarette, shocked to hear herself say it. 'Hell! I'm sorry Gerhard, I shouldn't talk like this about him, should I? You're a friend of his.'

Nervously, Elizabeth pulled a cigarette packet from her bag and offered one to von Hessler who refused. She lit up and the cigarette end glowed brilliantly as she drew on it to gain a little time. This was not going to plan. Why on earth was she blurting out her feelings to Gerhard, of all people? But she needed real help and, she realised with surprise, she wanted it from him.

'Gerhard, Klaus is going to get into trouble. I know it. We've got to stop him. What are we going to do?'

'That's precisely what I wanted to talk to you about, Elizabeth. It's a difficult position for me. I'm having to work behind Klaus's back and in a way behind your back. I don't like it.'

'I appreciate your gentlemanly diffidence.' She said, looking directly at him. 'But if we're going to help Klaus we need to be open with each other. You really don't need to work behind my back.'

'That's a relief!' He gave her a sort of smile. 'I'd better tell you - I'm certain Klaus was up in Stockholm last week removing documents, cash and God knows what else from Swedish bank deposit boxes.'

'That would make sense ...' She said slowly, her eyes narrowing. 'Willi found a used SAS ticket on the floor in Klaus's study and asked me if it was important. It was a bottom carbon copy and I couldn't read the destination and when I mentioned it to Klaus he told me he'd been to Copenhagen. I ... I'm not sure I believed him and now ...'

'I don't know where this is all going to lead, Elizabeth. It's not good is it?'

'No, not at all. But what did you actually find in Stockholm?'

'Two empty deposit boxes. They'd been emptied a few days before – it could only have been Klaus.'

'What do you think was in them?'

'Monetary instruments, Dollar bonds, compromising letters.'

'Oh God! This is awful.' She drew on her cigarette, lifted her head and blew a puff of smoke into the air. 'The next thing we'll discover is that he's selling Nazi gold and then he'll have Simon Wiesenthal and his Nazi-hunters on his trail.' She apparently contemplated this idea for a moment before her expression sharpened. 'But what will he do with those letters?'

'That's what worries me the most. He'll bring the house down on our heads. All sorts of people will suffer - my family, von Benz and his people. Not to mention that there's at least one letter that will make uncomfortable reading for your Royal family.'

'The Royal family? How do you know?'

'Fortunately I've got that particular letter myself and I showed it to Peter Anson who recognized the writer, he became a senior naval officer during the war.'

'Well if he's right, you can burn it. Why are you looking so distressed?'

'That's not the worst. There are yet more compromising letters ... and they involve my father. And there're about far more serious matters than the questionable relationships of an English naval captain.'

That admission had cost von Hessler, she could see that. 'So we're in this together,' she said softly and touched his hand for a second.

'I guess so, as the Americans put it! And up the creek without a paddle, as the English would say.' He gestured at their now empty cups.

'I do love your colloquialisms Gerhard! They're really quite diverting. And yes, I'd love another coffee, please.'

She watched him as he went towards the coffee bar. There was a steely determination in the man that she had not detected before; without doubt, he could be formidable, perhaps even a match for Klaus. She found the thought encouraging, heartening even. Her glance fell on the other occupants of the café, a woman nearby gave her a broad smile and Elizabeth realised she must have been smiling herself.

Von Hessler returned with the coffee. 'This is going to be a joint operation, Elizabeth. In my navy days everything depended on secure communications. You and I need to communicate without alerting Klaus – the question is how?'

For a moment Elizabeth recalled her schooldays and the ridiculous codes they had invented to use in letters to her brothers serving overseas in an attempt to evade wartime censorship. 'I don't think we need to resort to codes,' she said with a grin. 'You can write to me at the hospital or you can ring me there just after two on Wednesdays.'

'That sounds simple enough, I can do that. So what next? Those cartridges might as well be filled with real explosives. How are we going to stop him blowing us all up? Anson tells me that Klaus is being watched, most likely by one of the intelligence agencies – maybe a British one or even the Stasi. Does he realise this?'

'Oh he does. Especially after we discovered that bug in the study.'

'Well that's reassuring. It means he'll have to watch what he's doing.'

'He's very good at covering his tracks,' said Elizabeth. 'Half the time even I don't know where he is. But how are we going to stop him?'

'It may surprise you, Elizabeth, but there's only one way that I can think of, and it's not very ... very nice.' He grimaced at the word.

'Tell me.'

'We threaten to expose him, in a nutshell. Of course that could be counter-productive and lead to a stand-off, if that's the right word.'

'I've threatened to do that already, Gerhard. Klaus's response was that you're as involved as he is.'

'But I'm not about to sell bearer bonds or gold bars or whatever, which are the rightful property of the Bundesrepublik.' He argued.

She shook her head. 'It won't work, we have to do something a bit more subtle.'

'Elizabeth ... I regret to say this but all we have in our armoury is threats. However, he doesn't know that I have one of the cartridges, nor that I've been to Sweden, so I can drop in a fact now and then to create the impression that I know the whole story. It's a well-known interrogation technique.'

'You've got a cartridge?'

Von Hessler explained quickly.

'Oh, I see.' responded Elizabeth. 'But Gerhard, what if Klaus didn't tell me the whole story about those cartridges that he buried en route to Kiel in 1945. He claims they contained only jewels, letters and papers. What if they contained bearer bonds or cash? I've always wondered where he got the money to buy the Company.'

'That is a definite possibility. He's never told me where he got the money either. Of course, he'd have had to produce proof of ownership in order to sell bearer bonds ...' Gerhard shook his head. 'I don't know how we'd even begin to investigate that one, it's such a long time ago; the trail will have gone cold.'

'Could you check with the American States that issued the bonds you found in Stockholm? Surely that a large holding would have been split up between several cartridges.'

218

'That's good thinking, Elizabeth. I'll certainly look into it. But time's not on our side, he's had the stuff for over a week. I'm sorry to put the pressure on you, Elizabeth. You don't look at all happy.'

'No, I'm not. All this makes me angry. One thing is certain – Klaus must get rid of those cartridges and if everything else fails I'll force his hand – and he knows it.'

She sighed. It was all so stupid and unnecessary. But at least it was a problem shared with someone she could trust.

Von Hessler looked at his watch, 'Elizabeth, I think my next move is to hear what he has to say. Then I'll decide whether to tell him about Stockholm and that I know how he got the Letters of Authorisation for those deposit boxes.'

As Elizabeth drank the last of her coffee and put her cigarettes back in her handbag, she could easily picture the encounter between the two men. Stunned and alarmed, she realised which of them she wanted to come out on top. Where was all this oing to lead? She gave him an anxious smile.

'Be careful Gerhard. Don't rush it with Klaus.'

They left the coffee bar together and walked to the car park where she had parked. A moment of awkwardness as they stopped by her car - she held out her hand. She waved to him as she drove off, leaving him to pick up a taxi.

219

Chapter 8

In the taxi von Hessler ran over the uncertainties that he needed to resolve. He debated what excuses Schmidt might give for opening the cartridges and whether he had disposed of any of the contents. He felt he could deal with that aspect of the matter. More worrying was the prospect that Schmidt had his hands on official letters from the likes of Himmler or Ribbentrop and compromising private correspondence involving his family and relations in Germany or in England. His original astonishment on learning from Joachim von Benz that Schmidt claimed to have such letters from the 1945 cartridges had become alarm. He should never have trusted the man!

It complicated matters impossibly that he now found himself allied with Elizabeth ... against her own husband of all people. His meeting with Klaus was going to be totally unpredictable, reminding him of some of his war-time experiences in intelligence. He grinned to himself; he was getting the taste for it again. Well, if nothing else, he would give Schmidt a run for his money.

Paying off the taxi, he took the steps two at a time as he strode confidently into the headquarters of *Schmidt Elektrodynamik*. His approach appeared to disturb the receptionist's cool demeanour and he was amused to notice her blink. I must look threatening, he thought, but never fear, it's your boss I'm after – not you! He gave her a smile.

Klaus Schmidt greeted him effusively and immediately suggested adjournment to a restaurant. Well, the local restaurants were certainly benefitting from his fear of surveillance! As soon as the food had been selected and menus removed Schmidt took the initiative.

'You must forgive me, Gerhard, for opening up the cartridges before we had a chance to do it together.' He said, pouring on the charm and pulling a long face, his hands held up in a gesture of repentance. 'I just couldn't restrain my curiosity. Of course, I was worried that people might be on to us and was none too sure that you hadn't been spotted doing your illegal salvage job up in Fehmarn. Not to mention that there was the chance that one of the divers would talk. Anyway it's a big disappointment – there is nothing much to show for all your efforts.'

'Do you mean they were empty?' Von Hessler replied, ticking off the various reasons against his mental check list.

'No, no, they were filled all right but most of the stuff is worthless. Bearer bonds that were called 20 years ago, useless Reichsmarks, various banknotes that are no longer legal tender, stock certificates in companies such as Triumph Werke Nürnberg issued in 1942 and so on.' He cast a quick glance at his companion as if assessing how his words were being received. 'There are also some bank accounts which have been dormant for far too long to be worth investigating.' Schmidt shook his head dismissively and laughed. 'You're looking sceptical - most of the banks were in Berlin and the accounts in Reichsmarks.'

'Anything else?'

'There were some more letters of the type that I found in 1945.'

'Oh? What do you mean by that?'

'They're more of the sort that I had to frighten von Benz with when he tried to pressure me. That man bit off more than he bargained for! Did he tell you?'

'He did indeed. You certainly stopped him in his tracks. But let's not concern ourselves with that idiot. What else did you find?'

'Nothing much.'

Schmidt's pursed lips and an answer that was not quite spontaneous gave the game away, von Hessler also noted the giveaway vertical furrows in the centre of Schmidt's forehead. He was not a good liar! 'Tell me about the letters.'

'I haven't had time to go through them yet. Some are in English, some German. What is interesting is that one of them is from Grossadmiral Dönitz.' He paused. 'You look surprised.'

'I am. What does it say?'

'It's a Letter of Authority entitling the bearer to diplomatic status and addressed to the Swedish government. He signed it as Führer so it was valid.'

'Who was the bearer?'

'This will surprise you Gerhard. It certainly surprised me. It was your father.'

Von Hessler hoped that his face had not betrayed his shock nor the anger that instantly replaced it. If Schmidt was hoping to catch him off-balance he was mistaken. He moved into the attack.

'My father? Are you sure about that? There are plenty of von Hesslers and more than one served in the *Corps Diplomatique.*'

'I checked him out in the *Almanak de Gotha.* It's your father all right. Didn't you know?'

'No, I'd no idea he had had any contact with the Grossadmiral. I went to a naval reunion last year in Aumühle and met the old man, himself. I could have asked him if he remembered my father, had I known. He's got an extraordinary memory.'

'There's something else that's rather curious. The Almanak gives the date of your father's death as the second of May 1945.'

'Yes, that's right.'

'... but the letter is dated the third.'

'How very odd!'

'When did you say S103 was sunk?'

'The fourth of May.'

'Well there's a mystery. Maybe it was a typing error. Things were pretty confused in those last days.'

'I'm not impressed,' said von Hessler, shaking his head. 'That letter cannot be genuine. If it is dated the third of May how can it have been in the ammunition box which you had already delivered at the end of April?'

Schmidt swallowed, thinking fast. He was an appalling actor!

'Maybe someone inserted another cartridge after I delivered the box.'

Von Hessler shrugged, he needed to keep one step ahead of Schmidt. He put the letter to the back of his mind.

'What of the other letters?'

'Mostly from palaces, Schlosse, English castles, all big houses from the sound of them.'

'I need to see them, Klaus.'

'Of course, my friend. They're in the office safe. You shall have them. I can't say that all of them have survived. Water got into one of the cartridges and the contents are unreadable – just a mass of grey pulp. We will never know their dark secrets.'

Apparently Schmidt was determined to stick to his story, in which case, nothing of use would be elicited from him. The tale he had produced was unlikely but even so, von Hessler recognised that he was stymied by the lack of evidence with which to challenge it. Mentioning the trip to Sweden would doubtless produce another denial and only result in putting the man on his guard.

Back in the office Schmidt opened his safe and extracted a bulky envelope which he handed to von Hessler. Forcing himself to give Schmidt a warm, friendly handshake, he left, slamming the taxi door and snapping out the word *flughafen* to the driver who gave him a sour look.

He opened the envelope and rifled through the letters, none of which appeared to be of outstanding interest apart from that from Dönitz. His unease increased as he realised that the meeting had resolved nothing; that it had only raised more questions. He was now convinced that Schmidt was up to no good, but what was his game? The man might do anything if provoked. He needed to warn Elizabeth to delay putting pressure on him. At the airport he rang her and she readily agreed to meet in the departure terminal. Twenty minutes later she appeared and sat down next to him.

'Gerhard, you don't look too happy.'

'Oh dear, does it show?'

'Yes it does. How did the meeting go?'

'Well, the principle outcome is that Klaus completely denies that there was anything of value in the cartridges. What I wasn't expecting was this letter, signed by Dönitz after he became Führer. Have a look.'

Elizabeth read it. 'But this is pretty harmless. I thought you'd always had relatives in the Diplomatic Corps. '

'I agree, the letter's harmless, but what others has Klaus got that could drag in my father?'

'Are you sure you're not just being paranoid?' said Elizabeth with a sceptical smile.

'I hope not. But you've got to admit that he's withheld a good deal already, plus the fact that he's used letters to threaten Joachim in the past. It's his style. We've got to be careful not to push him too hard.'

'So where do we go from here?'

'The problem is, Elizabeth, that we've nothing to challenge Klaus with apart from his trip to Stockholm and I think it's better we keep that card up our sleeve. He holds all the trumps at present.'

'There must be something, surely.'

'There's still a chance that my man in the university will succeed in drying out the letters from the briefcase and that may lead somewhere. Who knows what they will reveal.'

'How long will he take?' asked Elizabeth.

'Days, possibly weeks. I don't know.'

'But we can't afford to wait that long. I'm convinced that Klaus is going to do something stupid and we've got to stop him.'

'I'll press him to get a move on. That's all I can do.'

Von Hessler paused while he checked the flight departure indicator and then turned to look at Elizabeth.

'God this is awful. Here I am attempting to thwart a man's dark designs and my accomplice is his own wife. It's bizarre.'

'You mustn't start having ridiculous scruples at this point, Gerhard. You said yourself that Klaus could be dangerous. We've got to stop him before he destroys all of us. Anyway I'm enjoying the excitement, these clandestine meetings are making me feel quite young again.'

'That makes two of us. Any minute now one of us will be saying something out of a romantic novel like 'We can't go on meeting like this'.'

'We haven't got that far have we?' Their eyes locked.

'That's in the next chapter.' He said with a laugh. 'In the meantime the Freiherr has to get his plane back to Hamburg. Elizabeth it's been a real pleasure seeing you. I'll ring you as soon as I have any news.'

'Have a good flight,' she said.

He smiled, picked up his bag and turned to walk to the check-in desks. Then he looked back and blew her a kiss. Demurely, her eyes sparkling, she blew one back to him.

As he drove north from Fuhlsbuttel airport the grey evening sky reflected von Hessler's dismal mood. There appeared to be no easy way of stopping Schmidt from exploiting whatever he had found in the cartridges. The discussion with Elizabeth had not produced a solution ... and worst of all, there was his father's presence on board S103 and his involvement with the Nazis to be explained. Perhaps the handwritten letters from the briefcase would shed some light. Arriving back at Haus Langenhorn he went straight to his study and pulled out the folder from his desk, switched on the lamp and started to read the letters once again.

Berlin

Dear P, The sun is shining today and breaking through an early morning mist. I am planning to cut the grass but first I must sharpen the mower. The man next to me has already performed a cut last night so I must activate myself.

Your Aunt has sent me an interesting volume on carpets so I will soon be in a position to help you choose ones from superior regions. It is a fascinating subject ... ...

He read no further, dropped the letter onto the desk and picked up another. This too he discarded after reading the first paragraph. He flipped through the remaining four and finally thrust them all back into the folder and flung it down onto the desk.

His father must have had a reason for placing them in the briefcase, but that was it? Anson had speculated that they contained coded messages. Who could he turn to for help?

Then he realised that he knew the very man - the expert crossword solver, chess champion and linguist who as a young man had had a big reputation in the Abwehr in its heyday under Admiral Canaris. Now he was Herr Doktor Professor Manfred Hirn. He had pleasurable recollections of intelligence briefings by Hirn during the war. The precision of his mind and the crystalline lucidity of his arguments had been a rare joy. He picked up the phone to invite Hirn over the following day, something to which the Professor readily agreed.

The Professor arrived in a battered Opel wearing a drab tweed suit set off by a crimson bow tie. A shock of grey hair covered his large head and his angular face was framed by a trim beard. Heavy black-rimmed glasses accentuated his dark blue eyes.

Von Hessler escorted him into the study, offered him a chair and after a brief enquiry into his work in the university, handed him the six handwritten letters. Hirn was not a man for small-talk. He read each one in silence and then carefully positioned the first over the second and held the pair up to the desk lamp, repeating the process with each letter. Von Hessler waited.

A patient under the scrutiny of an internationally famous consultant must feel like this; he chuckled to himself. Hirn positioned the last two letters against the lamp and as he studied them he spoke.

'This is promising Gerhard. We have a *prima facie* case for grid coding.'

'Forgive me, but how did you reach that conclusion quite so quickly?'

Hirn, with a barely perceptible movement of his head, swung his eyes round to bear on von

Hessler in a way that reminded him of a pair of guns sighting on a naval destroyer.

'Simple my dear Watson,' He said with a grin. 'Firstly, the way all the lines are filled to the right margin – quite unlike a normal letter. Secondly, the consistent length of the letters. Thirdly, the cultured hand. Fourthly, the alignment of the lines between each copy is exact. These letters were written with a lined guide-paper under them. Can you imagine a cultured writer needing the assistance of a schoolboy's aid to writing in straight lines? And last but not least, the trivial content. But that's only a start. Now let me look at the detail.'

Hirn pulled a large magnifying glass from his case and studied each letter. Von Hessler left the room to ask Frau Graubal to make coffee. When he returned Hirn was writing notes. He continued for several minutes.

'Very good,' he announced. 'I think we have enough here to start work.'

'Tell me how grid coding works would you, Manfred? I've but the haziest recollection.'

Hirn marshalled his thoughts for a second or two.

'So! We start with a piece of squared graph paper to provide the basic grid. Individual squares in the grid are cut out to create holes scattered at random along each line. The grid is then placed over the writing paper and through these holes the characters that constitute the message are written. The grid is removed and a

230

guide-paper whose line spacing matches that of the grid is placed underneath the writing paper. The text of a normal letter is then composed so as to embody the code characters already written.'

'It sounds easy enough,' said von Hessler. 'Decoding is presumably done by placing an identical grid over the letter at the other end. But how do you propose to decode without the grid?'

'That's when the serious labour starts,' said Hirn with another grin that took decades off his age. 'Fortunately you have six different letters which helps a great deal. As you are aware any code constructed by humankind can be decoded by humankind, so we look for clues. The first of these is found by examining each word to see if we can identify any of the code characters. These betray themselves by poor joining-up of the writing. Secondly we look for odd spacing between words which tells us that one of the two words, or maybe both, contain code characters.'

'Hence your magnifying glass. It does indeed sound like a laborious task! But surely a practiced code writer will develop the skill to make detection difficult.'

'Ah' exclaimed Hirn, 'You mustn't underestimate the problem of writing these letters. It's hard work constructing even short sentences that fit the positions of the code characters. Several drafts are needed before achieving something that reads like a normal letter. The final version has to be written with extreme care. One or two bad joins can give the game away and you have to start afresh. In practice some joins will always show up. Even a skilled man will get tired if he has to write several letters on the same day.'

'How much of the grid do you expect to recreate from just six letters? The chances don't sound too good to me.'

'You raise the question of chance, Gerhard. Now we're into interesting territory.' Hirn's face had become animated and he stood up, put his arms behind his back and began to walk up and down the length of the study. Von Hessler read the signs – he was in for a university lecture. His eyes sparkled with amusement.

'Do you want the simple exposé or the complex one?'

'You're the best judge of that, Manfred.'

'Good,' responded Hirn and swung his eyes around for a brief assessment of his pupil. Then he said with relish 'We'll take the complex one.'

Hirn continued talking as Frau Graubel brought in a tray and set it on a side table. Von Hessler, reluctant to interrupt him, automatically poured two cups of black coffee.

'So! We want to compute the chances of arriving at an adequate decode of your letters. There are about 20 lines on each page. Let us postulate that a typical coded message runs to 100 characters, which thus requires an average of 5 grid holes per line. Then let us assume we can detect only 1 out of these 5. So in our 20 lines we can detect only 20 holes in our first letter. Now we examine the second letter and find another 20 and so on until we have done all 6 letters. This you might think adds to a total of 120 probable holes. Are you with me so far?'

'Yes, that all seems quite obvious. Where's the catch?'

'Ha! I must remember that I'm speaking to a retired intelligence officer who has maintained his acumen and who questions everything put in front of him. Well, the catch is this – we must not *add together* the *probability* of finding holes as we assess each letter. Doing that disobeys a basic statistical law. We have to take the *improbability* of finding holes and *multiply* them together.'

'You're getting ahead of me here, Manfred. Let's have an example.'

'Very good. For any one hole we have already assumed that the probability of detection is 1 in 5 which is an *improbability* of 4 in 5, or decimal terms odds of 0.8 to1 against. Each time we examine a new letter we improve our ultimate chance of success so the improbability *drops*. This drop we determine by *multiplying* the odds of 0.8 for each new letter. So, for 6 letters we derive odds of just over 0.26 to 1, if my mental arithmetic is correct. Now we convert this back to the *probability* of finding any one hole by subtracting the figure 0.26 from one, which gives a figure of 0.74. In other words a probability of finding 74 out of 100 holes. Not as many as I would like but it gives us a chance.' Hirn ceased walking, and with a questioning look, turned to face von Hessler.

'I'm impressed, Manfred. You've lost none of your acumen either, in fact it seems to be sharper than ever. It must be university life that keeps you mentally fit. But please don't forget your coffee; it'll be getting cold.' Hirn sat down and Von Hessler waited while he emptied the cup.

'But now we come to the crunch – would you be able and willing to decode the letters for me?'

'Willing, yes. Able, remains to be seen. Everything depends on how many code characters we can discover. Naturally, I'll do my best. Incidentally do you have any idea who the writer was?'

'No, absolutely no idea.' Von Hessler shook his head. 'There's no address, as you can see, only the word 'Berlin' and that may be a fiction and, of course, only a first name signature.'

'Do you think it might have been a prominent person?'

'That's a good question. Judging by some of the other letters in my father's files, it could well have been.' Von Hessler paused for a second and added reluctantly. 'Even a very prominent person.'

'I'll get my wife, Frida, to run over her archives and see if she can match the handwriting.' Hirn seemed to relish the idea.

'That would be most kind of her. Of course, I'd forgotten that you met Frida in the Abwehr.'

Von Hessler instantly regretted raising the subject of the Abwehr. Hirn had been devastated by the hanging of its leader Admiral Canaris in Flossenberg camp by the SS in the closing days of the war.

'Yes, they were happy days, at least to start with,' responded Hirn. 'But the hanging of our chief Canaris was a dreadful, terrible way to end it all. The Admiral was a patriot, he cared for our country.'

Hirn stopped talking. Von Hessler looked at him. It was sad to see the sparkle of that brilliant mind dimmed by the trauma of past events. To fill the silence he poured some more coffee. Hirn drank it and suddenly continued.

'However, the Gestapo suspected he was no friend of Hitler and eventually he paid for it with his life. But on the whole we in the Abwehr fought a clean war, insofar as any war can be clean.'

'Does that view allow for dressing up German convicts in Polish uniforms and using then to attack one of our own radio stations in 1939? Just to create a pretext for our invasion of Poland?' asked von Hessler gently. 'That was an Abwehr operation and all those convicts were shot dead by us.'

'No it doesn't,' said Hirn firmly. 'I did say 'on the whole'. A 'clean war' is an oxymoron coined by uneasy men. War is dirty, but I will allow that it can be justified theoretically when all other methods have failed to overcome a manifest

235

evil. I was one of the fortunate ones. For me it was an intellectual challenge. When I was at Treunbritzen we cracked the English shipping ciphers but later they spotted it and after they changed them in 1940 deciphering became more difficult.' His voice dropped, 'No doubt my work cost the lives of many English mariners.'

Von Hessler noticed Hirn's avoidance of any reference to U-boats, and decided to move the conversation on.

'Curiously the British have never talked about their code-breaking efforts and I've no idea how successful they were. A few of us wondered if our naval traffic was vulnerable but hard evidence was lacking. Dönitz was suspicious but our senior men persuaded him that it was impossible to decrypt naval Enigma messages.'

'In the end our efforts in the Abwehr got us nowhere,' rejoined Hirn.

'We were on the wrong side, Manfred. Remember the Chinese sage who said 'Only fight on the winning side.'

'Ha! We're both on the same side now, but I'm not sure it's the winning one.'

'Have no fear. I've got the only remaining S-boat lined up to get us out of here if the Russians turn nasty. I can book a berth for you and Frida.'

'It will certainly need a fast boat. I heard that the Lieutenant-Commander who ran British naval intelligence in the Baltic after the war had an S-boat tuned up that could outrun anything the Russians had.'

'Strangely enough I met him once. Strange man, he seemed to enjoy the company of his late enemies as much as his own people and spoke good Russian which must have helped his work. Do you ever use your Russian?'

'Rarely. Every now and then I read a chess article in Russian. I hope I never have to use it in earnest.'

Again von Hessler noticed a sad look pass across his face. Then Hirn switched the conversation.

'So how do you keep that brain of yours in tune, Gerhard? Do you miss the intelligence game?'

'Yes I have to admit that there are few challenges today that equal it. I did think of taking up one of those complicated Chinese games but nobody around here plays. But more to the point, how do you keep yours in tune?'

Hirn removed his glasses, leaned back and gazed into the far distance.

'Music. I've developed an interest in the musical compositions of Johann Sebastian Bach. His development of counterpoint lends itself to mathematical analysis by computer.'

'And how about chess?'

'Well, that certainly keeps me on my toes. I'm following the games of that American, Bobby Fischer. If he wins it'll put the Russians' nose out of joint, I'm glad to say. I've been trying computer chess but they haven't yet reached grandmaster standard yet.'

237

'Who wins when you play against the computer?'

'I occasionally let it win,' said Hirn with a smile as he got up to leave. 'Gerhard, I'll have some fun decoding your letters. It'll be interesting pitting my wits against somebody who lived more than 25 years ago. I'll ring you as soon as I have something.'

They shook hands and he drove off. Von Hessler walked back into the house smiling as he pondered the differences between the two of them. He pictured the high intellectual mountains that Hirn inhabited, with their clear atmosphere and breath-taking views. It was not a bad life.

The call came two days later.

'Gerhard, I'm afraid your letters are not going to reveal their secrets without a fight. The man who wrote them was clearly a professional and has left me almost nothing to work on. I've concentrated on looking for poor joins but I've found only 1 or 2 per letter - altogether perhaps 8 or 9, so my guess of detecting 1 code character per line is too optimistic. There is another technique available. It demands equipment that I can probably borrow so don't abandon hope yet.'

'Is there any meaning in what you've found so far?' asked von Hessler.

'None. Before getting to grips with the text I need to do some experiments. Incidentally when

I showed Frida the handwriting it stirred something in her memory but she's unable to pin it down and we'll have to wait while she does a proper search.'

'Well keep up the good work, Manfred. I'm deeply grateful to you.'

Almost immediately the phone rang again. It was von Lauchert.

'I've just had your letter. I am sorry to disappoint you but I've almost no recollection of the matter you raised. It was a long time ago and there was a great deal on my mind. Of course I remember Major Schmidt - he was a first class battalion commander. But apart from him – almost nothing.'

'Oh well. It was rather a fond hope that you might have remembered what must have been a trivial incident in the middle of a great battle.'

'You're absolutely right. But it's surprising how we Generals were expected to deal with trivia. Army group headquarters were forever plaguing my staff for accurate returns of losses of *matériel*. But despite all the information we gave them they never seemed to moderate their demands. Come to think of it I seem to remember an incident involving transport for Schmidt. It must have been the very thing you're asking about.'

'Do you remember much about it?'

'Yes, it's coming back to me. HQ wanted Second Panzer to provide a staff car for a couple of my officers to go on a mission of some sort and wouldn't take no for an answer. In the end I had to ring them myself and point out that we had not a single serviceable staff car, no petrol, and most certainly no spare officers. I got quite heated, I remember.' He gave sharp bark of laughter.

'What happened?'

'Oh ... in the end they provided a civilian car.'

'Do have any idea what the mission was about?'

'No. But I tell you what I'll do. I'll have a look through my orders. What date are we talking about?'

'Probably the end of January 1945.'

'You may be in luck. One of my staff was a historian and during the final debacle he managed to acquire the copies of all my orders from when I took command of Second Panzer in December '44. He presented them to me a couple of years later. If I turn up anything I'll send you a copy.'

'That would be most helpful, Herr von Lauchert. I look forward to hearing from you.'

'It is a pleasure to be of service, Freiherr von Hessler.'

The days crawled past, the inactivity threatening to drive von Hessler crazy. Desperate for something to occupy his mind and his hands, he was more than grateful when he was forced to relieve old Graubal of some of the garden duties. The man's ageing memory had several times led to withered leaves and dried-out soil when the all-important watering was overlooked. When Doktor Hirn finally arrived in his Opel, von Hessler was busy watering the red pelargoniums in the urns placed along the top of the low wall that enclosed the ornamental garden at the side of Haus Langenhorn.

Despite the hot day the Professor was wearing the same tweed suit with leather patches on the elbows. Von Hessler smiled, it was all part of the man! He didn't believe in buying a new so long as the old kept going and definitely distrusted what others called 'progress'. Progress in his book had to be in the mind – in the understanding of the individual psyche, and the compulsions that so frequently led nations into disaster. For a moment Gerhard wondered what it would be like to exchange lives with him. To be free of the constraints demanded by his aristocratic heritage, their strict traditions, and the lifestyle that he had inherited. The two men shared many beliefs but only Hirn had found the courage to put them into practice. Maybe it would not be all that difficult to do the mind-switch.

Contemplating this idea, Von Hessler turned off the hose and walked over to the car.

'Welcome, Manfred. You seem to have brought your usual breath of fresh air and sunshine with you. Did you have a good journey?'

'Yes indeed. I've found myself a new route with almost no traffic. It's a trade between more cows and fewer cars ... and it's a good bargain!'

'Come and sit in the orangery and enjoy some of nature's perfumes.'

'What a charming idea! My mind works best if it is nurtured by good smells and good scenery, being close to nature. Do you know, I've discovered that I definitely play a better game of chess if I use ivory pieces. If I'm forced to play using plastic my game is deficient.'

Von Hessler nodded agreement as they sat down.

'Absolutely. I flew back from Düsseldorf a couple of days ago and everything about the meal seemed to be plastic. Even the brandy came in a plastic bottle, for God's sake! But let's get down to business. What have you got to show me?'

'Not a great deal, I'm afraid,' said Hirn. 'The man - it was probably a man - who wrote these letters was extremely careful and has left almost no clues as to where the code characters are buried. As I mentioned on the phone I have moved on to a comparison technique using epidiascopes that is yielding some results albeit with a fair amount of labour.'

'Is that a new method?'

'I doubt it, but I haven't seen it used before. The idea is to set an identical pair of epidiascopes side by side and superimpose their images on the screen. The two letters are then aligned precisely so that any exact superposition of characters becomes apparent. The method works best if the letters are displayed upside down so that the eye is not distracted by the character shape.'

'But surely there must be a vast number of accidental superpositions?'

'Exactly – that's the problem and where the labour comes in. When I started I put one letter in the first epidiascope and fed each of the other 5 through the second. It became clear where certain code characters lay but nothing like the 100 that I guessed at. So I decided firstly that each of the six letters has to be compared with the remaining five, which gives a figure of $5+4+3+2+1=15$ comparisons and secondly, that I would have to adopt a more statistical approach. So for each comparison the location of every single superposition has to be recorded. When all comparisons are complete the number of superpositions on each location is added up. The maximum will be 15. Those above a score of say 12 will almost certainly be candidates for membership of the grid.'

'Dear me, it does sound laborious. What sort of results have you seen so far?'

'I'm working on comparison number 8 at present so we have a few more days to go. Of course it's too early to deduce anything final but I've already found many locations with a high superposition frequency and they will certainly become candidates.'

'And what do you do when you've assembled the likely candidates?'

'Then we move to the interesting bit. Some of the candidates will be false positives and equally we will miss some real positives. Assuming that we have enough to start reading the coded message, we look for meaningful words. This is not as easy as it sounds because in a message block the words are run together without punctuation. As soon as we can extract meaningful words we are onto 'paydirt' as our American allies would say.'

'What if the message doesn't make sense?'

'Yet more labour. For example it's likely that we'll find words with gaps in them. A word such as 'meeting' with an 'e' missing is unlikely to be 'melting' in this context. The only likely complete word is 'meeting'. So we look for appropriately placed 'e's in the text. The chances are good that such an 'e' will lie on one of our medium scoring locations and thus we can promote it to candidate status.'

'Do I detect a note of optimism Manfred?'

Hirn shook his head disapprovingly.

'I work with theories Gerhard. All theories last only as long as it takes to prove them wrong. At present the epidiascope method works in theory. Let's hope that it survives the current inquisition. A grid code would probably yield to an Abwehr team and whoever wrote these letters may have been aware of this and used double encryption. That would be a devilish challenge. If it has been used then we have no real chance.'

'You're beginning to worry me,' said von Hessler and continued warily. 'Let us assume that we have simple grid coding only. Do any of the candidates correspond with the few that you detected earlier when you were looking for poorly joined-up characters?'

'You really are determined to get a prediction out of me,' said Hirn with a grimace. 'I can't answer that question because I've refrained from looking at the earlier work until I have the results from the epidiascopes. The history of science is full of examples of men seeing only what they're looking for, disregarding results that don't fit, and influencing their collaborators, often unconsciously. And you and I know how much that occurred in intelligence work.'

'Don't remind me,' said Von Hessler with animation. 'I thought we had accurate figures for the weight of shipping sunk by our U-Boats. It was a blow to my professional pride when the British revealed the actual figures after the war.' He leant back in his seat and stretched out his legs. 'The war was a strange time. I worked in a continuous fog. Was our information accurate? Had our plans leaked? What was to be the enemy's next countermeasure? Had he some new decryption technique? It was a world plagued by uncertainty.'

He paused and sat up.

'But Manfred, you didn't come here to reminisce about the war. Let's get back to grid coding. I'm clearly not going to get any predictions out of you but I am anxious. I don't want to push you but time is not on my side and if you can do anything to accelerate progress I would be extremely grateful.'

Hirn pulled out his pipe and filled it from a leather tobacco pouch with careful deliberation. He paused for a moment's reflection.

'I'll certainly do what I can. As you say I can't give you any forecast. It's too uncertain. Scientists are used to working with uncertainty - we all should be – everything becomes uncertain when you work at atomic level as Werner Heisenberg propounded years ago. Quantum theory holds that the mere act of observing a photon alters its state, so exact measurement of all of its parameters becomes impossible – who knows how much this applies further up the scale – perhaps up to macrocosmic levels. We live in a world where 'uncertainty' is President and 'probability' is Chancellor.'

'Men like you should go into politics. You might bring some science into it. You could shift some of that woolly thinking.'

'Sadly no-one would listen. Politics is all about feelings not facts. Regrettably I'm not in the feelings business. I think our politicians have a hard time in trying to represent an electorate who are deeply traumatised by the Nazi years - war and defeat, the death camps, the Nürnberg trials. We no longer feel secure within our national identity and little patriotism. We relate more to our *heimat.* We keep our eyes lowered and work like mad to prove that we can at least hold our heads up at a mercantile level.'

Von Hessler looked out of the orangery windows and suddenly felt cold. He was glad it was a warm sunny day. Hirn had mentioned the camps - was he aware of the fate of the liner *Cap Arcona*?

'You raise some profound issues, Manfred. I could add a few more horrors – nuclear war, the Reds just across the border, the Berlin wall, and nearer home, the Baader-Meinhof gang. On the good side we avoided national break-up at the end of the war. It could have happened if Göring had fought on in the South and ignored Dönitz up here in Flensburg. After all, the South was the cradle of National Socialism and incidentally, largely Catholic. Membership of NATO has been a factor in keeping us together ... that and the Marshall plan. General Marshall was a wise man cast in the same mould as Roosevelt. We were lucky. Moving on to today – how do you view Willi Brandt?'

'I dislike the posturing of politicians but Chancellor Brandt is different. I like the man's courage. Pursuing his Ostpolitik takes guts. And he outmanoeuvred Ulbricht by negotiating with the Russians and Poles at the same time. They want a resolution which Ulbricht doesn't and they will push him to get it. That's the sort of political skill I admire.'

Hirn was sucking his pipe – a sign that his mind was running at full speed. Von Hessler could

247

see that his ideas were bubbling up faster than he could deal with coherently.

'I don't think we understand our own history,' Hirn continued. 'It's wracked by instability going back to medieval times. We've no natural frontiers. The only invaders we avoided were the Romans and they were only stopped by the Rhine. In the thirty years war we had English, French, Dutch and Danish troops fighting across our German lands and we were finally saved by the Swedes. And that was a mere 300 years ago. In that war half the population of Prussia died and it took 100 years to recover! No wonder we're *angst* ridden, Gerhard. It's curious that the English have no native word for *angst* so they use our word!' He paused for a second. 'It's an advantage being an island.'

'So how do you interpret the process whereby Hitler was elected Chancellor in 1933?'

'Hmmm ... it started with Frederick the Great, then Bismarck, both playing the power game. Their driving force was our chronic instability and insecurity. Then along came Kaiser Willi getting into deep waters and drowning. He was no statesman and, inevitably, the outcome was the punitive Versailles treaty and President Hindenburg, an old man who was no intellectual match for Hitler. It was historically inevitable. I ask myself if we could have avoided Hitler in 1933 and I wonder: did we really want to?'

Von Hessler stiffened. 'Some did in my father's generation. If he was alive today I would dearly like to ask him that question.'

'What do you think your father would say?'

'I sincerely hope that he would repeat what he said about Hitler when I was a boy. He was very much against him then ... though now I'm not so sure.'

Von Hessler was at a loss how to break the bleak silence that followed. He had a need to talk about the dark side of war and of the men involved in it; to talk to someone with an objective view who was willing to enter the *verboten* territory of war-guilt. Friends or family who simply applied sticking-plaster were no help. Somehow he had to keep the conversation going; he invited Hirn to stay for lunch.

Hirn put his pipe in his pocket and looked at his watch.

'That's kind of you,' he responded 'but I've promised to take Frida out to lunch and as she is my researcher as well as my wife I need to look after her. So I must thread my way back through the cows.'

Von Hessler escorted him to his car.

'Good luck Manfred. Drive carefully. Hitting a cow is practically a capital offence around here.'

He watched the Opel depart, walked back into the house and slowly closed the door behind him. Then he remembered the pelargoniums and went out to resume his task. There was something calming about the sound of splashing water.

Von Hessler was feeling less confident of his ability to deal with Schmidt. The Dönitz letter was a setback. Harmless in itself, it implied that Schmidt had more such letters. He needed to move things along. When he rang the university archive curator, he was delighted to hear that several documents were ready for him.

After a hasty lunch he drove into Kiel and was shown a small pile of papers that had been successfully freeze dried. The first two appeared to be unimportant. The third was a schedule of the ammunition box contents. His spirits rising at each item, he read through it:-

Letters of Authorisation with keys 1129, 1130, 1131, 2301 for deposit boxes in Stockholm banks.
Letter of authorisation with key 42 in a Malmö bank
Letters of Authorisation with keys 3301A, 5123F, 5675B in Zürich banks.
25 State of North Carolina $5000 bearer bonds
20 State of New York $5000 bearer bonds
20 Stock certificates RM1000 Triumph Werke Nürnberg 1942
19 Stock Certificates RM1000 Elektrische Licht und Kraftanlagen, Berlin 1943
Gold coins 20 mark Kaiser Wilhelm II total 90
Gold coins 20 mark Hansastadt Hamburg total 30
10 kg Scrap gold

Currency - English £20 notes dated 1935 - total
40, American $50 - total 34, S.Fr50 total - 49
Jewellery – see separate list
Letters – 2 packets
Experimental high energy propellant (one
cartridge) [Note – handle with care.]

He could hardly believe his luck. Here was evidence that would pin down both Schmidt and Beckmeier. He paused at the last line and recalled a conversation with König who had mentioned warnings issued to divers about explosives that could become unstable after long periods of storage. This was experimental stuff – who knew about its long-term storage? Was it prone to instability? Should he warn Schmidt?

As he drove back he mulled over the situation. The gold coins would be a source of ready cash for Schmidt and difficult to trace, but any payments made by the bond issuer's agents would be traceable - if the bonds had proved to be valid. The major unknowns remaining were the contents of the deposit boxes, and of the cartridges removed in 1945. So far there was no sign of the list of jewellery.

Then he remembered the two packets of letters mentioned in the list. Schmidt must now have both packets – the first would have been in one of the cartridges he purloined in 1945 and the second in a cartridge which he had just opened and in which he had found the Dönitz letter. Was this just a sample of a whole series from Himmler and

251

von Ribbentrop addressed to his father? Perhaps Schmidt had the advantage over him.

As soon as he got home, he rang Elizabeth, only getting the answering machine. He tried the hospital and was told that she would not be in for a week. In desperation, he rang Anson.

'Peter, I need some advice. Things are becoming complex. No, don't laugh like that! I've found the list itemising the contents of the ammo box. We're dealing with substantial amounts of money and tradable instruments, and yet more correspondence. I need to talk to you about how I deal with our mutual friend.'

'Did you find the list in the briefcase?'

'Yes, it's just been dried out.'

'Have you made copies?' asked Anson.

'No, why should I?'

'It so happens that I've been talking to that chap Hutchison who visited me from Hermag Security in Bonn.'

'The outfit run by British Intelligence?'

'Yes. He rang me yesterday and things are hotting up. I would make copies of everything you have and put them somewhere safe.'

'*Mon Dieu*, you do make it sound serious, Peter.'

'Well, it could be. I really think you should let Hutchison know about this. You need advice from an independent source.'

'Independent from whom?'

'To put it bluntly, from your own people.'

'Now you have got me worried. Dark forces at work, eh?'

'Could be.'

'And outside West Germany?'

'Possibly.'

'But if I involve him I lose control - he could do anything. Elizabeth is involved and I wouldn't make a move without consulting her.'

'It may be too late. What's your security like? Who else knows about the list?'

'Hell – are you telling me that there's been a leak?'

'I don't know, Gerhard. But we've got one of those coincidences again. You get the document dried out by your paper expert and in no time I get a phone call from Hutchison which makes me suspect he has details.'

'It can only have been at the university. My man must have been using equipment that others had access to. He mentioned freeze driers. That could have been it.'

'Well however it happened it looks as if the cat's out of the bag.'

'Are you saying that this thing could go public?'

'Actually I think that's unlikely. Hutchison said they were going to play it quietly because of possible involvement of an important family with royal connections. So no, I don't think it will go public. The lady concerned is pretty safe.'

'God! Which lady are you talking about?'

'The Elizabeth married to our friend.'

253

'Oh ... oh good – then what's your view about how much I should tell her?'

'Tell her everything. If it's going to be handled with discretion it's better she knows the whole story. She could help get the thing sorted.'

'There's another problem. One of the cartridges is still filled with its original experimental propellant and a note on the list states 'Handle with Care.''

Anson gasped.

'Well that's a nasty complication. Maybe it was left in deliberately. The new material could have been a significant breakthrough and worth something in its own right. The question is, how safe is it now?'

'God knows! I wouldn't know where to start on that one. Have you any ideas?'

'This one is right up the street of your chap from Bonn. Get on to him, Gerhard. But don't forget that Schmidt is well used to handling ammunition. He'll be careful.'

'Thank God I rang you, Peter! Are you coming up this way again?'

'Maybe. I'll let you know. Keep me in the picture.'

'I will, and thank you for your help.'

Von Hessler put down the phone and cursing loudly and repeatedly, he stormed down the corridor, very nearly bumping into Frau Graubal carrying a tray of flower vases as he rounded the corner. She gave him a look which he interpreted as a mixture of reproach and concern.

For a quarter of an hour, he stormed around the gardens then, his mind a little clearer, he went back to his study, looked out the Bonn phone number and rang Hermag Security. It didn't surprise him at all that Hutchison wanted to meet as soon as possible, ringing back to confirm that he was booked on a flight that evening from Köln-Bonn to Hamburg and asking if von Hessler would put him up for the night. If so he would hire a car arriving at 8.30 pm.

This arranged, von Hessler glanced at the clock, decided that he had a chance of calling before Schmidt returned home, and rang Elizabeth. So much for their plans for communicating!

'Elizabeth, I need to talk to you ... now.'

'Oh.' He could almost hear her thinking. 'I'm just going out – can I call you in about ten minutes?'

As he anticipated, she rang him from a local phone box.

'What's happened?'

'The whole thing has leaked. I've spoken to Anson; he's had a call from Hutchison of Hermag Security in Bonn who already appears to know what I'm about to tell you, which is that I've found the schedule of contents of the ammunition box. Amongst a list of cash, gold and deposit boxes there's one cartridge filled with experimental explosive which could be dangerously unstable.'

'What do you mean, Gerhard?'

'It could blow up if he handles it carelessly. It could kill him.'

'We'll have to tell him.'

'Yes, I think we must. But he's going to demand an explanation and I'm not sure how much I ought to disclose.'

'Tell him that you know the whole contents of the box.'

'I don't know, Elizabeth ... I'm reluctant to show my hand at this stage. In any case I've got Hutchison from the British secret service coming tonight and I have to talk to him first.'

'OK, you talk to him, but please hurry.'

He put the phone down, ran his hand through his hair and stood looking out of the window. He'd always found strong women exciting, particularly ones as attractive as Elizabeth.

Hutchison was late. Von Hessler, waiting by the window in an upstairs room, watched him as he stepped out of the car. He saw a tallish man with a military bearing, black hair greying at the temples and a face of pink complexion that was both intelligent and determined. He heard as Frau Graubal ushered the visitor into the drawing room then he went down to greet him. They exchanged a few words on air traffic delays at Düsseldorf and agreed that was never a good idea to catch the last flight of the day. He noticed with amusement that the man was dressed in the traditional manner of a retired British army officer – blazer, dark flannel trousers and a tie which appeared to be significant.

First impressions were favourable. Von Hessler enquired if it was a regimental tie.

'Grenadiers,' Hutchison replied tersely.

'Tanks?'

'Yes, my battalion converted to armour early in the war.'

'Did you ever fight opposite Second Panzer division?'

'Briefly. I could well have taken on some of your friend Schmidt's tanks – I must ask him if we ever meet.'

'That seems highly likely the way things are going. But let me show you to your room.'

Von Hessler led the way up the broad oak staircase lit by stained-glass windows through which the evening light cast a warm glow, and along an oak-panelled corridor carpeted with old red Kazakh runners, each with curious symbolic shapes set in large octagons.

'This is your room. The bathroom is the last door on the left. I hope you'll be comfortable. My housekeeper has some food ready for us when you come down.'

Hutchison reappeared quickly and they sat down to supper. Frau Graubal served 'Lady Curzon Suppe mit croûton' while von Hessler opened a bottle of Schloss Johannisberg Riesling 1964. He filled the glasses and neither man spoke as they sampled the wine. Hutchison's face relaxed and he looked approvingly at the glass.

'This is a subtle wine,'

'A distant cousin who had some connections with the vineyard put me on to it, I'm glad you like it. But down to business - I gather from Peter Anson that things are 'hotting up'.'

'They are indeed,' responded Hutchison. 'That visit from von Benz started the ball rolling since when our people have been taking an interest in both you and Schmidt. I gather that you've been doing a bit of off-shore exploration.'

'How on earth did that story reach you?'

'You'd be surprised. We pieced it together from some unlikely sources including the Stasi. How they got to know remains uncertain; it could be leaks from high places. It's said that one can use Bonn to pass information to the Stasi faster than the Bundespost can deliver them a letter.'

'Now you've got me worried. The Stasi indeed! I thought they had bigger issues on their minds. So you know about the salvage job I did?'

'Only the outlines. Something to do with the cargo in a sunken S-boat in the Baltic. Perhaps you could tell me about it.'

'The cargo was an ammunition box filled with tank rounds from which the propellant had been removed and the empty cartridges stuffed with cash, valuables and various bits of paperwork.'

'I'm guessing it included some letters.'

'Why are you interested in these letters?' asked von Hessler cautiously.

'As you probably know back in 1946 Schmidt sold some letters to a dealer called Brenner in Heidelberg.'

Von Hessler swore. 'No, I didn't know that.'

'Ah ... well, this man realised their significance and put out feelers, eventually selling them on to one of our people who was acting in a private capacity on behalf of a member of our Royal Family. We knew this individual had been over here on official business at the end of the war so weren't entirely surprised when the letters surfaced. Independently we discovered evidence that at least one of the letters involved the Englishman who was previously the Duke of Albany.'

'That's the boy Charles who came over in 1900 to become Herzog von Saxe Coburg und Gotha. I've met his son Friedrich.'

'That's him. As you must know he fought on the German side in the first war, was subsequently stripped of his English titles in 1919. Possibly as a result, he ended up strongly pro-Nazi. He made contact with our King Edward the Eighth late in 1936 and presumably corresponded with him. Obviously correspondence of that sort would be worth a great deal of money. What we're talking about now is probably more of the same.'

'That certainly explains your interest in Klaus Schmidt.' Von Hessler paused to refill the wineglasses, weighing his words carefully.

'I should tell you that Schmidt cannot be completely trusted. Although he's an old friend of mine, I've learnt some surprising things about him recently. Specifically about his use of compromising letters to protect himself ...'

Hutchison interrupted 'A sort of reciprocal blackmail?'

'You could say that, yes. It's not just your English royal family who could be involved; it's several families over here as well, including my own. Of course I don't need to explain that we're talking about either passive liaison or active cooperation with the Nazis.'

'Where are these letters now?' asked Hutchison.

'I've a few involving my own family which I intend to destroy, and some that are illegible due to the effects of seawater. I also have one letter that Anson tells me involves a close relation of your Royal family and which I propose to burn. Would you care to read it?'

'Yes of course. It'll add a bit of colour to my otherwise drab report.'

Von Hessler fetched the letter from his study while the soup plates were removed and Frau Graubal brought in a dish of poached turbot. He passed the letter to Hutchison who read it quickly.

'Nothing dramatic here. It's fairly common knowledge that his Lordship had an interest in both sexes when he was younger. But the letter could still do harm.'

He handed it back and watched as von Hessler put his lighter to the tip of the letter; the ash fluttered into the fireplace.

'There's something I must ask you. The salvaged material was hidden in 50mm cartridge cases most of which Schmidt now has, which, I must add, is not the way it was planned. I've just recovered a list of the contents showing that one cartridge was filled with experimental high-energy propellant. There's a warning note that it must be handled with care. It's now 25 years old and likely to be unstable – should I warn Schmidt? Do you know any British explosive experts who could assess the risk? I don't want to ask the people here.'

'I'll ring HQ in the morning. They can probably produce someone on the phone. But why not warn Schmidt straight away?'

'I'd prefer that he didn't know that I've got the list of contents.' Von Hessler said. 'It's my only asset in keeping one jump ahead of him.'

'I see. So you're dealing with him at arm's length. That sounds like a good idea. Tell me about Schmidt and the business he runs? By the way, this is excellent fish!'

'My housekeeper is an excellent cook! As for Schmidt, he's got several hundred people working in his two factories, one in Düsseldorf and one in Hamburg and designs and manufactures control gear for big electric motors. He bought the business shortly after he was discharged, but how he raised the cash is a mystery though he's made a success of it, mainly taking risks. For instance, when he's chasing a big contract he'll place firm orders for long-lead components so that he can quote short delivery times. It's a risk, but he usually lands the contract. I've met a few of his competitors at the Industrie Klub in Düsseldorf and they regard him with something approaching awe.'

'How did you meet him?'

'At my sailing club. I needed a crew man and he volunteered, since then we've done quite a bit of sailing together in *Jasmine.* He's great company on the boat as well as being a good sailor. A few years back three of us had set off from Heiligenhafen heading for somewhere in Denmark with a dubious weather forecast. The wind gets up and we reef. I'm down below warming up some soup when I hear a shout from Klaus, so I put on my oilies and clamber up into the cockpit to find it empty. Not a sign of my crew!'

'Good God! Both of them gone?'

'Both of them. So I gybe her round and start looking for them. Of course there's almost no chance of spotting a man overboard in heavy seas once you lose sight of him, but then in the distance I see a yellow object sticking up out of the water and it's Klaus hanging on to the crewman with one hand and waving the lifebuoy with the other. He'd had difficulty in releasing it and when he finally got it free realised that he couldn't throw it far enough to reach the man in the water. So he jumps overboard with it and swims out to him - typical Klaus.'

'Well, the man's got courage. Would you say he was a crook?'

'He certain gets near the borderline. I reckon his overwhelming code is: Thou shalt not get found out! A psychologist would probably say he's in rebellion against some internal father figure. He's aggressive with men, but often as docile as a lamb with women. There's something of the actor in him too - he goes in for dramatic gestures.'

'What do you know of his war record?'

'Very little. On the Eastern front he survived the battle of Kursk, and was with the Panzers who broke through the American front in the Battle of the Bulge. He must have been one of von Lauchert's key commanders and once told me that after von Lauchert was promoted Generalmajor he expected to be upped to Colonel, but things had deteriorated so badly by then that it never came through. He must have been the obvious choice for the job of getting that ammunition box to Kiel.'

'Dare I ask – has there been any hint of war crimes?'

'No, absolutely none. As far as I know Second Panzer had a good record. They're not to be compared with the *Das Reich* Panzers and the massacre of the population of Oradour, that was an SS division. The architect of the Panzers, Guderian, was a decent man. One of the few generals who refused to agree to Hitler's battle plans and lived to tell the tale. No, Schmidt is clear on that count.'

'The reason I ask is that he's on Simon Wiesenthal's books. Apparently he sold some scrap gold to a dealer in Vienna around 1947. The man was a wealthy Jew who survived the length of the war by bribing the SS, which is pretty extraordinary. He found some dental inlays among the wedding rings and other scrap and strongly suspected that the gold had come from holocaust victims. So he informed Wiesenthal who was then working in Linz.'

'That must be the 10kg of scrap gold on the list of contents I mentioned. I've no idea who originally acquired it, but it certainly wasn't Klaus. Do you know what action Wiesenthal took?'

'As far as our chaps can discover it was followed-up but the trail went cold. But of course others may have got wind of it.'

Von Hessler looked quizzically at Hutchison. 'When you say 'others' who've you got in mind?'

'One of the Nazi-hunters working independently? Intelligence agencies on either side of the iron curtain, newspapermen? . It could even be one of the people who originally owned, or acquired, the material in the ammunition box.'

'Do you think that might account for why he was being bugged?'

Hutchison raised the palms of his hands. 'Anything's possible! It could even be blackmailers after him.'

'Now his odd behaviour and fears make some sort of sense – he'd good reason to worry, and it wasn't just paranoia.'

'When I first heard about Schmidt it struck me that he was an unusual choice of friend for a man with your background.'

'I suppose that's fair comment.' Von Hessler said. 'He's different from most of the people in my circle. A lot of them are very *korrekt*, very conscious of their connections with the royal families of Europe. Some kept their heads down during the Nazi era - withdrew from affairs of state and got out of touch- others took up Himmler's offer of honorary membership of the SS. For me Schmidt's a link with the real world of industry and commerce.'

'Yes, I can see that. Thank you for the portrait, it's useful.' Hutchison stopped to gather his thoughts. 'I suspect you're not going to be happy with what I'm now going to tell you. I've been doing my homework on him and made some curious discoveries. Did you know that he was previously married to a Fräulein Erda Richter before his marriage to Elizabeth Heath-Schofield?'

'No. I'd no idea. But then there's no reason why I should know. When did he marry Fräulein Richter?' He asked, frowning, why did the name Richter ring bells in his head?

'Early in 1948.'

265

'And when did it end?'

'That's an interesting question.' Hutchison paused. 'It appears it never did; they're still married.'

Von Hessler put down his knife and fork and stared at Hutchison. The room went out of focus and he saw the dark figure of a man sitting at the other end of the table looking at him intently. An image flashed across his mind of a Gestapo officer with a dead face and vacant eyes. He shook it off and tried to read the real expression on Hutchison's face.

'How did you find that out?' He asked coolly.

'Private detectives. They dug up evidence of the marriage via a circuitous route that started in a tax office, but there's no record of any divorce. If there had been one they'd have found it, so it looks as if Schmidt is a bigamist. And I might add, the father of a boy by that first marriage.'

Von Hessler leant back and drew in a deep breath.

'How in God's name has he got away with it?'

'By doctoring the records, and ensuring those in the know keep quiet.'

'But surely it must be next door to impossible to alter or substitute an entry in a marriage register!'

'He must have had a collaborator in the Lübeck *Standesampt*. Probably bribed him.'

'I find that difficult to believe!'

266

'Herr von Hessler, you've been in the intelligence business. How many altered passports have you seen? Forged documents, bogus visas and suchlike - they're the staple currency of agencies worldwide. With a name as common as Schmidt, a few alterations would throw most people off the scent. In fact what gave the game away was his wife's unusual first name which they came across elsewhere. She was born in Lübeck and once that was established it didn't take them long to track down the marriage record and detect his alterations.'

'OK, OK' said von Hessler. 'My intelligence work was in the Navy run by Admiral Dönitz, not the *Abwehr* run by Admiral Canaris! We didn't deal with doctoring public records or the sort of tricks that the *Abwehr* got up to.'

He filled Hutchison's glass as he pondered. 'So how did they track down the boy?'

'These detective agency people have suspicious minds. They ferreted out the birth registration. The boy's first name is Hans. Then they found that the mother had changed his surname from Schmidt to Richter a year later.'

The bells in von Hessler's head chimed loudly.

'God Almighty! Richter! Hans Richter. I know the man. He saved my life. You know about that?'

'No, not yet.' His knowing smile said it all. 'But can we get back to those letter? The reason I'm here tonight is that their authors want them back, so I'd like to discuss how we're going to prise them out of Schmidt. But first we need to establish how many he's got – either from 1945, or from your sunken ship.' He paused significantly and then added, 'and possibly from various banks.'

Hutchison responded to the ironic glance aimed at him with a fleeting trace of a smile.

'How do I know about the banks? It's simple – we checked airline passenger lists. Why does a man visit Zürich and then Stockholm on consecutive days and stay for just a couple of hours?'

'Why indeed. Actually I too had discovered the Bank connection. I got it from the contents of a cartridge that had escaped Schmidt's clutches, but by the time I got to Stockholm he'd already been there.'

It was growing dark and the nightingales in the shrubbery had stopped singing - a good moment to move to the drawing room. Von Hessler asked Frau Graubal to produce coffee and brandies. While they waited for her, he drew the curtains across and the two men settled into easy chairs and lit cigars.

'Those letters are going to be a problem' said Von Hessler pausing as he blew out a long plume of smoke. 'My friend Schmidt is a tough negotiator. We've a few advantages over him, but it's going to be like pulling teeth, and even more expensive. How much did the last deal cost back in 1946?'

'I've absolutely no idea. It was all done privately by one of our chaps who incidentally is rumoured to be a relation of our royal family. This time round all I can do is report back the sort of figure that Schmidt will settle for and get the go-ahead if it's reasonable.' Hutchison studied the glowing end of his cigar and added 'But we do have some leverage over him.'

'Bigamy? Falsification of records? Anything else?' said von Hessler.

'Certainly the first two. There's also the question of what Schmidt has done with the other stuff in the cartridges, none of which is his property. I'm only after the letters so I think we better keep quiet about the other stuff. We don't want official bodies taking an interest in any sales he's already made.'

'You seem to have acquired a remarkable body of knowledge. Tell me, von Benz's visit to your embassy in Bonn was well before I mounted that salvage operation, so who leaked the story about the letters? It can't have been Schmidt or his wife or Hans Richter, and Anson would have told me if it had been him.'

'Good question. This is how it goes – Schmidt decides to sell the new batch of letters and, being more cautious than he was in '46, uses Richter to approach Brenner in Heidelberg. But Brenner's son is now running the business and doesn't take to Richter, in fact he distrusts him. So he contacts our embassy to get authentication of the sample letter that he's been given. Fortunately the chap on the desk was one of those who interviewed von Benz and is instantly on the alert. So he takes it to the ambassador and I get a telex from London. I then ring Brenner junior and discover that Richter has given him a phone number which leads me straight to *Schmidt Elektrodynamik* in Hamburg. I put the sleuths onto the case and they discover, *inter alia*, the story of Richter and his mother.'

'Not bad for what sounds like less than a week's work,' commented von Hessler. 'Schmidt isn't going to be best pleased with his son. From what I saw of them, I'm sure Hans doesn't know that Schmidt is his father. There's another interesting side to this - Elizabeth told me that Richter has lived with his mother for years in a plush apartment in one of the more salubrious districts of Hamburg - Blankenese, I think. I wonder what game his mother is playing and who is supporting her. We need to know more about that woman.'

'Coming back to the son, are you thinking what I'm thinking?' said Hutchison. 'Why does he disclose his work number when it will lead straight to Schmidt? What's he up to?'

'God knows!' said von Hessler. 'Another string for a blackmailer? And another one for the pot - Elizabeth is insisting that Schmidt burns the letters – the whole lot.'

'That would be a cheap solution from my angle. But how do you rate the chances of that happening?'

'Quite high. She's a powerful lady.'

'But realistically, how much leverage can she exert?' Hutchinson asked sceptically. 'She's unlikely to bring in the police. Particularly if she suspects he's a bigamist. Will she really want to blow the lid right off?'

Von Hessler laughed.

'Highly unlikely. But if she did it would probably wreck his Company, to say nothing of their 'relationship' and anyway, who are we negotiating with? Elizabeth? Brenner? Richter? Or Schmidt? Or is it all four? It sounds like an international peace conference to me and just as tricky. I need to sleep on it.'

'Well let's do just that,' said Hutchison.

Von Hessler closed his bedroom door, sat on the end of the bed and kicked off his shoes. He cupped his head in his hands and muttered: 'What a damned mess.' Tomorrow was swathed in uncertainty – and complexity. Hutchison had a simple brief – just buy the letters and get out - lucky fellow!

Unmoving, he sat, trains of thought running through his head yet leading nowhere. Schmidt could be blown to pieces by that lethal cartridge ... surely, that wouldn't happen - he would warn him. Before that he had to speak to Elizabeth. *Gott in Himmel!* How could he break the news about that marriage to Erda Richter - could he trust Hutchison's information? Perhaps he could check by confronting Schmidt ... but that couldn't be done before he rang Elizabeth! And what about

271

the letters compromising his father? The thoughts led him round in circles.

He needed to sleep. The pain in his ribs was returning and he straightened up, stretching out his arms which brought some relief. Sedatives? No, he'd need a clear head in the morning to face further discussion with Hutchison. Reluctantly, he climbed into bed and switched out the light. He was in for a bad night – a rare event for him.

Eventually he drifted off, woke early and, meeting Hutchison on his way downstairs, escorted him to the dining room where they were greeted by the aroma of coffee wafting in from the kitchens. Hutchison seemed relaxed. Lucky bastard had slept well!

Frau Graubal had cooked an English breakfast and his guest rubbed his hands with delight as she served it. As she left the room he looked purposefully at his host.

'I really think that negotiating with Brenner or Richter would be a waste of time – they're just bit-players.'

'Yes, I agree with you there. I feel we need to get Schmidt away from his home ground in Düsseldorf.'

'Yes ... I can see that would be sensible. Where?'

'Hamburg, I think – and today.'

Hutchinson nodded. 'Yes, we'll have to use shock tactics, threaten to disclose both his bigamy and his attempts to sell the letters.'

'Hmmm ... I reckon you're right. Don't give him time to consider his options.'

Hutchinson went on to propose that they force an agreement for the hand-over of the letters within 24 hours, offering a cash sum.

'Will London agree to that?'

'I think so. Obviously, in recognition of your assistance the deal would also include the return of all letters involving German families.

Von Hessler pondered this *tour d'horizon*.

'It might work. I take it that your sole objective is cutting a deal with Schmidt at the lowest possible cost. Is that right?'

'Pretty well' said Hutchison, 'we can't pussyfoot around with that man, my job is to stop him at the lowest possible cost.'

'Have you thought of other ways?'

'Such as?'

'Using Elizabeth. She's demanding that Schmidt burn the letters and I suspect she might do something drastic if he doesn't.'

'Yes I have thought of her.' Hutchison stopped to finish his coffee and asked von Hessler for a refill. 'Their marriage is in trouble anyway, or will be when we've done our business. That being the case, I can't see that she is in a position of strength. Moreover there's another factor that I haven't mentioned. Our correspondent in Frankfurt tells us that Schmidt's company is underfinanced and yet is taking on orders that will require more working capital. If he can't get it, he'll lose control to the Banks. In other words he needs every pfennig he can lay his hands on. I can't see him burning those letters.'

Von Hessler got up from the table and walked up and down the room. Hutchison was a formidable operator. But he didn't like the idea of handing over control just like that. He stopped opposite Hutchison.

'Why the need to move so damned fast?'

'Let me draw a military analogy – naval battles are slow moving affairs - big fleets can take days to close on each other. Land warfare is different. Your Panzergeneral Heinz Guderian taught us some lessons in France in 1940. *Blitzkreig* is what I'm talking about. He used it with huge effect and that's my plan with Schmidt. We've got to overwhelm him. We can't risk drawn-out negotiations with small packets of letters sold off piecemeal.'

Von Hessler sat down again, picked up his coffee and sipped it pensively. He looked up at Hutchison, a wry smile twitching at his lips.

'Well I suppose for two tank commanders meeting in battle it makes sense. But let me raise another point. I imagine that Schmidt has long planned his response to possible exposure. He'll rely on that Register in Lübeck, from which all evidence of that first marriage has been removed.'

'That'll be his first shock,' said Hutchison with a glint of malice. 'In my briefcase I have photographs of the relevant Register page that reveal the alterations. They were taken in infrared and UV light by the agency I hired.'

'Clever move! Schmidt won't have reckoned on that. I'm beginning to think you just might get your letters. But one other thing - the unauthorised and hence illicit recovery of those letters from the wreck of S103. I'm thoroughly implicated and he'll doubtless try to use this and drag me down with him.'

'Not after you show him the letter from Admiral Lange which came through yesterday addressed to you. I have it in my briefcase.'

A smile flitted over Hutchison's face as he extracted the crisp sheet of A4 paper carrying the Bundesmarine letterhead and handed it to von Hessler. He read:-

Dear Freiherr von Hessler,

Following your recent request, I am pleased to grant you permission to carry out a limited salvage operation on Kriegsmarine vessel S103 lying on the seabed off Fehmarn Island. Only privately owned material may be removed. Great care should be taken during the operation to avoid infringement of the maritime boundaries of either the DDR or the Kingdom of Denmark.

May I wish you a successful expedition.

Yours sincerely,

GHPD Lange
Rear Admiral

Hutchison continued 'I expect you're wondering what's going on.'

'Indeed I am,' said von Hessler. 'How the devil did you come by that letter?'

'I can't disclose the whole story, but I can tell you this much. The arrival of that Volksmarine survey vessel off the Eastern tip of Fehmarn no doubt caused you some alarm. Unsurprisingly it also sounded alarms in official quarters. A leak was rightly suspected and ultimately traced back to Bonn. As I mentioned we ourselves first heard of your trip from the Stasi. It would have been embarrassing if an enquiry into your illegal expedition exposed this leak from such a highly placed source so tracks had to be covered. I thought it might help that process if your expedition was legitimised, thus eliminating the need for any such enquiry. So I put in a request.' Hutchison betrayed not a hint of triumph. Then he added 'It's interesting what diplomats can do when they set their minds to it!'

Von Hessler pulled a wry face. 'You cunning buggers! You really have fixed Schmidt! I'd love to see his face when he reads that letter. One more thing, Hutchinson, I wrote to his commander General von Lauchert and he confirms what Schmidt claimed about his orders in case he tries to deny them. This is a copy of what he sent me.'

Hutchison read the order.

'I'll keep it if I may? It may come in useful. Did you ask him about the contents of the ammo box?'

'No. He couldn't remember much about the affair and I didn't want to push too hard. No point.'

Hutchison looked at his watch and tapped it.

'It's time I contacted HQ about your explosive cartridge. I'll use your phone if I may.'

Left alone, von Hessler sat down and gazed into the mid-distance thinking through the conversation and the audacious proposals that Hutchison had expounded. But his mind kept returning to Elizabeth. How would she react to his part in the confrontation? She might see it as a plot to bring down her husband ... which, of course, it was. That was bad enough, but worse than that, it would expose her marriage as a sham. But how could he avoid telling her? There seemed to be no honourable way out. Klaus had to be stopped.

His ruminations were interrupted by the striking of the Vienna Pendeluhr that hung in the hall and he became aware of the distant sound of Hutchison talking on the phone. The man was taking an unconscionable time.

Hutchison returned and shook his head. 'The explosives chap can't really help without specific data on the experimental propellant. But he did say the bottom line is that anything made 25 years ago and carrying a warning like that is probably lethal.'

'I'll have to ring Schmidt.'

'Does that mean that you'll take on the job of getting him up here?'

Von Hessler grimaced. 'It looks as though I'll have to. I'll ring him now. Make yourself comfortable in the drawing room. It shouldn't take me long.'

He went to his office and sat down. It was all a dirty business but it had to be faced. He lifted the phone and slowly dialled the Düsseldorf number.

'Elizabeth, I need to talk to you alone. Is Klaus around? It's very difficult to …'

'What's the matter Gerhard? You sound terribly serious.'

'Well yes. There is. I've some … upsetting news concerning Klaus. He's landed himself, and you, in serious, even catastrophic, trouble.'

'Is it something to do with those wretched shells?'

'Indirectly, yes. He's been trying to sell the stuff that was packed inside them. This alerted the authorities and private detectives have been put on his tail. But I'm afraid they've turned up something far worse ... it involves you …'

'You're not telling me that he's been unfaithful are you Gerhard?' She paused, 'That's hardly the stuff of catastrophe!'

'Elizabeth, he's been deceiving you from the beginning.'

278

'You mean he's got a mistress?'

'Elizabeth, I'm finding this incredibly difficult ... it's not something that should be discussed over the phone ... but I've no option. I have to speak to you before I face Klaus.'

'Go on, tell me the worst.'

Von Hessler paused. In his head he raced through all the possible ways of avoiding the truth. But none came and he said abruptly

'Your marriage to Klaus is invalid. He's still married to another woman.'

Tense and rigid, he waited for her reply, hoping against hope that she would say 'I already know'. But no word came.

'Elizabeth, say something!'

'You're telling me that he tricked me into a bogus marriage?' She asked, her voice low and hard.

'Yes ... yes, I am. I'm so sorry Elizabeth.'

'And you expect me to believe this?'

'Elizabeth I know this is a terrible shock ... but ...'

'How can you be so credulous, Gerhard? You believe a bunch of private detectives against the evidence of your own eyes? You know perfectly well that Klaus and I have a successful marriage. Are you trying to destroy it?'

'For God's sake, Elizabeth! Of course I'm not trying to destroy your marriage. You don't really believe that do you?'

'Then why ring me out of the blue with this ... this preposterous nonsense?'

'Elizabeth, I've seen the evidence. It's going to be presented to Klaus and I thought you should hear it before he does.'

'And who's doing the presenting may I ask?'

'A chap from British intelligence – an Englishman.'

'So my marriage is now under international scrutiny. This gets more preposterous by the minute! I'm not going on with this conversation Gerhard. I'm too angry.'

'Elizabeth, hold on! You need to tell me where Klaus is. He's in physical danger. If he interferes with one of those cartridges it'll explode and kill him. I need to warn him.'

'Well you can't. He's just left to catch a plane to Hamburg. He should arrive in a couple of hours at most. You can get him there.' So saying, she hung up.

His heart pounding, he sat heavily back in his chair. What a mess! He cursed Hutchison and his English-upper-class ruthlessness. Maybe it was the way to deal with Schmidt but at what a price? On top of that, he fiercely, furiously, volcanically angry with Schmidt. Then he remembered Hutchison was waiting in the drawing room.

'We've just time for another coffee before we set off for Fühlsbuttel. Schmidt's on the first flight from Düsseldorf. He arrives in just over an hour.' He said as Frau Graubel brought in the coffee.

'My God! How the hell did you pull that off?'

'Co-incidence,' Responded von Hessler. 'He'd just left when I rang.'

'So you spoke to his wife?'

'Yes.'

'So she won't be able to talk to Schmidt before we meet?'

'That's right. The *blitz* will have maximum effect.'

'So we go ahead as planned?'

'Yes, we bloody well go ahead! I see no other way. I'll bring the original of the ammunition box contents list. It'll help with the *Blitzkrieg*. I think we can assume that he's already sold the gold and foreign currency, and probably tried to sell the bearer bonds.'

He stopped to gulp down his coffee.

'God, that man is a bastard!'

He turned to Hutchison

'Let's get on with it. We'll use the Aston Martin. That should get us to Fuhlsbüttel before Schmidt.'

Hutchison retrieved his briefcase from the bedroom and they got into the car. 'Better strap yourself in,' said von Hessler.

The indicator board in the Fuhlsbüttel Arrivals Hall showed the Düsseldorf flight due in 10 minutes. Hutchison went in search of the BEA

Station Manager whom he knew and returned to say that he had been lent an office and telex facilities. Conversation dried up as they waited. Von Hessler looked at the assembled drivers holding notices with the names of the passenger they were to meet. Then he saw Hans Richter standing among them, and went over and shook hands.

'This is a surprise, Herr von Hessler. Herr Schmidt did not warn me to expect you.'

'Well there's a reason for that. He didn't know! I and a colleague have sudden urgent business with him so he'll be as surprised as you are to find me here. Come over and I'll introduce you to my colleague.'

They walked across the hall and von Hessler effected the introduction. Minutes later Schmidt emerged and stopped in astonishment.

'Gerhard, what a pleasant surprise. What brings you to Hamburg?'

'I'm afraid it's some very serious business, Klaus. But before I go into explanations allow me to introduce Mr Hutchison who is *Geschäftsführer* of the firm 'Hermag Security' in Bonn.'

Von Hessler observed the faces of the two men - Hutchison's cold and hard - Schmidt's now puzzled and watchful.

'Klaus, we need a few minutes of your time on a matter of urgency. BEA have kindly placed an office at our disposal where we can talk in private. If you and Hans will follow me I will lead the way.'

282

Virtually herding the two men, Von Hessler set off at a smart pace in the direction of the BEA suite. The four men filed into a suite of offices equipped with grey filing cabinets and metal furniture standing on uncarpeted grey floors. Through the glass partitions they could see an animated group of air hostesses dressed in dark blue uniforms trimmed with red. Von Hessler led them to an inner office where there were some seats. To one side stood a bookcase laden with cardboard boxes full of timetables and publicity material and on one of the walls hung a large framed colour photograph of a Hawker-Siddeley Trident in BEA livery. Complimenting this, amongst a clutter of papers on the desk, stood a diminutive model of a Vickers Viscount.

Von Hessler turned to Schmidt 'Klaus, I must explain that the discussions that we are about to have are highly confidential and in your best interests I suggest that they should be restricted to the three of us.'

'You want Hans to leave?'

'That's your decision, Klaus. Perhaps that would be advisable for him to leave for a few moments while I explain what this is all about. You can then recall him if you wish.'

'Hans, go and get yourself a cup of coffee,' ordered Schmidt, turning to von Hessler with an aggrieved expression. 'So what the hell is this all about?'

'It's about the cartridges salvaged from S103 and your negotiations via Hans to sell part of the contents – some letters in fact.'

Schmidt's attempt at masking his surprise was pretty good, but not a good-enough. He was no poker player.

'I think this is where I hand over to you.' Von Hessler said, turning to Hutchison.

Abruptly Schmidt got up, seized his briefcase, and saying that he needed to make a phone call, stormed from the room.

Hutchison looked amused. 'D'you think he's going to do a bunk on us?'

'I don't think so,' said von Hessler, frowning. 'He's not the sort of chap to ring his wife or his lawyer. I wonder what he's up to.'

'Probably fixing up some box of tricks,' remarked Hutchison.

Schmidt returned after a few minutes, sat down and was about to speak but Hutchison cut him short.

'Herr Schmidt I am here to put a proposition to you and this is it - that you hand over all the letters that you obtained back in 1945 or from the S103. I will pay you a recovery fee of £25,000 on behalf of the owners of those letters. As they are technically stolen property, stolen by you, or to put it more politely removed by you from S103 without authority, this fee is conditional firstly on your handing over every letter in your possession, with no disclosures about these letters by you to any third party.'

Von Hessler's eyes never left Schmidt's face. Some pink patches were beginning to spread across his cheeks but otherwise his stony expression gave nothing away.

'Absurd,' said Schmidt contemptuously. 'I have been offered four times as much ...'

'If I may continue Herr Schmidt,' interrupted Hutchison. 'You have not yet heard my second condition. If you do not immediately accept my offer then the matter will be handed over to your local police together with a file containing, amongst other matters, details of items from S103 that you have already disposed of such as ten kilograms of scrap gold, your sale of which is currently on the files of the Simon Wiesenthal Bureau and under investigation.'

'What kind of stupid threats are these?' responded Schmidt with vigour. 'You assert that I stole the material from S103. I never went near the damn boat. Sitting next to you is the man who removed the box and its contents. The police will take a great interest in him, not me. You are wasting my time!'

'I don't think I am, Herr Schmidt,' said Hutchison in a low voice. 'Far from it. Take a look at this letter from Rear Admiral Lange.' He passed it over. Both men watched as he read it and then re-read it more slowly. Von Hessler wondered if he was having trouble taking in its contents or just buying time. If the latter, Hutchison did not allow him any.

'You will have noticed that the letter gives authority only to Freiherr von Hessler and that it refers to private property. The gold coins may have been either state or private property but they were certainly not your property and you were not at liberty to sell them. Nor indeed were you at liberty to sell the scrap gold stolen from concentration camp victims.'

'What gold coins?' Schmidt had raised his voice. 'I know nothing of gold coins. This is sheer invention on your part. Where's your evidence for gold coins? You have nothing.'

'If I may intervene, Klaus,' said von Hessler. 'I have here a list of the contents of the ammunition box. It refers amongst other items to gold coins and to Swedish bank deposit boxes. Some of these boxes were emptied by you in Stockholm just three days after you removed the cartridges to Düsseldorf. If you care to examine the list you will see that gold coins do indeed appear on it.' He handed the list to Schmidt.

After several seconds Schmidt looked up at von Hessler.

'Where did you get this?' He asked, a trace of alarm showing for the first time.

'It was in the briefcase.'

Schmidt remained silent. To von Hessler he appeared to be trying to calm himself, but suddenly a new wave of anger welled up and he burst out.

'I am not going to sit here and submit to blackmail by a foreign company no matter how much money it offers. I refuse to deal with you. Take your evidence to the police. I have friends who know how to deal with this sort of thing.'

Speaking slowly Hutchison responded: 'Herr Schmidt, I would point out that blackmail arises when a blackmailer demands money. I am not demanding money. I am offering money. I am trying to do a deal with you and putting all my cards on the table. I don't have time for long drawn-out negotiations. I need this deal sewn up by 3 pm tomorrow.'

'Then forget it,' said Schmidt. 'Your conditions are stupid.'

'Herr Schmidt, I hope that you have considered the implications of what you have just said. I'm referring to the involvement of your son, Hans, in your attempt to sell the letters.' Hutchison snapped back.

Schmidt recoiled in his chair 'What do you mean my 'son'?'

'I mean your son now named Hans Richter, originally Hans Schmidt, born to you and Frau Erda Schmidt.'

'Who is this woman Erda Schmidt? Schmidt is a common enough …'

'She is your wife,' interrupted Hutchison.

'Where did you get this preposterous rubbish?' Schmidt demanded angrily, his eyes darting from one man to the other.

Hutchison waited for a few seconds and responded icily 'From the Lübeck marriage register.'

'Then you cannot have examined that register. There is no such entry, except in your imagination. Go back to Lübeck and study it with greater attention. Meanwhile I have a meeting to attend.' Schmidt reached out for his briefcase.

'There is no need for me to go back to Lübeck, Herr Schmidt. I have with me photographs of the entry which I recommend you to study.' Hutchison opened a large envelope and extracted the photographs, handing one to Schmidt. 'This one was taken in natural light. Do you notice any peculiarities?'

Von Hessler watched Schmidt's tense reaction. It was as if Hutchison had served him with an arrest warrant. He studied the print intently, then he relaxed and handed it back. 'This does not even carry my name. Is that what you mean by a peculiarity?' He shook his head dismissively.

'Yes, I do mean just that. The peculiarity is that the original name 'Schmidt' has been altered to 'Schmid' by removing the 't'. If you examine the next two photographs you will note the evidence of that alteration and of others. One photo was taken under ultraviolet light and the other under infrared light.'

Von Hessler watched fascinated as Schmidt cautiously took them and placed them on the desk. He could not conceal his alarm - a forced casualness failed to mask the intense scrutiny to which he subjected the prints. He extracted a cigar from a case and lit it with a match. For a few moments he was silent.

'You have no doubt noticed the reappearance of the 't' at the end of your name, the reappearance of the '1' in your house number and of the '0' in your district number. I can point to other alterations if that would help.' Hutchinson said quietly.

'That will not be necessary,' snapped Schmidt. 'These photographs – are they part of the file that you referred to earlier?'

Hutchison held out the palms of his hands towards Schmidt in a soundless gesture of assent.

'Is that a yes or a no?' rasped Schmidt.

'I have made the consequences of your refusal clear,' said Hutchison, and in a menacing tone added. 'I am not going to repeat them.'

'I see. I must make another phone call.' Schmidt slowly got to his feet and left the office closing the door behind him.

'I think you may have cracked him,' said von Hessler quietly.

'I'm not so sure,' responded Hutchison. 'Back in '44 in France when we thought we were getting on top of the Panzers and they pulled back, they were not retreating – oh no - they were regrouping for a counter-attack. We shall see. We shall see. Perhaps he is going to ring his wife.'

'Well if he does he may get a shock. I've already told her the worst, although she wasn't inclined to believe me. I felt I had to. It was the only fair thing to do.'

'So you spilt the beans. If I may say so you were being very protective. I wouldn't have done it.'

'No damn you!' thought von Hessler 'you wouldn't.'

Hutchison got up. 'I'll try and talk some coffee out of the girls in the office.'

He returned followed by a stewardess carrying a tray with coffee and biscuits. After five minutes Schmidt reappeared and sat down.

He stared at Hutchison with a strange look on his face – it could almost have been triumph.

'I am not prepared to submit to threats. I have been tape recording this meeting,' and he tapped his breast pocket. 'The recording will serve to indict you both on a charge of attempting by threats to induce me to engage in an illegal transaction. It will go straight to the police when I leave here together with the photographs of the three of us in this office that have been organised by Hans on my instructions.'

Von Hessler could detect no reaction in Hutchison. The master poker player sat immobile for several seconds, then, imitating Schmidt's manner, speaking slowly and clearly he said:

'Herr Schmidt, I too have been recording our negotiations - an elementary precaution in view of their sensitive nature but that's by the way. It's clear that you have not fully absorbed the danger of any disclosures of your part in the handling and disposal of the ammunition box. One of my researchers was briefed to establish your war record. She found that you had been a member of Second Panzer Division when it was commanded by General von Lauchert. We subsequently contacted him.' Hutchison stopped abruptly, again waiting for a reaction from Schmidt. There was none.

After a few seconds Hutchison continued.

'One of his staff, a historian mindful of the need to preserve the division's records, obtained and hid the General's written orders. Two years later he handed them over to the General. Among them he has found for us the order he gave you and sent us a copy. It is hand-printed. I will read it -

Movement Order *No D85/362*
To *Major Klaus Schmidt,*
Date   *19ᵗʰ Jan 1945*

You are ordered to convey one box of experimental tank ammunition in Mercedes car No HH 24-7314 to Fürst von Benz in Kiel with all speed and maximum secrecy. If fuel is short or in case of other difficulties contact only Hamburg Gauleiter Kaufmann. Driver Beckmeier will accompany you.
Signed- *Meinrad von Lauchert*

Generalmajor
Second Panzer Division
Army Group West

I am taking steps to meet Driver Beckmeier in the next few days. He will no doubt cast some light on your journey to Kiel with the box.'

At the mention of Beckmeier von Hessler saw for the first time a flash of despair cross the face of the man in front of him. His arms, previously hanging limply down, now tensed. he matchbox in his left hand cracked and crumpled. He looked up and in a voice showing signs of strain said

'Very well. For the recovery fee of £25,000 I will hand over to you all letters to and from England. I will however retain the internal correspondence originating in my country. These are my final terms.'

Hutchison said nothing. He pulled out a notebook, pencilled a message, tore out the page and handed it to von Hessler.

'*Will accept. Was acting ultra-vires over the German stuff any way. Sorry.*'

Von Hessler scribbled the word '*Understood*' and handed the note back.

Turning back to Schmidt Hutchison said: 'In that case the recovery fee drops to £17,500.'

Schmidt's face relaxed. Von Hessler could see his almost palpable relief - he was now on familiar ground, doing a business deal. 'I will settle for £22,500 nothing less.'

For the first time Hutchison allowed himself a smile. 'Then we agree on £20,000.'

Schmidt looked hard at him trying to resist the smile but failed. With an embarrassed attempt at a grin he held out his hand.

'OK, we have a deal.'

'Good,' said Hutchison briskly. 'If you will give me details of the account to which the money is to be telegraphed, I will telex London immediately and get the transfer set up for 3 pm tomorrow. Assuming that you have the letters in Düsseldorf, I will come over tomorrow, check them and then phone the bank to authorise the cash transfer at 3 pm.'

Schmidt wrote down the bank details and handed them to Hutchison who left the office to send the telex, pointing out that it would take him several minutes to encrypt it.

The two men were left together tight-lipped in frigid silence glancing at each other intermittently. The second hand on the electric wall clock clicked on remorselessly. Then Schmidt turned to von Hessler.

'I thought of you as a friend.' He said in a low voice.

To von Hessler the words had a terrible finality, like an engraving on a tombstone. He saw between them a freshly-dug pit – what was to be buried in it? What feelings, what relationships? He could trace anger, regret, pain on Schmidt's face. He thought of all the ways he could reply but nothing could convey the complexity of his own emotions. He gave out a long sigh.

'How did we get into this mess?' He asked on impulse.

'Money,' said Schmidt in the same low voice. 'I needed money,' With a sweep of the hand he dismissed the matter. 'Does Elizabeth know?'

'Yes, Klaus, she does. I had to tell her. I rang her this morning. I couldn't work behind her back.'

Schmidt pursed his lips and nodded.

'It's probably just as well. I've lived with that deceit for too long. Sooner or later she had to know.'

He looked down and slowly ran his thumb over the palm of his left hand. His mind seemed far away.

Von Hessler waited, watching the face of the silent man. But a question forced itself into his mind and he rapped out

'Those German letters that you're hanging on to. What are you keeping them for?'

Schmidt jerked back to the present.

'I'm not going to burn them. They're my insurance policy. There are people around, like that young fool von Benz, who tried to take advantage of me as you know. They're my insurance against people like him.' Without giving von Hessler a chance to comment, he continued. 'About the money, Gerhard - some time I'll explain. Maybe you'll understand. But it's all too complicated to go into now.'

'OK. It can wait. But there's something that can't. One of the cartridges is filled with dangerously unstable propellant so watch what you're doing.'

'How the hell do you know that?'

'Remember, I have the list of contents.'

'Thank you for the warning ... but I have handled anti-tank ammunition - plenty of it.'

They relapsed into silence. Only the sounds of typewriters and telephone calls filtered in from the outer office. Shortly they heard Hutchison's military footsteps and he re-entered the room to say that the deal was fixed. Schmidt got up, unwilling to engage in further conversation, shook hands wordlessly with the two men, picked up his bag and walked out of the office in search of Richter. Hutchison watched the departing figure moving towards the exit.

'I wonder what he'll say to his son.'

Von Hessler added: 'I wonder what Elizabeth will say to him.'

Hutchison disconnected the microphone under his lapel and put the telex carbon copy into his briefcase. Von Hessler remained sitting, unwilling to make any further comment.

'Ringing General von Lauchert proved a good move. I bet he knows where the stuff in the ammo box came from.' Hutchinson mused.

'If he does, I doubt he'd ever tell me. Anyway it's all ancient history now.'

Von Hessler slowly got up and stretched his arms.

'I'm glad that's over. We better head back home and pick up your hire car.'

Chapter 93

Von Hessler awoke and immediately the grim recollection of the ~~fraught~~ phone call with Elizabeth lowered his mood. Was she going to make the first move and ring him - or had she written him off?

He tried to picture the scene between her and Klaus when he returned from Hamburg and shuddered.

There was a lurking uncertainty whether~~that~~ Klaus would actually go ahead and hand over the letters to Hutchison. Not to mention what sickening disclosures lay waiting to be exhumed in the letters that he was retaining?

Yesterday had been an unpleasant experience all round, but it must have been doubly appalling for Elizabeth. Klaus would undoubtedly have given her a one-sided report of how Hutchison and he had behaved. Would she even begin to understand why he, von Hessler, a close friend of theirs, had agreed to be a part of Hutchison's *blitzkrieg*? Did he understand his own motives? Perhaps he should have stayed out of it.

He dressed and went down to breakfast. Finding his attention wandering as he read the morning paper, he put on the radio. Why didn't she ring? Perhaps he should ring her, but he put off the idea. Once finished with breakfast, he raced back up the stairs and changed quickly into riding gear, striding round to the stables and saddling up his new stallion *Prinz*.   They were getting to know each other and he was waiting to give the stallion his head. Now was the time.

The morning was cool and sunny with a gentle south-westerly breeze. Before them lay a field of emerald green laced with gossamer spider webs glistening with dew. As he trotted the horse towards the track that ran across it he mulled over the events behind the crisis. Klaus's shady deals in the late 1940s were <u>on the same moral level as</u>~~comparable~~ ~~with~~ his sale of the letters to Hutchison. But <u>on</u>~~in~~ the scales of dishonourable conduct both were nothing when weighed against the man's deception of Elizabeth. That was contemptible, vile, unforgivable. Why was Elizabeth angry with him and not with her so-called husband?   Was it a case of shoot the messenger?

The track was clear and the horse was raring to go. A light tap of his heels and *Prinz* broke into a canter, then with another light tap he was off. The horse was fast – the slipstream began to make his eyes water. They thundered along the track, the speeding hooves eating up the distance, and after several minutes he could pick out the barn – the end of the track.

Exhilarated, von Hessler reined in the horse for the trot home while disturbing echoes of his discussions with Hutchison filled his ears. <u>The man</u> ~~He~~ had remarked: 'You're being very protective' about the call he had made to Elizabeth. That was undeniable. But why shouldn't he feel that way? She had been lured into a bogus marriage – an Englishwoman, living in a foreign country with a man who couldn't be trusted. She needed help – but he couldn't deny that there had been an element of self-interest in his concern. Why hadn't she rung him?

Re-entering the house he picked up the phone; then put it down again. If Elizabeth was furious at his part in the showdown with Klaus then it was sensible to let the dust settle – if she wanted to talk she would ring him.

His faith was rewarded later that morning. Her voice was cold and guarded.

'Gerhard, I'm told by Klaus that you brought in that man Hutchison to force him to sell the letters that he'd discovered in one of those shells. Why did you do that? I don't understand.'

'It wasn't like that at all, Elizabeth. Klaus is talking a lot of nonsense. The fact is I was approached by Hutchison and not the other way round. It was he who discovered that Klaus was trying to sell the letters to a dealer in Heidelberg and ...'

'Klaus says it was a forced sale conducted by Hutchison almost at gun point – is that true?'

'Partly. Hutchison was certainly using strong-arm tactics. But you need to look at what's behind all this. Klaus obtained those letters by breaking an agreement with me. They were not his property and he'd no right to try and sell them.'

The conversation was going badly. Surely she must realise that Klaus was never going to paint her a fair picture of what had happened. Elizabeth was a direct sort of person but why this confrontational approach? It was forcing him to respond with a hard tone of voice like a witness in the dock.

'Why were you there? Assisting with this business?'

'In the end, Elizabeth, it was because I felt I had to. It seemed to me that the whole thing was a powderkeg that was going to blow up in everyone's face. Someone had to stop Klaus selling them to that man in Heidelberg.'

'It doesn't sound so terrible to me.'

'Well it was a prospect that so alarmed the top people in England that they ordered Hutchison to buy the whole batchlot there and then. They virtually gave him *carte blanche* and he took it.'

'But you weren't given *carte blanche* and yet you joined in a forced sale.'

'You're right, it's not the way I would have done it. But Hutchinson works for the British secret service and they don't pussyfoot around. OK it's not the way business is normally done but this wasn't normal business.'

'So why didn't you let Hutchison get on with it on his own? Why team up with him?'

It was getting worse.

Flatly countering her questions didn't seem to be working, but surely the facts spoke for themselves ... not to mention justifying his actions!. He hoped she wouldn't detect a note of exasperation as he replied.

'For the simple reason that my family's reputation was also at risk. I thought that working alongside Hutchison I could kill two birds. In the event he sold only the letters compromising families in England and he's hanging on to those affecting mine and as ....'

'Well you seem to have ambushed him very successfully. If I'm to believe all that Klaus tells me, you and Hutchison made a formidable pair. It's a side of you that I haven't seen before, Gerhard. You must feel proud at having beaten him at his own game!'

'I'm anything but proud, I feel soiled, contaminated by it all. Klaus holding those other letters is a direct threat to me – it's he who's holding a pistol to my head – you don't expect me to ...'

'What makes you think that he'll use those letters against you? He's bitterly upset by what happened yesterday, but that doesn't mean that he's suddenly changed from friend to foe.'

'How can you maintain that after what he's done to you, Elizabeth? Do you expect me to trust him now? He was prepared to put the reputation of the English royal family at risk by selling those letters to a dealer. Why do you believe he won't do the same to me?'

'I don't think I want to discuss Klaus any more.'

'I see. Well that's going to restrict the conversation. What shall we talk about then – politics, the weather?'

There was a long pause.

'I'm sorry Gerhard. I'm overwrought. I'm terribly distressed about the whole business. I've got a really ghastly feeling about it.'

'So have I. I wish it had never happened. But it has. Come on, we mustn't get angry with each other. We really mustn't. ... where do we go from here?'

'I wish I knew. I've got an awful lot to think about. One thing I have decided upon is a trip to Hamburg in the near future. I need to find out more about ... I wondered ... as I'm going to be there... it might be sensible for you and I to meet rather than trying to talk it out on the phone.'
??????????

'That sounds like a sensible idea. Why don't you ring me when you've fixed up the trip?'

'Yes I will. I have to go now. *Auf Wiederhören,* Gerhard. No broken bones?'

'No. Nothing but some cracked ribs. Goodbye, Elizabeth. Ring me soon.'

Von Hessler put down the phone, staring into space. On the positive side, he and Elizabeth were still friends ... though she had been expectedly defensive about her husband. What rubbish had Klaus fed her? She'd not walked out on him ... why was she so trusting?

And what sort of deal was he planning for the remaining letters? Von Hessler had no illusions about Schimdt's intentions ... he'd got hold of them by reneging on his original agreement over the opening of the cartridges, h=e'd perverted

301

the aims of the salvage operation to enrich himself, and was unlikely to stop at tarnishing the reputation of the von Hessler family. The man was a false friend, a traitor.

He went to his study, lit a cigarillo, grabbed an ashtray and sat down. The first thing to be done was to mend his relationship with Elizabeth.

W~~Then~~ with a start he remembered the hand-written letters that he had passed to Doktor Hirn. They might be equally damaging to his father and family if and when they were decoded. Deciding that he needed to know the worst, he picked up the phone. Hirn reported some progress and sounded cautiously optimistic. Von Hessler immediately invited him over for lunch.

An hour later the aging Opel rattled up the drive and stopped with a swirl of blue smoke from its exhaust.

'Welcome Manfred. You made very good time. Meet any cows?'

'Just the usual herd. They were coming towards me so I forbore letting my impatience assume control and I pulled to a halt. They trundled past quickly enough! However, had they been going in my direction, it would have been another matter.' With just the hint of a smile Hirn continued, 'I must write a paper on the dynamics of automobile flow through a semi-fluid medium as exampled by a herd of cows.'

'What a splendid idea, Manfred. You must send me a copy although it's doubtful if I will understand a single word of it. Well come in and have some lunch. How is Frida?'

'Her usual busy self. She's convinced that she'll track down the handwriting in your letters, but it's a laborious business and difficult to forecast progress.'

They walked into the house; von Hessler ushered Hirn into the dining room and they sat down.

'And how about your progress?'

'Let me read you something of one of the letters on which I'm working.' Hirn pulled an envelope from his pocket and extracted some sheets of paper. 'Here we have it. You will note that the narrative material is convincing – the sort of harmless trivia that circulates within families. If the purpose was to escape the attentions of the censors then it's a good letter. I'll read it. There is no date.

BERLIN
MY DEAR PAUL ,

I AM SLOWLY LEARNING RUSSIAN WITH
MY FRIENDS. IT IS HARD WORK AND
TAKES MUCH EFFORT. I GO FOR WALKS
IN THE AFTERNOON TO CLEAR MY HEAD.
THE WEATHER IS LOVELY AND THE SUN
BRIGHT. SOON FROSTS WILL BE NO MORE.
I AM GOING FOR A REALLY LONG
GRUELLING WALK TOMORROW AS I NEED

THE EXERCISE. ......etc etc   I won't read any more.'

Hirn passed the letter to von Hesssler.

'The characters underscored in pencil are those that are picked out by such holes in the grid as I've been able to discover. Now let us move on to my attempt to assemble these characters into words and the message that results.' Hirn passed across a second piece of paper.

Original message block -

```
MYA*RESTSOON*LAUSFAILUR
EFINISGERMANIAECONTACT*N
LYGR*YMHIM*LERREPEACENE
*STHANKSFORMUCHH*LPA*IO*
           * =possible grid hole
```

Trial assembly into words -

```
MY  A  *  REST  SOON
* LAUS   FAILURE
FINIS GERMANIAE
CONTACT * NLY GR * Y M
HIM * LER RE PEACE NE * S
THANKS FOR MUCH H*LP
A * I O *
```


'Manfred, my curiosity is such that I really must read this stuff straight away. Do excuse me. Help yourself to the vegetables.'

Hirn busied himself with dishes of sauerkraut and celery while casting enquiring glances at his host. After a moment's hesitation he spoke.

'I should explain, Gerhard, that what you have there is currently the most meaningful of thedecodes.'

Von Hessler grimaced. 'I like your use of the term meaningful. My first reaction is that it's almost devoid of meaning. I take it that asterisks denote that you're unsure whether there's a hole in the grid at that point, rather than unsure about the character that might appear in it.'

'Yes indeed. If you take the first word of the second line it seems likely that we have a name, either CLAUS or KLAUS. I'm practically certain that it's a 'C' because 'K' is not present in that line of the letter, but I've yet to verify the presence of a hole over a 'C' in the same line.'

Von Hessler shook his head. 'I can't make much sense of line four. Can you?'

'I'm as puzzled as you are. There's no possible word containing the letters GR*YM   It could be a set of initials or one can postulate the word GRAY or GREY, but then how account for the 'M' ?'

'You're sure about that 'M' at the end are you?'

'Positive. But the start of line 5 is the most intriguing. The word that springs to my mind to fit those characters is 'HIMMLER'.'

Von Hessler looked up at Hirn and then at the decode for several seconds. 'If you're right, then ignoring the word GRAY it could read *'Contact only Himmler re peace news.'* I fear that that has implications for my father's reputation.'

There was a moment of awkward silence as Hirn dabbed his mouth with his napkin.

'Dare I ask - was he in touch with Himmler in the normal course of events?' He asked quietly.

'Yes. I'm afraid he was. Or so it would appear from other correspondence in his briefcase.' Von Hessler paused while he re-read the decode. He placed it squarely back on the table and looked up at his visitor.

'Manfred, you and I worked in intelligence - we need to get at the truth - whatever the decodes reveal.' He paused. 'After all, in the second oldest profession we must maintain standards.' He added almost apologetically.

With noticeable relief Hirn returned to his analysis.

'It seems that our man was prone to expressing himself in Latin. As he wasn't confining himself to German I did wonder if that group of characters at the end made the Spanish 'ADIOS'. As a way of signing off it does have the advantage of using a smaller number of characters than the German.'

'That's interesting. You may be right. So let's see what we can deduce about the writer. He's well educated, possibly a linguist, used to moving in high places and thinks at a political or philosophical level. He might even be a diplomat. The tone of the message is that of a leader. The fact that he writes in code implies that he is under surveillance or even imprisoned.'

Hirn nodded approval.

'Yes, I go along with that. I thought the tone of the ending was somehow ominous. There's something final about it. Whether this letter really is the last of a series we can only decide when I've finished working through the rest of them. Which reminds me - I did wonder if the writer was involved in espionage – he was a practiseed hand at this method of coding, quite professional in fact.'

'Yes, I think that's quite on the cards. Manfred, I'm deeply grateful for your efforts. You really have made a great deal of progress – far more than I had any right to expect. Before we move on to other matters can I round this one off with a final question? Have you any idea how long it's going to take before you reach the end?'

Hirn looked up at the ceiling and his fingers drummed lightly on the table as he pondered.

'Give me another week,'

'Oh, Thank God! You know the uncertainty surrounding my father's activities is preaying on my mind. It'll be a huge relief when it's resolved one way or the other.'

At his desk Von Hessler riffled through the morning post and picked out a plain envelope with a typed address and Bonn postmark that looked intriguing. To his surprise, the first of the enclosed sheets was handwritten on unheaded paper :

Bonn
                                                        15 May 1970

Dear Freiherr von Hessler,

I am enclosing a letter which came with the batch that I acquired from our mutual friend. As you will see it does not lie within the category of correspondence that I was expecting to receive. I am sending it herewith as it will no doubt be of significance for you.

I cannot explain how or why it came to be included with the other letters. It was near the bottom of a pile that was held together by a rubber band. It could have been included either accidentally or deliberately, I have no way of telling.

Neither its existence nor its content has any bearing on the matters in which I have recently been involved and therefore I do not intend to divulge either point to any other party.

With friendly greetings,
Astley Hutchison

The second sheet also on unheaded paper was typed and had been folded down the middle. He unfolded it.

Hohenlychen

3 April 1945

Dear Freiherr von Hessler,

It would greatly assist my negotiations with Count Folke Bernadotte if you would speak to him privately and mention that I am somewhat restricted as to the measures that I can take to move Jews from the lagers in Bergen-Belsen or Buchenwald to Neuengamme for the purpose of their release. The deterioration in the military situation has led certain people, including Herr Kaltenbrunner, to interfere with my orders and I cannot be certain that they will be carried out.

I attach importance to this release of some of the remaining prisoners as I wish to secure the goodwill of the Jew Stephen Wise who is a close friend of President Roosevelt.

I am glad to tell you that the implementation of the final solution to the Jewish problem is now virtually achieved enabling me to allow this minor relaxation of the programme. I am sure that I can rely on you to proceed with your usual discretion.

Heil Hitler!
Heinrich Himmler Reichsführer SS

Gerhard refolded the letter, repeatedly sharpening the fold between his thumb and forefinger, then put it back in the envelope and slung it across the room. It hit the bookcase and dropped to the floor. He closed his eyes and gasped 'Neuengamme'. The name of the lager reverberated in his head - 'Neuengamme – the origin of~~where~~ the prisoners drowned in the liner *Cap Arcona* ~~had come from~~. Now Bergen-Belsen and Buchenwald are added to the *Konzentrationslagern* named in letters to *his own father* - this one from Himmler, the father of the holocaust. He shuddered as he visualised Himmler in SS uniform, the pair of lightning-flash SS runes on his collar, the peak of his hat almost obscuring his eyes. The man was smiling and shaking hands with his father.

He staggered hurriedly to the toilet, shut the door and leant against the wall feeling his guts roiling as bile filled his mouth. Shivering with a sudden chill, he spat the foul stuff out, then filled the basin with cold water washing it away, before splashing his face. He caught sight of himself in the mirror. He looked jaundiced.

For several minutes, he stood there breathing heavily while his stomach settled before going back to his study. On his desk he caught sight of the photograph of his father dressed in diplomatic uniform, reaching out, he grab bed it, turned it face down and slid it into a drawer. He then sat, his head in his hands, while in his mind the image of his father appeared again, alone this time, it slowly receded into the distance until it was a mere speck. His thoughts a jumble of memories, regrets and anger, he eventually got to his feet and left the house taking the path past the stable block that led to the fields. Twhere he had placed a bench with a distant view of the sea: a sanctuary. Sitting there, breathing in the scent of the gentle breeze rustling the leaves on the trees behind him, the chill slowly left him as the morning sun touched him.

What the hell was he going to do?

There seemed no other explanation than that Schmidt had inserted the letter in the pile deliberately. His anger flared up again only to die back instantly – their confrontation in Fühlsbuttel airport had miserably failed to extract from Schmidt the letters compromising his own family, and now Schmidt was rubbing it in. Typical of the man!

He tried to think constructively. Perhaps the letter had got into the pile accidentally, but he wasn't going to ring Schmidt and ask him. It might be better to ask Elizabeth – he would ring her tomorrow. Maybe she'd have some idea.

His muscles stiff, he decided that he needed exercise so, heading back into the house, he picked up the phone and arranged a game of tennis.

Later that evening hevon Hessler received a 'phone call from Elizabeth to say that she would be in Hamburg at the Hotel *Vier Jahreszeiten* the

311

following day and suggesting that they met at around four o'clock.

Needless to say, it was at that precise hour that von Hessler strode up the Hotel steps, in through the revolving doors and went to meet her in the lounge. He couldn't miss the restraint in her greeting – a trace of formality and reserve. She accepted his suggestion that they should take English tea in the café and they sat down at a small square table covered with a plain white tablecloth and laid with white china.

'Do you stay here very often?' she asked rather stiffly.

Von Hessler smiled 'Only when I'm in Hamburg and none of my friends will have me. And you?'

'When I'm up here with Klaus, but that's not very often.'

'No Klaus today?'

'No Klaus today. But then I could hardly ask him to accompany me.' She looked at him and pursed her lips. 'You see I have been visiting his wife.'

'Oh I see. So you've been to see Frau Erda Richter. Is she ... Did it go all right?'

'I think the most appropriate word to describe our encounter would be 'icy'. We were polite to each other. I can't say I liked her – the truth is I came prepared to be shocked and I was. But I don't want to talk about her.'

Aware that the list of *verboten* subjects probably included Klaus himself he searched for another.

'So how are you in yourself?'

'Let's talk about you, Gerhard. How are you?' she responded coolly, ignoring his question.

'That's a big question. There's so much going on at the moment that I wake up every morning dreading what the day will bring.'

'The same goes for me.'

She bit her lip. For a second he thought she was going to cry.

'You must be finding it tough – are you coping?'

She sighed, fidgeting with a teaspoon.

'I don't know. Nothing feels the same. I tell myself that this sort of ... of crisis afflicts many women. It doesn't help knowing that my ... my pain is no different from theirs. The worst thing is the feeling that I'm on my own – there's no-one I can talk to.' She gave him a puzzled look. 'But here I am talking to you.'

'Are you still angry?'

'That's too small a word. Leaving Klaus out of this for the moment, I'm certainly angry with Hutchison ...~~and with that crooked lawyer in Lübeck.~~'

'And with me?'

'I try not to be. I try to think of you as a Greek messenger.'

'Does that mean you're going to shoot me nonetheless?'

'No, I'm not going to shoot you, Gerhard.'

'Well that's a relief ... it was a gruesome battle with Klaus - he was my friend.' He looked up briefly at the ornate ceiling of the café. 'There's something in the air about betrayal ...' He clenched and unclenched his fingers. Reluctantly he completed the sentence 'and not just by Klaus.'

'You're not feeling guilty are you?'

'It wasn't pleasant teaming up with Hutchison - helping him to do his dirty work.'

'It had to be done, I can see that. Better you than someone really out to hurt him.' She grimaced '*Betrayal* - it's a terrible word. But it's the right one. It echoes around the rooms in our apartment – never seems to die away. Waves of distrust pour over me - almost revulsion. They drown all the ...' she stopped in mid- sentence, disinclined to continue.

'I can imagine how you feel. Do you trust anyone now?'

'I don't know.'

'Do you trust me - after what I did to Klaus?'

'I don't think that's important now ... I mean what you did to Klaus. A nyway I don't think he holds it against you. As a negotiator he thinks you're a tough one - he's not seen that in you before. But he respects you for it. Certainly you and Hutchison gave him a hard time.' She paused, her expression grim.   'And he deserved it.'

He was aware that she was looking at him strangely, questioningly. Their eyes met for a long moment; she looked down first. 'I haven't answered your question, have I?' She heaved a massive breath and frowned. 'Do I trust anyone?'

'I suppose that implies the answer is no.'

'No, it doesn't mean *no*, Gerhard. I just don't know who I can trust.' Then quietly she said 'Oh God, I'm sorry. I ... I do ... I do trust you.'

'So I'm not holed below the waterline?'

She smiled for the first time. 'That's a very nautical way of putting it!'

Once they had finished their tea, von Hessler suggested a walk along the Alster. The lake sparkled in the late afternoon sun as they strolled along Neuer Jungfernstieg across to the gardens lining the banks of the Aussenalster. On the water a fleet of small yachts was assembling for a race – the wind was just enough to rustle the leaves of the trees. A water bus packed with tourists pulled into a landing stage nearby.

They walked in silence for a while; neither feeling the need to make small-talk. Then Elizabeth turned to him.

'Tell me more about all these things that are making you anxious, Gerhard.'

'They arise from that fateful salvage trip. Apart from the fact that it fractured several of my ribs and nearly cost me my life, it's left a trail of anxieties. One of them is that Klaus is hanging on

315

to some of the letters, the ones I was hoping to recover.'

'Which are they?'

'They're the letters exchanged mostly within Germany. The ones which didn't involve English families – at any rate not directly.'

'I'd no idea Klaus was holding any of them back. What's he doing that for?'

'He~~No doubt~~ ~~he'll~~ claim<u>s</u> they're his insurance policy against any repetition of the von Benz sort of threat.'

'Well, whatever he claims, he's not going to justify any more funny business.' Von Hessler saw again the determined look on her face. She went on.

'I've already stopped him selling the letters to Hutchison.'

'What did you say?'

'I said I've stopped him selling the letters.'

'But Hutchison told me that the deal was completed.'

'But no money changed hands. I'd already told Klaus several days ago that if he sold even a single letter I would go to the police.'

'So how did Hutchison get the letters, Elizabeth? I just don't understand.'

'Klaus told me that he was desperate for money. So, in a nutshell, I got it for him and he handed over the letters without any payment.'

Von Hessler looked hard at her. 'Are you saying in effect that *you* bought the letters?'

'No I'm not. I produced sufficient money for him by buying part of his holding of *Electro* shares - at the full market rate I hasten to add. That enabled him to hand over the letters to Hutchison gratis.'

'That must have taken some organising. You had very little time.'

'It was tight. I phoned my father the night Klaus returned and he lent me the money. He got the bank to telegraph it.'

'Well I'm damned. That was a smart piece of work. Hutchison would give you a job any day.'

She gave him a quizzical smile. 'I don't know how to take that remark.'

'It's only my juvenile side coming out,' he responded with a grin.

They sat down on a bench with a wide view of the lake. He thought – she's a beautiful woman – without a trace of animosity in her, but pity the man who stands on swampy moral ground!

As they watched, the yacht race got under way, von Hessler casting a critical eye over the proceedings.

'Did Klaus put up much of a fight?'

'Not really. He wasn't in a fighting mood. Anyway he knew I meant what I said. He didn't like parting with the shares as it meant losing absolute control of the Company. But he's still left with 45%.'

'Most people would say that's more than enough. Why does he need the money?'

'It's obvious really. He's supporting two wives.'

'Ah ... even so, Frau Richter must be spending a hell of a lot of his money. Of course there's his son Hans – he must have cost him something. That's before he gave him a job at *Elektro*. But then there's the possibility that Klaus could simply be buying her silence.'

'I wouldn't put it past her to indulge in blackmail.'

'Do you think that was what was happening?'

'It could certainly account for some of his black moods ... and for some of his angry outbursts.'

'Angry outbursts?'

'Oh yes. you haven't seen him at his worst. It's pretty rare but he goes berserk, loses control. When he feels he's losing a battle he becomes really angry - and frightening.'

'But that didn't stop you getting your way over the letters - you can be quite as tough an operator as Klaus.'

'Perhaps that makes three of us,' she replied with a half smile.

'Oh I'm not in the same league as Klaus.'

'But you're a very confident person, Gerhard. When you make your mind up you go straight ahead and achieve what you want.'

'Why do you say that?'

'Well look at that salvage operation. How many men of your age, if you'll excuse me saying it, would risk their necks out in the Baltic shipping lanes in a rubber dinghy in complete darkness, and navigate it to exactly the right spot. *And* with Ulbricht's patrol boats on the look-out for you.'

'That's not the bit that worried me. The Ossies wouldn't have kept me locked up for very long. I've got connections over there.'

'High enough up?'

'Oh y~~Y~~es. You'd be surprised how many people over there with family links over here remain in touch. All stout party members of course. Some high up too.'

'So what were the bits that worried you?'

'Oh, failing to find the marker buoy, getting run down by a merchant ship, finding bodies in the wreck, that sort of thing. But they weren't real worries.'

'If they weren't real worries then what on earth would be?'

'Oh more important things - things like personal relationships.'

She looked amused. 'From what little I've seen, your personal relationships are fine.'

'They haven't always been.'

'Now you're going to tell me it's something to do with women.'

'So you want to hear all about my love-life?'

'Of course.'

Von Hessler looked at his watch 'Have you got all evening?'

'Possibly~~Of course~~.'

319

'I'll tell you if you promise to join me for dinner.'

'Then I promise~~I'd love to~~.'

'I'm delighted. So~~Well~~ - let's sit here for a bit while I tell you.'

As they sat together on the park bench he related the story of Elke and their broken engagement. She listened attentively without comment.

'They say it's love that makes the world go round … but sometimes it seems to make it stop.' She commented.

There were a few moments of silence. They both looked across the water at the sailing dinghies slowly passing in procession – the crews silently engrossed in catching every breath of wind. After a time she turned to him.

'Did you ever try sailing dinghies when you were young?'

'No, never. My introduction to sailing was with my father on his yacht. Anyway the wind on these inland waters is much too flukey for me. How about you?'

'Oh yes, I used to sail dinghies in Chichester harbour when I was a child, but the war put a stop to that. Then I took it up again after the war and like you I sailed with my father and mother before coming over here. They had a lovely boat.'

'How did you come to work in Hamburg?'

'That was the Foreign Office. I read modern languages at St. Hilda's in Oxford and that got me into the FO. After a few months I was posted to the Consulate-General here. It's just up the road over there. That was in 1949.'

'How did you find it after England?'

'Hamburg was a really grim town in those days, especially once you got away from the centre. I found the bomb damage appalling. So many were killed. I don't know why people only make a fuss about Dresden. Hamburg was nearly as bad, and that was back in 1943. I read somewhere that over a million people were made homeless, yet few talk about it now.'

'What about life in the Consulate?'

'That was fine. There was a great deal of socialising and any number of young men to choose from.'

'Why Klaus?'

'The truth is that I didn't really take to those superior chaps in spurs wearing blue mess-kit with chain-mail on their shoulders. I think they were Fourth Hussars. There was always a number of them about in the Hotel when it was the officers' club. Then I met Klaus at a 'do' in the Consulate and he swept me off my feet. It sounds an awful cliché but you know Klaus. The panzer tank commander who knows exactly what he wants, closes the hatches and goes for it~~charges~~.'

'What did your parents think?'

'They were pretty appalled. But they came round when they saw I was serious. I think my father ended up liking Klaus.'

'Does he know about what's happened?'

'Yes. He's one of the few people who do. He's pretty well off and I borrowed the money from him to buy the shares so I had to tell him the whole story.'

'He sounds like a good father.'

'I used to think I was blessed with both a good father and a good husband. Klaus was a tremendous support when I lost my one and only child. But that was long ago. And now......'

She looked up at him and he saw the pain in her face.

'So what are your plans?'

'Do you mean will I leave Klaus?'

Von Hessler nodded. 'If you want to put it that bluntly - yes.'

'I don't know. I think I'm still in shock. I need time.'

'Look Elizabeth, why don't we walk back to the hotel and I'll stand you that dinner I promised.'

'That's a lovely idea, Gerhard. Let's do just that.'

Chapter 10

Von Hessler looked across the table at Elizabeth. He picked up his glass of champagne.

'Here's to what the future brings!'

They clicked glasses.

'What have you got in mind?' She asked with a quizzical smile.

'Something different from the past.'

'You're looking very serious, Gerhard!'

The orchestra was playing the march from Act Two of Franz Lehar's *Die lustige Witwe*. He smiled back at her and waved his hand in time with the music.

'This was one of my father's favourites.'

She looked at him. 'Was the *Horst Wessel* among them?'

'Why do you ask that?' He asked with just a trace of asperity.

'Only because Klaus told me that it was a popular marching song during the war.'

'Have you any idea of the words?'

'Good Lord, no! How should I know them? I was at school in England for most of the war. How does it go?'

'To be honest I've only a sketchy idea.' He admitted a little sheepishly. 'I've never sung it myself. The song was originally adopted by the SA and has references to the Brownshirts and Hitler-flags, and of course the Swastika. I never heard my father play it either on the piano or the gramophone though, occasionally, one would hear it on the radio.'

'So he wasn't a Nazi supporter?' She waited in vain for a reply. 'You've gone very silent.'

'I suppose examining the past does that to me. It can be painful.'

'I shouldn't have asked … I'm sorry, Gerhard. It just popped out.'

'No harm done. It's just all a bit sensitive at the moment … the past is coming up and hitting me rather badly at the moment. I'd rather not talk about it.'

'Why not?'

Von Hessler grimaced. 'It's something I've never spoken of to anyone. The last twenty years have revealed so much that is hard to bear about what it means to be German. Perhaps too hard.'

'Too hard to share? With me?'

Von Hessler looked hard at her and smiled.

'It's hard to refuse when you put it like that! Though I imagine you've a good idea what I mean.'

'The stuff in those wretched cartridges?'

He nodded and beckoned the waiter to refill their glasses. There was a moment's silence.

'Elizabeth, has Klaus mentioned the Nazis in connection with my father?'

He paused.

'This conversation appears to have got us into deep waters! Shall we talk of something else?'

'No, Gerhard, these things need to be said. To put it bluntly Klaus told me that your father was in league with them.'

'With Himmler?'

'That's what he said.'

'He must have gleaned that from the letters he found. I found similar letters in my father's briefcase and they seem to support that idea. I can't believe it! God! I wish I'd never I salvaged them!'

'I'm so sorry Gerhard. It must be awful for you.'

'I'd always prided myself that we had never had anything to do with the Nazis. And now this happens. It's nauseating.'

'Klaus was pretty surprised. He'd always thought that the army was lukewarm if not downright hostile to the Nazis. He certainly hated the SS after what their extermination groups did in Poland and Russia. Mind you, the killers who formed the *Einsatzgruppen* certainly had logistic support from the army so there must have been some. It's difficult to see how any adult German can feel completely free of responsibility?'

Von Hessler gave a long drawn out sigh.

'Perhaps people who were active in the resistance circles do. They were hopelessly ineffective in stopping Hitler, but at least they tried and many of them died for their efforts. But I don't think my father risked his neck in that way.'

Von Hessler picked up his glass and gazed at it as he gently swirled its contents around.

'Do you know, Elizabeth, when I was at school in England I felt at home. It seemed a gentler place than Germany. I didn't spend much time at Haus Langenhorn because my father was Counsellor in our embassy in London and I stayed with him in the vacations. He loathed Ambassador Ribbentrop. I remember him saying that the only thing he was good for was performing opening ceremonies at sewage works!'

'Really?'

'Yes, he actually did that at Mogden in West London in 1936.' He paused for a second. 'Oh dear, we seemed to have moved from Nazis to sewage – not much of an improvement.'

'Which school were you at?'

'Marlborough.'

'Why an English school?'

'Partly because my father wanted me to perfect my English. My mother died in 1926 when I was 6 and I'd had a succession of English governesses so I was already reasonably fluent. But then someone commented that I had a funny accent just like half the crowned heads of Europe, who had also been taught by English governesses, so maybe that was a factor. My grasp of English grammar was none too good. I remember I used to say things like 'I want to speak English proper'. I think another reason was that when he was appointed to the post in London he didn't want to leave me alone in Germany.'

'Did you enjoy Marlborough?'

'Yes, I was lucky with my housemaster. He understood us boys - a wise chap – and we respected him. The last thing any of us wanted to do was disappoint him and letting him down was unthinkable.'

Von Hessler had never talked to Elizabeth about his childhood before, it felt strange. Then he realised why – only one other woman had ever shown an interest in his early life – Aunt Hilda.

'So where did you go to school?'

'A posh girls' school in Sussex, near Brighton.'

'Was it fun?'

'Sometimes. We got up to all sorts of tricks. Academic attainment was not so important in those days and I found myself in a high-spirited set – rather head-strong. That's where I developed a healthy disrespect for authority.'

They moved to the lounge and von Hessler ordered coffee. Knowing the evening had to end shortly, he sought to defer the moment.

'I feel like a brandy, Elizabeth – will you join me?'

'Hmmm … I think I need one tonight. It might help me to sleep.'

They sat together on the settee, talking for half an hour and then von Hessler escorted her to the lift and pressed the call button.

'I hope you sleep well, Elizabeth.'

'It has been a lovely day, Gerhard.'

The lift arrived but they just stood looking at each other. As the door began closing, von Hessler leapt forward to hold it open. Elizabeth walked in and then turned towards him. He blew her a kiss and the door closed. Aware that his heart was racing, he walked back to the foyer where he stopped irresolutely. Why had he held back at the lift?

Needing another drink, he headed for the downstairs bar but before he could order his drink a man accosted him - Hans Richter.

'Good evening, Freiherr von Hessler. How nice to see you again. Would you care to join me and my friend, Herr Mau?'

His breeding overriding his irritation, Von Hessler was all smiles, following the young man and being introduced to Mau, a potential *Elecktrodynamik* customer. Richter ordered von Hessler a large brandy. Mau was a keen sailor and the conversation centred on their various nautical exploits, though no mention was made of the events on Fehmarn Island.

It was some hours, and several rounds of drinks, later that von Hessler found himself standing alone and irresolute in the foyer. Drink-driving was not a sensible idea! He'd have to stay in the hotel for the night, room service would provide sleeping gear and an electric razor

Lying in bed, his mind kept returning to Elizabeth – what was she going to do? Yawning he dismissed the question, requested a call for 7am and switched off the light.

Morning. He showered and dressed quickly, then called the switchboard to enquire if Frau Elizabeth Schmidt had checked out.

'No, sir.'

'Can you put me through to her room, please?'

There was no reply.

Taking the lift down to the breakfast room he could see no sign of her so raced to reception and asked again if she had checked out. This time he got the answer he wanted! She had just booked a taxi. Figuring she was likely to be coming down in the lift, he hung around. Ah! There she is! The familiar figure one of a mêlée of people moving towards the reception desk where she handed over her key and indicated her bag to a porter. Then she saw him.

Von Hessler caught her look of surprise – almost shock. But she quickly recovered.

'Gerhard! I didn't expect to see you this morning.'

'After you'd gone, I ran into young Richter and another man in the downstairs bar and after a few rounds of brandies I decided it would be sensible to stay here rather than drive home. I hope you slept well.'

'Unfortunately not. I lay awake half the night.' She hesitated. 'Gerhard, my taxi will be here any moment. I was going to write but it's better if I tell you now.' She looked anxiously at him. 'I can't leave Klaus … I just can't.'

'I see'.

He took a deep breath and looked up at the row of shaded lights above the reception desk.

'I don't know what to say … I think you know …' His voice trailed off into silence.

They stood like statues, neither willing to meet the other's eyes.

The doorman called 'Frau Schmidt – taxi!'. which jerked them both out of their reverie. Elizabeth touched his arm lightly.

'I really must go.'

She walked the short distance to the door then turned towards him and he saw a look of anguish on her face. He lifted his arm to wave, but she had gone. The door revolved endlessly, a stream of strangers moving in and out, all with some useful purpose – in a totally different dimension.

He ate breakfast, though would have been hard pushed to say what precisely, then checked out of the hotel, returning to where he had left the Aston Martin. The grey concrete walls of the car park mirrored his mood: unrelieved drabness leading to a grey world. He sat in the car unwilling to start the engine, pulled out a road atlas and stared at the *autobahnen* map for West

Germany, at the A7 heading South from Hamburg towards Düsseldorf.

'Pointless!'

He'd probably never see the town again. Then he started the engine and, slowly at first, started north towards Kiel.

Why was she sticking to Schmidt? Does she still love him? Or is it because her marriage vows hold meaning for her – despite their invalidity? Her English idea of honour? Not kicking a man when he's down? What did it matter what the reason was? He'd lost her! He pressed his foot down on the accelerator.

Parking the car in the barn, he paced into the house and asked Frau Graubal for coffee. As he sipped it he was seized with the need to get out to sea again. Picking up the phone he rang local friends none were available. He stared into space, searching for inspiration. Anson! Was he still in Amsterdam? Within minutes, he had fixed up a sailing trip starting in ten days' time. With the vestige of a smile on his face, he went out to saddle Prinz.

When he got back, he learned that Frau Graubal had taken a phone call from Herr Doktor Hirn.

'I told him you were out riding.' She said.

'Thank you, I shall call him.'

Could he have discovered something?

'I'm sorry I missed your call.' He said smoothly once the usual greetings had been exchanged.

331

'No matter … you must come for lunch tomorrow, Gerhard.'

Von Hessler frowned, detecting a totally uncharacteristic hint of excitement in Hirn's voice. Even when Hirn had been announcing a critical intelligence breakthrough at an Abwehr briefing when lesser men would have permitted themselves a note of triumph, he'd been renowned for his steady monotone!

'I'd be delighted.' He said, waiting for Hirn to mention what progress had been made with the decoding, though the man merely said he looked forward to their lunch and hung up.

Trying not to think the worst, and lacking Hirn's patience with the hazards of country lanes, von Hessler took the main road to Kiel, stopping to purchase a bunch of carnations en route. He parked outside the modern apartment block that Hirn had acquired on his appointment as Professor in the Faculty of Mathematics and Natural Sciences and, disdaining to use the lift, he bounded up the wide marble stairs two at a time.

His host welcomed him, quickly joined by his wife, elegantly dressed in an oyster silk blouse and a shapely-tailored skirt. As von Hessler kissed her hand the perfume she was wearing recalled poignant memories - *Je reviens* had been Elke's favourite. Frau Hirn looked younger than he expected. They had last met in the Abwehr office in Treunbritzen twenty-five years previously when she was barely twenty. Now her blonde hair was darker and a few tiny lines spread lightly from the corners of her wide brown eyes but her face showed the same sparkling intelligence that he remembered though now underscored by a new quality of serenity. Much as when with Elizabeth, he felt uplifted in her presence.

Hirn showed him around the spacious apartment. In the library tiers of white painted bookshelves extended to the ceiling on three sides and the centre of the room was occupied by a low square table piled high with more books, many with slips of paper protruding.

'I haven't enough space!' Hirn complained, kicking at stack of academic journals that lay on the floor. 'I can't bring myself to throw any of them out, and still they come!'

Von Hessler walked slowly round the room picking out book titles at random.

'You've some serious stuff here, Manfred. The titles are quite intimidating. Any novels amongst them?'

'A few, I admit to having some Hermann Hesse and Thomas Mann. But many novels are time-wasters'!' He grimaced. 'Anyway there's already enough fiction in some of the academic journals I have to digest!'

The drawing room was light and airy, the floor covered by a 1960s' Scandinavian carpet in pastel shades of pink, sky-blue and grey. The walls were covered with a pale brown hessian and a fresh scent diffused through the room from a bowl of sweet peas standing on a side table.

'I say, where did you acquire these?' von Hessler asked as he surveyed the paintings hanging around the walls.

'They're Frida's,' said Hirn in a voice that conveyed a hint of envy.

Von Hessler walked to the centre of the room and stood silently contemplating a series of *avant-garde,* turn-of-the-century landscape and portrait paintings, mostly by Austrian artists. Finally he turned to his host.

'You've some exceptional works of art here, Manfred. In fact I've never seen a collection of such quality in private hands. I'm very fond of the Jugendstil period; there's a sense of liberation, new ideas, raw creative power in these paintings. How did Frida acquire them?'

. 'Her maternal grandfather lived in the Vienna of the Hapsburgs and was an avid collector - but he never bought any Klimts, unfortunately.'

'Well at least these survived the war, which is more than you can say for a lot of paintings. Where were they stored? '

'Not in Schloss Immendorf for sure.'

'Why do you say that?'

'You know the story?'

'No, I don't think so.'

Von Hessler noticed Hirn's anxious glance and his hesitation.

'Many of Klimt's works were held in Schloss Immendorf 'for safe keeping'. They were deliberately destroyed in 1945 by an explosives commando of the SS as they retreated from

Austria. The Schloss was set alight and the flames engulfed them.'

'Oh my God!' said von Hessler slowly enunciating each word. He walked over to the window and stared out at the distant view of the waters of Kiel Fiord. 'Then they must have been 'extracted' shall we say from Viennese Jews. Don't tell me any more – I've become severely allergic to the activities of Reichsführer SS Heinrich Himmler.'

'Well, perhaps we should leave him until after lunch.' Hirn said, peering over his half-moon reading glasses, his expression concerned. 'But have no fear, what we have to discuss this afternoon will do nothing to exacerbate your ...um ... your allergy!'

Von Hessler almost smiled at the idea of Professor Hirn in the role of Consultant Psychiatrist. But what was behind that vaguely comforting remark? Dare he hope?

Over lunch Hirn steered the conversation away from anything touching the decoding of letters and the talk wove an edgy way from student unrest to the escape of Andreas Baader from prison aided by Ulkike Meinhof, via the frigidities of the cold war.

After dessert they adjourned to the library for a demonstration of image superimposition employing twin epidiascopes. Von Hessler paid close attention as Hirn detailed his technique. Then they joined Frau Hirn in the drawing room for (in von Hessler's case) much needed coffee. Hirn opened the proceedings with a certain formality. He could almost be conducting an Abwehr briefing except that the chairs were comfortable and the coffee hot and delicious.

'Gerhard, I have avoided any discussion of your letters until now as it was Frida herself who made the final vital contribution, enabling the first message to be interpreted and its significance understood. So it's entirely appropriate that she should tell you herself.'

Frau Hirn's animated expression reminded von Hessler of an actress waiting for her cue.

'Splendid!' said von Hessler 'I'm all ears, Frau Hirn.'

'Well, as you know, Manfred originally asked me to have a look at the handwriting, partly because it seemed familiar and partly because I had experience of working with forged documents in the Abwehr. I think you'll be glad to hear that I've succeeded in identifying the writer of the letters.' She smiled mischievously. 'But first let me deal with the message content. For that we need the final result of Manfred's efforts.'

Von Hessler saw a trace of relief on Hirn's face. Was it because his wife had taken charge of the proceedings? Perhaps he was uncomfortable discussing the von Hessler family and their history. That would make sense if what was about to emerge would reflect badly or even discredit them. Hirn handed him a piece of paper on which the final decode had been written, relaxed back in his chair and crossed his legs. Von Hessler stared at the words, trying to make sense of them.

```
MY ARREST SOON
CLAUS FAILURE
FINIS GERMANIAE
CONTACT ONLY GREY M
HIMMLER RE PEACE NEGS
THANKS FOR MUCH HELP
ADIOS
```

'As you can see Manfred has confirmed his suggestion about the name HIMMLER and he's filled in the other gaps. Frau Hirn said, waving a finger at the paper.

Gerhard frowned.

'Am I right in thinking that this message is instructing my father to contact Himmler about peace negotiations?' He asked, relief flooding through him? 'Is that what it means?'

He looked across to see Hirn nodding at him. The thought pounded through his head: least it's nothing to do with the SS! Thank God!

'But who or what is GREY M ?' He asked.

'The context indicates a person, probably on a similar level to Himmler.' Frida answered. 'I trawled the literature covering the Nazi period and concluded it has to be Johannes Popitz, the Prussian minister of finance from '33 to '44, known within the government and by Hitler as, would you believe, *Grey Eminence.*'

337

Von Hessler noticed the not very well concealed hint of success in her voice. She was a chip off the Hirn block!

'You've done a fine piece of work there Frau Hirn – this man Popitz fits 'Grey M' nicely! What do we know about him?'

'This is where things started to get exiting for me - he was a prominent member of the civilian resistance circle that had formed around Carl Gördeler in the '30s.'

'Resistance circle!' von Hessler exclaimed. 'Could that be what this is all about?'

'I think it is highly likely.' said Frau Hirn. 'As you know there were such groups both in the army and among politicians and thinkers, mostly functioning independently. Popitz was an activist; it was he who proposed to Himmler that as the war was going so badly the SS leader should take over from Hitler.'

Von Hessler shook his head. 'That was an extraordinarily brave thing to do! I wouldn't like to have been in Popitz's shoes.'

'Of course, Himmler did nothing at that point but the circle disapproved of Popitz's idea and he was side-lined. However, the next part of his story is not so good.'

He could see the distaste in her face. 'Go on.' He encouraged.

Speaking quietly she continued: 'After the failure of the bomb plot to kill Hitler in '44, Popitz was arrested, tried by the People's Court in Berlin and convicted of being a conspirator. He was hanged in February '45.'

'God!' Von Hessler covered his face with his hands. 'I don't like to be reminded of those last months ... the killings by the SS, the discovery of what went on in the lagers, the mass graves – the knowledge will never go away. Never!'

'You're not alone in feeling that way, Herr von Hessler.' She said softly. 'I think it's – it's something that ...' She pursed her lips and left the sentence unfinished.

Silence followed. Hirn glanced questioningly at her. With a rueful look she went on.

'As you may remember Himmler later attempted to negotiate peace terms with the Western allies, possibly Popitz's idea encouraged him ... presumably this is why the writer is asking your father to keep in touch with both of them. As the writer seems to be unaware that Popitz had already been arrested, the letter must have written immediately after the failure of the bomb.'

Von Hessler stood up, walked over to the window and looked out into the distance for a few seconds.

'Well it seems clear that the writer was asking my father to continue working for an end to the war. That's an immense relief! I don't have to tell you that when Manfred first mentioned the name 'Himmler' it raised some unwelcome spectres ...' He hesitated '... and other things have just come to light relating to my father's

339

dealings with him and other Nazi leaders – I can't say any more.' He saw her concern but something about her eyes, with their large dark pupils had a calming effect on him. She seemed to accept his silence - it was all right. He went back to his seat.

'Shall we move on to the name CLAUS in the second line?' She asked. He barely heard her but nodded agreement. 'I'm sure you'll agree this can only be that brave man Claus von Stauffenberg. I think that here the writer is expressing his feelings about the failure of Stauffenberg's bomb to kill Hitler – it's 'the end of Germany'. Just two Latin words convey his stark despair. It's so sad.'

With an effort he focussed his attention and responded: 'A fine piece of intelligence work on your part, Frau Hirn. You've made sense of the whole thing.'

To mask his anxiety he helped himself to one of the petit fours from a plate on the table and sipped some coffee.

'But can you tell me who this mysterious writer is?.' He asked abruptly.

This time Frau Hirn allowed pride full rein. 'This will come as a surprise to you! It was Admiral Canaris.'

'Canaris!' He looked at her disbelievingly. 'You're absolutely sure?'

'Absolutely.'

He looked at Hirn whose face clearly endorsed her findings.

'Canaris ... of all people writing in code! Extraordinary!' Surprised delight lighting up his face, von Hessler found himself without words. He laughed. 'I'm sorry ... I need a minute to take this in. It casts a completely new light on my father's role ... he was helping the Admiral, the head of the Abwehr – not Himmler.' Exuberantly he went on. 'Do you know I've admired Canaris ever since I learned about his persistent efforts to frustrate Hitler more barbarous plans.'

'We loved him in the Abwehr, Herr von Hessler,' said Frau Hirn quietly. 'He was a gentleman. The discovery that he'd been hanged in Flossenberg lager just before the end was one of the blackest days for me. Dietrich Bonhöffer died with him, you know. Ten days later ... only ten days ... and the camp was liberated. It still brings tears ...' She stopped, and looked away.

This time her husband did not intervene to break the silence. Von Hessler reread the message letting its meaning sink in and then asked Frau Hirn.

'Have you looked at the other letters?'

'Yes we have, but none of them has the same interest. This one is unique in that it appears to be the last of the series. It was just chance that Manfred started with it.'

'What are the others about?'

'They're mainly about meetings of the circle led by Gödeler. Guarded references to plotters in the army - also warnings about woolly-thinking in resistance circles.' Hirn replied. 'They also indicate that your father was a link with diplomats abroad and used by both the Admiral and Popitz, presumably because he was not suspected by the Gestapo.'

'That's an interesting point. Working with the resistance would have made my father pretty nervous. I suppose that could explain why he carried a letter of authorisation from Himmler for his trip to Sweden. It must have worked like magic at the SS checkpoint when he boarded the S-boat.'

Hirn leaned forward. 'Frida, tell Manfred how you identified the handwriting.'

'I was fairly sure that I was looking for an important person, so I searched all the top-level archive material that I could get my hands on. Most of it was typed although I checked signatures, but so often they were just scribbles and hence of little use to me. I was getting nowhere but the feeling that I'd seen that hand before drove me on. I concluded it could only have been here at home or in Treunbritzen when I was working for the Abwehr. Getting sight of their material today is tricky as a great deal of it went abroad, but I had a curious feeling that the evidence was right here, at home. So I searched through boxes of old correspondence and what did I find? A card from the Admiral, in his own handwriting, addressed to Manfred congratulating him on the decryption of a signal from the British embassy in Moscow!'

'A clear case of Frida's intuition at work.' interjected Hirn.

His wife flashed a tight smile at him with the words: 'Manfred, let me finish. At once I saw that the writing was a good match though I had to produce evidence to convince my sceptical husband! The standard tests confirmed they were identical with a high level of confidence – enough to convince him I'm glad to say.'

Von Hessler tilted his head back and a broad smile spread across his face. 'I must say you've done a remarkable piece of work Frau Hirn, and so have you Manfred.'

Hirn gave him a wry look. 'If I'd been using even the low-grade intuitive powers allowed to us men, I'd have followed up my initial guess about that last word ADIOS and asked myself 'Who would naturally slip into Spanish? Who was a Spanish speaker? And of course at the top of the list would have been the Admiral. But damn-it, I never did. Ah well.'

'The answer Manfred is to form teams mde up with members of each sex.' Von Hessler grinned at both of them. 'A small team with one of each seems to work extremely well – particularly in your case!' He consulted his watch. 'However, my intuition tells me that you're both busy people and it's time I made my way home. I can't tell you how much you've relieved my mind with your utterly brilliant work and I'm eternally grateful.'

Hirn put the letters and decodes into an envelope and handed them to von Hessler. After more profuse thanks, they all shook hands. With a light step von Hessler ran down the stairs.

He drove home in thoughtful mood. Although hugely relieved that his father's reputation had emerged intact, a small insidious niggle remained – could he have been playing a clever game, backing both sides? After all, some people maintained that Canaris was doing just that with the Nazis.

But the image of Frida Hirn interrupted his thoughts. Why had he never married a girl like her?

Go on admit it! You let family pressure steer you away from girls like her ... girls who were not considered 'suitable' on social grounds. And they say the English are class orientated! The only one who never interfered was his aunt Hilda. All the others were too concerned about maintaining the family's position in society. The pressure had ramped up since the end of the war too, no opportunity was missed of reminding him that he was 'Gerhard Freiherr von Hessler' and that he had to 'behave sensibly'. Somehow the idea coalesced that lacking either parent to advise him he would choose an unsuitable woman.

His anger smouldered - that mind-set was formed in the 19th century – two wars had been fought and still they talked about 1870, Bismarck and the French.

Oh, they'd approved of Elke but her family had been even worse at interfering ... though perhaps it's unfair to blame them – she must have had a reason of her own for breaking off their engagement and marring that man, Georg. Brought up to consider her life's ambition to marry into the Hohenzollerns! He'd loved her – and at times it still hurt.

Frida Hirn had touched a nerve within himself. Was it fear? Fear of allowing genuine engagement with a woman and the risk of the relationship then being sundered?

The loss of his mother floated into his mind.

Then he saw again Elizabeth sitting beside his bed in Fehmarn hospital. She was like Frida, perhaps a little tougher. Other images floated back – Klaus and Elizabeth on his yacht *Jasmine*, then the meetings with her in the café in Tonhallenstrasse, in Düsseldorf airport and their walk along the banks of the Alster. A new determination arose in him. He was not going to let Elizabeth disappear out of his life.

The next day Frau Graubal brought in a thick envelope with a Düsseldorf postmark. The address label had been typed – not from Elizabeth then. He put it on one side with a grimace but eventually curiosity overcame him and he opened it. Inside he found a wad of letters. He picked up the top one. It read –

Dear Gerhard,

As you are no doubt aware I have concluded the deal with your English colleague. I enclose herewith the remainder of the correspondence found in the cartridge cases. I sincerely hope that we can now put the whole unfortunate affair behind us.

When the dust has settled perhaps you will give me a chance to explain how I was forced to attempt to sell the other letters that have now ended up in the hands of your colleague.

With greetings from your old friend,

Klaus

He read the letter again. Cold-blooded analysis showed Klaus was attempting to mend fences. On one level this was acceptable ... but Klaus' betrayal of Elizabeth stuck in his craw. How could he maintain a friendship with a man like that?

Idly, he glanced through the letters - mostly handwritten - and dated before the war. Many came from well-known *Schlösser* and big country houses. He flipped through them and picked out a few that looked interesting. Three contained vitriolic remarks about the Nazi hierarchy from respected public figures whom von Hessler recognised as members of the resistance circles around Johannes Popitz and Carl Friedrich Gördeler, the mayor of Leipzig. Two were partly favourable to the Nazis and several were sycophantic, even adulatory. A few originated

346

abroad from men such as Franz von Papen, Reich's ambassador in Ankara. But none had come from top members of the Nazi hierarchy.

He put them away for further reading and his mind turned to the one letter from Himmler that had been included in the pile handed over to Hutchison. It was just possible that Klaus had failed to notice it, but equally there was the niggling thought that he could have kept back similar letters as part of his 'insurance policy'. The Himmler letter could have been another of Klaus's warning shots across his bows like the previous one from Dönitz.

The questions went round and round in his head – had Elizabeth pressured Klaus into sending the new batch or was this a genuine attempt at reconciliation? According to Elizabeth, Klaus had not taken the Fuhlsbüttel negotiations too badly so maybe it was a genuine attempt.

He needed to be sure.

Furthermore he knew Hans Richter must have mentioned meeting him at the hotel. He wondered how Klaus would react to the news that he'd spent the night in the same hotel as Elizabeth.

He decided to put the matter to the test and rang Schmidt, ostensibly to thank him for the letters. Schmidt responded in a tone that was businesslike but not unfriendly, going on to explain that he was planning to be in Hamburg in two days' time. They agreed to meet for lunch in a little restaurant overlooking the Elbe.

On the appointed day von Hessler drove across to Blankenese and parked outside the restaurant which was situated halfway up the hill with continuous windows along three sides giving a magnificent view of a long stretch of the river. It was a warm June day with a gentle onshore breeze that carried in a faint aroma of the sea. There was no sign of Schmidt at the table reserved for them so he sat down to wait. A waiter produced the menu; he ordered a schnapps.

Schmidt arrived late, full of apologies. He seated himself, immediately broke a bread roll and started chewing it. He seemed unable to sit comfortably and he looked around the room glaring briefly at each group of diners in turn. A second menu was produced and during a jerky exchange of pleasantries they placed their order. Then, and only then, von Hessler offered him a chance to explain the financial problems that had led him to sell the letters.

'Ah yes! It all began, Gerhard, when I was discharged from the American PoW camp and found myself a job selling electric motors in Hamburg. I had a cousin in Düsseldorf who owned *Schmidt Elektrodynamik* which was in financial trouble. He asked me to lend him some cash, but after examining the accounts and talking to people I became convinced that the real problem was poor management, so I refused. Eventually he had to sell up and I bought the business. Of course I then had to base myself in Düsseldorf and that's when the trouble started.'

He broke off as waiters arrived with a spirit burner to fry the *steak au poivre* that they had both ordered. While the waiters worked, the two men watched the bulk carriers, container ships, and coasters moving in stately procession in and out of the port.

'This is a much more interesting river than the Rhine,' said Schmidt. 'I used to watch this scene when I was a boy. I even wanted to go to sea but my father sent me into the army.'

Von Hessler smiled. 'That's ironic! I wanted to go into the army but my father insisted on the navy. But go on with your story Klaus.'

'As you say, ironic! Well, that's when the trouble started. You see, Erda refused to come with me. At first, I'd be at the factory during the week and come back here to Hamburg at weekends. I used to ring her regularly as well, but increasingly I got no reply when I called. Her explanations for this varied – usually it was that she was visiting her mother in Lübeck. But I became suspicious and eventually discovered that she was having an affair. In short, she refused to give up the boyfriend so I bought a flat near Düsseldorf and moved there permanently.'

'I can't say I blame you.'

'I couldn't see that I had any choice. Our marriage was over, but, all the same, I made one last attempt to mend it. But it was no good and I told her that I was going to file for divorce. That's when she dropped the bombshell. Erda had discovered how I'd found the money to buy

349

Elektro.' He rubbed his chin and hesitated. 'I'm ashamed to admit it – I funded it from the sale of jewels I found in the two cartridges that I'd acquired in 1945. You can probably guess the rest - she threatens to expose me and demands an increase in her maintenance payments. And here's the crunch – no divorce.'

'God! Why? What was her reason?'

'You can well ask. I was dumbfounded. What could I do? I had to accept the situation and get on with earning some money. So, I buried myself in the job and it paid off. The business thrived. But of course Erda's demands for cash also increased. Then I met Elizabeth.'

Schmidt stopped and seemed to draw in on himself. For a moment von Hessler was concerned that he might be unwilling or unable to continue.

'Divorce was impossible – Erda just would not agree and she knew too much for me to risk it - I was near to despair. Then I met a lawyer from Lübeck at a social event and, to cut a long story short, he fixed the Standesampt for me. But that didn't help with Erda's ever increasing demands for cash.' Schmidt gulped down a mouthful of wine and spread his hands out. 'You know the rest of the story.' He leant back in his chair and brushed some crumbs off his jacket.

Von Hessler gently tapped the table with the handle of his knife and pondered how to respond. Quite apart from the failure of a marriage, it was a sad tale of cupidity and human frailty, but even so, he sought to understand

Schmidt's actions at a deeper level. He shook his head.

'It's terrible how one thing leads to another. It seems that they've just gone on getting worse for you.' He hesitated over his next question. 'How's it going to end?'

Schmidt looked strangely at him.

'By you stealing my wife! That's how it will end.'

Von Hessler picked up his glass. His eyes focused on the deep red of the Italian wine; he took a sip and then slowly and deliberately positioned the glass back on the table. Then in a level voice, he asked: 'Why do you say that?'

'I think you know why.'

He looked straight at Schmidt, a wry smile on his face.

'Klaus, I can guess! Hans has told you how we met in the *Vier Jahreszeiten*, and you're jumping to conclusions. Yes, I'd had dinner with Elizabeth but, once she went to her room, that was the last I saw of her that night. Let me tell you what really happened. I bumped into Hans, and his friend in the bar and we got through a fair amount of brandy! When they'd gone, I decided to stay in the hotel rather than risk driving home. That was the sole reason.' Sensing Schmidt's scepticism he added tersely. 'Let's get this straight, Klaus – nothing untoward took place.'

'Or at any other time?' snapped Schmidt.

'For God's sake Klaus, this isn't the dark ages! If Elizabeth and I meet for a few hours every now and then it doesn't mean we're having an affair! Surely, if she was going to leave you she'd have done it by now.'

'So you have thought about it?'

'Of course I have. Any dispassionate observer would ask the question - *Will she stay with him after finding her marriage is a sham?*'

'That rather begs the question doesn't it?'

'What are you getting at?'

Schmidt made a dismissive gesture. 'Let's cut out this fencing Gerhard. OK, I accept that you haven't threatened my marriage directly. But you ganged up with Hutchison even when you knew he planned to hit me with that doctored marriage record. And you did that because you wanted Elizabeth.'

Von Hessler saw the first small flush of colour spreading on Schmidt's cheeks, and felt every one of his aristocratic ancestors lining up behind him at this calumny.

'Klaus, I appreciate you want this to be an honest discussion, but getting angry is not going to gain anything, is it?'

Schmidt sighed 'You know me too well. OK, I'm angry. I admit it.'

'We're both angry, Klaus.' Von Hessler's voice could have cut steel. However, he busied himself refilling their glasses. The sun was shining through the windows and he was getting hot in the sun; the tables were packed closely together and the woman sitting at the next table was paying them too much attention. He threw a polite smile at her, sufficient to make her turn away before giving Schmidt his attention.

'You asked about Hutchison - there were a lot of reasons, not all of them altruistic, behind my 'ganging up' with him, as you put it.' He said quietly. 'But the chief one was to stop those letters getting into the wrong hands. My particular concern was with the ones that you've just sent me.'

Schmidt looked put out. 'I always intended to hand them over to you.'

Von Hessler could not let the remark pass. 'Until you realised they could be turned into cash!'

'Yes, damn you! It's obvious you've never been on the receiving end of ... shall we call them threats – you know the word I'm looking for.'

'You're quite right, Klaus, and I'm not being very sympathetic. I accept that you must have been desperate. What happens now?'

'It will finish when Elizabeth leaves me. causing Erda to lose most of her power over me.'

'Steady on Klaus! Why are you talking about her leaving you, for God's sake! There's no sign of her doing that is there?' Von Hessler glared at the man beside him. It was bad enough that she didn't want him, but to have Klaus going on about her leaving ... it was too much!

The seconds ticked by.

'I've brought it on myself. It's nothing to do with you and Elizabeth. Let's talk about something else.' Schmidt said in an almost inaudible voice, staring fixedly at a tanker pushing slowly upstream against the current.

Von Hessler watched him. There was a glazed expression on his normally animated face. They used to be such good friends.

'Klaus, you've been under severe stress. You need a break..' He paused, scouring his mind for an answer. 'Ah ... why don't you join Peter Anson and myself for a bit of sailing in next week?'

Surprise suffused Schmidt's face, ruefully, von Hessler had to admit that he was almost as surprised himself - the idea had come out of the blue.

'You're a real friend, Gerhard. I'd like that. But I'll have to look in my diary, is it all right if I ring you once I'm back in the office? I'd be delighted to join you.'

'And what may surprise you – I'll probably pick you up just a little downstream from here. I'm planning to get her here via the canal.'

'What could be better?' said Schmidt with a grin.

They left the restaurant together and Schmidt, in a hurry to get back to the Hamburg office, immediately drove off in his black Mercedes Benz. Von Hessler decided to take a stroll along the narrow twisting streets of Blankenese towards the river. The houses dotted over the hillside were built in a mixture of architectural styles - comfortable family residences dating from the early days of the Second Reich, old Frisian buildings with thatched roofs, interspersed with occasional modern houses sporting plain white walls and enormous picture windows. The absence of traffic and the relaxed holiday atmosphere soothed his spirit.

Round a corner he found a small café with tables set out on a terrace; it looked charming so he ordered an espresso and lit a cigarillo. From his seat the panorama of the sweeping bend of the river was even more impressive. As he idly watched the leisurely progress of the ships moving up and down the river, billowing white clouds drifted slowly across the blue sky intermittently obscuring the brilliant June sun. Slowly it dawned on him how much his unquiet mood was at odds with the tranquil scene spread out in front of him and he realised that the lunchtime conversation he'd had with Schmidt had actually resolved little or nothing. He still had no idea whether the real reason for Schmidt sending him the letters had been pressure from Elizabeth.

You dolt! In a stupid, impulsive moment of compassion you invited Schmidt to join the sailing trip … to share the confined living quarters of your 12 metre yacht! This is the man who's married to Elizabeth … the man who lied to her about her marriage; who reneged on his agreement over the salvaged letters and who had robbed the owners of part of the crown jewels of the Kings of Württemberg! What were you thinking! His first wife's disreputable behaviour cannot possibly excuse any of this. Furious with himself, Gerhard pushed the ashtray across the table and rested his head on his hands.

The scene of their encounter over the lunch table manifested in his mind and he saw again the anger on Schmidt's face. Then the image became indistinct as if the man had withdrawn to a distance to avoid scrutiny and had half turned his back. As he watched the scene darkened as a black cloud gathered overhead.

There was something unsettling about the whole thing. Bitterness welled up in him. The vision changed as a sudden bolt of lightning struck the distant figure of his erstwhile friend. Aghast, signified. Never! He forced the thought from his mind - it was just a daydream.

Quickly finishing the coffee, he hurried back up to his car and set off for home.

He went straight to his study where he immediately opened the big envelope, pulling out the contents and sorting them by country of origin and language. The biggest pile was in German and from within Germany, but while sorting through them he found a letter in English. It read :-

BUCKINGHAM PALACE

12 March 1936

My Dear Charles,
I have had a talk with Leopold and assured
him that I will do my best to calm the situation that
has arisen over the remilitarisation of the
Rhineland.
I read with interest your report of the last
meeting of the Anglo-German Fellowship. Do
maintain your efforts to work for a better
understanding between our two countries.
My best wishes,
David
[At the bottom a pencilled note in German
handwriting -]
Charles Edward Herzog von Saxe-Coburg und
Gotha - former English Duke of Albany.
Leopold – our ambassador.

Von Hessler whistled with surprise. The
letter's inclusion in the 'internal' correspondence
appeared to be a mistake by Schmidt, what other
explanation could there be? If the presence of the
Himmler letter in the batch sold to Hutchison had
also been a mistake then maybe he was being
unreasonable in suspecting Schmidt of having an
ulterior motive. The Palace letter was a valuable

357

historical document which should have been included in that first batch. As Hutchison had taken the trouble to send him the misplaced Himmler letter, von Hessler he decided to return the favour and send the one from the Palace, along with a covering note.

HAUS LANGENHORN
19 June 1970

My Dear Hutchison,

Much to my surprise I have just found the enclosed letter among a large batch of 'internal correspondence' that I have received from Herr Schmidt. I suspect its inclusion is a mistake on his part.

I am sending it to you as it clearly should have formed part of the 'external correspondence' that you recently acquired from him.

I have been led to believe that you more than achieved your aim of recovering this at minimum cost – in fact at no cost at all. Quite a remarkable outcome!

With my best wishes.
Yours,
Gerhard Frieherr von Hessler

The remaining letters were of less interest, revealing little that was not already public knowledge and confirmed that none had come from top members of the Nazi government. He replaced the letters in the envelope and turned his mind to the sailing trip with Peter Anson which for the first part would now include Schmidt.

Where should they go? He needed a complete break and had no wish to sail anywhere near Fehmarn Island. His weary mind turned to a plan he had formed several years ago – to travel via the Canal from Kiel and revisit the East Frisian Islands. The last time he had made that trip had been in his father's yacht before the war and he remembered the fascination he had felt for the bizarre landscape: the endless mudflats sliced by sinuous creeks marked out with tree branches stuck in the sandbanks at intervals; the wildlife: black ducks, silver seals; the sense of remoteness that engulfed the island and the strange language of the Frisian islanders.

Yes, taking advantage of the long daylight hours of June, the 58 nautical miles of the Canal could be traversed in a day under engine at, say, 6 knots, and still leave time to sail down the Elbe to Cuxhaven for the night. Enthused, he unrolled BSH chart 'Ems to Helgoland' and inspected the vast swathe of treacherous sandbanks and shoals that stretched from Cuxhaven along the length of the Frisian Islands westwards to the mouth of the river Ems. No wonder this area had required local knowledge in the days before the electronic echo-sounder! Even with an echo-sounder providing accurate depth figures and thus reducing the risk of running aground, it was going to be a challenging trip – much more interesting than the tideless Baltic, and with more exiting weather.

If Peter were to join his yacht at the Kieler Yacht Club, he could help load *Jasmine* with supplies for at least a week's sailing. Then Schmidt could join them at the other end of the canal at the lock at Brunsbüttel or at the port of Cuxhaven across the Elbe.

Chapter 11

Von Hessler arrived at the Kieler Yacht Club at five o'clock well ahead of Anson. The Club was a handsome white building of three storeys that dated from the reign of Kaiser Wilhelm II who had been the main driving force behind its establishment. Immediately in front of the clubhouse the yacht *Jasmine* lay tied up stern first against the quayside. She looked beautiful with her new design incorporating a gleaming white glass-reinforced plastic hull, an aluminium mast and stainless-steel rigging. No expense had been spared in fitting her out with two-speed winches, the latest instruments, ship-to-shore radio, and electric water and bilge pumps. She was not only beautiful but functional as well!

He was just carrying back a stack of cardboard boxes that he had unloaded into her storage lockers when he spotted Anson. Together they transferred more boxes, sailing gear and kitbags on board. Soon all was ready for departure.

'Peter, we'll need to get something to eat straight away. We start at the crack of dawn; small craft are barred from using the canal during the hours of darkness so I suggest we sleep on board. They don't serve breakfast in the club early enough anyway.'

'That's fine by me. What's the weather going to do?'

'It's not perfect. There's a depression north of Scotland and a cold front arriving here shortly. The outlook for this evening, when we plan to cross the Elbe is strongish winds, force five to six, south-westerly veering to the northwest as the front passes across. You'll be delighted to know that it's the worst possible direction, as the chaps in the club lost no time in telling me! It's a notorious area when the wind is against the tide and has been known to throw up some really nasty seas but there's no way that we can get down the Elbe except with the tide under us.'

'We'll just have to face it!' Anson said with a grin.

'As you say! Anyway with the wind slap on our nose we can forget sailing - we'll be under engine all the way . '

'How far is it from the lock at Brunsbüttel to Cuxhaven?' Anson asked, looked slightly concerned.

'About 18 seamiles.' Von Hessler replied. 'Don't mean to alarm you, but for some of the passage we'll have nearly three knots of tide under us, so if we motor at say 3 to 4 knots we should do it in 3 hours - always assuming we can keep up that speed in the face of those mountainous waves.'

'We can only hope the weather boys are being pessimistic.'

They moved to the club restaurant, perused the menu and ordered.

'Have I told you the tale of my great-uncle's escapade during the regatta here before the first world war?' asked Anson.

'Not that I can recall,'

'My great-uncle had a really short temper and lost it with the skipper of a German competitor who refused to give way despite the fact that my great-uncle was on starboard tack and thus had priority. So pulled out his pistol and fired some near-misses at the offending yacht.'

'Very un-English behaviour, my dear chap.'

'Quite,' said Anson, amused. 'It gets better! Once back on his moorings he was shocked to discover that the offending boat belonged to the Kaiser, and even more alarmed when he observed two German naval officers sitting ram-rod stiff in the back of a launch coming alongside. The two officers wearing the aiguillettes of royal equerries climbed on board, saluted and presented my great-uncle with a large envelope closed by a seal of magnificent proportions. He imagined it could only be a warrant for his arrest signed by the King-Emperor.'

'Was it?'

'Well, the two German officers gave nothing away and waited while he slit open the envelope. Inside was an invitation to dinner on the Royal Yacht!'

'What a lovely story!' von Hessler said laughing. 'You could dine out on that many a time.'

'I have,'

After a final brandy and cigar apiece, they repaired on board. Anson was allocated the port cabin and Von Hessler took the starboard. Schmidt was to board at Cuxhaven and given a berth in the fo'c'sle cabin which would provide more space for his bulky frame.

Von Hessler woke at dawn the next morning. Birds in full song were already celebrating the new day by the time he crawled out of his bunk and unshipped the door panels, slid back the hatch, climbed up into the cockpit, stretching his arms. There was a chill in the air and a film of dew covered the deck. Looking up, he noticed that the dawn-pink clouds were being driven across the sky by a wind ominously rustling the leaves of the trees behind the clubhouse. No doubt about it, once they were through the canal, it promised to be an exciting sail.

He dived back into the main cabin, switched on the electric pump and filled the kettle. The racket made by the pump was his not-so-subtle way of waking the crew. He dressed quickly and made a pot of coffee by which time Anson had emerged from his cabin and inserted himself sideways between the cabin seat and the table.

'What's it like out there?'

'Cold and windy.   The usual south-westerly. Quite a lot of cloud.'

He switched on the radio and the shipping forecast confirmed that the front was moving steadily east towards them.

At 0500 hours they slipped their mooring warps and motored the short distance to the entrance of the Nord-Ostsee Kanal at Holtenau. The smaller of the two locks was already open so they quickly put out fenders on the starboard side, and tied up to the floating pontoon. Apart from a coaster of about a thousand tons that had arrived before them there were no other vessels within the lock though a huge bulk carrier sat in the adjacent lock emitting the deep rumble of a big marine diesel engine ticking over. Slowly the lock gates closed behind them and water surged in. Once it was up to the canal level, the onward gates opened. They waited for the coaster to get clear of the lock gates. Ahead of them a 150 m wide span of calm water stretched away into the distance.

'Now for ten solid hours of engine. You take the wheel for now, Peter, and I'll get breakfast. Will ham and eggs plus some cheese do you? Keep her at six knots but if you see a vertical row of red lights flashing you'll have to stop to allow one of the big ones to negotiate a narrow stretch.'

The cross-country trip to Brunsbüttel began. Perched on the helmsman's seat, Anson ate breakfast from a plate balanced on his lap. Von Hessler came up with further mugs of coffee and sat down in the cockpit. The two men watched contentedly as the panorama of green and fertile land slowly wound past them. Cows and sheep grazed in the fields, but apart from an occasional farm worker there was little human activity to be seen at that early hour. However, after three hours the town of Rendsburg hove into view with its immense steel bridge carrying the railway high over the canal.

'I'd dearly like to stop here for a meal, Peter, but our timetable doesn't allow it. But I persuaded Frau Graubal to make a casserole of *Boeuf Bourguignon*; I popped it into the oven at Holtenau.'

'That's an inspired choice for lunch on a boat.'

'Well actually it's one of my favourites and she does it well. We have a standard routine, you know. She asks me for a half-bottle of burgundy to put in it so I produce a whole bottle – she asks me what she should do with the left-overs and I tell her it's for the cook!'

Von Hessler brought up the casserole, some crusty bread and bottles of lager, and they lunched in the cockpit.

'This is a magnificent stew,' said Anson. 'I'm glad we don't have to share it with Schmidt. I took him out to lunch the other day. That man has the most enormous appetite.'

'I'm glad to hear he's eating well. When was this?'

'Last week. He seemed happy enough about business prospects but I could sense that he wasn't his usual ebullient self at all.'

'That's one of the reasons I invited him to join us. Things are not going well for him.'

Anson looked puzzled. 'I take it you're not talking about the business?'

'No – he's got other problems.' Von Hessler saw a look of expectation on Anson's face. 'Sorry not to be more specific. Let's say it's domestic.'

'Oh dear. I thought he seemed a trifle evasive when I made polite enquiries about his wife's health.' He paused and then added. 'She's quite a lady.'

'Yes, she's quite a lady,' repeated von Hessler rather abruptly.

'They seem an unlikely pair. He strikes me as being a bit of a chancer, but she's moral to the core. '

'Have you done much business with him yet?'

'Oh yes. My chaps have closed quite a few deals with *Elektro*. Your introduction was very useful.'

The canal was now changing direction and heading south-southwest. Von Hessler stood up and looked at the wind vane at the top of the mast.

'There's no advantage to be gained by hoisting the sails even on this course. We've still got a westerly, damn it!'

The level countryside of Schleswig-Holstein provided few diversions and they regaled each other with sailing yarns and tales of adventures on the high seas. A large flock of swans resting on the bank eyed them with disdain. *Jasmine* overtook a little girl on a bicycle, but she immediately started pedalling furiously along the path trying to keep up with them. They were so impressed by her efforts, that von Hessler tied some loose cash in a plastic bag and threw it across to her as a reward.

They took two-hour turns at the helm. At 1500 hours von Hessler produced coffee and chunky biscuits but the cloud was thickening as the weather front drew nearer and they heard a distant clap of thunder. The wind increased and became squally with the threat of imminent rain.

At last the lock at Brunsbüttel came into sight. They refuelled at the Esso bunker station and waited for the white light that would signal permission to enter the lock. Impatient to start the next leg of the trip, von Hessler called up the control tower on VHF channel 9 to learn that they would have a wait of about ten minutes. Resigned to the delay, they stopped in the still water of the canal occasionally using engine to counteract drift caused by the wind.

'Oh well, that gives me time to tidy up below and make sure everything is well and truly stowed,' said von Hessler as he climbed down into the cabin.

A few minutes later, Anson called down to him.

'Gerhard, the wind has started to veer! It's almost a Westerly now and it's getting up.'

'What do the instruments say?'

'Fifteen knots,' replied Anson. 'Occasionally up to seventeen. It's a bare force 5.'

'I expect it'll be a good 6 by the time we get out into the river. Better get out the safety harnesses and lifejackets. The seas are going to be vicious. Let's hope it doesn't veer any more.'

'What's our plan B?' asked Anson in a subdued voice.

'Put into Otterndorf which is about 10 miles downstream compared with 18 to Cuxhaven. I've told Klaus I'll contact him if we have to change plans.'

'How long will it take him to get to Cuxhaven?'

'He reckons about 2 hours from his Hamburg office. He plans to leave at about six so we'll have to make the decision within the next hour or so. I'll get him on a linked telephone call through Hamburg-port Radio if I need to.'

At 1610 hours the flashing white signal light came on, and they moved into the smaller lock, made fast to the floating pontoon and switched off the engine. Dense, dark grey clouds now hung low over the river, heavy rain pelting down slanting across the lock. The temperature had dropped noticeably. They waited silently as the level in the lock slowly rose to match the Elbe

369

outside, now at high-water with the ebb beginning to run then the gates opened and they cast off into the choppy water with moderate wave heights. The far bank was barely distinguishable - a thin line separating grey water from the grey sky.

'It doesn't look all that bad,' observed Anson.

'Hmmm, maybe, but we're in the lee of the North bank where we are now. Wait until we get across the river. The only way to cope with the seas in the estuary is to take them head-on. They could easily roll us over if we take them on the beam, so we'll have to cut straight across and go down the inshore lane on the other side. That'll put both wind and waves dead ahead of us, assuming it doesn't veer any more.'

'Are you allowed to go down the other side? I thought we had to keep to starboard.'

'No, not here. The river's over 1¼ seamiles wide so the shipping lanes in midstream are used for the big stuff and they keep to the rules, but the inshore traffic is bi-directional.'

Von Hessler stared pensively at the scene ahead for a few seconds. 'God! look at all that shipping! It's like an autobahn! Getting across that lot's not going to be easy.'

He looked at Anson 'All set?' pushing the throttle lever forward; they headed out into the Elbe.

Once they had cleared the west mole protecting the canal entrance, the full force of the wind struck *Jasmine.* The ebb tide had started to run and the muddy brown waters of the Elbe were steadily getting rougher as rain squalls swept across the river. The yellow oilskins and red lifejackets of the two men stood out against the prevailing murk and, as they headed towards the shipping lanes in mid-stream, the yacht began to roll wildly in a sea that was almost abeam.

'It's a pity we can't get the sails up to stabilise her. This sort of motion is not my idea of fun,' said von Hessler.

'Why don't we?'

'I don't want the jib blocking my view. Those shipping lanes are too damn busy. Mind you with the sails up I suppose we might be more visible.'

'Why don't we dispense with the jib and just put up the mainsail? '

'You're right. Let's get it up.'

Anson removed the sail-cover, undid the sail ties, inserted a handle into the winch and slowly and laboriously hoisted the sail. They were now moving faster and drawing close to the edge of the downstream lane.

'This is beginning to look like Hyde Park Corner!' Anson exclaimed. 'There are ships going in three directions where the canal traffic merges. Do they get many collisions here?'

'I believe so.' Von Hessler grinned – 'probably as a result of trying to avoid yachts! But seriously - vessels over 50 metres have to report in by radio and are controlled by the River Authority. They watch them on radar. They'll pick up our radar reflector and if we do something stupid they'll send out a police launch and we'll be locked up – assuming we survive.'

The two men scanned the river assessing the course and speed of the merchant ships. Von Hessler throttled back as they approached one of the many red buoys that marked the edge of the downstream lane. Three cargo ships in line and close together forced them to turn into the wind and wait for a gap. Across in the upstream lane the grey shape of a tanker could just be seen through the rain. They guessed it was about a thousand metres away.

'I'm going in right behind the last of these three and then straight across in front of the tanker,' said von Hessler. 'Keep your eyes skinned.'

He opened the throttle, and to allow for its greater speed, altered course to aim just ahead of the third ship. As they moved closer their view of the tanker was obscured, though once *Jasmine* had passed tight under the ship's stern, the tanker hove into view again - it was now decidedly close. They were at the midpoint between the two lanes and von Hessler swung the wheel hard over, heading her straight down the middle of the river. The tanker gave a short blast on its hooter and swept past them. A few hundred metres behind it another ship was coming down. He swung the wheel over again and crossed the lane ahead of it.

'That tanker was a bit closer than I was expecting,' He said, half apologetically.

The two men grinned at each other.

Ahead of them lay 18 sea-miles of the notorious Elbe estuary. The boat's predominant motion changed from roll to pitch. With the wind against them Anson set about the task of getting down the mainsail. Standing on the cabin roof, clinging hard to the boom he gathered in the sail and managed to lace up the sail-cover. Choosing a moment between the assaults of the waves he clambered back down into the cockpit. In front of them angry and confused seas could be seen spreading in all directions out across the widening estuary. Steering demanded concentration from the helmsman, who apart from keeping clear of other vessels had to avoid the worst of the waves. The wind gradually veered northwards which, with an accelerating tidal stream, was an unfortunate combination, but they were maintaining satisfactory progress at about 6 knots over the ground. [1]

After half-an-hour Anson took the wheel and von Hessler went below to consult the chart.

He reappeared quickly.

'What's it like down there?' asked Anson.

'Grim. I haven't had a chance to get my sea-legs yet. It's too early in the season.'

'How are we doing?'

'OK. I estimate that we should reach our halfway point at Otterndorf in about an hour's

---

[1] 'Speed over the ground' is distinguished from speed thru' the water' when tidal flow is significant.

time. I'm told you can see its church spire above the dyke.'

'That's our bolthole isn't it? '

'Yes,' said von Hessler. He glanced quickly at Anson. 'I need to make that call to Klaus if we're going to put in there. How are you feeling?'

'I reckon I can cope with a few more hours of this. How about you?'

'I'm OK. More importantly, *Jasmine* seems to be holding her own. I think we'll make Cuxhaven.'

Conversation flagged as she pitched and rolled and fought her way downstream against the wind. Anson, perched on the helmsman's seat, gripped the wheel firmly with both hands while Von Hessler grasped a winch or any other fixed object that afforded him a handhold. Every now and then a freak wave would rear up like a mythical sea monster and crash down on the foredeck. But it was obvious that the height and spacing of the waves was increasing, becoming more threatening.

A wall of brown water would advance on the boat, so high that it appeared impossible for her to rise fast enough to surmount it, but somehow she did. Then she would pitch down and accelerate towards the next wave, level out in the trough, and come almost to a stop as the bow plunged into yet another wall of water. They hung on, almost mesmerised, as the cycle repeated relentlessly.

'There's the church spire! We're half-way,' shouted Anson suddenly.

'That should warrant a glass of schnapps, ' said von Hessler 'but I'm not sure I'm capable of carrying the bottle up here under these conditions - apart from the problem of pouring it out!'

'Let's wait until Cuxhaven,' said Anson quickly. 'The thought of a safe harbour will keep me going – just!' The effort of holding on during the violent pitching was beginning to tell on him.

'This sort of thing puts a big strain on the rigging even without the sails up,' said von Hessler as he grabbed the backstay for support. 'We're pushing it. But she's a well found boat.' He had no energy left to say more.

Little could be seen along the bank of the river behind the grass slope of the dykes protecting the low-lying countryside from inundation. Dark grey mudflats were beginning to appear above the water and the occasional duck could be seen waddling about hunting for worms.

Squalls of rain continued to add to the spray blown off the creamy white tops of the waves: the speed of the tidal stream had reached its peak. The force 6 wind had veered and was blowing from west-northwest straight into the mouth of the estuary, making the seas higher than ever. Conditions were extreme and they each took the helm in half-hour spells. Each time a wave came at *Jasmine* she seemed to bury herself a little more. The two men exchanged glances occasionally, wondering, assessing how the other was coping. An hour had passed when a freak wave advanced on *Jasmine*. Accelerating fast as she slid down the back of the previous wave she buried her nose in the new one, forcing an avalanche of water to crash along the deck, swamping the cockpit. She stopped dead.

Would she recover? For a few seconds nothing happened. Then, like a whale breaching, she rose. Water poured off the decks draining back into the river, the self-draining cockpit slowly emptied, and she started to move ahead.

'We need to slow down,' von Hessler shouted as he eased back the throttle. 'We don't want any more of that!'

They pounded on, meeting wave after wave in regular succession. The North Sea now extended almost right across the horizon, the far riverbank, several miles away, now only dimly visible. At this point the deep water channel ran close up against the dyke which was protected by groynes reaching out into the river. Behind the dyke they spotted a squat stone light-tower painted white with a black top.

'That must be Altenbruch,' said von Hessler. 'It means there's a mere three sea-miles to go.'

'A mere 45 minutes,' parrotted Anson.

Gradually the dock cranes of Cuxhaven hove into view and the *Jasmine* ushed her way past the Amerikahafen, then the two Alten Hafen. At last they swung in by the three posts that marked the southern side of the mouth of the Jachthafen, and calm water.

'We've made it,' grunted Anson as they found a slot amongst the yachts on one of the pontoons and tied up. It was just after 2200 hours. Both men sat down in the main cabin, cold and exhausted.

'My God! I'm glad that's over.' said von Hessler. 'How about that schnapps?'

Anson nodded. He pulled out the bottle and filled a couple of small glasses. In a minute they were empty.

'Let's have another,' said Anson.

'Sorry about the small glasses,' responded von Hessler as he refilled them.

After changing into shore clothes, they set off to meet Schmidt at the yacht club. But when they got there they were told that Herr Schmidt had phoned to say he would be late. Leaving a message for him, they walked up over the dyke, along a street lined with old red-brick houses with Dutch gables, found a restaurant and enjoyed a large meal.

Schmidt appeared as they were returning to the boat.

'My dear Klaus - Welcome to Cuxhaven,' said von Hessler as they shook hands.

'What sort of a trip did you have?' asked Schmidt. 'The club told me it was bloody rough out there. In fact they were surprised that you hadn't cancelled.'

'Yes, we had a tough time of it. We're both damn near exhausted. Have you eaten?'

'Oh yes. They brought me something in the office. Sorry I'm late but I had to wrap up a deal and it took longer than expected.'

'That's okay. Now, plans for tomorrow - we need to be up early. High water's at 0517 and we leave as soon as the ebb starts. Peter and I are heading straight for our bunks. You're in the fo'c'sle with plenty of space, Klaus, so you should be comfortable.'

Daylight was fading as they climbed on board. Around them the sound of wind whistling through yacht rigging made a tuneful counterpoint to the roar of breakers crashing against the harbour walls and the low rumble of heavy shipping not far offshore. In the west, blue sky emerged as grey clouds now tinged with pink retreated over the mainland. In the boat the three men wished each other Good Night and crawled into their sleeping bags.

The alarm rang at 0530 hours by which time a brilliant sun was rising over the misty estuary, a fresh breeze blowing in from the west and the blue sky dotted with white clouds promised a pleasant day. The noise of the breakers had moderated although the air was filled with the squawking of gulls circling around as the boats of the fishing fleet chugged out to sea.

On *Jasmine* hardly a word was exchanged as the crew made themselves ready and prepared the boat for the day's sailing. They let go the

378

mooring warps, von Hessler reversed her down between the rows of yachts tied up to the pontoons of the Jachthaven and out into the estuary.

'Right Gentlemen, now we're all awake, I'll give you the plan for today.' He said brightly, refreshed after his good night's sleep. The intention is that we motor downstream keeping close to the training wall. The wind will be against us until we reach the end of it but then we'll get the sails up and head across to the Islands. The wall stretches for nearly seven sea-miles off the tip of the land here though we should be clear of it in an hour as we've got the tide under us. I'm hoping that things will be a bit calmer when we get into the lee of one of nearer islands, either Scharhörn or Neuwerk, and, if so, we drop the hook and I'll cook up some breakfast. Any questions?'

'Yes Captain,' said Schmidt 'who is our navigator?'

'Well Klaus, if you're thinking of volunteering I have to warn you that it's going to be a tricky business. We'll be threading our way across mudflats along narrow twisting channels that are hidden below water and often unmarked. Some are marked by withies planted at intervals but they're not always reliable and this is an odd bit - if the branches are upright like normal saplings then they're on the northern side of the channel. If they are bent downwards then they mark the southern side.'

'And what happens when the channel runs north-south?' asked Schmidt with a chuckle.

'Good question. You have to know the direction of buoyage which is shown on the chart. If heading north in the direction of buoyage then the withies are on the west side. OK? You can forget the compass – the only things that matter hereabouts are the echo-sounder, a good pair of eyes and a well-developed intuition. It's really quite easy. Any more questions?'

'It sounds to me that the chances of running aground are about one hundred percent,' remarked Anson. 'How much do we draw?'

'Just under a metre. She's got twin keels so we've a good chance of staying upright if and when we do run aground. '

'OK. Volunteering is postponed until we've studied the chart,' said Schmidt with a broad smile. 'If it looks really difficult then it's a job for the English Navy,' He emitted a deep guffaw.

'Oh no,' replied Anson, 'that's a German chart you've got there. Soundings are in metres. I'm a fathoms man. Can't think in metres.'

'I have a feeling,' said von Hessler, 'that there's some buck-passing going on here! I'll navigate for the first hour, Peter you do the second, and Klaus does the third. You take the helm now, Klaus, if you would.'

Although the seas had moderated overnight no-one felt inclined to spend any length of time down in the cabin studying the chart. They followed the curve of the training wall built to force the current to scour a channel through the vast area of silt deposited by the river. The early morning mist had cleared and in the middle distance they could see a gaunt black shape standing on the island of Neuwerk - a substantial brick-built light tower constructed in 1300 by the town of Hamburg and the oldest surviving building. They passed close by a rescue beacon planted in the water covering the mudflats and surmounted by a steel cage.

'What the devil's that?' asked Anson.

'That's for walkers caught by a rising tide,' replied von Hessler. 'They climb up those rungs welded to the sides of the pole and take refuge in the cage.'

An hour had elapsed by the time they approached the shallow water covering the Mittelgrund mudflat at the end of the training wall. Von Hessler surveyed the sea ahead with binoculars.

'I think you'll have to give Mittelgrund a wide berth to the north before we turn south. I can see breakers on the far side.'

He handed the binoculars to Schmidt.

'Agreed,' he said after surveying for himself. 'They look rather nasty.'

However, despite their attempt to evade them, the waves sweeping towards the northern end of the mudflat mounted rapidly in height and gave them a rough time.

'This is what we had yesterday, Klaus. But we'll be out of it soon. I'll have a look at the chart and tell when you can start altering course.'

Von Hessler returned to the cockpit and checked the buoys and beacons in the surrounding waters. After several minutes he gave the nod and they swung round into the calmer waters in the lee of Scharhörn Island and headed almost south.

'The channel we want is coming up. See red spindle buoy over there with a can on the top? It's a Weser-Elbe channel marker. They run from 32 down to 26 in even numbers. This one's marked WE32. Can you see it?'

'Yes, I've got it,' replied Schmidt.

'OK. When we reach it, bring her up into the wind and we'll get the sails up.'

They passed the buoy. Schmidt brought her up and throttled back while Anson winched up the mainsail and von Hessler unfurled the jib. Then with the engine switched off and the wind on the beam *Jasmine* headed south – southeast, sailing fast down the channel.

'When we reach WE28 we'll be in shallower water. It'll be calm enough there and I'll get breakfast.'

'It's great to get under sail,' said Anson. 'I've had enough of that engine.'

They passed WE30 and closed on WE28.

'How much depth have we got, Klaus?'

'Two metres.'

'OK, chaps. If you go for the west side of the channel, I'll drop the hook.'

Von Hessler went forward and started to free the anchor chain as Schmidt brought her up into the wind. Suddenly, above the flapping of the

382

sails he heard an ominous sharp crack and, from behind him, came a sound like the swoop of an enormous predatory bird. With a violent thud the mast crashed down onto the cabin roof, the hull shuddered with the force of the impact.

Horrified, Von Hessler swung round to see the deck swathed in white sails - for a second it looked just like a shroud and his heart sank - there was no sign of either man in the cockpit. Quickly heaving the anchor overboard, he carefully picked his way aft over the tangle of sails, halliards and rigging but it was only furiously wrenching away the mainsail that he managed to reach the cockpit in the ruins of which he could just see the two men - lying on the floor. Anson was starting to move but Schmidt lay motionless immediately under the mast. Von Hessler helped the confused and white-faced Anson to his feet.

'Are you all right?'

'Yes … just dazed … what happened?' He collapsed onto a seat, his eyes on the fallen mast. He swallowed. 'That was a near thing!' Then the prone figure of Schmidt took his attention. 'Oh God! he's bleeding! Gerhard, his head's bleeding!'

'I'll get the First Aid kit. You okay for a moment?'

'Yes, yes … I'm just shaken and a bit bruised. Are we anchored?'

'Yes. I let it go. With any luck it'll bite.'

Von Hessler hurried off. After a moment, Anson started trying shift the boom and the tangle of rigging; he got down beside Schmidt.

'Klaus!' He called, but there was no response. 'Klaus! Can you hear me? God! The blood!'

Von Hessler climbed up the cabin steps carrying a red box and a Nautical Almanac. He handed the Almanac to Anson. 'Is he still out?'

'Yes'

'Look up the First Aid section. We may need it.' He got down beside Schmidt. 'Hell! He's bleeding a lot. I'll get him into the recovery position first.'

'Is he breathing?'

'Yes, he's still breathing. God! He weighs a ton! I can't shift him on my own; give me a hand, will you?'

The two men turned him on his side, shoved a folded towel under his head and covered him with a sleeping bag. They stood up and exchanged an alarm glance.

'I'll try and get a bandage on him,' said von Hessler. 'Anything to stop the bleeding!'

Anson gently supported Schmidt's head while he wound the white fabric around and around, fastening it with a safety pin.. They stood up, hands and knees covered in blood. Von Hessler sighed 'You clean up. I'll stay with him.'

'We ought to radio for help,' said Anson as he climbed back into the cockpit.

'Not a chance. The aerial's damn-all use on the end of a horizontal mast. We'll have to get ashore.'

He went below, dropped into the navigator's seat and studied the chart.

'Peter, you won't believe this! There's a seaman's hospital right on the coast. It's about three miles away. We should be able to get pretty close before running aground. Let's have those sails out of the water and we'll make for it.'

They pulled and wrenched and hauled and finally reduced the deck to something like order. The mast was shifted to one side to clear the wheel, and lashed down.

'That's the best we can do,' said von Hessler. 'If you motor us up to the anchor, I'll get it up.'

He went forward and furiously hauled in the chain.

'We're free!'

Anson swung the wheel over, headed *Jasmine* towards the next channel marker WE26, and grabbed the chart.

'There's a tiny channel leading off from the end of this one, but it's not marked with withies. I'll feel our way up with the echo-sounder.'

'OK,' said von Hessler. 'I hope to God we're going to get close enough. He could have a fractured skull. What a bloody shambles!

'It's not your fault. Any idea what caused the mast to fail like that?'

'I've just had a look - the forestay deck fitting's failed. It must have been weakened by the pounding she took yesterday. What was Klaus doing when it came down? He obviously didn't see it coming.'

'I don't think he did. I think he was looking back at the buoy, presumably checking the current running past it.'

As they moved steadily along the channel they watched the depth reading fall, forcing frequent course changes and reducing speed as it narrowed. They were close to a refuge beacon when they finally ran aground.

'I'd say we're about a mile offshore,' said Anson as he switched off the engine.

Von Hessler examined the coast with binoculars.

'It looks an easy enough walk. I think it's sand rather than mud and we're in less than a metre of water. I've got the longest legs so you stay with Klaus and I'll go raise a stretcher party. I should be back in less than an hour and she'll be dried out long before that.'

He lowered the swimming ladder from the stern, climbed down into the water and set off.

Anson watched him as he plodded towards the shore. Deep soft mud would have slowed him up but he was making good progress. The chart showed a marked footpath nearby leading to the island of Neuwerk which implied that the going was firm. He bent down over Schmidt.

'Don't worry, old chap,' he said in a loud voice. 'Help is on the way,' and wondering if the unconscious man could hear him. He watched his slow but regular breathing for several minutes then, after dropping the anchor, he went down into the cabin and rummaged through the food lockers for something to eat.

Periodically he checked to see that Schmidt was still breathing relieved to see that the vivid blotch of red blood on the bandages had at last ceased spreading. As predicted, the ebb continued and before long the boat was high and dry. After forty minutes he heard shouts and looked up to see a wagon drawn by a pair of horses approaching, crossing the sand on four rubber-tyred wheels. It drew up alongside *Jasmine* and von Hessler climbed on board followed by a young hospital doctor who after a brief examination announced that the casualty needed immediate admission to the main hospital in Cuxhaven. A stretcher was produced and Schmidt was lifted gently onto the wagon.

'I'll go back with them and ring Elizabeth,' said von Hessler. 'But hang on, the tide won't come in again for another three hours, so why don't we both go?'

They climbed up onto the wagon which set off across the smooth surface, sometimes sand varying from light fawn to dark brown, sometimes dark grey mud with a sheen of iridescent violet. Clumps of wiry seagrass sprouted at intervals around scatterings of sharp-edged shells and small pools of water where brown seaweed grew.

Schmidt lay motionless on the stretcher buy as soon as they reached the shore the doctor hurried off organise an ambulance. Once inside the accident department of Cuxhaven hospital, Schmidt was wheeled away for immediate x-ray.

'Once I have called Elizabeth and explained what's going on, we'll have to shift the boat to somewhere less exposed. There's a fishing port at Spieka-Neufeld about 6 miles from where we left her. That should do us.'

'OK by me,' said Anson.

Von Hessler made the call but returned looking pensive. 'She wants me to ring again as soon as we know what the situation is. She's planning on driving up here'

The two men sat down in the bare waiting room. A little later a serious-looking doctor came in to announce that the X-ray revealed no evidence of cranial fractures.

'The patient has been moved into a room, but he's not regained consciousness, and I have to say I am concerned.' He said.

Von Hessler rang Elizabeth again. She decided to leave immediately and asked him to book a hotel room for her. She thought the drive would take her about 4 hours.

'There's nothing more we can usefully do here, Peter. Let's get a taxi back and move the boat as soon as she's afloat. I'll leave a note at the desk here to tell Elizabeth what we're doing.'

Arriving back at the shore they climbed the dyke and stood for a moment surveying the scene. In the distance they could see rivulets and creeks running down from each side of the watershed that marked the highest points of the ground between the coast and the island of Neuwerk. Over the horizon breakers pounded the mudflats but the only sound that reached them was a faint hissing. In the distance, merchant ships, their hulls partly below the horizon, moved imperceptibly, like beetles crawling over the land. The day's on-shore breeze was now well established and wafted a rich marine odour over them as they set off across the flats. It was very peaceful, a few ducks pecked intermittently at the sand and, further out, a pair of seals basked in the sun.

It was past 10 o'clock by the time they boarded *Jasmine* ; the water had just reached her and was beginning to rise up her keels.

Von Hessler produced a large breakfast while they waited for the tide to creep in. Once they were afloat, it took less than an hour's motoring for them to cross the watershed and, heading for the fishing port, they were soon tying up to one of the jetties in its little harbour.

'I am so sorry for all this, Peter. It's not what we intended at all! Obviously Klaus won't be rejoining us so I think the best plan will be to get *Jasmine* to Bremerhaven and have the mast fixed. According to the chart there's a Weser-Elbe route across the flats that's marked with withies. We'll reach the watershed after about 6 miles and should just be able to cross it provided we can get out of Spieka-Neufeld before high water. After that it's 14 miles along the Weser up to Bremerhaven. Are you up for that?'

'Oh yes, I'll stay on. What about tonight?'

'Well we … I don't want to leave Elizabeth here on her own. Let's see how Klaus is getting on.'

They walked into the village, rang for a taxi to take them back to the hospital and were shown into the patient's room. Schmidt's head was heavily bandaged and dark bruises had appeared on his face; he looked terrible. Reassuringly, the heart monitor displayed a regular pulse.

'If he shows any signs of coming round, call me.' The nurse said firmly before leaving the room.

Von Hessler looked at his watch.

'She should be here soon.' He drummed his fingers on the arm of the chair. 'What bloody bad luck! Still, at least his skull is intact. He must have a tough one – like the rest of him.' Restlessness seizing him, he rose. 'I'll see if I can find some coffee.'

Five minutes later he returned to find Anson and a nurse leaning over the patient. Anson looked up.

'He's coming round,' and then surreptitiously nodded his head towards the door. As the two men reached the corridor he continued. 'Schmidt started saying something when he heard Elizabeth's voice.'

'She's arrived? Where is she?'

'I don't know,' said Anson with a puzzled expression. 'Whatever it was he said obviously upset her; she just walked out.'

'What did he say?'

'I couldn't make it out – he repeated a word I 'm not familiar with, something like Edda or Erda. He was almost shouting.'

'Oh Lord! What else did he say?'

'After he'd opened his eyes he kept saying 'Why? Why?' in an aggressive fashion, but that was after she'd left the room. I couldn't make out whether he was asking why Elizabeth had disappeared or was just rambling. Anyway I simply said 'I don't know'. He seemed reasonably compos mentis and he asked where you were and I said you'd gone off I search of coffee and that seemed to agitate him even more.'

'I think I'd better find her,' said von Hessler.

He hurried down the stairs to the entrance hall and asked reception if Frau Schmidt had left the building. The receptionist was unsure but said that a lady in a camelhair coat had just asked her for a cigarette and had gone outside. Out in the car-park he quickly spotted her sitting in her red Audi, smoking. Undecided what to do, he stood some distance away and waited. Before long she got out of the car again and headed back towards the entrance.

'Elizabeth!' He called. She stopped and turned towards him; he'd never seen her so tense. 'I'm so sorry, Elizabeth. Peter told me what's just happened.'

'I can't bear it Gerhard. I thought I had something left to cling to, but …'

'I know what you're thinking but I wonder if … if you're wrong. For what it's worth, according to Peter, after you left Klaus called out 'why', twice, very angrily. Peter thought he was rambling as he's no idea who Erda is and couldn't understand why Klaus was so angry. I reckon it was because of her treachery.'

'Let's go back to the car,' said Elizabeth. 'We can't go on talking out here.'

They walked to the Audi. 'You're very kind, Gerhard. You don't have to defend Klaus. Anyway what precisely he meant is irrelevant. I'm sure he knew I was in the room. Did you get me into a hotel?'

'Yes. It's a decent one, so they tell me, in the town centre. .'

'What are you going to do?'

'I've got to get the boat to Bremerhaven for repairs. For the moment it's in a little fishing port along the coast. What are you going to do?'

'Wait until he's fit to travel and then, I suppose I'll take him home.'

He noted a hint of resignation in her voice.

'Shall we go back in and find out what the doctors think, now he's come round?'

'Yes – we'd better.'

The consultant was taking a cautious view, concerned about the danger of a haematoma developing inside the skull – a swelling due to internal bleeding which could press on the brain. They would need to keep him in for several days.

'Does that change your plans?' Gerhard asked Elizabeth.

'Yes … I'll probably go stay with friends near Hamburg. Klaus has plenty of relations up here so between us we can keep him amused. When are you leaving?'

'On the first tide out of Spieka-Neufeld. The harbour dries out so we can't get away until an hour before high-water. That means sailing at about five in the morning.'

'Do you have to take the first tide?'

'Yes, I'm afraid we do. It's a 20 mile trip to Bremerhaven, a lot of it across mudflats. It's not a major problem if we run aground in daylight but if we leave on the second tide and it happens after dark we'd be in trouble - we've lost our riding light. It was at the top of the mast along with the ship-to-shore aerial.'

'So what will you do tonight – sleep on board?'

'We'll have to. But we'll join you for dinner in the hotel if we may.'

'Yes, of course.'

They returned to the room and sat talking to a rather dazed and confused Schmidt until the nurse drove them out. In Elizabeth's car they travelled to the hotel and after dinner she drove them back to Spieka-Neufeld, claiming she wanted to see *Jasmine* in her dismasted state. The light was fading as they walked down to the little harbour and the boat looked rather sad, lying on the dark grey mud at the end of a row of fishing boats, their hulls painted in bright colours, blue, red, white and sometimes black. The sea had retreated far out to the horizon and the withies marking the seaward channel stood planted in the mud, stark and forlorn. Only a trickle of water remained winding its way down between the boats and the other side of the harbour. Even the gulls had given up for the night and found themselves safe perches. The gentle sea breeze that carried ashore a complex odour of marine decay slowly died away.

Elizabeth shuddered when she saw the smears of blood on the cockpit floor. She looked round the main cabin – and commented that it was not so very different from her parent's yacht in which she had sailed after the war - before collection Schmidt's bag and belongings and climbing back up onto the jetty. Anson stayed on board while von Hessler escorted her back to the car.

'I'm so sorry that I can't stay here with you Elizabeth but I can't abandon Peter after having promised him a week's sailing and then putting him through all this.'

She looked at him and silently nodded her understanding.

'I would have liked it if you could have stayed … I … I want you to stay. But life is up to its tricks again. Klaus's first words were an awful shock. It made me realise what a fragile thing is trust, once it is broken ….' She sighed. 'The past looks different now. I find myself asking what all those expensive bunches of flowers meant … but I mustn't burden you with my miseries.'

'Isn't that what friends are for?'

'You're more than a friend, you know that.'

She turned towards him; their eyes met and for a long moment they just stared at each other. H

Gently, he wrapped his arms around her, just holding her close … an eternity passed before she quietly disengaged herself.

'I'd better go.'

Without a word, she got into the car, they waved to each other and she drove off.   It was getting dark now and he could see the lights in *Jasmine's* cabin as he walked back to the jetty, his heart soaring.   How was he going to sleep? Grinning at the thought, he lit a cigarillo, sat himself on one of the wicker baskets littering the jetty and gazed at the red clouds on the horizon as they darkened above the thin line of the coast of Ostfriesland.   A wisp of a musical note danced across the mudflats on the soft breeze – it was a magical evening.

During the night the sea began its slow advance, reached Spieka-Neufeld and started to flood into the harbour. Von Hessler woke to the sound of water lapping against the underside of the hull. Quickly climbing out of his bunk, he dressed, and emerged into the cool morning air.   It promised to be a beautiful day.

Full of energy, he leaped ashore and headed towards the village.   Although the dawn had barely broken, already fishermen were loading their gear and sounds of their activities inside the long grey sheds of the fishery that lay behind the dike filled the air. In the village he came across a van delivering bread and milk. He bought both and carried them back to the boat.

One by one the engines of the fishing fleet burst into life. It was time to leave. Anson and von Hessler cast off and for about a mile followed the closely-spaced withies marking the creek that led from the harbour. Once in deeper water, they swung off to port and after a further two miles picked up the withies that marked the route of the *Weser-Elbe-Wattfahrwasser* which would lead them to the river Weser. The tide was ebbing as they nervously crossed the *Meyers Legde* watershed with less than 30cm of water under the keels and it was with relief that they headed for the river with no further hazards to face.

A moderate breeze blew from the west setting up innocent wavelets in the Weser estuary. They hugged the port bank to avoid the worst of the tide and arrived at the southernmost basin of the port of Bremerhaven a mere five hours out from Spieka-Neufeld. Tying up on the pontoon at the mouth of the river Geeste so they could obtain some local advice, they locked into the Schleusenhafen, then motored round into the Hauptkanal and through the swing bridge into the yacht harbour tying up near the Weser Yacht Club.

'Not a hope of getting it fixed in under two days.' The chief rigger said, shaking his head after inspecting the damage.

Von Hessler grimaced, this would leave only a day's sailing before the week was up. After discussing their options and deciding exploration of the Frisian Islands would have to wait, they left *Jasmine* in Bremerhaven, packed their sailing gear and returned by train to Kiel. With mutual feelings of regret, they parted and Anson returned to Amsterdam.

The report from the hospital was good - the patient was recovering well, demanding to be discharged with 24 hours. Von Hessler's eyebrows raised at this news, though he wasn't surprised. Doubtless Schmidt would be back at work in a day or two.

Should he write to Elizabeth? No, putting his feelings on paper was difficult – and risky. After their recent conversation he didn't want to excite Schmidt's suspicions - and he recognised that he was no good at dissimulation. He'd phone her. The two days passed slowly; he spent the time engaged in some of the more inconsequential social activities that he usually avoided.

The phone rang. He waited. Willi answered.

'May I speak with Frau Schmidt, please?' He asked, giving his name.

His heart pounding, again he waited.

'Gerhard, I was going to ring you.' Schmidt's voice boomed down the phone at him.

'You're back on terra firma now? What have you done with *Jasmine*?'

'Yes, I'm home.' Von Hessler said, disappointment churning. 'Jasmine? She's in Bremerhaven being fixed. But how are you? Not at work?'

'Good Lord no. I can't …. I can't appear swathed in bandages like this. Once the stitches are out next week, so they say, I'll be back in the saddle.' He paused and it was a good few seconds before he went on. 'Meanwhile I'm here, working from home … which of course irks Elizabeth.'

'How is your head now? You had us worried for a while there!' He didn't sound like his usual self – was concussion still affecting him?

'Occasional throbbing pains – nothing serious. Don't worry about me. But as you've called, I can tell you … um … there's an invitation on its way to you. Earlier this year I booked a … a shooting lodge near Hanover. Hoping you … um … can join us for a few days. It should reach you tomorrow, I think.'

'That sounds an excellent idea. It's probably safer than sailing! I'll look forward to it.'

'Here's Elizabeth … I'll say goodbye for now!'

No, Schmidt definitely did not sound like his usual self. It was a long half a minute before Elizabeth came to the phone.

'Gerhard, nice of you to call.' She said in a guarded voice.

'I was wondering if we were going to be able to talk - I presume not.'

'How is *Jasmine*? Have they done the repairs?'

'Yes. She's ready to sail again but I don't know how soon that will be. How are you?'

'Oh I'm fine. Did Klaus mention the shoot?'

'Yes. He said an invitation is on its way to me. Will you be there?'

'That rather depends on who accepts.'

'Well, I shall accept.'

'Good. Well, thank you for ringing Gerhard. Don't worry about Klaus. He's mending fast. Auf Wiederhören.'

'Auf Wiederhören.'

He put the phone down slowly wondering just what was going on between Klaus and Elizabeth, neither sounded normal. Would tensions surface during the shoot? Worrying.

A few days later, just as he was setting off for the shooting lodge near Hanover, a letter arrived from Bonn. Inside was a pale buff complements slip from Hermag Security GmbH. On the back Hutchinson had scrawled a message:-

In haste

Many thanks for passing on the errant letter. I am puzzled by your reference to my acquisition of the 'external correspondence' <u>at no cost</u>. Our friend *was paid the contract price in full. What game is playing now? Regards, AJPH*

'*Scheisse!*' He muttered, 'That bloody man's up to his tricks again!'

His first thought was to cancel the trip but caution prevailed. Klaus's 'game' looked like a nasty and dangerous deceit. What would Elizabeth do if she discovered he'd deceived her yet again? Should he tell her? But perhaps it was only fair to talk to Schmidt at the shoot, give him a chance to explain and then he would decide what to do. He put the note in his bag and set off.

The lodge was set in undulating wooded country at the end of a long gravel road some distance from the nearest village. A plain white two-storey building covered by an arched shingle roof with large projecting eaves, one side of the roof had been extended downwards to create a balustraded veranda. It looked very pretty with ivy covering the walls and the wooden pillars supporting the veranda roof.

As he drove into the parking area he was surprised to see Elizabeth's Audi parked next to Schmidt's black Mercedes - apparently they had travelled separately. What does that mean? His mind racing, he parked and let himself in through the open front door. There was a faint, not entirely unpleasant odour that seemed to be a mixture of mushrooms and floor polish but no obvious signs of people. Pushing open a door, he found himself in a square dining room in the centre of which stood a vast dining table surrounded by heavy oak chairs carved with patterns of acanthus leaves sprouting from intertwined branches, and the mysterious foliate face of the Green Man on each back panel. The pine floor was sparsely covered with Persian carpets, several almost threadbare and crudely carved candelabra hung from the dark wooden ceiling. A circular wood-burning stove adorned with green ceramic tiles around its massive girth occupied one corner and the room was lit by four rectangular stained-glass windows, each depicting a different hunting scene. The net effect was to create a sombre, dark atmosphere. It seemed to von Hessler that nothing about the interior had been modernised apart from electric lighting, some modern plumbing and a telephone.

Deciding that perhaps he should unload his bags and the pair of guns he had brought, Von Hessler returned to the car. Willi appeared apparently from nowhere and offered to help.

'Thank you, perhaps you'd take the guns Willi. These bags are too heavy for you. Haven't you got a young assistant to help you?'

'No sir. Only the maids who come in from the village and the cook.'

'How is your master?'

Willi shook his head, his old face anxious. 'That was a terrible bang he had, sir. He ought to take it easy … I've told him but he takes no notice.'

As they reached the entrance, Schmidt, his head still in bandages, emerged through the door and greeted him effusively.

'Welcome to *Jagdhütte Bismarck* my old friend. Elizabeth and I are delighted that you're joining us. But why are you looking so serious?'

'Klaus, any chance we can have a few minutes alone?'

'Of course. We'll go into gunroom, shall we?'

Dumping his bags in the hallway, von Hessler relieved Willi of his guns from Willi and followed Schmidt along a corridor into the gunroom. The room occupied the whole of a single story wing at the rear of the lodge. Heavily varnished beams of pine formed the high arched roof with cupboards, lockers, gun racks and benches distributed around the walls. Above these were fixed a double row of wooden shields carrying the heads and antlers of deer that had fallen to the rifles of shooting parties over the past hundred years. Each shield carried a brass plate with a name and date, and at the end of the room, positioned slightly higher than the others, was a mount sporting a particularly magnificent pair of antlers. On the brass plate was engraved:

Fürst Otto von Bismarck   10 August 1877.

Von Hessler looked around admiringly.

'That's a fine collection. Any of them yours?'

'No. I'm sorry to say none of them are mine. I simply haven't the time for deer stalking.'

402

'How is your head?'

'My head?' The question seemed to confuse him. 'Ah, yes. It's fine … takes more than a bang on the head to stop me! But what's on your mind?'

'Letters are on my mind, Klaus. I don't know if you're aware of it, but the batch you sent me included one from Buckingham Palace addressed to Herzog von Saxe-Coburg und Gotha.'

'Oh, really? My mistake,' responded Schmidt. 'Is it important?'

'Not in itself. But as it should have been included in what we termed the 'external correspondence', I sent it on to Hutchison. In my covering letter I referred to something that Elizabeth said about the cash element of our deal in Fuhlsbüttel…'

'What's she got to do with this?' interrupted Schmidt.

'That's easy. She'd already made it clear to me that she was opposed to the sale of the letters and was astonished that I'd any part in it. In fact she was furious and we had quite an argument. I was surprised to hear she had persuaded you to hand them over to Hutchison for nothing, and that she paid out of her own pocket. So I'm asking you to explain exactly what did happen.'

'What is that to you?'

'I would have thought that was obvious. I'm concerned because of my role in recovering the letters, and hence my right to be told about any transaction in respect of their disposal, and whether these developments put me at risk in any way.'

Schmidt shook his head in exasperation.

'Yes, Elizabeth produced the money. But forget what you call 'developments'. They applied to the amount to be paid, that's all … you weren't affected. Anyway, your letter from the Admiral authorised the salvage operation …so how can there be any risk?'

'Klaus, let me remind you that the Admiral's letter permitted me to remove only *privately owned material*. But that's a side issue. What I want to talk about is this compliments slip I've just had from Hutchison. It's handwritten and it's in English so you may not find it easy to read.'

Schmidt peered at it for several seconds, his eyes screwed up with the effort of reading the words then, with a sharp intake of breath, he threw his head back and half turned away. Unsteadily he swung back and glared at von Hessler.

'What d'you want me to do for God's sake? Hand the money back to Hutchison? I've told you my position. Cash is bloody tight. If you think …'

'I'm not asking you to *do* anything. I'm simply asking you to tell me *exactly* what's going on.'

'All right then,'… He started to wave the note in the air and then froze. 'Have you shown this to Elizabeth?'

'No. I'm not out to make trouble.' Von Hessler said, forcing down his anger on Elizabeth's behalf.

'So why mention payment in your letter to that bastard Hutchison?'

'Klaus, I'm asking the questions here and I'm asking them because I don't think you're playing straight with me. I need some straight answers.' Von Hessler said, his eyes flashing. 'Forget Hutchison! I don't suppose he gives a damn.'

Schmidt hesitated, groping for a response. But they both heard footsteps coming down the corridor towards the gunroom. Schmidt immediately left by the outside door. Von Hessler hurriedly picked up one of his guns and opened a cupboard apparently in search of oil as Elizabeth entered from the corridor with two of Schmidt's male guests. He couldn't miss the trace of restraint in her greeting and the formality with which she introduced the two guests - Herr Doktor Rosen and Herr Selig. Rosen was a small man with a trim grey beard and a quizzical expression. Selig looked every bit the successful businessman – a corpulent middle-aged figure wearing an expensive watch.

They chatted for a few minutes and von Hessler broke off to oil his gun while Elizabeth showed her guests the Bismarck trophy. Then Selig spotted the pale buff compliments slip which had floated to the floor, picked it up and attempted to read it.

'This is in English,' He said. 'It must be yours,' and handed it to Elizabeth.

'That's mine!' Von Hessler said, but it was too late; she was already reading it. He caught the look on her face – it was the same mixture of pain and despair that he had seen at Cuxhaven hospital. But by the time she met his eyes, her expression had changed to one of unhappy resignation. She held out the note to him.

'We need to talk about this.'

At that moment Schmidt returned through the outside door carrying an opened shotgun with the stock over his arm and the barrels pointing down. He caught sight of the pale buff slip in her hand, stiffened and stopped. The whites of his eyes showed as turned to von Hessler.

'So you've betrayed me.'

An embarrassed, shocked silence fell across the five people in the room. In a steely voice von Hessler replied: 'One of us is a betrayer, Klaus, and I think you know very well who it is.'

The red spots on Schmidt's cheeks spread across his face but he said nothing. A gust of wind slammed the outside door shut with a bang making them all jump. Then, he pulled out a cartridge from his pocket and pushed it into one of the chambers, closed the gun with a snap and deliberately raised it, aiming at von Hessler, his finger on one of the triggers.

Everyone froze. The only sound in the room was the gentle rattling of a trolley being

406

pushed along the corridor outside. The sound slowly receded.

'Nobody move!' shouted Schmidt. 'This man ... this so-called friend of mine .... is trying ... is trying ... to dis...,' he stumbled unable to find the word he wanted, '... to destroy my marriage. He will not succeed.'

'For God's sake put that gun down, and stop these dramatics, Klaus.' Elizabeth said calmly. 'You're not well. You should have stayed in hospital. I'm going to ring for an ambulance.'

'I don't need an ambulance,' he hissed, 'but your loverboy will!'

'Klaus, put that gun down *now*! You don't know what you're doing.'

'I know exactly what I'm doing. I know exactly what is going on here. This man...... this aristocrat with his high moral tone, is trying to take you from me. He wants to smash up our marriage and I am not going to let him. Not him ......nor that English blackmailer Hutchison.'

With deliberation, Elizabeth stepped towards von Hessler. She turned towards Schmidt.

'Now you can kill both of us.' There was steel in her voice as she spoke.

Schmidt raised the gun to eye level and sighted down the barrel at von Hessler. As he did so, a blinding white flash and an ear-ripping explosion burst from the corridor. The gun was shot from Schmidt's hands; it crashed to the floor and skidded across the floor. A jet of grey smoke reeking of burnt explosive set the occupants of the room coughing as shards of glass fell out of the shattered window onto the paving outside

His face white with shock and pain, Schmidt staggered sideways, cannoning into a steel locker then, doubled over, his left hand pressed into his stomach, he collapsed to the floor. Von Hessler leapt across the room and bent over him.

'I'm a doctor.' Rosen said quickly joining him. 'Here, give me a hand to get him onto that bench.'

He gently pulled Schmidt's arm away from his body and raised it up to examine the hand.

'Some of the pellets have gone clean through, don't think they've hit an artery. Looks like his watch took the brunt of the damage. Hold his hand well up like this … it will reduce the bleeding.'

He straightened up and addressed the others.

'Any bandages? There's got to be a first aid kit somewhere!'

'I'll go and see what I can find,' said von Hessler, almost running down the corridor to the kitchen. A white-faced Willi was sitting on a chair. He was trembling. The cook, Gretl, was holding a shotgun; she looked distraught.

'Is there a first aid kit?'

'Yes, sir!' She dropped the gun and ran to a cupboard.

'Is there any schnapps?'

'Yes sir.'

'Pour out a stiff one will you Willi.'

Restored a little by the task he had been given, the man stood up, lifted out a bottle from a cupboard and produced a tumbler. His hand shook as he poured out a generous measure. He held it out to von Hessler.

'No Willi,' He said gently. 'It's for you. You've earned it! Where the devil did you learn to shoot?'

'In the trenches, Sir, during the spring offensive. In 1918.'

Von Hessler leant against the dresser, folded his arms and regarded Willi benevolently as the man gulped down the schnapps, laying the empty tumbler on the wooden drainer.

'I had no idea shotguns were used in the trenches. But that accounts for your marksmanship!' He paused watching the man visibly recovering. 'Now look, Willi. If we have to come up with an explanation, I reckon our best bet is to say that it was an accident. I was cleaning my gun. You were here in the kitchen all the time. Got that Willi? I'll take your gun and put it with the others that have been fired this morning. Now don't worry – we'll keep you out of it.'

'Is he dead?' said Willi almost in a whisper. 'I was aiming for his gun.'

'No Willi, he's not dead. He's just got a badly damaged hand. We'll get him to hospital, they'll dig out the pellets and bandage him up. If you can, just carry on as normal.'

'Very good, Sir. Thank you, Sir.'

Von Hessler turned to the cook who had produced the first aid kit and said with a smile

'Look after him won't you.'

Back in the gunroom, he handed the first aid kit to the doctor and put the gun in the rack. Elizabeth had disappeared. Schmidt was lying flat on the bench, his arm held up by Rosen. An ashen-faced Selig was sitting puffing a cigarette. Blood dripped onto the floor, running down between the gaps in the stones.

Von Hessler picked up Schmidt's gun, broke it and removed the green cartridge which he examined.

'You'll be relieved to know that this had already been fired.' He announced.

'I wonder if he realised. Maybe he did. Our ... our friend is a bit of an actor.' Rosen commented wryly.

Von Hessler replaced Schmidt's gun in the rack and picked up the one used by Willi and spoke to the men in the room.

'We need to be careful. We don't want this thing escalating. Have you all got that?' He said firmly. 'I'll take responsibility ... it was an unfortunate accident while I was cleaning this gun.'

A murmur of assent followed.

'I've rung for the ambulance.' said Elizabeth as she re-entered the room. 'And I've warned the ladies that there's been an accident.'

'Right,' said von Hessler, 'I'll go to the hospital with Klaus and drill him to tell the same story.' He looked round at the others. 'If I know Willi, he'll be bringing the drinks any minute.'

'Thank God!' muttered Selig.

'And what about me?' growled Schmidt suddenly finding his voice. 'Get me a bloody stiff one!'

The sound of glass clanking on glass and the wheels of the trolley presaged the arrival of a white-coated Willi. Casting an anxious glance at the figure of Schmidt lying on the bench, he turned to Elizabeth, addressing her in English.

'Can I a drink serve, Milady ?'

but she had already turned to leave the room and shook her head, gesturing to the others.

Rosen took a bandage from the first-aid box and wound it tightly round Schmidt's hand as Willi poured the drinks. The other two men watched silently while they gulped their drinks. Von Hessler turned to Selig, excused himself and left the room.

He found no sign of Elizabeth on the ground floor so hurried out to the car park where he found her sitting in her Audi, smoking a cigarette, staring straight ahead. Walking straight up to the car, he opened the door and sat down beside her. Neither of them spoke - words seemed pointless. He watched the slender birch trees around the lodge as their branches gently swayed in the breeze, casting flickering shadows on the gravel. The quiet rural scene was a relief after the charged emotions in the gunroom.

Partly aware that he was suffering from delayed shock, he seemed to be floating, freed of all constraints. It was simple, he would take Elizabeth away with him there and then.

But he heard an ambulance siren and the dream collapsed.

'I must get back to the lodge before the ambulance arrives.' He said, his voice appearing to belong to someone else. 'Do you want to come with me to the hospital?'

'No. I'm not going to the hospital. Anyway I have to see to the guests... though I can't see them staying for long after this. After that, God knows where I'll go!'

'You could stay with me?'

She smiled at him her gaze on her fingers slowly picking tiny flecks of cigarette ash off her skirt.

'I dare say Doctor Rosen will bring you and Klaus back here – he's an old friend. I don't suppose Klaus will be able to drive ... I expect he'll get someone from the works to collect him and his car tomorrow.'

'I wonder if the hospital will check to see if he's still concussed.'

'It's not concussion, Gerhard ... that is the real Klaus. Once he's possessed by an *idée fixe* anything can happen ...for better or for worse.'

'Do you think he was acting?'

'Only partly. We all act don't we? We all put on a face to meet the people we meet. The

412

trouble is that Klaus comes from the *Sturm und Drang* school of acting.'

She drew on her cigarette and stubbed it firmly out in the ashtray.

'For me the crunch point isn't the stuff that he's acting out, the jealousy and the anger. It's his dishonesty. It's deep and it's cruel … and I've had enough!'

Von Hessle's heart went out to her – she was near to tears but determined to hold it together.

'I don't know what to say. I can't imagine what that must be like to live with.' He paused uncertainly. He looked at her again. She seemed withdrawn. He wanted to pull her back to reality.

''What will happen to Willi?'

She shook her head.

'Oh God! I don't know! I'll probably put him on a train to Hamburg. He's got a brother there.'

'He's a great little chap. If it's any help I'll give him a job. My man Graubal is getting terribly doddery.'

She gave him a thin if genuine smile.

'That would be kind. Life must go on.'

The ambulance arrived; Von Hessler opened the car door.

'I don't know how long it's going to take at the hospital. If they think it's going to be a long job I'll ring you.'

As he walked back towards the lodge he spotted a smallish rock lying on the gravel and booted it hard across the car park towards an iron water butt; the resultant collision created a highly satisfying clang.

As promised, von Hessler rang Elizabeth from the hospital.

'The doctors don't see any problem in digging out the pellets.'

'Is there any serious injury to his hand?'

'No, the X-ray was clear on that.'

'Thank you, Gerhard.'

Two hours later Schmidt emerged from the operating theatre with his arm in a sling and his hand heavily bandaged. A nurse handed him a bottle of pain-killers.

'You'll need these, they'll help you sleep.'

As arranged, Herr Doktor Rosen arrived at the hospital to collect them and unobtrusively handed a letter to von Hessler. He pocketed it while helping Schmidt into the back seat of the car where he slumped without saying a word and closed his eyes. Schmidt appeared to have fall asleep on the journey back to the lodge so von Hessler took the opportunity to read the letter -

Dear Gerhard,

Most of the guests have gone and I am now going myself. I am taking Willi. The cook Gretl is staying on until all have left.

Do forgive me for departing so abruptly and also for leaving you to deal with Klaus – It may be a challenge but I am sure you will cope.

I am driving home to pack my things and will be away by tomorrow midday. Would you be an angel and somehow or other delay Klaus to prevent him arriving before I leave. This is the end of my life in Düsseldorf, although I am still 'married' (and that is a problem I need to sort out).

My final destination depends on several phone calls, but will probably be either with my friends in Denmark or my parent's place in London.

I will ring you as soon as I can. We <u>must</u> meet again.

With love,
Elizabeth

He read the words 'The end of my life in Düsseldorf' again and again extracting every possible meaning. Rosen attempted to strike up a conversation about Schmidt's injuries but von Hessler's lack of response soon made him give up. By the time they reached the lodge, Schmidt had opened his eyes and they helped him out of the car into the hall. Lying on a hall table was a letter addressed to Schmidt in Elizabeth's hand. Schmidt pinioned the envelope to the table with his elbow, ripped out the letter and read it. Then walking slowly to the sitting room he slumped down in a chair. His chest swelled and he emitted a long sigh.

'She's gone.' He said and relapsed into silence.

Von Hessler regarded him, watchfully, unwilling to respond. It's your own doing, he thought to himself, so totally unnecessary … pathetic really. But still tragic. A decent man brought down by folly.

Schmidt stirred in his seat and looking around as if waking.

'Where is everybody?'

'All gone I'm afraid. You look as if you could do with a drink.'

'I could, and a bloody large one. Where's Willi?'

'Elizabeth has taken him off.'

'Why's she done that? Where the hell's she taken him? Where's she gone?'

'How should I know.'

'Don't bullshit me! You two are planning to meet. Don't tell me you don't know where she is!'

'There are no plans, Klaus.' He sounded dispirited. 'I'm not planning anything, other than going back to Kiel.'

Von Hessler gave him no chance to respond and went to the kitchen. There he found some Bols *Zeer Oude Genever* and poured two fingers from the tall brown ceramic bottle. Schmidt took a large swig and pretended to choke.

416

'What the hell's this? It's monkey's piss! Where the devil did you get it?'

'In the kitchen. I presume you organised the drinks ... as host.'

'You're trying to bloody well poison me!'

'I wouldn't do that Klaus. Not to a friend.'

'But you'd steal his wife.'

'Wife?'

Schmidt raised his right arm and made a wild frustrated swipe in the air.

'I could punch you for that remark.'

'I think we need another drink before we get into a fight. What would you like?'

'I bought a bottle of 'The Macallen' for you,' said Schmidt, looking down at the floor shaking his head. 'You should be able to find it.'

Von Hessler left the room, returned with the bottle and two fresh glasses. He lifted it up to the light and slowly turned it round.

'Twelve years old!' He said in a reverential tone, before easing out the cork and pouring generous measures. Handing a glass to Schmidt he raised his own: 'To your rapid recovery.'

He looked reflectively at the golden brown liquid. 'It was kind of you to remember my favourite scotch.' He added.

'Why did you give her that note?' Schmidt asked.

'I didn't. You let it fall to the floor, and Selig picked it up. He saw it was in English so he gave it to Elizabeth.'

There was another long silence and then Schmidt repeated almost inaudibly: 'She's gone.'

Von Hessler got up, walked across to the open window and peered out. The evening was drawing in, the air was still and the forest trees were silhouetted darkly against the fading light in the sky. One or two stars were already shining. Memories came back of sailing trips with Klaus, of sitting in the cockpit at the end of the day as one by one the lights on distant buoys became visible. He turned and looked down at Schmidt who was staring straight ahead. There seemed to be nothing worth saying and he turned back to the window.

From behind him he heard Schmidt mutter

'I've handed her to you on a plate. This is the worst moment of my life.'

Von Hessler nodded but made no comment.

'Why has she left me?' He looked at von Hessler angrily. 'Come on, I'm asking you.'

'For God's sake Klaus you're not seriously expecting me to answer that question?'

'I am.'

He turned back to Schmidt who was looking at him expectantly.

'Perhaps it's because you don't share the same values.'

'What does that mean?'

'If you want me to spell it out – you cut corners and Elizabeth plays by the rules.'

'Everybody cuts corners. You can't run a business without cutting corners.'

'Marriage isn't a business.'

'My first marriage was a business – based on hard cash as I later discovered.'

Von Hessler opened a box of small Dutch cigars and offered it to Schmidt who took one and examined it curiously.

'*Wilde Havana* - I used to smoke these. But Elizabeth didn't like the smell.'

He lit the cigar for him. Schmidt shifted in the chair and crossed his legs.

'Erda was a bitch. I'm not shot of her even now. Elizabeth was like a fresh breeze. I'm not letting her go.'

'I have to remind you Klaus that she's already gone. And how are you proposing to get her back?'

'She'll come back.'

'I think a bit of plain speaking is required here. You've got a cat in hell's chance.' Von Hessler left the window and started pacing slowly up and down the room.

'You've driven her away and she's not coming back. A lot of women would have walked out long ago after what you've put her through, Klaus. You've destroyed her trust. Not only did you deceive her over your previous marriage, making her what? A common-law wife? Little more than a whore in some people's eyes! But now, despite all she's tried to do for you, you've lied to her and cheated her over the sale of the letters! On top of that, you've covered your tracks with more lies about trips to Stockholm and God knows where-else.' He paused for breath 'And as if that were not enough, you threaten me and her with a gun. Your situation's irretrievable and you'd better face it.' Von Hessler flung himself back into his chair.

There was a knock on the door, the cook entered to announce that supper was ready. Both men got up and with exaggerated courtesy Schmidt motioned von Hessler to proceed first. They moved to the dining room and sat down opposite each other across the wide table. The cook brought in a tureen of consommé. Von Hessler opened the wine bottle which stood on the table, filled the glasses and ladled out the soup.

'Would you like me to break your roll?' He asked.

Schmidt nodded. The next course was venison steak with pommes duchesse and a side salad. Von Hessler looked across the table and felt a pang of sympathy for his adversary.

'I think we better call a truce. I'm obviously going to have to cut that up for you. Cut the steak that is, not your throat.'

'Agreed.' was all Schmidt was prepared to say.

They continued eating in silence, von Hessler refilling the glasses at frequent intervals.

Suddenly Schmidt's fork clattered onto the table and he lowered his head, his huge frame heaving with a suppressed sob. When he raised his head Von Hessler saw a face of overflowing with misery.

He looked fixedly at Schmidt for several seconds.

'I'm afraid I've been rather hard on you Klaus.'

'No, you bloody haven't!   You're totally right - I brought this on my own head! I've driven her away. I've ruined a perfectly good marriage. Everything I've worked for is in ruins.'

'Everything? Including *Elektro*?'

'Yes, including *Elektro*.   I lost control of the company when I sold Elizabeth that bundle of stock. She'll sell to the bank and that will be that.'

'You'll still be running the show.'

'And when I want to take the sort of risk on which I built *Elektro* some banker will block me. I don't want to become a branch of Siemens or AEG. I'm used to having my independence.'

'Sell up and start again.'

'Start again!' He shouted. 'Rebuild my business? Rebuild my life? You don't know what you're asking.'

'People do it. Why can't you?'

'I've been here before – on the Eastern front.' He stopped seemingly unwilling to explore the feelings that had surfaced.

'Go on; tell me about it.'

Schmidt seemed to be fighting an internal battle with himself. He forked a large chunk of venison in his mouth, chewing it slowly then swallowed and washed it down with a mouthful of wine.

'We'd crossed Poland into Russia, fought our way to the horizon 60 km away across the steppes. But when we got there we found that we had the same battle opening in front of us. So we did it again ... and then again and again, for one thousand kilometres. It wasn't until I looked at the big map that I realised that we'd hardly penetrated into Mother Russia.' He paused, reliving the moment. 'We were exhausted, but we were in sight of Moscow ... we thought we'd made it! Then the weather got worse and worse, and like a bolt from the blue their Siberian army counter-attacked. Our guns were frozen solid and we had to light fires under our tanks to get them started, for God's sake! They drove us back.' He paused again and emptied his glass. 'It was then I knew it was all over - and I was right. I've got that feeling again now. It's no good, Gerhard. Pour me another glass, would you?'

Schmidt pulled out the small bottle of painkillers from his pocket, put the cap between his teeth and attempted to unscrew it, but failed.

'Here' let me do that.' said von Hessler. 'How many do you want?'

'Three.'

Von Hessler looked at the label. 'It says here 'Dihydrocodeine. Take one or two tablets every six hours'. It also says 'Not to be taken with alcohol'.'

'Bugger what is says on the label. My hand is giving me hell. I want three.'

'On your head be it,' said von Hessler handing over three pills.

'I won't get any sleep without these,' Klaus said as he put the pills in his mouth and chased them down with a gulp of wine. 'My bloody hand is throbbing! Eleven entry punctures and four exit. Every puncture's hurting. Seven pellets dug out. One tendon damaged, one bone cracked. I'd be dead if I'd been a rabbit - would have been better if I had been.'

Von Hessler shot him a sharp glance. 'It's not like you to talk like that.'

He screwed the cap back on the bottle and passed it over to Schmidt who held it up, scrutinised the label. 'Loosen the cap will you? I'll need some during the night.'

. The cook cleared the table and brought in an apfel-strudel. Once she had left the room, Schmidt pointed to the empty bottle.

'There's plenty more in the cellar.'

Von Hessler returned with a fresh bottle and refilled their glasses. Having eaten the apfel-strudel they left the room in search of more comfortable chairs.

'Bring that bloody bottle with you, Gerhard. I'm going to get pissed.'

'We're half bloody pissed already! You shouldn't be bloody drinking with those pills in you.'

'I don't give a damn.'

'Well I do. I'm not carrying you up those bloody stairs. Too bloody dangerous.'

They entered the sitting room and Schmidt dropped heavily into an easy chair and took a gulp of wine. His eyes closed for several seconds. He opened them, raised his head and, after looking around the room as if trying to work out where he was, finished the rest of his wine.

'Now my bloody head's aching. If we're not going to talk I'll go to bed,' he growled, and with difficulty levered himself up out of the chair.

'*Schläfft du gut*,' was his parting remark as he walked slowly towards the door waving goodbye with his right arm. Von Hessler listened with a tinge of anxiety as he clumped up the stairs, and was relieved when he heard his bedroom door slam.

The next morning von Hessler came down to find himself alone. Standing on the gravel drive, he breathed in the fresh morning air; it was going to be a sunny day. And you will be spending it driving back to Kiel!

Three cars stood parked near the lodge - his own, Gretl's and Schmidt's – silent testimony to the collapse of the shooting party. He reflected on the evening's conversation and its abrupt end. Had he been too hard on Klaus ? No ... every word had been true. Anyway, Klaus was a tough character, resilient – he would bounce back.

Concluding that Klaus was still sleeping, and remembering Elizabeth's request that he delay Klaus' departure, he decided not to disturb him. Back inside the lodge, he crept up the stairs and listened for signs of movement at his host's bedroom door; nothing! Then he asked Gretl to produce breakfast for one.

An hour and a half later there was still no sign of Klaus. Was he okay? Von Hessler, knocked loudly on the bedroom door and, after getting no response, opened the door. Klaus was breathing heavily and still asleep.

'Wake up Klaus. It's time you were up. You'll miss breakfast.' He more or less shouted in the man's ear. Schmidt stirred and blearily opened his eyes.

'Where am I?'

'Near Hanover, in a shooting lodge.'

'Good God! I thought I was in *Jasmine*! How did I get here?'

'You drove – you were hosting a party. Don't you remember? Have you lost your memory?'

'I haven't got a memory. I've got a bloody awful headache.' He reached across to the bedside table, grabbed the pill bottle and swallowed down several pills with a gulp of water. 'That'll sort it out. That whisky's potent stuff.' He pointed to the bottle of 'The Macallen' von Hessler had last seen in the sitting room. There was no more than a centimetre left.

Schmidt appeared downstairs half an hour later, unshaven, beads of sweat glistening on his forehead. He refused breakfast and demanded coffee, gulping it down. Then he seized the telephone, attempting unsuccessfully to dial a number.

'You do it!' He demanded.

'Who are you calling?'

'*Elektro* ... get me a driver!'

With that, Schmidt returned to his room, muttering under his breath and unsteady on his feet.

Having called as requested, Von Hessler decided to get out for a walk, leaving a message with Gretl to tell Schmidt that he would return in a couple of hours.

The rustle of the wind in the trees and the singing of the birds was reassuringly eternal reminding him that life would go on ... despite the chaos of the last 24 hours. He wondered how Elizabeth would shape her new life without Klaus. Would it include him? Where would she go? How soon would he hear from her?

Navigating by the sun, he walked in a wide circle along the well-used footpaths and worn tracks interlacing the forest. Apart from one short salvo of distant gunshots accompanied by the barking of dogs far in the distance, nothing disturbed the peace and he found himself grateful for the absence of any human presence in the woods.

426

Perhaps it was in contrast to this sense of peace, but as he returned towards the lodge he became conscious of a sense of foreboding. Calling himself a fool, he shook it off.

There was no sign of Schmidt and Gretl claimed she hadn't seen him for over an hour. Minutes later the car from *Elektro* arrived so he went and knocked loudly on Schmidt's bedroom door. The man looked awful as he emerged unsteadily, carrying a suitcase. Von Hessler offered to take it from him but he refused. At the bottom of the stairs he snapped out of his subdued mood and greeted the driver with something like his usual cheer, appearing almost excited at the prospect of his return to Düsseldorf. The driver loaded the suitcase and Schmidt turned to von Hessler holding out a folded piece of paper for him to take. The two men then shook hands, unsmilingly and, after uttering a few words of farewell, he climbed into the back seat of the car. Von Hessler watched as car was neatly turned and headed off towards the road. He stood immobile looking in the same direction for over a minute before he turned and walked back into the lodge in pensive mood.

Then he read the note from Schmidt. It was written in an almost illegible scrawl and appeared to be unfinished –

My old friend you said strong words but they carried truth. I have been stupid STUPID. I go back to home and business afloat in rough seas.

They are heavy - everything goes up and   down.
I cannot see. Where is the tiller? Where is ... ...

Frowning, not sure what to make of it, Von Hessler went and paced up and down in front of the lodge, reading and rereading the note. In the end, he shook his head, carefully folded it and slipped it into his wallet. There was nothing more he could do at the lodge. It was time to go. He handed her some money, said goodbye to Gretl and set off for Kiel.

Several times over the next day he tried ringing Schmidt's home number from Haus Langenhorn but there was no answer.

A further two days elapsed before he received a call from Elizabeth; she was speaking from England.

'Gerhard, it's me. I've got to tell you. It's terrible news. Klaus died on his way back home. It's taken them three days to find me. I'm devastated.'

'Oh God! How awful! What happened? Was it a crash?'

'No. The hospital in Bielefeld say that from the blood samples they took from him they think it was a mixture of alcohol and the pills he was taking. They found the pill bottle in his pocket – it was empty. He must have swallowed dozens. I've got the most dreadful feeling that it was ... it can't have been accidental.'

'Oh ... you don't mean ...'

'I think he took his own life.'

428

'Suicide? I don't believe it, Elizabeth, he was a fighter! Oh dear God!' The words of the note came back to him.

'He *was* a fighter and I loved him. What have I done, Gerhard?'

'You haven't done anything, Elizabeth! I think I ought to tell you that I gave him a very hard time after you left – maybe too hard.'

There was a long pause before she replied. 'Whatever you did can hardly compare with walking out on him after nearly twenty years of marriage... Oh! I can't talk about this on the phone! I'm leaving this afternoon for Düsseldorf. I'll ring you tonight.'

Von Hessler replaced the phone and put his head in his hands. He should have realised! He saw again Klaus reading the warning on the pill bottle, the nearly empty bottle of whisky, his feelings about the fighting in Russia and the words in his scrawled note - *I cannot see. Where is the tiller?* Dare he tell Elizabeth any of this? Had he and Elizabeth unwittingly conspired to bring about this ghastly ending? He pulled out the note again and reread it. An image of a tombstone rose up before his eyes. Chiselled into its polished granite surface was the message: *You said strong words but they carried truth*

That evening Elizabeth rang him from Düsseldorf. This time there was pain in her voice. He wondered if she had been crying.

'No-one here knows that I'd left him, Gerhard – apart from you and Willi. I couldn't bring myself to tell them,' she said. 'They're going to do a post-mortem in the next two days and I have to arrange the funeral. I'm telling no-one about it, just can't face people now. There won't be anyone there except myself ... and Willi.'

'Not even Hans?' said von Hessler.

'Not even Hans! I can't face anyone, Gerhard! I can't! I simply can't!'

'Does that include me?'

'It's nothing personal, Gerhard, I just can't bear anyone or anything that reminds me of Klaus or the past. I know I can't undo the past or bury it. But I need time come to terms with everything ...'

'So you don't want to talk about it?'

'No. I'm sorry.'

'I'm sorry too. There's a good deal that I need to say about my part in all this. But obviously it'll have to wait.'

'Yes.'

'So there's nothing I can say?'

'No.'

'OK, but we must talk soon. Look after yourself, Elizabeth.'

'Goodby,e Gerhard.'

He banged the phone down on the rest. Why the hell was she determined to take all the blame for what had happened? It was irrational. She hadn't even been present during the last 24 hours of his life. It was *he* who had kicked Klaus when he was down, and *he* who had driven in the final nail. Now in death he saw clearly the humanity of the man within the uniform of the

430

ruthless *Panzer Offizier*. A chance encounter in the sailing club had brought them together. He had been closer to Klaus than he had acknowledged even to himself ... he was a fellow sailor.

His thoughts turned back to Elizabeth – she had rejected her husband and now she was rejecting him. Everything had unravelled at alarming speed. She wasn't the only one who needed time to think.

There and then he decided to leave for Bremerhaven. A few days single-handed sailing in the calmer waters inside the Frisian Islands would restore his equilibrium. In a flurry of activity, he rang the boatyard and asked them to fill *Jasmine's* fuel and water tanks and check the batteries, looked up the tide tables and listened to the weather forecast, packed his gear and early the next morning he left.

Chapter 12~~1~~

Comment [P]:

Von Hessler stepped aboard *Jasmine*, unlocked the main cabin door, slid back the hatch over the companionway steps and, picking up the cardboard boxes, carried them down into the saloon. Systematically, he stowed the contents in the food lockers, checked the readings on fuel and water gauges and opened the forward hatch.

Up on deck he examined the welding repair to the forestay deck fitting and relived for an awful moment the sounds of the mast crashing down on Klaus. It made him shudder. Quickly he checked~~turned his attention to~~ the tension in the new rigging. All seemed in order.

He~~and he~~ laid out the chart *Approaches to the Jade and Weser* on the navigation table. Immediately he realised that sailing to the island of Wangerooge was not a simple matter of laying a course straight from Bremerhaven across the bay ~~which~~ embracing~~ed~~ the estuaries of the two rivers because bang in the middle stood a large mudflat known as the *Mellum Plate* which could only be crossed at or around the time of high water. He sighed. In order to arrive at the optimum hour, he would have to sail 11 nautical miles down the Weser against a 3 knot current as the tide flooded in.

'*Schiesse!*' He muttered, staring at the chart.

As an alternative he could leave on a favourable ebb tide, carry on a further 10 miles to the northern tip of the mudflat, then leave the Weser and head west across the Jade estuary. Then, once across he could turn south and enter Frisian Island waters through the seegat known as the *Blaue Balje* which lay between Wangerooge and the islands of Minsener Oog. Perusal of the tide tables showed that an early start the next morning would do the trick. If he tied up for the night to the pontoon in the Geeste basin near the Bremerhaven~~harbour~~ entrance from the Weser t~~h~~is would~~to~~ avoid delays waiting for the swing bridge to open and the time spent negotiating the Schleusenhafen locks.

A delicious cooking smell drifted across the water making his mouth water. He rolled up the chart, climbed out of *Jasmine* and walked over to the restaurant in the Weser Yacht Club.

It was darker and colder when he returned, the mercury vapour lights in the boatyard lending a colourless ashen hue to the scene. The damp air reeked of varnish and paint doubtless emanating from two large yachts standing on the concrete hard resting on their deep keels. From where he was standing, they resembled a pair of dead whales awaiting the butchers' blubber hooks. He grimaced at the image as he made his way back to his boat and stepped down into the cockpit. Inserting the key he found the main cabin door was already unlocked. Cautiously he peered into the dark saloon and for an instant saw clearly the figure of Klaus reclining on a bunk.

Shaken, he backed away, sat down heavily in the cockpit and lit a cigarillo. Reassuring himself that ghosts did not exist, he peered into the cabin again - it was only a shadow, a trick of the boatyard lighting. He would never sail with Klaus again.

How would Elizabeth feel about his death once the initial shock had dissipated, and equally how he would feel? Neither of them had cause to feel guilty – though that was something he preferred not to dwell on. He needed to get moving NOW!

Arriving at the pontoon in the Geeste basin half an hour later, he tied up and looked around. The red and green lights marking the harbour entrance were flashing their message to mariners across the dark expanse of the Weser. High above on the radio tower, fixed red lights carried their warning to aviators. The lights on channel marker buoys in the river winked at slightly different intervals, as if sending memos to each other. He soaked up the marine atmosphere: the infrequent blast from a ship's hooter, the rumble of a big marine engine, and, over everything, the alluring, eternal salty scent of the sea. Below him, the inky black water flowed past the boat.

'What the hell am I doing here? Why am I planning this absurd trip? Sailing up winding creeks running throughof deserted mudflats with nothing for company but seals and birds?'

434

A jumble of reasons jostled in his mind. Abruptly, unable to endure them, he got to his feet stepped down into the saloon and poured a double whisky. Whatever the reasons, he was going ahead. He sat over the chart and forced himself to memorise the names and positions of the buoys that would mark the turning points in the passage to Wangerooge. Then he downed the whisky, climbed into his berth and switched out the cabin lights.

He rose next morning to find the sky beautifully clear with a fresh wind blowing from the south-west. After a quick breakfast of coffee and hard-boiled eggs, he slipped the moorings, pulled in the fenders and motored out into the Weser, bringing *Jasmine* up into the wind. Then he hoisted her sails. As he swung her downriver a force five filled them and with relief he pulled the fuel cut-off to the engine. With the wind on her beam *Jasmine* was well balanced and, after trimming the mainsail, he was able to hold a steady course without any trouble. At that point the Weser was just under half a mile wide, so he took her well out from the bank to take advantage of the current. River traffic was less of a problem than it had been on the Elbe and the wind, blowing across rather than along the river, created smaller waves. The sun burst through the clouds at frequent intervals and burnt off the lingering traces of mist.

Bremerhaven was soon left behind and only the tops of isolated buildings could be seen behind the grassy slopes of the dyke. Gradually the deep channel veered away from the river bank and, as the tide dropped, dark grey mudflats emerged. Hungry birds circled overhead, calling to each other and selecting a safe place to land. He spotted a flock of common redshanks with long reddish legs wading about, busily pecking for lugworms.

After 90 minutes the redbrick light-tower of Robbenplate came abeam. This was 10 miles out from Bremerhaven giving him a speed of 7 knots over the ground. On that reckoning he would reach the tip of the mudflat *Mellum Plate*, 11 miles further downstream, well before lunchtime. When its tip drew abeam he brought *Jasmine* up into the wind, started the engine and dropped the sails. Altering course to true west, and watching the depth on the echo-sounder, he made across the Jade estuary towards the buoys that marked the narrow deep-water channel of the seegat *Blaue Balje,* thankful that he didn't have to face the combination of a strong ebb-tide running against an on-shore wind, the cause of the violent and vicious seas in the seegats. He made the *Blaue Balje* passage without difficulty.

Time for lunch. He motored up the creek leading westward close to the southern shore of Wangerooge and dropped the hook when he was about to run aground. A little over three miles away to the south, across the sand and mudflats, he could just see the dyke that lined the coast of Friesland. Away to the north lay an ancient navigational beacon resembling a huge inverted conical flower vase perched on a giant table with four enormous legs. It sat on the shore next to a disused harbour of which only ruined stakes remained. The nearby beach and sand dunes ~~nearby~~ were deserted. He went below, set out the cold lunch prepared by Frau Graubal and opened a bottle of beer.

Now he had a four hour to wait for the tide to rise and allow further progress along the seaway marked with withies and known as the *Wangerooger Wattfahrwasser* which led to the little port on the western end of Wangerooge. Lunch consumed, he tossed the scraps overboard and watched as the circling gulls dived and snapped them up. Then he climbed back into the cockpit with his binoculars.

All around stretched mud and sand relieved by only by intermittent clumps of seagrass and a few basking seals. Small pools of water remained in depressions in the sand and there were seashells apparently scattered at random, some providing anchors for strands of green seaweed. The large numbers of birds that had arrived were busily searching for their lunch. Clouds obscured the sun and a dyke shut off the view of the village on the island. All that could be seen in its centre was the top half of a red and white light tower and a church steeple. Having examined everything of interest he went down into the saloon and searched among a small collection of books for something to read; he picked out *The Riddle of the Sands*. It had been his long-standing ambition to sail the waters of the

Frisian Islands ever since reading the book as a schoolboy in England. But Erskine Childers had never taken his yacht *Dulcibella* down the Wangerooge Wattfahrwasser, and even the island itself received hardly a mention. He would have to sail further west to Norderney to explore the scenes in the novel - but the project seemed less attractive without Klaus.

He replaced the book in the rack and searched in vain another. Returning to the cockpit, he grabbed the boathook and prodded at the brown sand – it seemed firm enough. He jumped down and set off to see what he could find. A pair of silver seals were sunning themselves on the bank of a creek but as he headed towards them they raised their heads, warily examining the intruder, and slithered back into the water. Ahead of him withies marked the route along the Wattfahrwasser and he remembered the reconnaissance done by the crew of *Dulcibella* and the importance Davies had attached to careful recording of its twists and turns, and of points where the sands had shifted so that the withies no longer accurately marked the channel. Sensibly, he went back to the yacht for a notebook and hand-bearing compass.

The sun emerged and started to dry the strand, lightening both the colour of the sand and his mood. Gas made tiny popping noises as it burst through patches of dark mud and added its contribution to the smell of the sea. From behind him the comforting, continuous sound of breakers reached him from the sands bordering the seegat.

The entire universe from one flat horizon to the other comprised an immense blue sky flecked with brilliant white clouds. However, the landscape would have presented a dull almost lifeless scene had it not been for the birds, exploring for unsuspecting worms and leaving trails of footprints in the mud.

He completed his survey of the Wattfahrwasser and returned to the boat where he had another look at the chart, gleaning little from it. There appeared to be nothing better for him to do but tidy up the confused heaps of rope and halliards that inevitably develop on the cockpit floor while a boat is making a passage. Elizabeth's last phone call floated up in his mind. She had been so hard and dismissive. Reluctantly, he faced his feelings of rejection desperate, even at the risk of a further rebuff, wishing he could talk to her. He could make a linked phone call via Elbe-Weser radio station, it would be possible. But conversation over the ship-to-shore was inhibiting, with each remark having to be ended with 'over' and the mike button released. He abandoned that idea and decided to ring from a phone box when he reached the harbour.

The tide crept back and covered the mudflats so he started the engine again and gingerly moved ahead, following the withies that marked the winding channel. With her keels only a few centimetres clear of the bottom, *Jasmine* finally crossed the watershed after which the depth slowly increased. Four miles on, and an hour later, they reached the end of the Muschelbank which extended way out past the end of the island. He swung her around in a wide circle, followed the withies that led to the harbour and tied up alongside another yacht. This was a stark uncomfortable place, with poor protection from heavy weather but fortunately the wind had veered west and moderated. Other than some cranes and a tall tripod, nothing broke the skyline apart from a pair of sheds perched high above the sand on steel legs, and occupied by the harbour master and customs. The only object of interest was a train waiting for the arrival of the ferry. It was bizarre - Wangerooge, a mere eight km long and just over one km wide, had a railway! This was something to investigate. Stepping across the foredeck of the boat lying inside *Jasmine* to the jetty, he wandered along to the harbour master's office. Harbour dues were just a few Deutschmarks. The public telephone box nearby was occupied and he decided to take the train to the village and find another.

He crossed the track, passed the little diesel locomotive and climbed into a carriage painted bright red and white, as if to match the broad bands of colour painted around the light tower close by. In due time, the ferry arrived bringing with it a crowd of passengers carrying all sorts of bags and holiday clutter, laughing and making a great deal of noise. With a full load of passengers the train set off and, amid much clanking and jolting, headed out over the mudflats along a track that was precariously supported on wooden piles. Leaving the mudflats, it then ran along the seaward side of the dyke, on sand that looked reasonably firm but bore the marks of many inundations. Finally it made its way across to the landward side and drew up in the station. He caught himself smiling as he alighted.

He found a restaurant with a phone and ordered a coffee and a piece of cake from the waitress, neatly dressed in a white bonnet with a long white and blue skirt which he took to be Frisian national dress. Then he pulled out his diary and wrote Elizabeth's phone number on a beer mat, drank the first coffee while he debated the wisdom of ringing her and ordered a second. He looked at his watch - she would be sitting down to dinner shortly. It was now or never! He got up abruptly, went to the phone and dialled the number. She answered almost straight away.

'Elizabeth, it's me,'

'I've been trying to get hold of you for the last two days, Gerhard! Where have you been?'

'Sailing.'

'You must tell me about it. But first I have some news. It's the post-mortem results; it's not at all what we expected.'

'What do you mean?'

'I don't know how you're going to feel about it but this was the finding - *the cause of death was an extensive subdural haemorrhage occasioned by a severe blow to the head'* It wasn't a deliberate overdose, Gerhard!'

'Thank God! … I don't know what to say… That blood-test was a total red-herring! – Do you know, Klaus was beginning to haunt me. I thought I saw him in the boat last night – but it was just a shadow – nothing but my overactive imagination at work! Oh Elizabeth! This must be such a huge weight off your mind!'

'Yes. It was hard to live with the ~~ghastly thoughtidea~~ that … my leaving Klaus had driven him to … to kill himself. And the haemorrhage would explain his behaviour with the gun as well. If only I'd realised that at the time … but he would have died anyway. The post-mortem made that very clear. At least the funeral is easier to face. It's tomorrow. In Bielefeld at eleven.'

'Oh Lord! Elizabeth, I doubt I can get there by eleven. I've left the car in Bremerhaven. I'll have to check train times, but it's very unlikely. Hang on a second – I'll ask the people here …' He turned aside and threw a question at the waitress. 'No, there isn't chance. It means getting the first ferry, then a taxi to the station at Wihelmshaven, then a change at Bremen and then again somewhere else. It would take me until mid-afternoon. As it is I can't leave the boat here. It's a poor harbour and I'll have to move her in the next couple of days.'

'Oh well it can't be helped, Gerhard. It would have been nice if you could have come but please don't worry. Everyone's rallying round. My parents are here so it won't be too much of an ordeal. Where are you now?'

442

'I'm on Wangerooge - one of the Frisian Islands. It's the first you come to after leaving Bremerhaven.'

'Who are you sailing with?'

'No-one. I'm on my own. I wanted to get away for a bit, though I have to say single-handed sailing doesn't suit me. In fact it's all been a bit dismal. I'm sorry I rushed into it.'

'Gerhard, we must meet up ... don't stay at sea too long will you? Though from what you say, you've had enough of your own company!'

'I certainly won't. What are you doing over the next few days?'

'Top of the list is talking to the lawyers in Düsseldorf again, getting various things moving. It's all been a bit exhausting then I'm planning to visit friends in Denmark.'

'OK. I'll ring you when I'm back home, shall I? I'm so glad that things aren't as black as they looked. It's good to talk to you. I'm feeling a lot happier already.'

'So am I – a lot happier.'

'Goodbye then, Elizabeth.'

'Goodbye, Gerhard.'

He settled the bill and, leaving the waitress an unusually generous tip, he walked briskly through the village out onto the pale sands on the shore, and from the top of one of the highest dunes surveyed the blue seas of the German Bight. The westerly had dropped to a pleasant gentle breeze. He sat down on the warm sand, lit a cigarillo, and

443

relaxed to the mesmeric rhythm of the breaking waves that rolled in from afar.

Klaus was to be buried tomorrow, and he wouldn't be there for that final journey. That was sad. The confined life on board had brought them surprisingly close and they had formed an unlikely friendship. Perhaps even *Jasmine* would miss his rumbustious presence.

It was an awful, terrible irony that an accident at sea had severed the link between them, one that had held despite the shocks of the last few weeks. He wondered what would have happened if they had completed their cruise. Would Elizabeth have gone back to Klaus? If she had, his suspicious mind would have made it difficult for them to meet. And if they had met? That didn't bear thinking about!

He switched his attention to the people on the beach and saw a fair-haired woman walking towards him. Good God! - it was Elizabeth! But her expression froze him. She came closer and then he realised it was someone else, a complete stranger. She carried on past him without so much as a glance. He looked away, and shook his head feeling a fool. After a while, he got up, stamped the cigarillo butt into the sand and took a last look around ~~the island~~ before setting off back into the village to find an evening meal and discover the departure time of the little island train.

Later, at the harbour, he checked the tide tables posted outside the harbourmaster's office. Back on board *Jasmine* he planned the next morning's five mile trip to the little harbour of Harlesiel. The passage ran along a buoyed channel called *Carolinensieler Balje* and ended in a creek which dried out well before low water and was marked by posts set in a training dam that ran along its western edge.

After a good night's sleep he set off early, reached Harlesiel without running aground, moved through the lock into the inner harbour and tied up. A taxi took him to Wilhelshaven station and later that afternoon he reached Bremerhaven, collected his car and drove back to Haus Langenhorn. It was the end of a foolish expedition conceived in haste and abandoned before it had really started. Now he had missed both the funeral and with it the opportunity to see Elizabeth. His mind kept coming back to her.

The next morning he rang her again and learnt that she was leaving for Denmark in two days' time and would drop in to see him en route. Two days was a long time, he thought, surprised at his own impatience. As a diversion he decided to deal with correspondence that had built up in the study and enthusiastically ripping open the envelopes, he flattened the letters into a pile, but his concentration was lacking and he ended up shoving them into a folder.

He took himself into the drawing room, folded back the lid of the ninety year old Bechstein and slid out the rack with its pair of candlestick rests. Searching for something that matched his mood he opened the music cupboard, flipped through the sheets of sonatas that lay on the top shelf and pulled out Beethoven's 'Moonlight' – he had been told that it was his mother's favourite and he had faint childhood memories of her playing it. Partly because of this, he had practised it more than any other piece and could perform most of it competently by the time he was sixteen. The note of quiet joy and expectation in the second movement was exactly right and the energy and pace of the third brought to his mind a picture of Elizabeth driving north fast on the autobahn, heading for Denmark, and stopping off at Haus Langenhorn.

In the music was a yearning for resolution, an end to uncertainty - something perhaps they both shared. After finishing the piece he sat reflecting on his choice ~~then got up~~ and stared at the photograph of his mother that stood on the piano. For the first time he saw in her a fleeting resemblance to Elizabeth. As he mused over the feminine influences in his life he became conscious <u>of</u>~~that~~ a strange old warm feeling ~~had been released, a feeling~~ that ~~up till now~~ had been overshadowed <u>ever since</u>~~by~~ his mother's death. He closed the piano and headed towards the kitchen with the intention of asking Frau Graubal to make some coffee, but she surprised him coming the other way. She greeted him with a smile and for a ridiculous second he felt the urge to take her by the arms and dance along the corridor.

The hours before Elizabeth could reasonably arrive passed tediously slowly. He had assumed that she would ring before setting out for Denmark but the phone stubbornly remained silent. The afternoon of the second day being warm and clear, he took himself out into the rose garden with a spray gun and the intention to deal with a mass of aphids. At long last he saw her red Audi coming up the drive. He almost ran across to greet her but as she stepped out of the car, he detected an uncertain look on her face - almost as if she needed reassurance.

'I can't tell you how glad I am to see you,' He said impulsively. 'I've been on tenterhooks all day.'

'I am sorry Gerhard. I should have rung you. But I had to stop off in Düsseldorf and I wasn't sure what time I was going to arrive.'

'Do come in.'

'Can I walk round first and have a look? I need to stretch my legs after that drive. You've got a lovely house.'

'I'm glad you like it. The old place has been in the family for generations. It was originally a typical Schleswig Holstein farmhouse and my ancestors added on bits over the years. The last addition was the orangery when they became fashionable. Of course it's much smaller than the family Schloss which is now owned by one of my cousins, but this is ideal for a single man.' He could hear himself gabbling and cursed inwardly.

'So would you move out if ever you got married?' She asked with a hesitant smile.

'Good Lord, no! I'm far too attached to it, although actually I didn't live here much as a child.'

'Klaus seemed taken with the place when he stayed with you a couple of years ago.'

'Yes I think he was. God! It's tragic how things turned out - he spent the last night of his life alone with me.   And what is so awful is that neither of us enjoyed it.'

'So what actually happened then?'

'We both had had a fair bit to drink and he tried to persuade me that everything would be patched up, that you would go back to him. As if nothing serious had happened at all. It hit me on a nerve, I can tell you, so I did a bit of straight talking, tried to introduce some reality into his illusions, perhaps rather harshly.'

'This was the hard time that you said you gave him?'

'Yes,' he said with a grimace. 'I'm afraid it was.'

He noticed her frown. She quoted Eliot. 'Human kind cannot bear very much reality.'

'No. Klaus couldn't that night. He got pretty angry.'

'The anger was always there.'   She said with a sigh.

'I suppose it was, though I was surprised when you first mentioned it. It was a side he kept hidden from me, that is until he aimed his gun at me. Y ou were magnificent – I'll never forget the way you just walked across and stood beside me. I

448

don't think I've ever felt such a bond with another human being. Shared adversity brings people together, in a way rather like sailing when the weather turns nasty.'

'Do you know Gerhard, I felt the same. Writers would talk about it being 'a defining moment', I suppose. It certainly was for me.'

He glanced at her and saw that she was smiling softly. They walked slowly across the grass towards the stables. Nether spoke for a few seconds.

'How did the funeral go?'

'More or less as I expected. There wasn't a big turnout – in fact I arranged it in Bielefeld with the intention of keeping the numbers down as I think I told you. Hans was pretty shaken. In fact I wondered if Erda had told him the truth about his father. She might have done.'

'And how did you find it?'

'I think I was pretty upset as well.'

'I used to wonder about you two.'

'In the early days we were close, but in a different way – but then I was young, a long way from home and, looking back, rather lonely. You know he wasn't really a hard man - his ruthlessness was on the surface. But *Elektro* and the business world were powerful; he got sucked in. I could see his standards slipping. I thought I could stiffen him, but in the end every man has to master his own demons.'

'You'll miss him.'

'Yes, I shall. But the truth is that we'd drifted apart. Loss of trust of that scale can never be repaired.'

'Did you think he was having affairs?'

'It crossed my mind. I was never sure.'

'He was so damned suspicious of me that I began to wonder what he was up to himself.'

'He brought a whiff of the battlefield with him. Danger, the unpredictable, even heroics ... I shall miss that.'

'He didn't lack courage.'

'No. Not many of my friends would have jumped overboard to rescue a man with only one lifebelt between them. It's grim that it had to be *Jasmine* that dealt the fatal blow. Of course the skipper's responsible for his boat and what happens to his crew; I can't escape that. It leaves me feeling bad.'

'I can understand how you feel that, Gerhard.' She said. 'I'd just walked out on him and I felt truly dreadful when I realised he was dead. I'm afraid I wasn't much help to you over the hard time you said you'd given him.'

'Oh don't worry. I put it down to you distancing yourself, just like you used to.'

'Just like I used to?'

'Yes. You used to keep me at arm's length ... at least that is how it felt.'

'Well, I was a respectable married woman, and you're a dangerously attractive single man.'

'Yet you came to visit me in Burg hospital.'

450

'You were almost the only one of Klaus' friends that I really liked.'

'I'll never forget waking up and finding you sitting beside the bed. That was my defining moment.'

Elizabeth stopped and turned towards him. 'I hope you don't think I'm still distancing myself.'

He took her hand, kissed it, and said 'No, I don't. Not now.'

'You're a model of gentlemanly restraint,' she said with a teasing smile.

'Yes, I suppose I am. But I have to be a little circumspect you know – Frau Graubal is a tremendous gossip.'

As they approached the paddock where Prinz was cropping the grass, the horse looked up, came over to the gate and they stroked his head.

To restart the conversation, he asked 'When are you due in Denmark?'

'Oh that's flexible,'

'Would you like to stay here en route?'

'Does it have to be en route?'

'Indeed not. I'll rephrase the question. Would you like to stay here?'

'Yes I would, very much. How long will I be allowed to stay?'

'Well,' he said, sensing it was a far from casual enquiry, 'for as long as you like.'

'For ever?'

'That is a serious question calling for a serious answer,' he said looking gravely at her 'Yes – I would like you to stay for ever.'

'Hmmm... ' she said after a pause. 'My friends in Denmark are expecting me. But I shall be driving back this way, so your invitation to stay en route would still be open?'

'Of course'

She smiled. 'So all I need say for the moment is *auf Wiedersehen.*'

'Don't stay too long in Denmark, will you.'

'I think it'll be a very short stay.' She laughed as he kissed her.

About the Author
Peter Maguire

Peter's debut novel published in 2018 in his 91st year was inspired by his period of National Service September 1947 to November 1949 where as a young RAF officer he was based in Hamburg in the aftermath of the 2nd World War. Shortly beforehand he had graduated from Imperial College as a qualified engineer and was commissioned to work in the airfield construction branch of the RAF at Fuhlsbuettel Airport, better known as the present day Hamburg Airport. He was responsible for overseeing the approach lighting on the Airport's new runway.

Peter later worked for ten years for EMI developing their radar systems before moving to Cirencester becoming the technical director for Ticket Equipment Ltd where his work included organising the Rotterdam Metro ticketing system taking him further afield across the world until he retired. Since that time he became actively involved in many local projects and took up interests as diverse as furniture restoration and training to become a qualified counsellor as well as fund-raiser for Cotswold Counselling. He also joined a flourishing writing group based in Cirencester which prompted him to write many entertaining short stories culminating in the extensive research and writing of this novel. As a tribute to 'The Riddle of the Sands' by Erskine

Childers, it too has a maritime theme because throughout his adult life Peter has been an enthusiastic sailor. He has crossed the English Chanel on more than one occasion and sailed around the French and Spanish coasts. Until his mid-eighties he was sailing up and down the Dalmatian Coast.

Peter has three children and eight grand-children from his first marriage. He now lives with his second wife, Sarah, in a beautiful village outside Stroud in Gloucestershire.

Printed in Great Britain
by Amazon